PIRATES
OF THE
NARROW SEAS 1

The Sallee Rovers

SECOND EDITION

M. KEI

KEIBOOKS
PERRYVILLE, MARYLAND, USA
2011

ISBN 978-0615521367

Printed in the United States of America, 2011.

KEIBOOKS
P O Box 516
Perryville, MD 21903
Email: Keibooks@gmail.com

With deepest appreciation to Chele
for inspiration, support, and vast quantities of proofreading.

~K~

PIRATES OF THE NARROW SEAS

BOOK ONE : THE SALLEE ROVERS
BOOK TWO : MEN OF HONOR
BOOK THREE : IRON MEN
BOOK FOUR : HEART OF OAK

The ebook versions of the series are published by Bristlecone Pine Press, Portland, Maine

POETRY BY M. KEI

Slow Motion : The Log of a Chesapeake Bay Skipjack (2nd edition)

Heron Sea : Short Poems of the Chesapeake Bay

Take Five : Best Contemporary Tanka, Volume Three (editor)

Take Five : Best Contemporary Tanka, Volume Two (editor)

Take Five : Best Contemporary Tanka (editor)

Fire Pearls : Short Masterpieces of the Human Heart (editor)

Atlas Poetica : A Journal of Poetry of Place in Modern English Tanka

TABLE OF CONTENTS

CHAPTER 1: ENGLAND

Lieutenant Peter Thorton did not want to get up. The sun, if so dark and dreary a thing could be called a 'sun,' had risen, but the change from night to day was nearly imperceptible due to the cold rain falling. Moreover, Thorton had been sick in bed for several days and the habit of indolence had acquired a certain appeal. Yet he was a naval officer and racked with guilt that it was now after seven of the clock in the morning and he was still in bed. Guilt warred with illness, but the bed was warm and the room was cold, so guilt alone was not sufficient to haul him out of his berth to get under way. Yet he felt that, if only the room were not so cold, he was recovered enough that he could very well get up and about. Which meant he would have to. Rising compelled him to wash and shave, which was followed by donning his least dirty linen shirt, a fresh stock, a shabby wool coat and thin breeches, freshly darned wool socks, worn out shoes, and gloves with holes in the fingers. He clamped his battered tricorn on his head, and thus properly attired, went down two flights of stairs to the privy.

Coming in from that errand he passed through the kitchen where a thin cook was at work. A thin cook is never to be trusted and the runny eggs and scorched oatmeal she gave him were proof why. "Your friend is in the breakfast room," she told him.

He gladly took his plate into that mean room with its remnant of coal-fire and exclaimed, "Perry! I didn't hear you come in last night." He set his plate down and took a seat opposite his friend and fellow lieutenant. The two, being lieutenants without positions, were on half-pay and sharing a garret room at the top of a narrow house to save on expenses.

Perry smiled and said, "I didn't come in. I had agreeable female company last night." He flicked his fingers across the lapel of his coat and raised his eyebrows for emphasis. Thorton noticed that the coat was fine and new, a good thick dark blue wool with shiny brass buttons stamped with the Tudor rose. It was double-breasted, but he wore it fastened with hooks and the lapels buttoned down flat. The skirts were ample and the white boot cuffs deep. "She gave me this and much more yesterday. Of course I spent the night."

Thorton momentarily envied his friend's good fortune, but he realized how he had acquired it. Perry was a fine looking man with curly brown hair and dark eyes. He cut a very dashing figure in his brand new frock coat. There on the table, next to his breakfast, was a brand-new tricorn. "She must like you very much. Who is she? A rich widow?"

"Almost as good. She is a butcher's wife. She's going to send round some mutton for you and I tonight which Cook will happily ruin for us." His tone was jovial.

"A married woman?" Thorton was scandalized.

Perry waved his fork at him. "I see you haven't entirely given up your plan to become a preacher. Ten years of service with the British navy ought to have taught you that many a woman is married to a cuckold."

Thorton eyed his friend's fine coat. Many things chased through his mind, not a few of which were the sordid transactions he had endured in the middle deck in the days before he became an officer. He sighed and stirred his congealing mass of disagreeable oatmeal. "I couldn't do it, Perry. But if you and she are content with the arrangement and her husband doesn't find out, I suppose that's the way things are."

Lieutenant Roger Perry grinned at him as he lounged over the remains of his own breakfast. "I plan to go up to the Admiralty today and see if there are any orders. There won't be, but if there are, I'll beg them to give me yours since you've been sick. Which they won't, but maybe we'll get a piece of luck and find a new clerk that hasn't yet had his humanity crushed by the British navy." His tone was cheerful. "There's no reason for you to go out in this rain when you aren't well."

"I'm much better, thank you. I'm bored and restless. I'll walk up with you and you can tell me all about Madame Butcher and her mutton. I wouldn't mind a pair of mutton chops tonight."

"Are you certain? 'Tis powerful cold and windy and the rain is coming down in needles."

Thorton smiled across at his handsome friend and said, "Yes, I'll come." His hair was a sandy blond and his face had paled over the winter, but there was a slight blush of color in it.

"You are looking better. You're getting your color back," Perry replied, unaware of anything more than the obvious state of his friend's health.

Thorton realized he had gazed a little too frankly and started shoveling oatmeal. "Let me finish, then we'll go." He kept his eyes down and tended to his food. He couldn't taste it which was just as well.

Perry said, "I'll get your cloak then." He ran lightly up the stairs to their mutual room.

Thorton sighed. He wished for orders. To room with Perry and never betray his true feelings was an ordeal he didn't think he could withstand much longer. At first it had seemed like a delightful opportunity: share a room, a bed, a day, a week, a month . . . But while close quarters had lead to certain confidences, those confidences included Perry's reports on his successes and failures with various women. So Thorton had taken to rolling over in bed with his back to his voluble friend and saying crossly, "I'm tired Perry. I can't run about all night like you do," then lie there pretending to sleep.

Perry for his part did his best to inveigle his friend to loosen up and enjoy himself in the public houses, but Thorton was a man who could make a pot of small beer last all night. He was exceptionally parsimonious with his money which Perry attributed to having been raised by an equally parsimonious parson with the same career in mind for his stepson, but in truth, money came easily to Perry and just as easily went, thanks to his charm and good looks. Never was this more on display than this wet soggy morning as the two young gentlemen went along the street.

A girl was standing in the door of a bakery looking out. When she saw them, she sang out, "Lieutenant Perry! My goodness! Why are you out on such a rainy morning?"

Perry swerved over her way and stood under her door's awning to say, "Why Sissy, you know I'm an officer in the King's Navy. This is my friend, Lieutenant Peter Thorton. We're going up to get our orders. You never know what adventure His Majesty is going to send us on. I might not see you after today!"

"Oh!" Her blue eyes widened and her hand went to her mouth. "Will it be very dangerous?"

"I'm sure it will be. It always is," he replied solemnly.

She wrung her hands. "Oh dear, oh dear. To think you're going away! Maybe to be killed!"

A sharp voice came from inside. "Matilda! Don't be blocking the door! Let the gentlemen in, girl!"

So she stepped aside and they entered. Perry surveyed the buns and cakes and other treats with a very judicious eye. "Can I have a sample of that? If it is good I'll recommend it to Admiral Throgmorton when I see him." Instantly the case was opened and the girl handed over the hot cross bun. Perry took it and waved to Thorton. "What do you think, Thorton, what else might the Admiral like?"

Thorton had never heard of an Admiral Throgmorton and wondered who Perry was talking about. But he was an officer and that meant never admitting when he was lost. "Maybe some of those crescent rolls? I hear they're all the rage in France, thanks to their alliance with the Turks," he ventured. So a crescent roll was handed over to him, very moist and tender and flaky.

Perry expressed his approval with his eye on Sissy's bosom. "Excellent. I will recommend you to Admiral Throgmorton when I see him. I'm sure he will be most pleased to see what you have to offer."

The girl tittered; she was not at all adverse to the compliment he paid her wares.

The two went on their way. They'd gone about ten paces down the street when it dawned on Thorton what his friend had done. "Perry! You can't go off without paying! That poor girl will be in trouble if the pastries are missing!"

Perry kept walking and Thorton had to hurry to catch up. He grinned at his friend. "But I was completely honest. If I ever meet an Admiral named Throgmorton I will be sure to recommend the shop to him."

Thorton stood stock still, then ran after him. "You're horrible. That poor girl!" But he was laughing all the same.

CHAPTER 2: ORDERS

The lieutenants hiked a mile to the Admiralty. Since a treaty had been concluded between Britain and France the previous fall the navy had been sharply reduced. Three-fourths of her vessels had been laid up in ordinary and their officers placed on half-pay. The whole pay of a lieutenant wasn't very much to begin with, but there was always the hope of prize money and promotion. Thorton, having become a lieutenant just before hostilities ceased, was still feeling a bit awed that he had actually been promoted. He was only three spots from the bottom of the list in seniority so it would take many years of deaths, retirements, and promotion for him to climb that list, especially now that Britain was not engaged in open war with anyone. Perry was higher up the list, but an orphan without friends or family in high places was going to have to wait for an opportune moment to distinguish himself in battle. In either case, they had to be assigned to a ship first. There were a great many officers in similar straits, each of whom made the monthly pilgrimage on the first to inquire for orders.

The atmosphere at the Admiralty was positively glum, what with thin, poor men attempting to warm themselves by the fire and get the damp out of their bones before reluctantly making their way up to the desk to have their names checked off with a shake of the head from the clerk. A small (very small) stack of neat white envelopes was by his elbow, and so, even though they knew they lacked the seniority and influence, each dared to think for a brief moment that one of those luscious white packets would be found with his name on it. It wasn't, and they went away berating themselves for having entertained hope when they knew better.

Perry presented himself hat in hand. "Lieutenant Roger Perry reporting for orders, sir."

The clerk, a disabled captain in a wicker wheelchair, checked Perry's name on the list, riffled through the packets, and handed him one. Perry gaped with astonishment. "Sign here," the captain-clerk told him. Perry took the quill in a dream and signed.

Other officers crowded round. "What did you get?" "Damn me, Perry, that's lucky for you!" "What is it? Tell us!" they chorused.

The captain-clerk rapped his knuckles firmly on the desk. "Gentlemen! Stand back. You are in the way."

They all stepped back, but Perry lingered nearby as Thorton stepped up. "Lieutenant Peter Thorton reporting for orders, sir." He saluted briskly.

The captain clerk returned the salute in his half-hearted fashion, then ran through his list and checked off his name. Thorton started away. "Mr. Thorton!" He turned back. A bony hand extended a packet to him.

Thorton gaped. "For me?"

"You're Peter Thorton, aren't you? That's what you said," the man snapped in irritation.

"Aye, sir." Thorton held his hat over his heart, took the packet, and signed the receipt. That took three hands so he fumbled a bit before he got himself sorted out and the quill scratched legibly across the receipt.

The two friends were stunned—and the envy of disappointed officers all around—to receive orders. They stepped out of the way.

"Where are you ordered?" Perry demanded, breaking the seal.

"The *Ajax*. Down at the Pool," Thorton replied in wonder.

"The *Ajax!* Why, I'm assigned to the *Ajax* too!"

They gaped at each other. With so much difference in their seniority, it was astounding that they should receive orders at the same time when so many others did not, and even more astounding that they should be posted to the same ship.

The other officers crowded round to ask questions, but they could no more explain the Admiralty's orders than they could explain what kept the sun in the sky or made the clouds to rain. However, the scuttlebutt garnered them some knowledge. The *Ajax* was an elderly French corvette that had been taken and refitted during the last war. Officially classed as a frigate, she was hardly a prime assignment. But she was an assignment.

The old clerk cleared his throat officiously. "Gentlemen! You have your orders. I suggest you attend to them. Promptly!"

So they were banished to the delirious joy of searching out their new vessel and transferring their belongings to it. Perry made sure to drop by his butcher lady. Thorton idled a long while outside while Perry said his farewells and received the lady's remonstrations—and the promised mutton, along with a slab of bacon and a pair of summer sausages for their private stores. A man might survive on the king's board, but he wouldn't be happy about it. Being lieutenants who had been a long time on half-pay, the gift was a welcome one.

They paid a man with a cart to haul their sea chests to the wharf, then paid a wherryman to row them to the *Ajax*, riding at anchor in the Pool below the London Bridge. She was small and old-fashioned with a lateen mizzen brailed up to her shebeck yard, but she had triangular headsails. Her sails were all taken in, but she had the yards for courses, topsails, and topgallants. Her lines were low and fine.

A minimal crew was aboard and lined up rather raggedly to receive their lieutenants. The boatswain, a red-faced Scot bawled, "Straight lines, men! 'Tis an officer, not a trollop! Stop your gawping!" He carried a piece of rope which he snapped against the legs or arms of men out of order. They straightened up, but a few dared to scowl at him, thereby showing that they were new to the Service.

The boatswain turned to face the lieutenants and knuckled his forehead. "Lewis MacDonald, boatswain. Welcome aboard, sirs."

He was a red-haired fellow with a nose that had been broken and never recovered. It remained squashed flat. His hair was streaked with grey and receding from his forehead. He compensated for this with a bushy pair of greying muttonchops. The rest of his hair was thin and bound into a tarred braid down his back in seamanly fashion. His features were broad and honest, with the usual expression of feigned stupidity that the lower orders reserved for dealing with their betters.

There was no sign of the captain yet. The captain would be a man of substance who would have several days grace in which to put his affairs in order and arrive aboard. This would give his lieutenants time to press him a crew and set the vessel to rights. Assuming he had effective and vigorous subordinates.

"I'm Lt. Roger Perry. My companion is Lt. Peter Thorton, reporting for duty. Who's the senior lieutenant?"

Thorton let him speak for both of them.

"I dunno, sir. You're first aboard."

They didn't know where to stow their dunnage until the other lieutenant was aboard. Cabins were allotted in strict rank from the captain on down. Although the captain could order the lieutenants as he pleased, he generally did so by seniority, with exceptions for political influence, favoritism and ability. In that order. Although since Thorton was a man with no seniority, no friends or relations in high places, and since that unfortunate event that had caused him to run away to sea at the age of sixteen, effectively no relations at all, he was quite resigned to being last among the lieutenants. It was a distinct improvement over being a midshipman. Laid off midshipmen received no pay at all.

"Well, I'm Number One for the moment," Perry joked. "Best get busy."

Thorton climbed to the quarterdeck and started memorizing everything about the ship and her men that he could observe. A hundred and twenty-seven feet long, give or take a little, thirty-four feet wide, she was narrower than an English-built frigate. She'd be fast if properly trimmed he thought. She was pierced for twenty-six guns on her weather deck and six more on her forecastle and quarterdeck. He asked the quartermaster, "What weight of metal do we throw?"

"Twelve pounders on deck and six on the castles, sir," the man replied. He was a short, thin fellow with a scarred face and a very long tail of tarred hair down his back. An experienced hand.

"Stout," Thorton grunted in approval. During wartime a mere frigate probably would not have received such guns; they would have gone to bigger ships. With three-fourths of the ships in ordinary, luxuries like bigger guns could be handed out to a smaller vessel. Thorton was a keen proponent of superior gunnery and pleased to have something more than the nine pounders he expected.

"Aye, sir. I hope the deck will hold them."

"I'm sure it will. What's our draft?"

"Fifteen feet, two inches, sir."

"A little shallow," Thorton remarked. "I'll bet she can really fly."

"She's a fast little barky when properly handled, sir," the man replied.

"You've been with her a while?"

"Four years now. Last captain was William Williams the second, God rest his soul."

"Your name, mister?"

"Smith, sir. Billy Smith."

"Thank you, Smith. Is there anything I ought to know about her?"

So the man began to tell him about the various actions she'd been in and the quality of her standing officers. Thorton walked all around the quarterdeck, looking at this and that, noting the mended wood and aging guns, and made dire predictions to himself about gun explosions and misfires. He'd have the crew drill immediately—hopefully they'd blow the weak guns to pieces before they left the Thames, allowing them to get more before going to sea. That he or some of the men might be killed in such an explosion barely entered his mind. Better now than in the midst of battle. If they would even see battle.

The remaining lieutenant came aboard after lunch with an assortment of midshipmen. Thorton went to meet the man.

"Welcome aboard. I'm Lt. Peter Thorton, sir." He saluted the newcomer, a fleshy, brown-haired fellow in a decent coat and hat.

"Lieutenant Albert Forsythe, reporting for duty," the newcomer replied. He returned Thorton's salute. "What's your commission date?" he asked.

"I'm the third for sure. I'm barely made. 'Tis between you and Roger Perry for first." To one of the side-boys he said, "Pass the word for Mr. Perry. Tell him Lt. Forsythe is here." To the midshipmen he said, "You boys can get yourselves stowed in the cockpit." The midshipmen disappeared below decks.

Perry arrived. He and Forsythe saluted each other, then compared dates. Forsythe had three weeks seniority on Perry. Seniority wasn't everything when it came to promotion, but if a man lacked friends in high places, it might as well be.

Perry saluted and gave his report. "You're Number One then. Captain's not here yet. We're dreadfully short of men. I'm thinking of pressing a crew. I'd think we could get forty or fifty men tonight. Nobody will be expecting a press. With your permission I'll go get the warrant this afternoon. What do you think?"

Forsythe opened his mouth. "I think we should wait to know the captain's pleasure."

"Aye aye, sir," they both replied. Perry was disappointed, but Thorton wasn't sure if he was disappointed or relieved.

The next two days sped by. Perry, being the charming one, went to recruit and came back with sixteen men with some sort of seagoing experience and twelve landlubbers whom he'd gulled into believing in the glory of naval service. They were all beguiled by Perry's implication that there would be prize money for snapping up pirates as easily as picking berries on a picnic. The new hands had to be trained so Forsythe put them into sail evolutions and the raising and lowering of topmasts. Rumors were rife and the men had a nasty habit of congregating into groups to chatter instead of working. Thorton called them to order and the slow man felt the sting of his tawse. He knew his job well and he made them learn it, too. He had been a foretop hand himself before becoming a midshipman. He consulted his watch.

"Twenty-five minutes to set the topsail! What a sorry lot of misbegotten landlubbers you are! You couldn't even suck your mother's tit if she handed it to you! I want it done in ten! Do it again!" They groaned and tried harder but with scant improvement.

On the second afternoon the captain came aboard. He was wearing a newfangled epaulette in the Continental fashion—decidedly not regulation. All the same, officers had considerable discretion in the design of their uniforms. When the captain's hat reached the level of the deck, the single snare drum gave a ragged roll. The side-boys came to attention.

"I am Captain Horace Bishop. You are?" He was a man of fifty with a good hat and coat, a portly build, silk stockings, a sensible wig, and jowls. He had their names and commission dates, then ranked them in strict order of seniority without comment. He gave a first impression as a solid, orderly sort of captain.

"Aye aye, sir," they replied. Seniority worked as well as anything to arrange men whose skills and qualities were unknown. Forsythe seemed a little dazed to find himself first even though he'd known it was coming.

Bishop said, "All hands on deck."

Boatswain MacDonald piped the call and the hands hurried to assemble. They'd learned to move briskly at the end of Thorton's tawse if nothing else. The seasoned seamen elbowed the landlubbers into position. The landlubbers slouched and scowled. Forsythe did not correct them.

The captain pulled out his commission and proceeded to read it in a stentorian voice. The reading of the commission made him second only to God and King with power over these men. That done, the men were dismissed. Work on board took on a more serious air. The captain was no longer an abstraction but a real and present power. He could hang any of them if he thought it necessary.

"Mr. Chambers, Mr. Thorton, come with me. The rest of you, carry on."

Chambers was the midshipman Bishop had brought with him: the captain's pet. They accompanied him to the great cabin and stood with their shoulders hunched under the low deckhead. Bishop was short enough that he could stand up without his hat.

"Mr. Thorton. You are to vacate your cabin and berth wherever seems convenient to the wardroom. We will have a passenger."

"Aye aye, sir." It was the only answer he could make.

"A Sallee man," the captain said with some distaste. Thorton's eyes nearly bugged out of his head. "Stop goggling like an idiot, Thorton."

"Aye aye, sir," Thorton replied, pulling himself together. He longed to ask more but dared not.

"Mr. Chambers, inform the cook that no pork is to be served to our guest. Mohammedans are like Jews. They don't eat pork." The contempt he felt for Muslims and Jews was plain in his voice, although he made no overt statement.

"Aye aye, sir," they replied.

So the word was passed and Thorton went to move his dunnage in with Perry. Perry's cabin was more commodious than Thorton's by a matter of inches. The cabin had a small square window that let in light and a bunk which was neatly made up with Perry's straw mattress, linens, and blue wool blanket. His seachest and other stores were under the bunk. Thorton stowed his things on the other side, leaving a narrow aisle down the middle. The room was about the size of four bunks if three been had laid side by side and the fourth at their feet. In other words, about eight feet by nine. He went in search of Perry and found him on the weather deck, calling for a boat.

"Did you hear? We're taking on a Sallee man as passenger!" Thorton announced to his friend.

That was extraordinary news. "Well, that explains why he's sent me to requisition two lambs."

"Mr. Thorton!" Bishop's voice rang out. Thorton turned and saluted. Perry was half over the rail, but he paused and saluted, too. "Did I direct you to announce our business to the world?"

"No, sir." Thorton gulped. "Sorry, sir."

"I count myself a reasonable man, so I was kind enough to explain to you why you must move your berth. I did not instruct you to repeat my private remarks to the crew!"

"Aye aye, sir. No, sir. Sorry, sir." Thorton was sweating.

Bishop's rounding on the young lieutenant had gathered onlookers. The captain roared at them. "Back to your posts! What kind of discipline do you enforce on these men? I'll have to whip the lot of you into shape!"

"Aye aye, sir," the two lieutenants replied.

"Get on with it." With that dismissal Perry finished going over the side and Thorton fled to the wardroom. The crew was grinning to see Thorton, their driver, get a dressing down, even though the captain's words boded ill for them.

CHAPTER 3: LOADING POWDER

Bishop called his officers into his cabin. One of the officers needed to remain on watch, and since Thorton was in *mal odeur* with the captain, he was the unlucky man. He paced the deck with his hands clasped behind his back and bent all his mental powers to trying to guess what was going on in the captain's cabin, but beyond the most general of outlines, he couldn't.

Bishop was explaining, "Gentlemen. This evening we will receive on board His Excellency, Achmed bin Mamoud, envoy from the Sallee Republic to England and his servant. His servant will be housed with the midshipmen. Mr. Achmed will occupy the third cabin. Has Thorton vacated it?"

Perry replied, "Aye, sir."

Bishop raised his eyebrows and remarked sarcastically, "Strange, I was sure you were the number two lieutenant, Mr. Perry. Mr. Forsythe, answer!"

Forsythe jumped. "Aye aye, sir, he has."

Bishop scowled at Perry. "Do not think that just because there is only a few week's difference in your commission dates that you can jump precedence like that, Mr. Perry."

"No, sir, I'm sorry, sir. But Thorton's bunking with me, so I knew he'd moved his things, sir."

"Did I ask you a question, mister?"

"No, sir." Perry shut up, his cheeks burning.

Forsythe was pale, dreading to be called upon with a question for which he had no answer. He was not a quick-witted man. He stood stiffly at attention, waiting for the next blow to fall, certain that he would feel the axe in his turn as keenly as Perry and Thorton had.

"As I was saying. They will come aboard tonight. By no word or deed are they to obtain the slightest inkling that the condition of this ship is in any way out of the ordinary."

"Aye aye, sir," Forsythe responded. He was not aware that there was anything out of the ordinary about the vessel himself, and he shot a beseeching glance at Perry. Perry was pretty sure Forsythe was the only one expected to reply to that and kept silent.

"Now then, where was I?" Nobody answered him. He collected his thoughts. "Ah, yes. The Mohammedan is coming aboard this evening. We are to convey him to France and wait on him while he confers with the French officials. We are to convey him to any port on the Atlantic coast of France he wishes to visit and deposit him wherever on that coast he directs. We are to look into the French ports and give a report of their naval readiness. Likewise, we are to keep a sharp eye out for Spanish traffic and report on it as well."

Their eyes were fixed on him as they ate up his words like hungry men. Since the peace between Britain and France there had been no cause to go nosing about French ports, but the Admiralty was not so ready to trust the temper of the French and wanted information. Their pulses beat more quickly.

The captain continued, "I understand that you each speak fluent French and that Mr. Thorton speaks French and Spanish as well. Is that correct?"

The officers chorused, "Aye, sir." If some of them thought their command of French a bit weak they dared not admit it. Under ordinary circumstances there would be no need to have so many men aboard who spoke French; to arrange things thus bespoke spy missions and secret errands ashore. Cloak and dagger stuff. Perry was looking forward to it with relish. It was fortunate Forsythe did not grasp the significance of the arrangements; if he had he would have been petrified. Not that he was lacking in physical courage, but he was sorely lacking in initiative and the ability to think on his feet, both which would be required for such reconnoitering. Perry, on the other hand, with his charm and good looks, was the perfect man for the job.

"We are going to receive a contingent of hands from the vessels in harbor. The *Indomitable*, *Intrepid*, and the tenders are all contributing. Tonight we will press a crew. *Indomitable* and *Intrepid* will help. We get first pick of the press, and we sail as soon as we have them on board and read in. Mr. Forsythe, you'll remain here with me. Mr. Perry, you'll lead the press gang. Take Midshipmen Chambers and . . . one other." He did not recollect the names of the midshipmen. "Do not convey anymore than absolutely necessary to Mr. Thorton—he has a loose tongue. We don't want them to fly before we catch them. The powder and shot will be coming alongside this afternoon. Mr. Forsythe, who do you want to handle the powder and the new recruits?"

Forsythe was relieved that he had escaped unscathed so far, and he was glad not to be part of the press gang, but the latest question was burning him. He glanced at Perry, then at Bishop. His voice was tremulous as he said, "I think Mr. Perry ought to take the recruits on board. He has a knack for it. Mr. Thorton can take the powder." His voice rose in a question mark as he sought desperately to see if his decision met his superior's approval.

Bishop stared at him and Forsythe blanched. "If it pleases you, sir."

"Don't you dare forget 'sir' again, young man. I will not tolerate insubordination on my ship."

"Aye aye, sir!" Forsythe squeaked.

Bishop turned his eye on Perry. "So you have a knack with recruits, do you?"

Perry was now on the fire. To say yes would sound boastful, to say no would call Forsythe's judgment into doubt. To say too much would earn another rebuke. "Since we were short handed, Mr. Forsythe directed me to recruit and I obtained twenty-eight hands, sir."

Bishop's eyebrows went up. "Twenty-eight, you say? Good hands?"

"Twelve landsmen and sixteen seamen, sir."

Bishop grunted. After a moment of consideration, he said grudgingly, "That was well done, Mr. Perry."

"Thank you, sir." He kept his expression blank and his tone bland.

The captain fixed his eyes upon Forsythe again. "Loading powder is a dangerous business. Why did you pick Thorton for the duty?"

Perry longed to interject a good word for his friend but dared not try it. Forsythe was sweating. "Well, sir, I thought Mr. Perry would do a better job with the men, so that left Thorton for the powder, sir. I'll change it if you think I should, sir." There were entirely too many 'sirs' in that statement, but Bishop accepted it as his due.

"Why did you not select yourself for this highly responsible duty?"

Forsythe was holed below the waterline and in danger of sinking. He racked his brains and came up with the only possible answer that would satisfy Bishop. "I thought it best to keep myself in readiness for whatever command you might give me, sir."

"To load powder requires a very exact understanding of load and safety, Mr. Forsythe. Do you think Mr. Thorton up to it? He seems a careless fellow."

Perry made a great effort to restrain himself. He had to bite his lips.

Forsythe saw his reaction and feared the worst. "Perhaps Mr. Perry knows something about Mr. Thorton that I don't, sir."

"Well, what is it, man?"

Perry wanted to burst out with a great many things, but he schooled himself to the brevity and dignity that Bishop seemed to expect. "I have served with Mr. Thorton, sir. He has a good head for figures and is scrupulous about his duties. I believe he is an excellent choice to load the powder, if it pleases you, sir."

"I didn't ask your opinion, Mr. Perry. I deal in facts. I will form my own opinion about the man and it is not off to a good start."

"Aye aye, sir." There was only so much cover Perry could give to Thorton without sinking himself.

Bishop was musing. "A head for figures and two languages. He must be proud of his intellect."

Perry wanted to argue that Thorton was anything but proud but dared not. He resorted to guile. "Perhaps Mr. Thorton should be summoned and questioned regarding his capabilities directly, sir."

Bishop fixed a glare on Perry and he knew he had ventured too much. He cultivated a wooden face. Bishop ignored his advice. "Very well. Thorton shall supervise the powder and I shall supervise Thorton. Call me when the powder comes along side. Dismissed."

"Aye aye, sir." With palpable relief they fled his presence.

Perry sought out Thorton to update him on all that had transpired as tersely as he could. He longed to tell him more, but was under orders not to. "I have more to tell you, but I can't because the captain thinks you're a blabbermouth. He's going to watch you with the powder, so watch yourself. Make sure you get a good nap, too. We've got business tonight."

Thorton's jaw dropped. "A blabbermouth? Me?" Even Thorton thought he was not a loquacious man; one of the reasons he resisted strong drink was for fear it would loosen his tongue.

Perry spread his hands."He makes large judgments from small details."

"Boat!" a hand sang out.

Perry looked over the side. "There's the first of the new crew coming up. I've got to get them." He hurried away.

Then another call from the other side. "Powder boat coming along side!" The word was passed to the great cabin.

"Captain on deck!"

Thorton hastened to present himself. He saluted smartly and said absolutely nothing.

"Mr. Thorton. If you were to have the honor of bringing the powder on board, how would you do it?"

"I'd order MacDonald to select the hands and see that they were barefoot and beltless, not so much as a brass button on them, sir. I'd not raise more than sixteen barrels of powder at a time because the winch line is old, sir."

"If it is old, why hasn't it been replaced, Mr. Thorton?"

"Shall I ask the boatswain, sir?" It was the boatswain's duty to make sure everything about the ship was in good repair.

"I'll ask him myself. Make a note of it."

"Aye aye, sir."

"Carry on with raising the powder, Mr. Thorton."

"Aye aye, sir." Thorton stepped forward and gave his orders with a minimum of words. An error would blow them all sky high, so MacDonald selected sound men who removed their shoes and tightened their trouser strings. Thorton inspected them before they began to work, checking their buttons and making them turn out their pockets. Knives and coins and other metal objects were confiscated and set aside. "Swabs ready, MacDonald?"

"Aye aye, sir."

Swabs and buckets of seawater stood by to extinguish any stray sparks and avert a conflagration.

"Lower the net handsomely, if you please." He leaned over the side. "You men. Sixteen barrels at a time. No more."

The men in the lighter looked up and called, "Aye aye, sir."

The first load of powder was swayed up and placed in the hold without incident. Thorton said not a word except to give and acknowledge orders. The second and the third loads were hoisted in. Bishop continued watching, hands behind his back. To get her five tons of powder and accompanying shot, cartridges, and other items, plus the shot for the swivels and muskets, required seven loads. At last it was done, and Thorton said, "Swab the decks, MacDonald."

The swabs were brought out to wash down the decks to make certain any stray grains of gunpowder were doused and swept away. Thorton went down to the hold to inspect the stowage, found it satisfactory, and climbed back on deck. He approached the captain, saluted, and reported, "Powder stowed, sir."

"Very well, Mr. Thorton. Carry on."

"Thank you, sir."

Thorton thought he'd done a good job of it and had hoped for some sign that his work had met the captain's approval, but it wasn't coming. He would have surely heard about it if something were amiss. He resigned himself. His last captain had been chary of compliments as well. It was much too soon for Bishop to pamper his junior officers with a kind word.

Thorton had something else on his mind. He hardly dared to broach it but finally screwed up his courage and asked, "Do you have any orders regarding gunnery practice, sir?"

Bishop gave him a freezing look. "Mr. Perry will see to it."

"Aye aye, sir." Thorton's face burned red even as it froze into a mask of no expression.

"That will be all, Mr. Thorton."

Thorton saluted and fled.

CHAPTER 4 : THE SALLEE ENVOY

The Sallee man and his servant hove alongside that evening. The shadows were lengthening and the watch was lighting the lanterns. The envoy was a portly gentleman of average height with a curled mustache and thick beard streaked with grey. He was sumptuously dressed in a large white turban and a green brocade coat decorated with a pattern of vines. The sleeves were narrow and the skirt was full, worn over green pantaloons. His scimitar hung from a red sash around his waist. His servant was a tall thin blackamoor dressed in a red shirt and fez and black pantaloons above red leather slippers. Their arrival attracted considerable attention, but the Turk was used to being stared at by infidels and beamed benignly at them.

"Peace be upon you. I am Achmed bin Mamoud, the Sallee envoy." He flourished his fingers in their direction. "Permission to come aboard?" His voice was simultaneously congenial and booming.

Thorton received him. "Welcome aboard, Your Excellency. I am Lieutenant Peter Thorton. This is Midshipman Archibald Maynard. Mr. Maynard will show you to your quarters."

Maynard rolled his eyes at being called 'Archibald' instead of 'Archie' but said nothing.

Achmed gave Thorton a little bow, so Thorton bowed back, deeper and longer. He had never seen a Turk up close before. He was quite curious. Maynard was staring in fascination at the African.

Achmed noticed Maynard's look and explained. "That is my servant, Keb. He is a eunuch." He spoke English with a moderate accent. "Is Captain Bishop here?"

Maynard was titillated; Thorton was scandalized. They were hard pressed to keep a professional demeanor. Thorton replied, "He is, sir. I will notify him immediately."

"Excellent." Achmed remained where he was, clearly waiting for the captain to appear.

Thorton fidgeted mentally, then he said, "Mr. Maynard, go tell the captain that Mr. Achmed has come aboard, then show his servant where to stow his things."

The blackamoor apparently did not speak English, so Maynard directed him with gestures. The two went off. The envoy studied the lieutenant as he waited for the captain. The man he saw was above average height, but not remarkably so, broad enough in the shoulder to be manly, but not of exaggerated size, and broad also in the hip so that his torso was something of a rectangle. He was lean, so could most properly be called a sturdily built man of no special proportions. He had a sallow complexion and facial features that were somewhat square. His nose was a triangle no bigger nor smaller than it ought to be, his lips tightly closed, while his grey eyes gazed levelly back without revealing anything. He was an expressionless man.

Achmed's brown eyes regarded him with something like sympathy as he chatted. "How long have you served under Captain Bishop, Mr. Thorton?"

"A few days, sir."

"That isn't very long to get to know a man. What is he like?"

"He is an Englishman, sir," Thorton replied as if that conveyed all that needed to be known. Perhaps it did.

Achmed waved a hand. "I had assumed as much," he said pleasantly. "I was more curious about the man than his nationality."

Bishop appeared on deck and Thorton realized the captain had deliberately snubbed the envoy. Word had been passed when the turban had been spotted, so Bishop should have been on deck to greet the dignitary. Achmed knew he had been snubbed and was summoning Bishop. Tit for tat. Achmed continued smiling and nothing about his look or voice conveyed any resentment.

Captain Bishop forced a smile and gave a little bow. "Your Excellency. Welcome aboard the *Ajax*. Mr. Thorton, you were remiss not to notify me immediately when you sighted our guest."

Thorton shot a look at Bishop that told Achmed that Thorton had done his duty and did not appreciate being blamed for the captain's boorishness. Thorton remained stiffly at attention and gave a gravel-voiced answer, "The wherryman was quick, sir." Not my fault, he was protesting inside—but that could not be said.

Achmed waved a be-ringed hand and smoothed it over by taking control. "Say nothing of it, Captain Bishop. In fact, I would be delighted if you and your officers would join me for supper. I suppose you have had your dinner already, but I have brought some delicacies with me, including Turkish delight and good Madeira wine. I'd like to share. My man is an excellent cook."

The only place capable of hosting such a dinner would be either the wardroom or the captain's cabin. Achmed was very politely intruding himself into their affairs and offering a bribe that he knew would be irresistible to men fed on the king's largesse: good food and wine.

Bishop was hooked. "You are very gracious to offer. We would be pleased to join you during the last dog watch. Mr. Thorton, make it so."

"Aye aye, sir."

"May I have a tour of your very handsome vessel, Captain? Yc look to have everything in excellent order. How soon will we be leaving?"

The envoy fell into step beside the captain who could not help to be flattered by the compliments. He gave the foreigner an officious tour, lauding the excellent condition of the vessel, the sated state of her stores, the excellence of her men, and other self-serving superlatives. The men who overheard were surprised and pleased. "He's strict, but he appreciates us," they told one another. They warmed to the captain immediately.

Thorton sent messages to the galley to make ready to receive the envoy's man and to give him whatever he wanted to cook. The blackamoor proved fluent in French. With the number of men aboard selected because they could speak that language, he was able to make himself understood. He drafted the cook and boys and put them to work. Soon delicious smells were wafting up from down below and Thorton's mouth was watering. He sincerely hoped that he would be invited to the table. The captain and envoy passed him and paid him no mind as he stood at attention.

Thorton caught up to the captain. "Sir, may I ask if you would prefer dinner in the wardroom or your cabin?"

"My cabin, of course. That is where dignitaries ought to be entertained. You shouldn't ask stupid questions."

Thorton burned but replied, "Very good, sir."

Bishop went into his cabin and Thorton started away. Achmed was waiting in the coach. He had overheard their encounter. "Ah, Mr. Thorton. Would you be so good as to attend me? I have some questions."

"Your servant, sir," Thorton replied, stepping over.

"My first question being, exactly where is my berth? My servant knows, but by the smells issuing from the hatchway, I assume he is busy in the galley."

Thorton was chagrined. Of course the stranger would not know his way below decks. "This way, please. I will show you the way, sir."

Thorton descended the ladder to the gundeck. With a turn, he arrived in the wardroom, which was nothing more than the space in the stern aft the guns. It was lined with little cabins for the officers: commissioned to starboard, warrant to larboard. The cabins were made of deal boards, and unlike the usual English frigate, would not be struck for action. She carried her guns forward of the cabins. The mizzenmast raked through the space and the dining table was built fore and aft of it in a continual run. Passing the salt from one end to the other required maneuvering it around the mizzenmast. Square windows in the upper portion of the stern lit the space.

Thorton took Achmed to the cabin that was third from the rear on the starboard side. The four cabins there housed the first, second, third, and marine lieutenants in order from the stern forward. The marine lieutenant was technically below Thorton in rank, but being the senior marine officer aboard, reported directly to the captain. The cabins on the opposite side housed the sailing master, surgeon, chaplain, and pursuer. The midshipmen slept in the cockpit, but messed in the gunroom with the gunner and boatswain. The *Ajax* was small for a frigate and did not have as many officers or gradations of status as a regular British frigate. On the other hand, she was graced with a chaplain who would also serve as schoolmaster for the boys, and a proper surgeon instead of a mere surgeon's mate. Peacetime provided a superfluity of officers needing berths.

Thorton stopped before the louvered door of what had briefly been his cabin. He opened it politely for Achmed. What a sight to behold! The spartan cabin had been turned into one of luxury. The bed was draped in blue and green silk comforters and blindingly white linen sheets. Two pillows were upon it. A portable cabinet had been set up and a mirror in a gilt frame was on the wall above it. The envoy's shaving things were stowed in the pockets provided for them—the Turk had been to sea before and knew that everything needed to be secured so that it would not go rolling around. A carpet of green and gold was on the floor and cushions were stacked in a corner. The lamp hanging from the deckhead was bronze work of Oriental delicacy. It seemed to Thorton that he must be staring into an Ottoman harem. He was quite dazzled.

Achmed had no trouble recognizing his room once the door was opened. He stepped inside. "Come in, come in. Have a seat. I'm afraid I have no divan to offer you, but take a cushion."

Thorton stepped onto the carpet and remained stiffly standing. "I am on duty, Your Excellency. What can I do for you, sir?"

Achmed was opening his cabinet and producing a bottle of ruby red wine and a gold cup. "Wine?"

"No thank you, sir."

If Achmed was taken aback by a man who refused the opportunity to enjoy Oriental luxury when given the chance, he showed no signs of it. He looked over the man's shabby coat and found it at odds with his demeanor which was correct to exactitude. "Have you ever been to Brest, Mr. Thorton?"

"Aye, sir."

Achmed looked at him for further information. None was forthcoming. "Yes?" he encouraged the English officer. Thorton nodded. No sound passed his lips. Achmed had to make his request explicit, but as was his nature, did not ask it straight out. "I have never been to Brest myself. I wonder if you could acquaint me with any details about it."

"When my other duties are completed, I would be happy to do so, sir."

An officer that would rather work than satisfy his own curiosity about an important guest was a novelty. Achmed was accustomed to being stared at and whispered about, queried and laughed at, secretly or openly. He knew exactly what an exotic bird he was to English eyes and used it to his advantage. He extended the golden cup with a smile. "You should try this Madeira. It is excellent."

"Thank you, sir. I look forward to supping with Your Excellency." He made no move to take the wine.

Achmed was not one to force a battle he couldn't win. He inclined his head graciously and gestured. "I look forward to getting to know you better. It is going to be a long trip. We should be on comfortable terms, yes?"

"Very good, sir. If you don't need me . . ." Thorton bowed, stepped out, and shut the door behind him.

'A long trip?' France was merely across the Channel.

CHAPTER 5 : THE ENGLISH CHANNEL

The English Channel was choppy and gusty as they beat against a west wind. The ship crawled along and the landsmen received numerous lessons in tacking and wearing ship, often delivered with the sting of a starter. Thorton swore at them a great deal but had little to say otherwise. The inexperienced sailors fouled the lines and crimped the sails. At one point he even had the sensation of retrograde movement so thoroughly had they mismanaged the operation of the sails. The seasick landsmen did not take kindly to being corrected and three men were promptly sent to the gratings to be flogged. Bishop was a man who believed in immediate consequences.

The hands were called to the pumps to wash the decks of vomit rather frequently. Bishop was a spit and polish sort of captain who wore his dress uniform on deck unless it rained. Fortunately, it rained often, which made cleaning easier, and excused the officers from formal dress. They were all grateful that Bishop had instituted three watches. It was an affordable luxury since Britain was not at war with anyone.

Thorton had more than the usual work. Perry was moderately seasick while Forsythe was so ill he could not come on deck for some of his watches. Perry and Thorton had to make up for him. Thorton was a little uneasy in his stomach but still able to eat while Perry grew peaked. Captain Bishop was ill and therefore surly. He railed against the helm for making too much leeway, and when it was pointed out to him that her shallow draft could not help it, snarled in response and threatened punishment.

The only happy person was Midshipman Maynard. He was young enough to think pitching up and down the waves qualified as 'fun.' He spent a lot of time on the foredeck to enjoy it the more. He didn't have a jot of seasickness.

Perry and Thorton were both off watch on a particular afternoon. They had retreated to the questionable comfort of their cabin. The *Ajax* was heeled over enough that the starboard gun ports could not have been opened. A seam was working and letting in the sea so that a slowly growing puddle sloshed about the floor, but it was hardly the sort of thing to cause concern. They had put their backs into it and raised their sea chests up on billets finagled from the store of firewood. Perry was lying casually in his bunk with his feet propped on Thorton's seachest. He had stripped down to his smallclothes to save his uniform while they were laboring with the sea chests. Thorton had strung a hammock over his sea chest and was lying in it. There was no place to sit other than the sea chests and he couldn't bear to share such a tiny bunk with Perry. Perry, with the state of his stomach, couldn't bear anything.

"God, I hope Achmed is seasick. 'Twouldn't be fair if he wasn't," Perry opined.

"When was the navy ever fair?" Thorton replied philosophically.

"Well, we do have a position when most men of our seniority don't, so sometimes it works to our advantage," Perry pointed out.

"Yes, that's true. I was tired of half pay."

Perry laughed a little, then his stomach rolled. "God, you've been so tight since Bishop came aboard I was beginning to think you'd lost your sense of humor!"

Thorton sighed and the hammock swayed. "Bishop doesn't like me."

"You ought to ingratiate yourself with him."

"How? You know I have no skill at that sort of thing."

"I could teach you. For one thing, smile when you meet him coming along the passageway. You come across very cold to someone who doesn't know you."

"I do?"

"Forsythe and Chambers think you're a dead fish. I defend you and say Bishop has you cowed, but they think you don't like them."

"Well, I don't. Forsythe is barely adequate and Chambers is the captain's pet."

"Damn it, Peter! You'll never get anywhere in life by letting people know you don't like them. Forsythe's all right as a person, even if he's not much of an officer. If I smile at him he does what I suggest. I can do his job and mine, too."

"He depends on you a great deal."

"Promise me that you will smile at someone once a day."

Thorton rolled his eyes.

"Just once a day," Perry persisted.

Thorton knew he was not good at ingratiating himself with people. He preferred to keep to himself. "I don't think a smile will overcome my naturally taciturn nature."

"You talk to me so that proves you're capable. We'll take it step by step. Smile first. We'll go on from there."

"If you insist."

Perry held his stomach through another corkscrewing roll. He braced his feet against Thorton's sea chest. Water sloshed across the floor. Unbeknownst to either of them, Achmed was on the other side of the wall with his ear pressed to a glass and the glass to the wall. He was able to hear Perry and sometimes Thorton. Perry was less than a foot away from him with only the thinness of the bulkhead between them.

Thorton spoke again. "The captain thinks I'm shabby. I heard him say so to Chambers. He thinks you cut a fine figure, though. He said, 'Perry looks like a naval officer. We'll make something of him yet.'" He puffed out his cheeks and chest in imitation of Bishop's face and figure.

Perry smiled. "Did he? I'm glad the old duffer is starting to cotton to me."

"I wish I had a new coat."

"Hey. I've got three, you know. I'll give you one of mine."

That piqued Thorton's interest. "I couldn't," he demurred.

"I've got a new dress coat and a decent frock coat. You can have my old dress coat."

Thorton sat up. "Really? But you might need it."

Being a poor lieutenant with no family and no line of credit, he'd gotten his ordinary uniform but had not been able to afford the dress coat, a coat he had not expected to need any time soon. Not when he was third from the bottom of seniority and had been furloughed on half pay shortly thereafter. Thank God he'd gotten promoted when he did; the war had ended almost immediately and after that there were no more promotions.

"Bah. I like my new coat very much. Bishop's never seen the old one; he'll never know."

So the sea chest was opened and the coat tried. It was a little short on Thorton, but a decent fit. Perry was an inch shorter but with the same breadth in the chest. Thorton sat on the sea chest with his feet on the billet ends to keep his feet dry.

"There! You look much better. Very dashing. Who on earth made that old coat for you? It doesn't do you justice."

Thorton considered himself in the glass and had to admit that the cut flattered him. The white facings were very handsome. He smiled. "Thank you."

On the other side of the wall Achmed withdrew the glass and pondered. So. The junior lieutenant was poor and condescended to because of it. He finally knew how to get to the man. He put away the glass and considered how to make use of his discovery.

The lieutenant's cabin was warm and stuffy with the two of them in there. Spray rattled against the little window. Thorton put away the glass and grabbed Perry's hand. "Roger, you're the best friend I ever had!"

Perry grinned at him. He let Thorton hold his hand, then suddenly Thorton lifted it and kissed it. He wanted to do and say so much more —although a laconic man by nature, he was not completely silent, and the reduction in his speech enforced by the captain's judgment had been hard to bear. At the same time he thought he had done and said too much and he looked away. Perry was surprised but not offended by the hand-kissing. Men kissed each other's hands as a sign of respect and that was how he took it, and indeed, how Thorton meant it. It was only that he felt so much more than he intended to convey. Perry gave Thorton's hand a tug and patted the bunk for him to sit down. Thorton sat next to him.

"See? This is better. This is more like the Peter Thorton I used to know. You have to keep your lips locked around Bishop but not the wardroom. I'm sure Forsythe and Chambers will like you once you open up to them."

Thorton swallowed hard. "I'm afraid that if I say anything, I'll say too much."

Perry snorted. "Next time you see Forsythe, how about a simple, 'How are you feeling? I hope your seasickness is better.' The little human things endear a man—they think you don't care."

"Well, I don't! They'll get over it soon enough."

Perry rolled his eyes. He wrapped his arm around Thorton's shoulders and pulled him close. He put his lips conspiratorially close to Thorton's ear. "That's why they don't like you. I don't especially care if they're sick or not, but I pretend to care and they like me for it. You should, too." With his other hand he tapped his friend's chest right over the heart. "We call it 'being a gentleman.'"

Thorton's heart hammered. Perry was being avuncular and nothing more; even though he was a couple of years younger than Thorton he acted like his older brother. Thorton licked dry lips.

Perry tapped his chest again. "Practice on me. Say, 'How are you feeling today, Roger?'"

Thorton whispered wordlessly, cleared his throat, and tried again, "How are you feeling today, Roger?"

Perry replied. "I'll be glad when I get my sea legs back. I was seven months ashore. What about you, Peter? How long did you have to wait for a commission?"

"Seven months."

Perry explained, "This is 'small talk.' That means you talk about small things. For example, you could have said, 'Seven months. I was on the old *Dauntless*.' Then they will know something about you. They might follow up by asking, 'Did you know old What's-His-Face, the cook? He's my mother's cousin's husband.' And now you have a conversation started."

"Oh." Thorton was intensely aware of the warmth of Perry's body next to him and the friendly arm around his shoulder. "I'd like to talk with you, if I could." He thought it came out well.

Perry gave him half a squeeze and lay down on the bunk and put his feet on Thorton's sea chest again. He propped his hands behind his head. "I'd like to talk to you, too. What shall we talk about?" He was smiling as he teased his friend.

Thorton turned to face him, but Perry's dishabille made him flush. The well turned calves in snug wool stockings, the strong thighs limned under the long cotton drawers, the bulge of his groin concealed under a thin cloth, the thin white jersey hiked up to show a line of his belly . . . These things made the blood run more hotly through his body. He tried to find a way to approach his deeper feelings. "Do you like me, Roger?"

Perry laughed at that. "Yes, I like you." He grabbed the pillow and belted Thorton with it. "God's blood! After seven months of rooming together we're both still alive, so we must like each other."

Thorton fended off the pillow. "Why do you like me? Other people don't like me, but you do. I'm not cadging for compliments. I just don't understand why some people take to me and some don't."

Perry considered the question. "You're a good officer. You work hard. You don't complain. You don't bother people more than necessary. You're dependable. You're intelligent. Once in a while, you even make me laugh!"

Thorton smiled to hear such a flattering assessment of himself. He leaned on his elbow next to his friend. He stared at the chest and shoulders that were so broad above the narrow waist. He wanted to reach out and touch that handsome body and feel its warm strength. "I'm very fond of you," he whispered. He didn't look at Perry's face as he said it.

"Well, I'm rather fond of you," Perry replied gruffly. "I thought you knew that."

Thorton's heart soared. He turned to look Perry full in the face. There was a genuine warmth in those brown eyes and they drew Thorton in. He slowly lowered his lips to brush against Perry's. As he did Perry's warm expression turned puzzled, then surprised. He stared in astonishment as Thorton gave him the lightest of kisses right on the mouth. Thorton's eyes were closed and he lingered there a moment to savor the feeling. Perry said and did nothing. Thorton lifted up and opened his eyes and stared into Perry's. Suddenly Perry sat up and drew a deep breath.

"I'm not *that* fond of you," he said roughly.

Thorton's face turned scarlet. His heart plummeted and would have put a hole right through the bottom of the ship if it had weighed anything. He didn't speak. He sat up just as suddenly and sat trembling on the edge of the bed. He shouldn't have said anything. He shouldn't have done anything. He shouldn't have opened up. He shouldn't have listened to Perry. He should have kept himself clamped tight in iron self-control. It was better to be thought cold and left alone than to betray himself like this. Oh God, he was ruined! What if Perry told the others? He and Perry certainly couldn't be friends after this. He jumped up from the bed and moved as far away as the little room would permit. He didn't even notice the cold water soaking his shoes.

Perry's eyes were wild and his jaw tense as he watched the other man. He grabbed his shirt and started pulling it on.

"I'm sorry," Thorton whispered. He squeezed his eyes shut and felt faint. The rolling of the ship pitched him backwards and his butt met the wall. He slid down to land in a heap on the floorboards. Water soaked his shins. He held his head in his hands. "I'm sorry, Roger. I'm sorry. I knew I shouldn't say anything. I knew I would say too much. Please don't tell anyone. I'll see if I can sleep with the midshipmen. I'll get out."

He reached blindly for his sea chest and started to drag it towards the door. Tears were welling up and he hated them, hated himself, hated the navy, hated England, hated the entire world. After what he had just done no one would want to associate with him. The men wouldn't respect him. He'd have to apply the tawse constantly to make them obey and Bishop would be breathing fire down his neck at every instant. They would never trust him and they'd tell coarse jokes at his expense. His career was over. There would never be a promotion or any consideration from his fellow officers. The future would be a hell not worth living.

Thorton's reaction gave Perry an even greater shock than his action. He put his hand on the sea chest to stop it moving. "Peter, I don't know what to say. I had no idea."

Thorton knuckled his eyes to blot out the tears that weren't falling. He swallowed and took a deep breath. He mustn't cry. He hadn't cried in years. He mustn't prove himself a poltroon as well as a pervert. "I've tried to be a good officer, Roger. I've tried to do my work as well as possible without complaint. I've tried to be everything a naval officer should be. I've applied myself to my studies and striven to master every detail. All in the hope that someday, if somehow, I gave myself away, maybe . . . it wouldn't matter. But it does matter. It will always matter. There is nothing I can do that will compensate for this." He gave Perry a despairing look.

Perry released the breath he didn't realize he was holding. "My God. 'Tis not just me, is it?"

Thorton shook his head. He dared to glance at his friend who was looking at him in horror. He hung his head in shame. He hated himself for giving himself away, but sooner or later it had to happen. He couldn't keep on this way. He was only human. There was nothing he could do to prove himself so that the British navy would overlook this once it came to light. He'd be whipped around the fleet and hanged. If he had been drunk and derelict on duty the punishment would not be so harsh. Even a drunken fool could enjoy a long and respectable career in the British navy. But for this there was no excuse and no forgiveness. He pushed his sea chest back against the wall. He wouldn't be needing it anymore.

"Goodbye, Roger. I'm sorry." He rose to his feet and like a sleepwalker headed out the door.

CHAPTER 6 : REPRIEVE

Perry sat stunned on his bunk, trying to absorb the immensity of the secret his best friend had kept from him for more than two years and seven months of living together while sharing the same bed, only to break his silence now. He felt supremely guilty as if it were somehow his fault—that as long as the secret had not been shared, it didn't exist. He had never dealt with something like this before. He'd heard about it. Lewd jokes, whispers about this officer or that, the randy rampages of men cooped up below decks for months at a time without female relief . . . Never could he picture Thorton involved in anything like that. He had respected him.

Meanwhile Achmed heard the cabin door open and put his plan into action. He had not listened after the discussion about the coat. He was busy with his own schemes and therefore ignorant of that which would have mortified Thorton had he known. He stepped into the wardroom, spotted Thorton walking toward the ladder with heavy steps, and said, "Good afternoon, Lieutenant. You're looking well today."

Thorton stopped and stared at him. Could the man not see it written in his face that he planned to kill himself? He would go on deck and slip quietly over the gunwale so that there would be no cry of 'man overboard' and no rescue attempt. He thought about the *Ajax* sailing away while he foundered in the sea. He would swim—he knew how. He couldn't bring himself to simply sink and drown. He'd swim until he was exhausted, then drown. Thus did the urge to live war against the urge to die.

Achmed was smiling at him, waiting for his answer. "Good afternoon, sir," he forced himself to reply. Rote courtesy. He meant none of it. Please God, let Achmed not detain him. He couldn't simply walk away; Achmed would follow him. He couldn't commit suicide in peace with Achmed yammering at him. He forced himself to smile. Perry had made him promise to smile once a day, so he smiled at Achmed. His head was reeling.

Achmed smiled back. "I see you've been saving your good coat until we were under way. You look very dashing today."

Not even a suicidal man is immune to flattery. Thorton blinked blankly at Achmed, then looked down at himself. The brass buttons marched evenly down his chest and the gold lace was in good condition, even if it was Perry's second best coat. Perry liked fine clothes and had spent the necessary money. Or one of his mistresses had. He should give it back before he killed himself. It would be ungrateful to take the man's coat with him when he would have no need of it where he was going.

"Do you think so?" he asked, surprised out of both his taciturnity and his depression.

"You look every inch the naval officer," Achmed assured him. Thorton was listening. Achmed was pleased that he'd found the key to the man at last. As much as he smiled and blandished others, he hated to lose the secret games he played with them. Thorton was a challenge he was determined to overcome for the sake of his own pride as well as for any information that might be gotten out of him.

Thorton straightened up and squared his shoulders. His hair brushed the deckhead. "I have forgotten my hat," he said. His voice seemed distant and tinny to his ears.

"I wouldn't wear your good hat today, Mr. Thorton. It has been spitting rain and it would be a shame to spoil it. You'll want your greatcoat, too."

"I haven't got a good hat, sir," Thorton replied as honest as ever. It was a fault in his character that he had never learned to dissemble. His life would have been easier if he had.

Achmed feigned surprise. "You haven't! You must have reported immediately to your ship without taking time to shop for yourself. You're a very efficient officer, Mr. Thorton. But really, it is no sin for a man to think about himself a little. Come in, come in." He opened the door to opulence.

Had Thorton been in a normal state of mind he might have thought Achmed was laying it on a little thick. However, he wasn't in his usual state of mind and Achmed had touched a nerve. He did not realize that his plan to drown himself in misery had been temporarily put on hold. He was curious about the man, his cabin, and whatever he would do or say next. For some unfathomable reason the wily Turk appeared to like him.

"Come in and shut the door. The weather's damp," Achmed called to him. So Thorton stepped onto the thick carpet and shut the door behind him. "Have a seat. I hope you don't mind sitting on a cushion. It is our custom." Achmed was lucky enough to have a dry cabin; Thorton experienced a moment of envy. Had there been no Achmed he would have the dry cabin himself and not have been forced into intimacy with Perry.

Thorton selected a gold cushion and sat down cross-legged like a Turk. He flipped his tails back and they stuck out at angles across the rug. The blue breeches pulled a little tight in that position; English clothes were not made for Turkish habits. Achmed dug through his luggage and moved parcels and tins.

"When I first came to England people stared at me so much I thought I should buy some of your local fashions to blend in, but I'm afraid didn't it work. I am a Sallee Turk and there's no hiding it. As it happens, I have a hat and cloak and some other things I don't need." He produced the hat. It was a very good black hat with a trim of gold braid around the brim and a naval cockade on it. In truth, Achmed had used it as a disguise to nose about English dockyards. Unlike Thorton, he was a very good dissembler.

Artlessly the Turk said, "I was taking it home as a souvenir, but I understand I've put you out of your cabin, so please accept it as a small compensation for the inconvenience I've caused you."

Thorton was stunned. "'Tis a very fine hat, sir." He did not question why Achmed had a tricorn with a naval cockade. More than one landlubber had adopted a nautical air to flatter himself he shared something of the dashing look of a naval officer. Thorton was gratified the man knew he'd troubled the lieutenant by taking over his cabin. Still Thorton made his demurrers. "'Tis damned civil of you, sir, but really, I can't accept."

Achmed put the hat in his hands and smiled warmly at him. "I insist."

Thorton clutched the hat to his breast while Achmed sat cross-legged on a cushion of his own right in front of him. He opened up the cabinet and said, "You are off-duty, yes? Now you can enjoy some Madeira. I admire your sobriety. It was very prudent of you to refrain from drinking that night when you knew you had to press men before we left."

Thorton was pleased to be called 'prudent' and ducked his gaze. "Just doing my duty, sir." He accepted the golden of cup of ruby wine and sipped cautiously.

Achmed poured a cup for himself, then secured the bottle and shut the doors again. The ship rolled along. "How long have you been in service, Mr. Thorton?"

He realized that this was what Perry called 'small talk' and that Achmed was good at it. Mindful of the lesson he had received, he replied, "I ran away to sea when I was sixteen. Three years of that, then I was pressed into the English navy. I was on the *Marigold*, so four years in the Spanish navy. All told I've been to sea thirteen years."

"You were in the Spanish navy?"

Thorton realized a foreigner most likely had not heard about the incident. "Oh, that. The Spanish stopped the *Marigold* in the West Indies, claimed we were supplying the Dutch, condemned our cargo, and pressed the lot of us. It was a scandal, I'm told, but we were at war with France, so aside from the usual protests, nothing happened. The officers were released, but the rest of us were stuck."

"How did you get away?"

"I jumped overboard at Sint Maarten and swam to the French side of the harbor. A rice schooner hauled me aboard and wouldn't give me back. I got to France that way, and from there, an English wine sloop took me back home."

"What an adventure! You must speak fluent Spanish then."

Thorton drank more of the very good wine and nodded. "A little French too."

Achmed was very curious now. He kept Thorton talking. "So you would be twenty-nine now. My son is almost that old. He's married and has children. Are you married, Mr. Thorton?"

"I'm married to the service," Thorton replied. He did not correct the man regarding his age since his birthday was coming up soon anyhow.

Achmed wasn't sure if the straitlaced young officer was joking or serious. He smiled. "Yes, I've heard it said that a British naval officer should never marry. 'Tis a hard duty. In Sallee things are much better. Our officers and corsairs see their wives and children quite often. I miss mine. I have been away a long time. God willing, I will be home in a month."

"Where do you live, sir?"

"Zokhara, the most beautiful city on the Middle Sea. Your health, Lieutenant." He tipped his cup high but drank little.

Thorton drank deeply. "And yours," he replied politely.

"Pity you won't be coming all the way with me. We could stop at Madeira. Wine is as cheap as beer on the island."

"You've been to Madeira?"

"Oh, yes, many times. Have you?"

"Not to go ashore. The Spanish take on water and supplies there."

Achmed smiled and kept silent. The conversation stalled. Thorton slowly realized that he was expected to say something. He cast about for something to add. "Have you been to France before?"

"Many times. I went over often when I was young. I used to be a Sallee rover myself. When I was much younger. After that, a fat merchant." He patted his belly and laughed good-naturedly.

That got Thorton's attention. "You were a corsair, sir?"

Achmed grinned self-deprecatingly." I wasn't always fat. Or married. Or old." His good humor was infectious.

"I don't think you're old, sir."

"But you do think I'm fat and married!" Achmed teased him.

Thorton was horrified. "Oh, no, sir! I didn't mean that at all! I would never mean to imply any such thing, sir!"

Achmed couldn't resist teasing him a little further. He feigned surprise. "You think no one would marry a fat old man like me?"

"Sir!" Thorton was aghast. He was offending their guest and Bishop would have him caned for it.

Achmed patted Thorton's knee. "Forgive me. I have been amusing myself at your expense."

Thorton blinked. Slowly it registered that he had been made an object of mirth and he grew hot. "Sir, if you think I—"

The Turk raised a hand and cut him off. "Peace be upon you, Lieutenant. Peace," he said more softly. "It is you who must forgive me. Enforced idleness on a ship has bored me, and I disported myself at your expense. It was unkind of me. I beg your forgiveness." He bowed low to the lieutenant. He watched through his lashes to see how Thorton took having a great dignitary humble himself to him.

Thorton was baffled. "You've no need to apologize to me, sir. I'm only a lieutenant."

Achmed rose and raised his glass. "You won't be a lieutenant for long. Cheers." He clinked cups with the Englishman.

"Cheers," Thorton replied. Having that damnable streak of honesty about him, he added, "I am the third most junior lieutenant in the navy, so it will be a long time before I get a promotion. I don't have any patrons or influence."

Achmed, being a retired corsair, was a good judge of seamen. He knew that Perry and Thorton were worth their weight in salt and was quite surprised to find Thorton was such a junior lieutenant. "Did you have trouble with the examination? I understand the mathematics are damnably difficult."

"No, the mathematics were easy. I passed the examination a long time ago. But I had been an enlisted hand, so I was stuck at midshipman for a long time."

"You were promoted to midshipman based on merit?" Achmed made a note that this man thought the fiendishly obdurate mathematics of navigation were 'easy.'

"Aye aye, sir." Thorton wasn't sure where this conversation was going or why he was saying so much about himself. Still, he was a person of no consequence, so talking about himself seemed much safer than say, talking about how many frigates were anchored at Plymouth, which was one of many details that the wily Achmed had extracted from the other officers.

He looked into his cup and cursed himself for a fool. He was being pumped for information. He had been sunk so far in his own personal misery that he had not realized it. He was holding a gold cup of excellent wine in one hand and a very good hat in the other hand, a hat which he had already accepted so couldn't give back even though he didn't want any more. He set the cup on the carpet. "Please pardon me, I have something to attend."

Achmed collected the cup and rose with him. He smiled. "Of course. Thank you for spending a little time with me. I was bored but you have lightened my day."

Thorton said, "Sir," and fled.

CHAPTER 7 : THE COAST OF CHERBOURG

Thorton returned to the small cabin he shared with Perry. He didn't know what to say and he was holding a very fine hat. Perry looked at him in surprise. "Where did that come from?" He was fully dressed which relieved both of them.

"Achmed gave it to me to compensate for turning me out of my cabin."

"Say, that was damned decent of him. The hat is nice, too. Have you tried it on?" So Thorton put it on his head. He had to bend his knees to keep from mashing the hat against the deckhead. "Zounds! You look positively dapper!"

A knock sounded on the door. Thorton opened it and the blackamoor handed him a triangular tin. It was the hat storage box.

Thorton said, "Thank you. My compliments to Mr. Achmed." He shut the door.

Perry laughed. "You should see your face."

"I'm having a very strange day."

"You certainly are." There was a pregnant pause. "Look here. We're still friends, right? Your personal affairs are your personal affairs. I won't say anything."

Relief flooded through Thorton and he sagged. He put a hand against the wall. "Thank you," he said with great feeling.

"Well then, no more of that. Best put your fine hat and coat away to save for the right occasion."

That was a practical action to take, so Thorton opened the tin, packed the hat in its tissue paper, and put it away under the bunk. He folded the coat and stowed in carefully in his sea chest. He cheered up thinking that he had both a new coat and a new hat and was still friends with Perry.

Suddenly feet scrambled overhead. The cry of 'Land ho!" came down to them.

"Grab your sou'wester, we're going out!" Perry scrambled into his sea boots and Thorton got out his oilskin.

Arriving on deck they discovered land in the offing. It was quite sunny on the shores of France while it was drizzling and dripping in the English Channel. The idlers congregated at the rail. The crowd included lieutenants and midshipmen as well. They continued to approach the coast and the French fishermen looked up from their nets and shielded their eyes. It stopped raining but water kept splattering down as the sails dripped. Achmed came out dressed in an oiled robe with a hood over his head. The *Ajax* changed course to parallel the coast. Headlands passed and they saw whitewashed cottages with thatch roofs clustered at the edge of the water: fishing villages. The bucolic scene continued throughout the afternoon. As the sun slid down the western sky fish-boats headed home. By evening the *Ajax* had raised Cap Levy and the town of Cherbourg come into view.

Cherbourg was a decent harbor, made better by French moles and forts, and worse by English bombardment during the late war. The French were at work rebuilding the mole damaged by the English. It was a substantial improvement over the old one. It formed a long causeway that protected the harbor from the northeastern waves. There had been many windmills on the old mole because of the constant wind, but they had been reduced to rubble by the English assault. The rubble was now being used to fill in the enlarged embankment.

"Hoist the colors," Captain Bishop ordered. The sight of the British ensign must have alarmed the townsfolk. "Take us in." The sailing master gave directions and Perry and Thorton were pleased to be idle watchers as Forsythe attended Bishop. They remembered the last time they had been here.

Perry pointed. "Look. That is where the *Dauntless* grappled the *Martinique*. We caught a Tartar that day!"

"And the *Hermes* under Horner came to our rescue. I admit, I was pleased to see her."

Perry laughed. "You were formidable that day. I think the men were more afraid of you than the French!"

"Do not tease me about it!" Thorton objected.

"You made lieutenant, didn't you? But you never tell the story, not even when you are drunk."

"I don't get drunk."

"You should."

"Besides, the *Dauntless* went down anyhow. 'Tis not the sort of thing to brag about."

"But you saved me and some other men from drowning when it did."

Thorton was uneasy with praise. "You would have done the same for me."

"I can't swim! I couldn't have."

It was not a difficult thing to enter a harbor in the late afternoon with a steady wind and a broad channel. The hands were calling the bottom as the *Ajax* eased into the channel. Fishboats parted and hugged the shores to either side to let the frigate pass. Suddenly a cry went up, "Line fouled!"

Then came a series of thuds and scrapes along the bottom. Thorton was amused and sorry for the officers on duty. Cherbourg was a deep harbor, but they'd managed to find shoals anyhow. A sudden hard thump jolted them and they grabbed the rail.

"Balls, that's bad," Thorton said.

"Back sails! Fall off!" Bishop roared. "Damn it, Mr. Blakesley! Aren't you minding your way?"

Blakesley was the unhappy sailing master. "I am, sir. The channel's supposed to be eighteen fathoms deep! The chart must be in error!"

Many hands, Thorton and Perry included, were peering over the side. The water was murky, but there was a line of something in the water. A log . . . no, a mast.

"My god. The *Dauntless*!" Thorton exclaimed. He turned to Bishop, "Sir, there's a wreck in the channel!"

Bishop swore again. "Damn ye, I said BACK SAIL, ye foul lot of teagues! Mind your business and cane the laggards, Mr. Thorton!" His stentorian bellow carried the length of the ship. Properly motivated by threat and insult, the foretop hands backed the sail and the rotation of the vessel slowed a little.

Bishop bellowed again. "Mr. Forsythe! Take the launch and set the stream anchor. Take Mr. Chambers. Teach him the importance of not swinging your stern like a doxy. Mr. Thorton! Take the pinnace and Mr. Maynard. Show him how to set a kedge off the larboard bow." With the wind blowing from the north they could not sail off. Worse, the stern continued drifting forward, causing the ship to slowly pivot on the wreck.

The captain continued issuing orders. "Mr. Perry, you will supervise the warp. Smartly, men, smartly!"

"Aye aye, sir!" came the various replies. They moved quickly to their posts, bawling orders as they went. "Kedge detail on deck! MacDonald! Forsythe! Chambers! Maynard! Prepare the launch! Prepare the pinnace! Hands to the capstan! Hands to the hawse!"

MacDonald piped up the boatswain's mates and sent one to each of the boats and another to the capstan. The launch was launched and the crew climbed into it, Thorton followed them down the ladder to drop into the pinnace as it came along side. They waited for the kedge anchor to be brought to them. Although it was nowhere near as big as the bower anchor, it was not a trifling object, and the hands had to wrestle it forward. It took a few moments to run the cable out through the hawse-hole, then bend it back and bind it to the ring at the top of the stock. That done, it was carefully lowered over the side. The men received it into the boat.

"Haul away easy!" Perry shouted.

Thorton repeated to his men, "Haul away easy, boys." They began to row away from the *Ajax*. Thorton took his bearings and told the mate, "Make for that windmill on the shore. Handsomely lads, handsome does it." The men rowed slowly and the line paid out.

Thorton ran out far enough and waited. He asked Maynard, "Have you ever kedged?"

Maynard shook his head. Blond curls flopped over his shoulders and gleamed in the French sun. "Not personally, but I've seen it done. We were aground on the Fair Banks in the *Courage* last year."

On board it was Perry's job to supervise the anchor cables and capstan. They had to wait while the stream anchor—a much larger beast than the kedge—was lowered gently into the launch and rowed away. It disappeared beyond the stern.

Bishop bellowed orders from the quarterdeck, then Perry's voice came across the water, "Heave!" The men relied, "Ho!" The boatswain's pipe pulsed with short rising notes, setting the rhythm for the haul. Chanteys were not permitted in the British navy; the boatswain set the pace with his call. As the men worked the capstan, the stern pulled on the anchor. The cable tightened and the anchor bit into the sea bottom, and slowly the stern was dragged back towards the north.

Bishop shouted, "Mr. Thorton, are you ready!"

Thorton stood and yelled back, "Ready on kedge, sir!"

Bishop broke out into a stream of invective and the heaving of the hawser stopped. Perry must have run into a complication with the cable. The men in the boat waited. Thorton stayed alert; he did not want to be found deficient in any way. His own self-respect required it. He was still smarting from the emotional turmoil of the afternoon, but there in the boat with work to do and the sun shining on the water he was rather glad he hadn't killed himself. What a fool he had been to think such melodramatic thoughts! Still, he felt a bit wobbly inside.

The matter on board was sorted out, and the stern was warped a little further. Finally Bishop bellowed, "Kedge away!"

Thorton rechecked everything, then relayed the order to his own hands. "Down anchor!" Down it went with a splash. He watched it go, then commanded, "Out oars. Take us two fathoms off." Once the boat was clear, he sang out, "Kedge away!"

The capstan creaked and the boat slowly pulled off the obstacle. There was a loud scraping noise and the hull shivered once or twice, then suddenly the line went slack. There was profanity on board, and he could hear both Perry and Bishop cursing. The boatswain's pipe shrilled 'belay.'

Bishop screamed, "You said the kedge was set, Mr. Thorton!"

Thorton pressed his hand to his brow. How could he know the kedge had not bitten until they hauled the line? It was certainly not his fault it had pulled loose from the bottom. Anchors did that. It was not unusual to have to reset an anchor.

"Your pardon, sir!" Thorton called back.

On deck the men righted themselves. The kedge was hauled up and the boatswain's pipe recalled the boat. They rowed in and received the kedge again.

Perry looked over at him. "Ready?"

"Aye aye, sir."

"Let the line run," he heard Perry tell his work gang. Again the pipes passed the order.

Thorton said, "Out oars. Row, men." Once more they rowed away. Once more the kedge was dropped and the line hauled. He heard the 'heave-ho' on board, the ship scraped a little, then suddenly glided free.

"She's clear!" he shouted.

Perry looked over, word was passed, and the 'boat return' was piped. Thorton ordered his men to give wide berth to the anchor rising up. He thought he spotted something unnatural below the waterline of the larboard side, but it was difficult to discern through the murky water. He didn't dare come in too close while they were getting the kedge up, so he said, "Let's go around the other side." They did, he came up the starboard ladder.

"Mr. Thorton!" Bishop roared. Thorton hurried to the quarterdeck and saluted. "What do you think you were doing skylarking at a time like this?"

"I beg your pardon. I was inspecting the hull, sir."

Bishop screamed until his face was red. "THAT IS THE CAPTAIN'S PREROGATIVE YOU INSOLENT WHELP! Six stripes of the cane before sunset tonight! Your behavior has been entirely SLACK today!"

"I'm a commissioned officer! You can't beat me!"

Those were not the words to ameliorate the captain's temper. "I CAN and I WILL! I will teach you a LESSON for your impudence! I will have ORDER and OBEDIENCE on my vessel!"

Thorton's face fell. "Aye aye, sir," he said woodenly.

Bishop was beside himself. "It is my duty. MY DUTY! And you, running off with my boat to prevent me from carrying out my duty!"

There was nothing he could say that would help. "I'm sorry, sir."

"SILENCE! I'll deal with you when I get back. Go to your cabin."

"Aye aye, sir."

So the captain went over the side into the launch and inspected the hull for himself. When he came back aboard he said, "All is well."

Perry had finished getting the anchor up. The great ship, finding herself balked by the wreck, moved abreast of the mole that was being rebuilt and anchored there. Thorton was worried. He put his head out of his cabin door but didn't dare leave. When he saw the wardroom steward, Humphrey by name, he inquired, "Are we holed?" The man assured him that all was well. "Quietly tell Mr. Perry I want to see him, please."

Perry came back from supervising the stowing of the boat and stuck his head in. "Hullo. You're having quite the day, aren't you?" he said cheerfully.

"Are we holed?"

"Captain Bishop says no. Why?"

"I think I saw something in the larboard bow, but I couldn't be sure. Will you check the cable tier, just to give me peace of mind?"

"The boatswain's making an inspection now."

"Good."

Perry returned to the deck. A few minutes later word was passed to Bishop, "Boatswain says we're taking water in the cable locker, sir."

Bishop was angry again. "I'll inspect it myself. You young idiots couldn't tell bilgewater from your own piss." He stormed down from the quarterdeck.

MacDonald and his mate were moving wet cable and had found the source of the leak. They touched their forelocks respectfully.

"As I thought. Bilgewater."

"No, sir. A hole." The whole was about two inches by four inches. Water was running down the inside of the planks, dripping through the grated floor, and into the bilge with a steady trickle.

"What! We didn't hit that hard."

"No, sir. We ran onto a spar from the wreck and it punched a hole in the bottom."

Bishop swore. "That rascal Thorton delayed me in my inspection. This could have been caught sooner."

MacDonald stared at him. "Aye aye, sir." The captain hadn't spotted it; the boatswain had found it during routine inspection. He really didn't see how it could possibly be Thorton's fault, but it wasn't his place to say so. "I'll need the carpenter, sir."

"Pass the word, Mr. Chambers."

As leaks went it was minor and soon mended. In the meantime, the call of 'all hands on deck' was piped. A marine came to the wardroom and escorted Thorton out onto the weather deck where the grating had become a permanent fixture.

Forsythe called, "Hands to witness punishment." He wore his dress uniform with its white facings. With calm water his seasickness had subsided and he was no longer green.

Bishop stood before them and in his abominably loud voice, informed them, "Mr. Thorton has willfully usurped his superior officer's authority by taking the pinnace on a lark, thereby delaying his captain in the execution of his duties and endangering the safety of the vessel. He is hereby sentenced to twelve stripes of the cane."

Thorton groaned inwardly. There were no arguments on this vessel, no careful considerations of additional evidence or mitigating circumstances. He handed his hat and coat to Humphrey to hold, then his waistcoat, stock and shirt. Stripped to the waist he took his place before the grating.

"Prepare to receive your just punishment, Mr. Thorton." Bishop's voice was spiteful.

Thorton leaned forward and grabbed the grating. He set his jaw resolutely. The cane whistled down. MacDonald was a philosophical sort and set about thrashing him. Even if Thorton didn't deserve to be caned for delaying the captain's inspection, he probably deserved to be caned for something. Young men always did. The first red welt laid across his back, then another, and another. MacDonald worked methodically until Thorton had twelve welts crisscrossing his back. It stung like hell but the blond lieutenant pressed his face against his forearms and didn't cry out. He comforted himself with the thought that it didn't hurt nearly as bad as the humiliation of revealing his secret to Perry. But it hurt enough. Finally it was over and he was allowed upright.

The caning had restored Bishop's good humor. "Let this be a lesson to you not to overstep your bounds, young man."

"Aye aye, sir," Thorton replied mechanically.

Bishop inspected his back. "Ha. That's nothing. Get dressed and report for duty."

Thorton pulled his thin white jersey over his torso, grimacing as the fabric scraped across the welts. Some of them were bleeding. Well, it wasn't the first shirt he'd ruined in naval service. He pulled his linen shirt over top of it and buttoned it up, then carefully redid his stock. Humphrey helped him into his coat and handed him his hat.

"Sir," he saluted Bishop.

The captain replied. "You know the quarter bill. To your place."

"Aye aye, sir." He did know. This was his watch below. He wasn't due on until midnight. Apparently Bishop did not know the quarter bill. His lieutenants had it memorized.

Achmed was standing in the back of the officers and off to the side, arms crossed over his chest. Thorton never looked at him, just passed him by and descended the ladder to the wardroom.

Captain Bishop said, "Dismiss hands, Mr. Forsythe."

Forsythe shouted, "Dismissed!"

The hands went their various ways. Naturally Thorton was a topic of conversation. "Initiative doesn't pay on this boat." Achmed overheard it. No, he thought to himself, it certainly doesn't. He would have to befriend Thorton. Surely resentment against his treatment would make him receptive to Achmed's blandishments.

Bishop went to his cabin to write reports. The sailing master recorded the punishment in his log. Perry was off duty, so he came to check on his friend. Thorton was lying on his stomach his seachest, still dressed.

Perry spoke softly. "Let's get you cleaned up." His hands were gentle as he helped the miserable lieutenant ease off the coat and bloody shirt. Salt water stung, but Perry got Thorton's back cleaned up, then washed Thorton's jersey in the bucket. "I got the bloodstains out before they set," he told him.

Thorton grunted.

"Move over."

Thorton scooted over next to the hull. Perry sat down next to him. "About earlier. When I said I'm fond of you, I meant I love you like a brother as Christ commanded. I'm an orphan. You're like family to me."

Thorton smiled a little. He leaned his shoulder against the side of the ship and winced. "I don't have a brother, either. Well, I have a stepbrother, but that hardly counts."

Perry clasped his hand. "Brothers then?"

"Aye, brothers," Thorton replied. He could live with that. It gave his heart some ease. He was able to close his eyes and rest a little.

CHAPTER 8 : STORM AT THE END OF THE WORLD

In spite of gloomy predictions, the fair weather held and they left Finistère behind. They traveled south through the Bay of Biscay without complications. The swells were immense. They had the entire width of the Atlantic Ocean to build into mighty rhythmic heavings like the regular respiration of a giant's chest. The masts described corkscrews as the frigate mounted the waves. First, as the bow rose up on the swell, she tilted to the larboard. Anything loose rolled aft and then to port. As the wave passed under the midships, she righted herself, then her stern lifted and her bow plunged down the other side, her masts leaning to the starboard. Everything aft rolled forward. When the next wave came on she righted herself and began the climb again, repeating the cycle endlessly.

Perry and Forsythe were seasick again, Forsythe very much so. Thorton and Maynard were not. Perry found his sea legs, but Forsythe continued to be miserable. As they sped on the wind shifted to the northeast and they ran free and fast before it. The motion became more violent as the winds were at cross purposes to the waves. Spume flew up and the foredeck was wet and slippery. Sometimes spray burst over the waist and speckled the weather deck with fat cold droplets. Dark clouds piled up in the north.

"Storm-breeders," Thorton told Maynard as they stood watch on the poop. "Go tell Captain Bishop."

Maynard dreaded the captain but went below and delivered the message.

Bishop came up. "In topgallants. Stow the flying jib and set the small jib. Stow the main and mizzen topgallant staysails." He watched a while, then gave further orders. "Two reefs in the topsails and mizzen. In middle staysail and mizzen topmast staysail.

"Aye aye, sir."

The orders were given and the men swarmed aloft to neatly bundle up the sails. The pressed men had learned that much at least. They'd feel the sting of the starter if they didn't. Satisfied, Bishop went below. The *Ajax* scudded along merrily and Thorton enjoyed the ride. Privately he thought it was early to be reducing sail. They had been making spanking good time and the seas were merely confused, not truly rough. To his mind at least. The landsmen were puking in the scuppers.

Over the next half hour the corkscrew motion grew more violent, punctured at intervals with sudden slaps and shudders as the waves worked themselves into white horses that galloped across the seas. The jarring drops and sudden whooshes added to the motion. Thorton kept looking over his shoulder to watch the storm chasing them. He thought it might pass mostly north of them. As he watched, lightning dropped from the clouds.

"Lightning. Go tell Bishop." So Maynard ran down again.

Bishop came up and gave more orders. "Goosewing the main and fore topsails. Take in the mizzen sail. Set the storm staysails. You'll be wanting your oilskin shortly, Mr. Thorton. Send the hands to dinner, then extinguish the galley fires."

"Thank you, sir. Mr. Maynard! Pass the word, early dinner, then lights out. Men to don foul weather gear. Run life lines. Bring me my oilskin and sou'wester when you come back and be wearing yours."

"Aye aye, sir. Thank you, sir." Maynard ran down.

"Call me if anything changes, and I do mean *anything*." Bishop gave Thorton a glare to underscore his command.

"Aye aye, sir."

"See that you do." Bishop went below.

It had been like that all down the Channel and around the corner of France. Thorton tried to avoid both Perry and Bishop. Instead he found himself spending time with Achmed. The Sallee Turk was voluble in relating tales of the North African corsairs, and quite by accident Thorton was learning a little Arabic. He was sure that Achmed would not lavish such education on him unless he thought it would be useful, and it would only be useful if they were to brave the Spanish coast and carry him all the way to the Sallee Republic. Thorton was looking forward to it. He'd been to France, to Spain, the Azores, and the Antilles, and he'd been born in the Maryland colony, but he'd never been to Africa.

The wind freshened and the first sting of rain hit his cheek. Maynard wasn't back. Ah well, he soon would be. The rain started down in torrents. He checked his watch, checked the sandglass, checked the binnacle. Only an hour more on his watch. Perry was after him. Poor Perry. He was going to get poured on. Thorton let his legs flex like springs as the angle and level of the deck constantly changed. Meanwhile the ship scudded along under just her mizzen and storm sails.

MacDonald came up. He was wearing his oilskin. "Begging your pardon, sir, but you remember that hole we got at Cherbourg? It opened again."

Thorton swore. "Inform the captain. If you see Mr. Maynard, tell him to hurry up."

"Aye aye, sir."

Maynard returned, but Thorton was shivering and soaked to the skin as the sky opened. He donned his oilskin about one minute too late. He exchanged the tricorn for the sou'wester. "Thank you, and put my hat in my cabin!" He handed off the wet hat. Maynard ran down.

MacDonald returned. He was looking disgruntled. He went up to Thorton and knuckled his forehead. "I told 'im, sir, but he just barked at me to fix it. He was eating his dinner, sir."

"Well then, you'd better hop to it. The weather is getting worse. Run the pumps."

"Aye aye, sir."

The captain had told him to send word when anything changed, and it had changed. It was wrong of him to snap at MacDonald for delivering the message he had asked for. Thorton thought hard things about a captain that would sit for his dinner after being told there was a leak in his ship. It wasn't a very serious leak, but getting knocked about by the seas could cause the whole seam to split and then they'd be in serious trouble. Perry was going to have an interesting watch.

The wind moaned in the rigging and lightning cracked closer at hand.

"Ahoy the deck, a sail!"

The lookout couldn't be heard on the quarterdeck, but the call was carried from man to man. Thorton pulled out the glass and tried to spy what the lookout had seen, but could hardly make it out. It did not alarm him. In this weather there wouldn't be speaking or battle.

"Where and what?" he called to the lookout.

"Fine on the starboard bow at extreme distance. Lateen sail, two masts."

"Mr. Maynard, go tell the captain."

"Aye aye, sir."

Maynard was soon back. "He snarled that he would be up when he finished his dinner and to quit crying to him over every little thing, sir."

Thorton rolled his eyes. "Very well, Mr. Maynard. Stand by." He used the glass again. What vessel was it? He wasn't sure. "Mr. Maynard, go to Mr. Achmed and ask him what sort of two-masted, lateen-rigged vessel we might encounter in these waters."

Meanwhile, Thorton climbed to the top and had a look himself. Fixing the image in mind, he climbed down again. Maynard came back with Achmed and a crockery mug full of a steaming brown beverage. That is to say, Achmed had the mug, plus an oiled robe with a hood

51

over his turban and clothes. They met Thorton on the aft deck and took shelter by the windward stair.

Achmed looked out to try and see what the English saw. His eyes weren't as good. "Are her masts well-forward, or spaced evenly?"

"Forward."

"Are the masts stubby or tall?"

"She's longer on deck than her masts are tall."

"Striped sails or plain?"

"Plain."

"I think you've got an ordinary galley then. If it was a lateen barque her masts would be evenly spaced. If she were taller, she'd be a xebec. Could be Spanish, French, or corsair. The corsairs rarely run past Eel Buff these days and the French are still in port. I'll wager it's Spanish."

"Thank you, Mr. Achmed."

Just then Captain Bishop came out of the coach. When he saw Thorton on the weather deck instead of the quarterdeck, he roared, "Mr. Thorton! Why aren't you at your post? This is an intolerable lapse of discipline and in the face of a gale, too! You'll be caned for this!"

"I was returning from the top, sir!"

Achmed had been a corsair before he had been a diplomat. He was a Sallee man still. Every nerve urged him to give chase. "A Spanish galley, Captain!" he interjected.

"Nobody asked you, sirrah! Get to your cabin!"

Achmed's eyes widened at the insult. He took a moment to master himself.

"Captain! Mr. Achmed is an expert on lateen craft, sir!" Thorton protested.

Bishop glared at Thorton. "That is no excuse for you to be skylarking when you are on watch!"

Achmed was already slipping around the captain to turn into his cabin. It was not his ship and not his problem. Maynard was eavesdropping nearby. Achmed paused and handed the hot mug to Maynard. "Give this to Thorton when you can. He's going to need it."

Maynard looked down wonderingly into the mug. "What is it, sir?"

"Coffee."

Maynard had no idea what that was. The English empire ran on tea. "Aye aye, sir."

Achmed buried himself in his cabin before he had to witness the rest of Bishop's tantrum. Thorton stood woodenly as Bishop chewed him out. Barely a week since his last caning. He sighed silently. He made no response to Bishop's ranting. Finally Bishop turned to study the lateen sail that was slowly growing as it made way towards them. "Looks like a galley." He held the glass to his eye and studied it further. As he did, water poured across the deck from the pumps.

"Who ordered the pumps!" Bishop whirled to face Thorton.

"I did, sir. I wanted to get ahead of the water," the lieutenant replied without expression.

"I didn't order pumps! I told you to notify me the moment anything changed! You are defiant, Mr. Thorton! Insubordinate! Subversive!"

Maynard was still holding the mug of coffee but it made him mad to see Bishop rail at Thorton like that. "You said you weren't to be disturbed for little things, sir!" His boyish voice cracked as it piped high and clear against the wind.

"Pumps are not a little thing, Mr. Maynard!"

Thorton was getting angry in spite of himself. "The pumps are no more important than the leak you wouldn't leave your dinner for. SIR!"

Bishop was beside himself. "You are relieved, Lieutenant! Go to your cabin and stay there. Send Mr. Perry!"

"Aye aye, sir. You have the conn, sir." Thorton went down the companionway.

He slammed the door as he entered the little cabin he shared with Perry. He announced, "I've been sent below for the crime of running the pumps because we've sprung a leak. Bishop is calling for you."

Perry jumped at the violent entrance. "By God's left ear. What is it now? I'm not due for an hour." He grumbled but opened his seachest to fetch out his oilskin.

"There's a galley out there too. Achmed knows what it is, but Bishop won't let him talk. I'm going to see if I can get any more information out of him. I'll pass word if I do."

"Don't let Bishop see you."

"Could you knock up Mr. Achmed and ask him to see me then?"

"Aye. I'll have a word with him myself."

A few minutes later Achmed presented himself at Thorton's door. He was smiling pleasantly. "How may I help you?" Belowdecks the noise of the gale was not so loud, but he still had to raise his voice to be heard over the creaking of the timbers and the rushing of the water past the hull.

"I was wondering, sir, if you could tell me how to tell the different kinds of galleys apart."

"If a Sallee rover or other corsair, they'll only have shrouds on one side. The Spanish and French have them on both. They can't sail as close to the wind as the rovers because of it. The Spanish build an *arrumbada* above their foredeck. That's a sort of platform or castle.

The corsairs don't. The Spanish and French like a fantail lazyboard on their xebecs, but the corsairs have a pintail. There are other details, but by the time you're close enough to see, they'll either be shooting at you or speaking to you."

"Thank you, sir."

"Glad to be of service." He remained in the wardroom to observe what Thorton did next.

Thorton went to the foot of the companionway and shouted up to the idlers taking shelter in the coach, "Pass the word for Mr. Maynard!" A minute later Midshipman Maynard stuck his head down the ladder. "Go tell tell Mr. Perry . . ." Thorton repeated what he had just learned about lateen-rigged vessels.

Maynard repeated it and disappeared. Thorton returned to his own door and lingered there. "Didn't the Spanish mothball their galley fleet years ago?" he asked.

Achmed replied, "So they did. However, in times of war all available vessels are put into service. They make excellent amphibious assault craft, you know. I put my galiot on many a *ferenghi*[1] beach when I was a young man."

Meanwhile Maynard got Perry's attention and relayed the message. Captain Bishop was busy screaming at the hands to reef all sail and pump harder.

Perry put the glass to his eye and studied. "Shrouds on both sides. Not a corsair then." He watched as the antennas were lowered. Turning to Captain Bishop he raised his voice to be heard over the wind, "The galley has sent down her yards, sir."

For a shallow craft like a galley the great weight aloft was dangerous in foul weather. Then again, almost any kind of weather was dangerous for a galley. Basically they were very large canoes. The galley buried her head in a wave and it broke over her foredeck, flooding the *arrumbada*, and washing into the benches. She labored to right herself, water pouring from her scuppers, only to be pooped by a rising sea. Her lanthorn swung crazily. She carried no lights, not in this weather. Perry took a dim view of anything that didn't have the apple-cheeked bow of an English ship. The *Ajax* herself shipped more water than he wanted, although nothing like a galley.

England was at war with neither France or Spain. Bishop gave orders. "Make a signal: *Ajax* to galley, 'Query.'"

Certain signals were international in nature, such as those of identification and requests for aid. They watched and waited.

---

[1] *ferenghi* Turkish lit. 'French,' by extension, European

After a bit the galley ran up a signal, "Help."

Caught far out from shore, the galley could not run into a safe shelter and must weather the storm or founder. In these heavy seas, she was foundering. Bishop was a cautious man and not inclined to show a stitch of canvas in this weather, but he couldn't very well let the galley go down without making a token effort at rescue.

"Give me the main top close-reefed, Mr. Perry."

Perry passed the word. Hands swarmed up the ratlines and pulled the earrings down on the main topsail. A single reef was let out. The *Ajax* increased her speed a trifle.

"Make a signal: *Ajax* to galley, 'Take station on my lee, two cables.'"

The galley continued closing. The sea boarded her again and again in spite of her slaves straining at the oars. Perry hazarded a suggestion, "I think we could make a little more sail, sir."

"I will not endanger my ship to save another!" Bishop snapped.

"Of course not, sir. But we're holding well. Maybe let out another reef, sir?"

"Don't tell me what to do, young man! I was at sea while you were still sucking your mother's pap!"

"Aye aye, sir." It sat ill with Perry to watch the galley struggle for her life when he had the power to save her. Or at least make a manful attempt.

Bishop swept her with the glass again. "Spanish, I think. Her officers are in blue with red breeches."

The galley was being pushed to leeward. Being such a shallow vessel, the blowing winds pushed her across the surface of the water, like a skater on ice. The harder it blew, the more she slid, the oars not withstanding. Perry saw that she was being blown far to leeward, too far to be able to take up the two cables length distance on her own. The *Ajax* would have to come around.

Bishop saw it, too. "Prepare to wear ship!"

All required hands took their places. She would have to make a U-turn to starboard to come up along side the galley. The galley was trying to turn her head into waves and the sea was pushing her backwards, towards the frigate. With her sails down she was governed more by the motion of the waves than the wind, whereas the frigate, presenting more surface to the wind, was governed more by the wind than the waves. The waves would push the galley towards them and the wind would blow them towards the galley. The galley captain had made use of that. Perry hoped Bishop saw it.

He didn't. He made a wide U turn and came up on the galley's lee instead of the other way around. A scrap of Spanish invective came across the water to them, born by the wind, then snatched away. Bishop started cursing the damn Spanish for not doing as they were told. They were close enough that had the wind permitted, they could have shouted across to each other. The galley's lee rail was swamped and her marines were pumping like mad. The galleyslaves were doused to their waists and higher as she heeled. Meanwhile, with the vessel on the wrong side, the wind was blowing the *Ajax* to the west and the waves were pushing the galley to the east, widening the distance between them.

Bishop yelled at Perry, "Get Thorton up here. Tell him to tell the damn Spanish to hold their position, we'll come around again."

The word was passed and Thorton came running up. He shouted Spanish through the speaking trumpet, but the wind carried his words away. The two vessels were drifting farther apart. The galley was backing oars to try and hold position.

Perry said, "Let's just come around and make a figure S to wind up on the windward and pointing the right way!"

Bishop swore. "I am in command, I give the orders!"

Perry shouted into the wind, "What are your orders, sir?"

"Tell the galley to come around and we will, too."

For the galley to turn one hundred and eighty degrees in these seas would be suicide. She was much too narrow and shallow to have purchase against the broaching waves.

"She'll be rolled, sir!" Perry shouted. "Let her hold while we maneuver!" Suddenly he knew how to persuade Bishop. "We are the more seaworthy craft, sir! We can maneuver better! We are better seamen than they are!"

An appeal to Bishop's vanity was always in order. "Drop back, let her go ahead, then tack across her stern and come up along her starboard side!"

Box-hauling a square-rigger in a gale could go horribly wrong, but if properly executed, would work. "Prepare to tack!" Perry roared.

Thorton was astonished that Bishop was even willing to try it. 'Bold' was not a word that generally appeared in descriptions of the *Ajax's* current captain. Thorton raised the speaking horn. "Hold your position!" he shouted in Spanish. Whether they heard or not he didn't know, but they were holding position anyhow. They knew the folly of turning broadside to sea and wind.

CHAPTER 9 : THE SPANISH GALLEY

The Spanish galley held her position as best she could but continued to drift farther and farther to leeward. The *Ajax* backed sails, lost way, and stalled. The Spanish captain studied their actions and figured out their intention. The galley rowed harder and pulled ahead. This enabled them to resist leeway a bit, but they dared not turn head to wind because that would give them a beam sea. They compromised between the two, pitching and creaking wildly with their free men pumping like madmen. The slaves threw themselves on the oars and rowed for their lives. The *Ajax* came ponderously across the galley's stern then up along her starboard. As they cut so close across her stern they could read her name: *San Bartolomeo*. With the *Ajax* for a shield against the wind the *Saint Bart* turned more directly into the waves. She backed oars and tried to match the frigate.

"Brace those yards hard around!" Perry shouted.

They creaked and turned as far as they would go, the *Ajax* heeling hard to larboard. It was a poor position that they would not have chosen on their own, but it gave shelter to the galley. The galley pitched and plowed her head under. Waves of water cascaded along her deck, nearly drowning the slaves in their chains. She struggled up again and water poured from her concave deck. A bridge ran down her middle between the oar banks but nobody dared traverse it. Her two boatswains with their whips were clinging to the antennas on their gallows. The gale blew on.

Thorton looked down from the quarterdeck to marvel at the tenacity of the frail craft full of hundreds of lives. He counted fifty oars with four slaves each. Some of the seats were empty; she did not have her full complement of miserable souls.

The action of wind and waves served to bring the two vessels together again.

"Prepare grappling hooks!" Perry shouted.

Bishop whirled on him. "What are you doing?"

"I'm going to lash her to our side. Look how she founders!"

"She'll take us down with her!"

"Then we must save her crew! We can't send boats in this sea. Grappling is the only way!"

Bishop had no experience with galleys. Until he was staring down into her waist he had no inkling how many men were in her—twice as many as his frigate. The galley was as long as the frigate and much narrower and shallower; it hardly seemed that she could hold so many souls. His men were safely sheltered in the bowels of the hull except such crew as were necessary to work the sails, but for the galley, nearly two hundred slaves were exposed on deck. Exposed they were, for they were chained naked to the oars. Another two hundred freemen—sailors, marines, gunners, and officers, occupied her decks. They were pumping, bailing, swearing and praying.

"We don't have room for them!"

"Then let her ride lashed to our side to keep her from sinking!"

Bishop wavered. Nonentity that he was, he was not ruthless enough to condemn four hundred men to their deaths. "Make it so!"

"Aye aye, sir! Stand by with grappling hooks! Make fast!"

Bishop looked around for Forsythe, but Forsythe was bending over the taffrail puking out his guts. Perry was officer of the watch. Neither of them spoke Spanish. "Thorton! Take a party and board her. See what you can do to make her right."

"Aye aye, sir! MacDonald and two hands! Maynard!"

The lad was there in his foul weather gear, bright and curious, his blue eyes dancing with excitement. He would not panic in a pinch and was clever and brave enough to make himself useful. Boy that he was, he *wanted* to go aboard a foundering galley.

As the grapples were set, they swung their legs over the side and met Spanish marines scrambling up. The Spanish officers shouted, "Abandon ship! All hands into the English frigate!"

Thorton understood the Spanish and paused on the gunwale. "Sir, they're abandoning ship!"

Bishop swore about cowardly Spanish who couldn't stand a gale, then said, "Carry on, Mr. Thorton."

Thorton reached the deck of the galley and scrambled up the stairs to the poop. The Spanish captain was there in his cloak and tricorn. The ostrich feathers of the hat and everything else were thoroughly drenched and downbeaten. Thorton saluted and spoke urgent Spanish to him.

"Lieutenant Thorton of His Britannic Majesty's frigate *Ajax*! We rescue you, sir!" He had to shout to be heard in the wind. The rigging thrummed and howled and the waves crashed and beat. A great wave broke over the larboard and drenched the slaves in the waist.

The Spanish captain returned his salute. "Captain Alonso Renaldo y Villanueva of His Most Catholic Majesty Carlos' galley *San Bartolomeo*. Thank you very much. I will join you as soon as my men are safe."

Thorton turned to watch the *Ajax's* men running forward and aft to inspect and some go below. Then he realized something terrible: no one was moving to release the slaves' chains. "Release the slaves, sir!"

The Spanish captain made no move. "They are criminals condemned to die in the galleys."

The two vessels heeled together, banging and scraping violently. One grappling hook snapped free. The slaves pulled frantically at their chains. Others raised their hands and clamored to the rescuers in Spanish, French, Italian, Turkish, Arabic, Dutch, Hebrew, and African tongues. One voice bellowed above it all, "I am an Englishman! For the love of God, save me!"

Thorton searched but could not pick out one naked brown and sunburnt body from another. "I heard English! I can't leave an Englishman on board. For God's sake man! Release the prisoners!"

The Spanish captain remained like stone. He could not leave the poop deck as long as Thorton was there. His own pride, to say nothing of naval tradition, required the captain to stand his post until all other hands had been saved. Galleyslaves didn't count; they were dead to the laws of Spain and he could dispose of them as he pleased.

MacDonald ran up. "Her seams have opened in the bow. She's head down and filling, sir." Thorton knew what awful fate that portended: the rushing power of the waves would peel the planks away from the ribs to leave gaping holes where the water poured in. The *San Bartolomeo* was doomed.

Thorton was desperate. "The keys!" he screamed.

The Spanish captain was sweating. Thorton wouldn't leave until he had the keys, and the Spanish captain couldn't save his skin until the Englishman had left his poop. Finally the man put his hand into his pocket and drew out a key ring.

"They'll mutiny!" he shouted at Thorton, but Thorton didn't wait. He ran down to the waist. The Spanish captain followed him, muttering about mad dogs and Englishmen. Renaldo checked to see that no more of his own free men were aboard the vessel, then went up the side of the frigate and left the Englishmen and slaves aboard.

The slaves were chained by fours with a lock securing each chain to a staple that was in turn secured to an iron band that went round the bridge-posts. It could not be pulled free. The iron bands were welded together. Only by unlocking the lock could the slaves be freed. Thorton hurriedly put the key into the first lock on the port side. Waves kept coming over and crashing down, drenching him in spite of the oilskin. The lock opened and he left it to crawl to the next one. The slaves tore loose the lock and ran the chain through their manacles. All eyes were on Thorton. They called him to hurry in half a dozen tongues.

"Thorton! Belay that!" Bishop bellowed down at him.

Thorton stood up and shouted, "There are Englishmen in chains!"

His shout caused consternation and anger on the frigate's deck. Angry English eyes turned on the Spanish. The galley captain did not speak English, but he saw the mood well enough and stood up haughtily, hand to his sword. He barked orders and his marines formed a defensive formation.

The slaves were not willing to wait for the debate to be settled. Suddenly the keys were wrenched from Thorton's hand and a black-haired slave shoved the key in the lock to free himself. More hands reached to take the key away from him. A babel arose as each demanded the key to freedom.

"I need you here!" Bishop screamed at him, but Thorton couldn't hear him over the tumult.

Filthy hands grabbed at his bestockinged legs as if he could magically produce a bushel of keys from out of his pocket. The galley pitched and rolled and water cascaded in sheets across her bridge. Thorton fell. The slaves knew they were being abandoned. They had been desperate before, but now they were wild. Those closest to the frigate could reach out and touch her. They held up beseeching hands and begged for rescue. Suddenly, somewhere near the mid-deck, a tall figure rose. He was a Turk with dreadlocks of matted hair down past his shoulders and a filthy beard to match. Naturally swarthy, the sun had turned him to mahogany then dried him up. He was a tall, cadaverous man of whom nothing was left but sinews and skeleton. His voice boomed out in excellent Spanish, "Silence! Hold your positions!"

Many slaves turned to look at him. Thorton scrambled to his feet. Maynard, although only a boy, was laying about with a belaying pin to break through the slaves that were assailing the bridge to come to his defense. The slave with the key turned it frantically in the lock, then another snatched it from him. The slaves who could reach were grabbing and fighting each other for the key.

The Turk roared out, "Belay that! Number Three Bench! Number Four Bench! No fighting or I'll whip you myself! Order men, order! Number One Bench! Get below and inspect!"

Thorton shouted at the Turk, "She split her bow seams! We must abandon ship!"

The Turk shouted, "Number One Bench! Belay that! If you love your lives, seal the forward bulkhead!"

The four freed slaves leaped for the hatch. Number Two Bench was free and Number Three running their chains out. Number Four Bench was unlocking. The slaves fell silent, waiting tensely for their turns and orders.

The Turk boomed out again, "Number Two Bench! Number Three Bench! Man the pumps!"

Aboard the frigate, Bishop was bellowing in French at his belligerent guests, "Surrender! Lay down your arms!" Several of the Spaniards spoke French and held a hurried consultation with their captain.

"Cut loose the galley! Let it sink!" the Spanish captain demanded. His officer translated for him.

There were Englishmen aboard, both the crew Bishop had sent over and an unknown number of English slaves. Bishop hesitated, torn as always when forced to choose among ugly options. His duty was to his own ship. The slaves were nothing. Condemned criminals. Nothing to concern himself about.

"Mr. Thorton! Return!"

Thorton heard and called, "Aye aye, sir!" The wind tore his words away, but his salute was plain.

He shouted to his men, "*Ajax!* Return! Maynard, make 'em go!"

One of his men scrambled up the side, but the two ships were tossing and bucking and not in cadence with one another. He fell between the ships. Although some slaves reached over to help him, they had to jerk back when the two hulls slammed together. The man was crushed.

"Mind your step!" Thorton bellowed.

MacDonald, the Scottish boatswain, was still below and not heard the orders; he had a man with him. Thorton ran to the hatch, dropped to his knees by the coaming, and shouted down into the darkness, "*Ajax!* Return! *Ajax,* return!"

The galley's head was well down even as her pumps started to work. She was lashed stem to stem and stern to stern with the frigate, and her head going down was pulling the bow of the *Ajax* down with her. The *Ajax* lolled further onto her side, twisting before the combined pressures of wind and waves. So the broach began.

Bishop bellowed, "Cut loose the galley! Mr. Thorton! Save yourselves!"

MacDonald scrambled out of the hold. The ruddy-faced Scot turned to give a hand to the man behind him while English axes hacked away the lines holding the bows together. The *Ajax's* bow came up immediately, but jerked short as the ropes amidships still held. The axemen ran to them and began hacking.

"Run for the ship!" Thorton barked.

The second man leaped and grabbed the channels on the *Ajax*. Willing hands helped to pull him to the *Ajax's* deck.

"Mr. Maynard, get aboard!"

The midship lines were cut as Maynard ran to the side. The two ships bounced together one more time, then parted. He did not make the jump. Maybe his nerve failed him, or maybe it was good sense that told him not to try jumping between two behemoths as they writhed in their salty beds. The last line parted. Thorton, MacDonald and Maynard were stranded aboard a sinking galley.

The tall Turk shouted orders, first in Spanish, then in Arabic. "Out sweeps!" The galley plunged deep and the waves washed across her. "Head to waves! Back starboard oars!"

More men were free from their chains and went to the pumps.

"Key to Number Twelve Bench starboard side!" the Turk roared. There was a momentary hesitation, then the key was passed across. "You and you, take the first bench port side!" Since the key had been handed from back to front on the larboard side, that side was developing many empty benches and the galley could not pull evenly. The Turk was redistributing men to get her in line.

Thorton awoke from his frightful paralysis. "MacDonald! Maynard! The tiller! Come with me!" The three Britons ran up to the poop.

The Spanish had switched out the wooden tiller and replaced it with an iron one when the weather turned foul. It was an iron club a fathom long thrashing back and forth across the poop. Maynard saw it, and perhaps to make up for his hesitation in leaping for the frigate, sprang for it. It smacked him in the middle and he hung on. The iron rod swept him off his feet like so much dust. MacDonald sprang and grabbed it from the other side. Thorton came on. With the three of them on it they made it mind.

"Are you hurt, Maynard?" Thorton shouted over the storm.

"No, sir!" the boy shouted back, although he'd taken a powerful thump to the stomach.

The rudder bit. The Turk felt the change in the vessel's behavior and shouted new orders. Wave after wave plowed over the sunken bow.

A freed slave ran up to the poop. He saluted and said in perfectly good English, "If you please, sir, Cap'n Tangle says to shift weight aft." He was tawny, skinny, and naked like all the slaves. His red hair was thin, but he had an excessive amount of beard as if to make up for the loss on top.

"Who the hell are you?" Thorton demanded. He also wondered who 'Captain Tangle' was, but one thing at a time.

The man braced his legs to the pitching deck. "Joshua Foster, gunner's mate from the old *King Henry,* sir." He saluted.

"Tell Tangle to send me a pair of helmsmen so that I may send the boatswain down to make weight aft."

"Aye aye, sir."

A minute later a pair of men were scrambling to the poop. They knew what to do. MacDonald and Maynard yielded the tiller to them. MacDonald ran down the steps and found a gang of men coming up to meet him. He had no Spanish, so barked in execrable French, "Down, you sons of bitches! Move those cannons aft!"

All of the guns had been safely stowed below when the weather started. The larger guns weighed three thousand pounds. They were wrapped in netting and lashed to keep them from rolling. The boatswain's gang rigged tackle. With the benefit of blocks and eight stout backs they hauled them aft and secured them. It was slow work. Meanwhile, up on deck, the Turk, still in his chains, was giving more orders. He had a petty officer in charge of the pumps who was rotating hands every few minutes. They were pumping like mad and no man could sustain the pace more than five minutes at a time. New hands jumped in and grabbed the moving pump handles while the others simply dropped and rolled out of the way to lie panting and gasping. When they could breathe again, they dropped into benches to row. He had boatswains in charge of each side who shouted at the men, but the oars were not in rhythm. One of them started clapping his hands to set the beat. With that to steady them they found their pace. The Turk sent a lookout to the masthead and another to the bow.

Thorton glanced up. He did not know how much time had passed. A lifetime, it seemed. The frigate was disappearing in the west. Rain poured and thunder boomed, facts of which he had scarcely been sensible so intent was he upon the needs of the galley. He saw a patch of golden light far to the south and hope flared within him. He began to search the winds. No, the waves were too rough; he could not turn her head south. He could only hope that the sunlight would catch up to him. As he watched, the hole in the clouds closed up again and the world was nothing but grey water everywhere. He noted that the stern was starting to ride lower and the slope from stem to stern was no longer so sharp. Were the pumps gaining on the leak? He looked over the side. No. She was settling deeper in the water. She had very little freeboard and had lost a foot of it already. She was slowly going down.

Well then. He must plan for all eventualities. His eyes searched the deck, but there was only one ship's boat. It might carry twenty men. He looked over the tafferel and found the captain's gig bobbing there. So. He might save a few. Whom to pick? He would not be among them. He was now the captain of a sinking ship. He would go down with it as her Spanish captain had not.

MacDonald came up and saluted. "Guns shifted aft, sir."

Thorton said, "She's riding a little low, but her trim suits me."

A ghost of a smile tugged at the corner of MacDonald's mouth. "Aye, sir. I do believe she's low enough to slip under the door to your mother's parlor."

Thorton smiled. "Good work, MacDonald. Now see if you can do anything about that leak."

"Aye aye, sir." He went below.

CHAPTER 10 : CAPTAIN TANGLE

The galley wallowed. Wave after wave broke over her bow and cascaded down her foredeck. The slaves pumped and rowed, but their strength was failing. They were cold and naked, starved and battered by the Spanish. There was only so much they could do. Thorton stared at the great lateen sails bound to their gigantic antennae. They were down but ran the length of the deck from poop to prow. The Spaniard had sent them down when the weather worsened (as well he should). So much weight! Above the waterline, too. Thorton was tempted to heave them overboard to lighten the load and improve the balance.

Foster came up. "Begging your pardon, sir, but Cap'n Tangle sends his compliments for the trim of the hull and wants to know if you've experience in galleys, sir."

"No, none at all. This is it."

"Aye, sir. Then he told me to tell you not to open the forward hatch nor bulkhead, not if you fear God and love your life."

Thorton's eyebrows shot up. "Why is that, Foster? We need to patch that hole."

"A galley's hull is divided into watertight compartments. That forward hold is sealed off from the others. 'Tis full o' water, sir, so can't take any more. Her head won't drop any more than it has. If you open the bulkhead door, you'll never get it shut again and the middle hold will flood. Then she'll go down, sir."

Thorton snapped, "Run to MacDonald and tell him what you just told me! He's in the middle hold!"

"Aye aye, sir!" Foster practically leaped off the poop deck, bellowing, "MacDonald! Belay that!" He didn't bother to climb down into the middle hold—he simply leaped over the coaming and plummeted into the dim light below.

"Mr. Maynard, send my compliments to Mr. Tangle. He's that tall Turk in the port waist. Ask him to come up."

"Aye aye, sir." The blond boy ran down.

A couple of minutes later Foster came limping back up to the poop. "MacDonald says to tell you he's astonished, but the forward bulkhead is holding. He took a measure of the middle bilge and has got three feet of water, sir."

Maynard came up before Thorton could answer. The boy saluted, "Cap'n Tangle says to thank you, sir, but it won't be convenient for him to come up until the irons are off."

The slaves were busy rowing. They had given up trying to free themselves for the moment. With the frigate nowhere near there was no hope of rescue but their own strong backs.

"Who has the key?"

"I don't know, sir."

"Mr. Maynard. You are to find that key and take it to Mr. Tangle. Unlock him. Tell him to select a reliable man and send him round to unlock the other chains. Then return the key to me."

"Aye aye, sir." Maynard ran down again.

Maynard had lost his sou'wester and his blond curls were limp and plastered to his head. Still, with all the naked men aboard, it was very easy to spot the midshipman. Thorton watched Maynard free the tall Turk, who then handed the keys to the man in the next bench. The vessel was still pitching and rolling so that the men had to struggle to throw themselves onto their oars and fall back at the proper time to pull. This was a galley; men did not sit and scull like a rowboat on a lake; they put their whole bodies into it and used their weight and legs as much as their backs and arms.

Thorton's knees were flexing like organ peddles, one rising as the other fell. His right leg was straight while his left was bent, then his left straightened while the right bent. It was like marching, but his feet never left the heaving deck and he never went anywhere. He was pleased to discover he was not seasick. He felt very proud of himself for that, then excited as he realized his situation. How many Englishmen had commanded a galley for even a short time on a doomed exercise? The news about the bulkhead cheered him; he might not sink. The Spanish had panicked and abandoned ship prematurely. His first independent command! His heart was joyful. He squared his shoulders and wished he had a spot of tea. He might feel positively celebratory if he weren't so cold and wet.

The gale settled down to a good hard blow. The thunder gave up booming. The rain came down cold and steady. The galley wallowed with wave after wave sweeping over her bow and washing her waist. Then a matted and sodden tangle of black hair appeared at the top of the windward stairs, followed by a gaunt brown face containing hollow eyes and a hooked nose. Next came a neck corded with tendons and a matted beard with a white streak in the middle. It did not cover a chest of broad shoulders with small dark nipples barely distinguishable from the mahogany skin. Far more noticeable was an ugly pinkish-tan scar the size of a hand that blotched the upper chest from clavicle to the right armpit. Powerful pectoral muscles were attached to chiseled abdominals that would have been admirable if they weren't sunk so near to the spine that supported this bag of bones. Hair on the chest and arms did little to obscure the figure. Bony knees connected to well-defined calves and narrow ankles. The feet were almost comically large compared to the emaciated flesh. The frame was there to support a goodly physique two inches over a fathom high, but Spanish captivity had wasted the flesh. Thus the man called 'Captain Tangle' came on deck, water sluicing down his skinny shanks. Thorton avoided looking at the dangling genitalia, although it was hard to pretend that they weren't there.

The creature—for it was hard to think such an apparition was a man, in spite of its form—saluted. Thorton saluted back. A baritone voice that once might have been melodious rasped out, "Isam bin Hamet al-Tangueli reporting, sir." He spoke excellent Spanish, much to Thorton's relief.

"Mr. Issa, ah, bin-um, tan-tangle," Thorton stumbled over the Arabic syllables. He switched to Spanish. "Thank you for your good work."

"Thank you, sir," Tangle replied in the same language. He studied the English lieutenant. The body might belong to a filthy animal, but a cool intelligence gleamed in those brown eyes. He was quite composed for a galleyslave who had nearly sunk, been abandoned to die by his masters, rescued by his own wits and God's good fortune, and not yet certain of survival.

Thorton, who had felt himself to be in charge of the galley, was seized by a strange insecurity. "You are an experienced galley hand, Mr. Tangle?" he asked timidly.

Lips so thin as to barely deserve the name cracked into a wan smile. "I am, but I prefer a xebec."

Thorton noticed he had omitted the 'sir' that British protocol required. Thorton also realized that should Tangle decide to take command, there was very little three Englishmen could do about it. Foster was standing near, but he was standing nearer to Tangle than to Thorton, which was evidence of where his loyalties lay. Thorton decided not to mention the omitted 'sir.' He did not want to pick a fight he was not certain he would win.

"Your advice regarding the handling of the vessel will be appreciated, Mr. Tangle," he told the man.

Was that amusement in the Turk's eyes? His expression didn't change, but he replied drily, "It was good of you to give the ship to us, and even kinder for you to accompany us on our journey."

Thorton stiffened. "We will make for Correaux, Mr. Tangle. It shouldn't take more than three days to get there."

"As long as you don't meet the rest of the Spanish squadron and can get the bow up, I agree. Have you ever commanded a lateen-rigged vessel, Mr. Thorton?"

Thorton never had, but he refused to be bested. He changed tactics, "Are you a Turk, mister?"

"I am. A Sallee Turk, but a Turk all the same. Why do you ask?"

"Because the Ottoman Empire has a treaty with England that requires us to succor one another's seamen when they are in peril at sea. Thus, at the risk of my own life, I have saved yours. It would be ungrateful for you to turn pirate and steal this ship away. Either she belongs to the Spanish, poltroons that they are, or to her rescuer, the English. She does not belong to the men on board, no matter how much they might long for revenge on the Spanish."

Tangle played his trump. "I am *Kapitan Pasha* of the corsairs of Zokhara, and the Sallee Republic is at war with Spain. She is lawful spoils for me. I appreciate your kind assistance, so I will be happy to set you ashore where convenient, but since there is no treaty between my country and yours, I have no obligation to you."

"There may not be a public agreement, but I think there is a private one," Thorton countered. "It is the duty of His Britannic Majesty's frigate *Ajax* to convey His Excellency Mr. Achmed bin Mamoud, envoy for the Sallee Republic to England, to his choice of ports in France. He carries a document to submit to the Dey in Zokhara for approval. I would hate to jeopardize the growing amity between our two nations by a premature bout of looting."

Tangle's forehead wrinkled as he absorbed the import of that. A louse crawled out of the white streak in his beard onto his lip and he brushed it away with his hand. Thorton took a step back. Now that the wind was dying the galley's stench lingered. So did Tangle's. The expression on Thorton's face reminded Tangle that he was naked and filthy. He had been that way for so long he had ceased to notice. He looked down at himself, then down at the waist of the vessel where his comrades were still plying their oars. He rubbed his nasty beard in thought. Then he spoke.

"I have galley fever, Mr. Thorton. My days are numbered. What happens to me doesn't matter, but what happens to these other men matters very much. Once their chains are struck, not one of them will endure having them replaced. We will die rather than submit."

Thorton didn't know what galley fever was, but he knew that men condemned to the galleys wasted away until they died at their oars. It took about two years—if a man had been strong and healthy to begin with. He said firmly, "The only submission I ask is what a free man may honorably give to another. I ask for the safety of the ship, good order, and a landfall at Correaux."

"What happens if we meet your English master and his Spanish guests?"

Thorton shrugged. "That is not under my control, Mr. Tangle. I can give you no surety but for my own deeds."

"Your concerns have been duly noted, Mr. Thorton." Tangle turned to watch the men at work. He clasped his hands behind his back with his legs well braced. His pose was very much that of a captain at his post.

Thorton would not yield the point and stood beside him to gaze down into the waist. He also clasped his hands behind his back—the habitual pose of a man who had learnt not to put his hands in his pockets. He was accounted a tallish man among the English, but he was short of Tangle's height in spite of wearing shoes when the Turk was barefoot. He could not help noticing the contrast. He was properly dressed, but Tangle wore his nakedness like ermine and velvet. The Englishman's face was a coppery color because of the sun, but Tangle was a deep mahogany all over, including places where it was improper for a man to be tanned. The Turk was so hollow he looked like he must fail to carry his own weight and cave in, but he stood as erect as any English captain. Down below the men looked up at Tangle and their hearts cheered. They paid no particular attention to Thorton. It was Tangle they looked to for leadership and him they willingly obeyed. Slowly it dawned on Thorton that he had never had command of the galley and never would.

CHAPTER 11 : A CHANGE OF CAPTAINS

The wind dropped and the rain moderated. Ashore it would qualify as a spring shower, but on the Bay of Biscay it was a rough ride. The swells were long and rolling but made turbulent by cross winds. To the north it was still storming with waves running away from the storm. To the south the sun broke through occasionally.

Tangle suggested, "We can turn south now, if we are careful about it. We might be able to get out from under the eaves of this weather and put a mend on the bow."

Thorton looked around, then nodded. "Make it so."

So Tangle went to the rail and called out orders in a loud bellow that rasped in places. Next he gave the helm orders. The galley backed oars on one side and swept on the other. She began to rotate in place.

"A neat trick," Thorton said. "No sailing vessel can do that."

Tangle grinned wolfishly at him. "You *ferenghi* are wrong to give up the galley so easily. They have their drawbacks, but there is nothing better for coastal raids. When I was a boy my father ran his galiot onto many a Spanish beach. She can hold her own in most kinds of sea combat as well."

"Our frigate could take such a low and fragile boat as this."

Tangle shrugged. "Perhaps. But had you met a squadron of galleys, you would have been the loser."

"Five against one is not a fair fight."

Tangle cast him an amused look. "War is not about fairness. War is about finding the advantage, seizing it, and never letting go."

Thorton knew it was true, but he would not say so to Tangle. "We carry six and twenty twelve-pounders on our gundeck. You would not care to receive our broadside."

"If I found you becalmed, I would row up on your stern where they would be of no use to you. A galley's centerline guns are a pair of thirty-six pounders. The advantage in numbers does you no good if your stern is stove in and you cannot bring them to bear."

Thorton privately admitted that those thirty-sixers were worrisome. They could blow a hole in the *Ajax* with ease. Without the benefit of watertight compartments she would drown if she could not patch. Previously he had thought of galleys as something antique and useless, clung to for the sake of vanity. She was a beautiful vessel with crimson sides and gleaming brass. Her tafferel was highly decorated with skilled carving covered in gilt paint. However, he was English. Moreover, he was Peter Thorton, so he would not yield. "Our marksmen in the tops would make a murder of your men exposed in the waist."

Tangle wisely did not put an oar further into Thorton's stew. Instead he changed the subject. "We could raise the main with all reefs in and let the hands rest. There is no point using them up. They need water, food, and clothes."

"Perhaps. I don't want to peel open her bow."

Tangle studied him with an inscrutable expression. Finally he said, "A ship cannot have two captains, Mr. Thorton. With all due respect for your courage, I know galleys. You don't."

Thorton's ears burned and he wanted to squirm. He forced himself to say calmly, "I value your advice, Mr. Tangle, but I am in command."

Tangle's hands clenched at his sides. "You seem a right good lieutenant, Mr. Thorton. How long have you been in service?"

"Thank you, Mr. Tangle. I have served with British, Spanish, and French vessels, both merchant and naval, for thirteen years now."

"Mr. Thorton, I have been a captain longer than you have been at sea. I was a lieutenant when you were still in nappies."

Thorton flushed, but remained dogged. "I am under orders and have a duty to fulfill. The conn is mine and I don't intend to give it up."

"'Tis folly to be stubborn, Mr. Thorton. I have given orders and the men have obeyed me. At least those that are willing to obey. Some will ignore both of us until we get some discipline on this ship. That won't happen as long as you are parroting what I say."

Thorton burned even redder. He clenched his fists at his sides. "I have given orders of my own, mister."

"The men look at me to see if I am going along with them. It doesn't matter what you say. If I say nay, they won't budge for you. That's not mutiny, Mr. Thorton. Just a simple statement of fact, a fact that existed long before you came aboard."

"You were going to mutiny against the Spanish?" Thorton was both shocked and titillated.

Tangle gave him a lopsided smile. "If I ever got the chance, yes. You would have done the same."

Thorton was disconcerted by the Turk's perspicacity, but he had it right. Had Peter Thorton been condemned to a Spanish galley his brain would have been in a constant foment thinking how to turn the tables.

Tangle was speaking softly. "You're a good and able officer. I need you, Mr. Thorton. Most of the men condemned to the galley are not sailors and few are qualified to be officers. Once the danger of the storm has passed, they will riot. We must have them well in hand before we stow the oars. That means her officers, few as they are, must be united."

Thorton chewed his lip. "I can learn what I need to know to conn this ship."

"Yes, you can. I will teach you, regardless of any other consideration. I like an able man, and the ship needs you. She needs us both."

Thorton thought about all the differences between Tangle and Bishop that were manifest in this meeting. Bishop would have roared and strutted and Thorton's heart would have rebelled. He would have argued and gotten caned for his troubles. However, there was nothing to argue with concerning Tangle's handling of the ship and men. He knew what he was doing and did it well. If Thorton clung to all the niceties of rank and rule the poop deck was his. Those rules would give the vessel to Bishop when they rendezvoused. If he bowed to merit, the poop belonged to Tangle. If he yielded, he might not see England again. How he longed to see a wider sea under the command of an able captain where merit was rewarded over favoritism and a man could be who he truly was!

His mental tumult was writ in his face. Tangle waited. He was curious to see what sort of man Thorton turned out to be. He had an inkling, but he plumbed deeper by keeping silent. Most men could not abide a silence and must fill it with noise from their own mouths. Tangle was not most men.

Finally Thorton spoke. "I yield to your superior knowledge, sir." He gave a little bow.

Tangle released the breath he didn't know he was holding. "Very good, Mr. Thorton. Do you know anything about gunnery?"

"I do, sir."

"Very good. You passed your lieutenant's examination, so you must know something about navigation as well."

"I do, sir. It comes easily to me."

"Excellent. You shall be first lieutenant and sailing master. Hizir here will be the captain of marines and the third lieutenant. Foster, that makes you quartermaster and second lieutenant. I'm short on officers, so we'll have to double up until I can find somebody else to serve. Now I need a boatswain."

Hizir was a Swedish man with an Arabic name; in other words, a renegade. Sometime in the past he had converted to Islam and become a corsair. He was a tall blond man well tanned all over. He had a scar over his left eye and another on his left cheek. His flesh was pocked with other scars and his nose was somewhat flattened. He had pink nipples and—no, don't look below the waist, Thorton told himself. He turned his attention to Tangle and noticed the Turk's nose wasn't straight, either. He had a small hump at the bridge where it had once been broken. Thorton put his mind to business.

"If you please, sir. Maynard is a midshipman and a likely lad. MacDonald is a good boatswain." Thorton was rapidly slipping into the subordinate position. Tangle's aura of command made it easy, but it was a relief, too. Thorton was a very junior lieutenant.

"Your men?"

"Aye, sir."

"Very well. Maynard and MacDonald. Do they speak Spanish?"

"No, but they have passable French."

Tangle shook his head. "Some of us speak French, but not enough. We'll have to speak Spanish as the common tongue. It will do for now. I'll drill all hands in Arabic later. First, we'll want men to guard the spirits, the bread room, the powder magazine, the armory, the captain's cabin, and so forth. Mr. Hizir, you're also in charge of the water ration. Once everything is secure, you may dole out a pint per man."

Hizir snapped a salute. "Aye aye, sir." He headed off briskly to do as he was told.

"Pass the word for Martínez."

Martínez was a small dark man, wiry and scruffy. He regarded the men on the poop warily as Tangle addressed him. "You're the ship's purser now, Mr. Martínez. Don't let the men loot anything. Gather what clothing you can find. Make them bathe and delouse, then give them clothes. Mr. Hizir is the lieutenant of marines. Make recourse to him as necessary to preserve the goods of the ship and compel the cleanliness of the crew."

Martínez saluted rather sloppily. He had never been to sea before he was condemned into the galley. "Yes, sir." He headed below to find the keys and do his duty.

Thorton felt impotent. He had taken the water ration for granted. On a British ship the capacity for stores was very great. The frigate could put several months of water in her hold, so there was generally no need to keep a strict guard on the water (the spirits were another matter—nothing equalled a British sailor for ingenuity when it came to sneaking alcohol), but the galley had to be strict with her limited supply of water, water that was all the more precious because it was the prime ingredient needed to keep the slaves fit for rowing. Having battled the storm and being still at their oars they would be thirsty indeed. Once the oars were put up they would start to forage for their wants—a man who had been chained to a bench had powerful wants. The marines and purser were needed to protect the ship against her men. Such a state of affairs had never prevailed aboard any British ship in which Thorton had served and never would; slaves were never used. Pressed men might feel themselves to be abused, but they were neither chained nor naked, so no matter how bitter they might feel, it came nowhere close to the sentiments of men who had been brutally bound in their own filth and expected to die like that. The stench of the vessel was making Thorton ill and he pulled out his handkerchief and pressed it to his face.

Tangle was studying the sky. "Raise the mainsail, all reefs in." To the timoneer he said, "Bring her bow into the wind."

Thorton was lost in his reverie and did not realize he had been addressed. Tangle said more sharply, "Lt. Thorton!"

Thorton jumped. "Sir?"

"I said to raise the mainsail, all reefs in. Do not make me repeat myself, mister." His voice was stern.

"Aye aye, sir." Thorton saluted for good measure.

Being a stranger to the vessel he had no idea who the mainmast hands were. He went down to the deck and shouted, "Mainmast hands! Make sail!" A quarter bill had not yet been devised so the crew did not know their assignments, but a few who had been mainmast hands before their captivity supposed they were wanted and showed up. He surveyed the naked brown and black men.

"How many will it take to raise that antenna?" he asked them.

A man answered, "Twenty." He was short with curly dark hair down to his shoulders and a beard grown out to a short length. He still had some flesh on him and his brown eyes were bright. He didn't stink as badly as Tangle, from which Thorton deduced that he had not been long in the galley.

"What's your name, mister?"

"Rabah bin Rafi, sir." His Spanish was heavily accented.

"From what country?"

"Morocco. I am a Moor, sir."

"A sailor?"

"A corsair, sir," the man replied proudly, drawing himself up to the fullness of his diminutive height.

"What was your duty aboard the corsair?"

"Mainmast hand, sir."

"You're captain of the mainmast." Thorton counted off additional men from those standing by. "These men are now your mainmast gang. Raise the main with all reefs in."

Rabah took over. He put two put at each end to control the tack and the peak, the rest to haul the halyards. He inspected the sail and reported, "Reefs already in, sir. The Spaniard tied them in."

"Very good. Raise sail."

Rabah's gang was mostly landlubbers with no experience of sails, let alone lateen ones. He put his experienced hands where they could serve as guides to the uninitiated. They spread the bitter ends across the bridge to untangle them but kept the bights cleated on the belaying pins. The lines would not be loosed until all was ready.

Tangle called down, "Put another five men on those halyards, Mr. Thorton! They're spent and won't be equal to the task."

"Aye aye, sir." Thorton counted off another five from those nearby. There was no expression on his face at being publicly corrected by the Turkish captain. He glanced up at the poop, but Tangle stood at the rail and said nothing further.

"Haul away," Thorton told the captain of the main in Spanish.

Rabah called out, "Haul away!" in Spanish, then repeated the order in Arabic and an African tongue Thorton could make no sense of. Thorton committed the Arabic to memory. It was his nature to learn everything he could about his duty, and that included how to command the Muslim hands.

Slowly the great mainsail swayed up. The men groaned and sweated, but Rabah began to sing an Arab sea chantey. His Moors took up the song and hauled in time to its rhythm. The Christians could not understand the words, but they caught the melody and worked to it. Thorton had learned a few words of Arabic from Achmed, so he knew that the men were asking Allah for help, but beyond that he did not understand it.

"Handsomely!" he called out in English as the huge antenna wavered. It was instinct that spoke. He required a moment to translate into Spanish. The chantey was interrupted by an Arabic oath as the men lost control of the antenna and it dipped and swayed.

"Avast!" Thorton roared in English then Spanish. There was a confused pause. "Rabah! Put those men in order!"

The newly appointed captain of the mainmast ran among them to sort them out. Once they were right, he called to them and the great antenna began to rise. The singing resumed. The parrel creaked up the mast. It was a majestic sight to see the main raised, and it moved Thorton greatly to see the sail going up on a ship that he had feared was going down.

They hauled the antenna into place and secured the halyards. Panting men dropped aside, but the Moors, who were sailors and recent enough additions to the galley to still have strength and pride, started coiling the lines.

Tangle called down, "Keep the coils off the deck."

"Aye aye, sir," Thorton replied.

Rabah's Spanish was imperfect, so Thorton had to step forward and demonstrate by picking up the coil from where it lay and hang it on the mast. The mast, like a British mast, was surrounded by a piece of sturdy furniture to which the halyards were belayed, and the coils were hung from their pins. In this short exchange, Rabah learned the Spanish words and Thorton the Arabic ones.

Thorton looked up to the poop deck and reported, "Mainsail raised, sir."

The lubbers thought it unnecessary to state the obvious, but sailors knew that the obvious is not so obvious. That a great spar has been raised does not mean that it has also been made fast.

Tangle nodded, then measured the wind. "Make sail."

"Make sail!" Thorton turned to Rabah, and Rabah repeated the order in three languages. The great sail should have opened like a curtain when the brails were loosed, but the ragged crew did not move as one. The lower portion of the sail opened first, then the upper, but the bunt was caught in the middle. The big sail flapped like thunder. Water poured out of its furls, but the men below were already wet enough to not mind. Rabah sprang forward to correct the defect. The big sail opened fully and luffed a terrible racket.

Tangle was leaning over the poop rail to watch. "Are we foul?" he called.

Thorton was watching all the lines and Rabah's work, too. "No, sir. We're fair."

"Very good." Tangle turned away from the rail and ordered the helm about. The ship turned as the rudder bit and wind caught the sail. The luffing quieted and the pregnant-bellied sail began to draw. Her ride smoothed and she began to run with the wind abeam. The men gave a ragged cheer.

Tangle called out, "On point!" Thorton hesitated. Tangle saw his confusion and explained further. "Get the antenna as close to horizontal as possible with the clew down. She'll run better and heel less."

"Aye aye, sir." Thorton memorized all these new facts. He was grateful for the explanation. The orders made sense when he understood the reason. "On point, Rabah." The change allowed the vessel to sail more upright.

"Ease the sheet," Tangle ordered.

Thorton relayed the order and Rabah made it so.

Tangle watched the trim of the vessel, then called down, "Stand by to set the foresail. She's riding her nose too hard. Sheet her loose so she rises high."

Thorton now had a grasp of what he was to do. "Rabah and mainmast hands, to the foredeck!" He would have to organize a foremast crew, but for the moment he preferred men who had an idea what they were doing.

Rabah and his gang went to the foredeck and distributed themselves with some forward and some aft the *arrumbada*, the forecastle that protected the bowchasers when the guns were on deck. Several of the men scrambled out on the wooden netting that ran along either side of the prow—a perilous post. They were lateen sailors and accustomed to it. Anything was preferable to chains and filthy benches. The foresail was not as large as the mainsail, and there was not as much room on the foredeck to work, so Rabah stood down four hands. The foresail swayed up. Thorton set it on point as well. That done, the waves did not break over the bow as often as they had before.

More orders were passed. Thorton got the foresail trimmed as Tangle ordered: very high and round and full, like a kite on a string trying to pull the bow up after it. It was not ideal for speed, but speed was not the purpose.

"Lt. Thorton! Assemble a team to patch the hull from the outside. When you're ready, let me know and I'll heel her over."

Thorton called for MacDonald and gave the boatswain the task. The Scot went among the crew to inquire for anyone with carpentry skills, and found a man who had been a furniture maker and another who had been a prentice to a caulker. Thus equipped, they went below to fetch the carpenter's tools. When they returned, Tangle heeled the vessel over to accommodate them. They went over the side in slings to do their work.

Things were settling into order and Thorton started trying to work out a quarter bill in his head. It was a difficult task when he didn't know how many hands he had or what sort, nor exactly how to carry out all the myriad duties of a galley. Those tasks were both like and unlike the tasks aboard a frigate: the watches must be kept, the glass turned, the bells rung, the bilge pumped, and so forth, but the details of how that was all done and the best way to do each differed.

Foster came lurching along the bridge to salute him. "Yes, Foster?"

"The captain says to assemble the crew into two watches and scrub the decks and then themselves. He's tired of the stink. Turkish watches, sir."

The rain had washed a lot of the filth out of the galley, but as the sun came out and the day began to warm, the ship's odor was becoming rank in the extreme. "Aye aye. What's a Turkish watch?"

Foster explained, "Five watches corresponding to their prayers. Four watches of five hours each and one of four. That's the night watch. I like it better than the English way. You might get five hours of sleep at a time which is almost enough to rest a man."

"I see. With the odd number of watches there is no need of a dog-watch because the hands will pass through each of the watches in their turn," said Thorton.

The Spanish, French and English all used the same system so it had never occurred to him that the watches might be ordered any other way. It was strange to him, yet the prospect of getting a whole five hours of sleep in one solid chunk held great allure. It predisposed him to regard the system favorably. With the English system a man was lucky to get four, and for an officer standing watch and watch in time of need, it was often less. He had to roust up early enough to shave and brush his coat and make himself presentable while the crew had nothing to do but turn out of their hammocks and take a piss.

Thorton sorted out more work gangs and made them scrub. The pumps played over the decks but with less fervor than when they were in danger of sinking.

"Mr. Maynard, go inspect. I want to be sure every slave is out of his chains. If they are, you may go around and remove the manacles from the working men. The idlers are to be last."

"Aye aye, sir." Maynard went on a hunt and finally found the key. He was glad that Thorton had not caught him remiss in that matter. He started removing shackles from the scarred and filthy ankles.

Tangle watched the waist being scrubbed out, then gave the conn to Foster. The tall Turk descended the windward steps and walked into the play of the pumps. He began to wash himself. Maynard hurried over and removed his leg iron. As Thorton watched, a barber began to shave the Turk's head. He took off all the foul and matted hair, then his beard and even his eyebrows. After that he shaved Tangle's arms, back, armpits, chest, legs, groin—every inch of him. The filthy vermin-infested hair was washed into the scuppers and overboard. Once shaved, Tangle scrubbed again in the cold water then took a towel and dried off. Thus shorn he retired to the captain's cabin.

Maynard ran up. "Captain Tangle says to send word if anything changes."

"Aye. Thank you, Mr. Maynard."

The crew had not been keen to exposed their naked bodies to the cold stream of the pumps, but after Tangle's example, they went willingly. A good many of them followed his example and shaved their heads and beards and sometimes more, but others simply had their hair cut short. A certain amount of horseplay accompanied the bathing and the harsh lye soap was thrown and went skidding along the deck. Men slipped and fell by accident as they shoved each other in merriment.

Thorton shouted, "No horseplay! If you're clean, get dressed! I'm going to inspect you all!"

After they came out of the pumps he inspected them visually and by sniffing. If he spotted any sign of lice, he sent them back for a shave. It was bad enough to be on a damaged and stinking galley, but he could not abide a lice infestation. Having gotten the ship and crew cleaned, he ordered out the hammocks. They were in the hammock nettings and had been thoroughly drenched by the storm. He ordered them scrubbed and scraped and hung up to dry. The same with the blankets.

The weather continued blustery and the wind chill, but the sun was warm. Thorton attended to business, even got an inventory of stores and a cook. The man he picked, a skinny African named Guillermo the Negro (to distinguish him from Guillermo the Spaniard), was happy to have the job. Of all the men on board a ship, the cook never went hungry. Rice and peas were plentiful, but bread, firewood, water, wine, and all other comestibles were in low supply. So time passed.

CHAPTER 12 : THE CHASE

"A sail, a sail!" the masthead lookout cried. Thorton ran for the ratlines only to discover there weren't any. He wondered how the lookout had made the climb. The English lieutenant was sure he was not equal to the task of climbing a wet, vertical mast. He looked up and called, "What do you see?"

"Sail north by east, sir!"

Thorton got his bearings. The frigate had disappeared to the north, could it be her? Or the galley's consorts? That sent a shiver along his spine. "Mr. Maynard! Inform Captain Tangle we've spotted a sail." Maynard ran off.

The lookout continued watching, but at that distance he could not make it out. The sail could not be seen from the deck.

Tangle came out in a minute. He wore a white linen shirt looted from a Spanish sea chest that was too small for him. He couldn't button the top several buttons and a slice of muscular brown chest showed. The cuffs stopped short of his wrists and the lace barely brushed the backs of his hands. He wore brown velvet breeches unbuttoned at the knees because they were too short, but the waist was gathered in and belted because it was too big. He had tied a white cloth over his shaved pate to save it from the sun. He was still barefoot. With the sun out the deck was steaming, but drops of water continued to drip from the sails in a constant shower on the decks below. The laundry added its own humidity. It dripped on Tangle and he slapped his shoulder reflexively as if a flea were crawling on him. Somehow he seemed more animalisticly naked than he had before. Perhaps it was because nudity was a natural state, but to be half-dressed with his shirt undone drew attention to the fact that he was not properly attired. Thorton found himself staring at the man's chest and pulled his eyes up to the face.

Tangle gave him a stern eye that said he had been dilatory. Thorton snapped a salute. "One sail north northeast, sir."

"Bring me the tack, Mr. Thorton." He started along the bridge.

Thorton hesitated, then ran after. "I'm not sure what that means, sir."

"Lower the tack end of the main antenna. I'm going up."

So the orders were given and the lateen yard was tilted so that the forward end came near the deck. Tangle grabbed the wooldings to pull himself up, wrapped his legs around the antenna, and started climbing like a boy shinnying up a tree trunk. Seeing how it was done, Thorton thought he could do it, but ratlines would have been easier. Tangle climbed all the way to the peak of the sail about a hundred feet above the sea. He studied the stranger, then looked around. He came down again, moving slowly and carefully. At last his bare feet thudded on the deck.

"The frigate. Mr. Thorton, how are relations between England and Spain these days?"

"Amicable, sir."

"I've no wish to meet an English frigate with Spanish guests on board. I expect the Spanish will want their galley back and I don't intend to give it to them. How's the hull?"

"MacDonald has patched her, sir, and we've pumped out the forward hold. We've kept the bulkhead sealed as per your orders."

"How much drinking water do we have?"

"Four days, sir."

"Damn it. Make all sail. Run northeast."

That would put the galley on a course to intercept or be intercepted by the frigate. It puzzled Thorton that Tangle should run towards the frigate when he wished to avoid capture, but he was pleased to be going towards the frigate rather than away from it. He turned and bawled orders. The hands, now divided into proper fore and mainmast hands, went to their tasks. They swarmed up the antennas and let loose the reef knittles. The great sails flapped out. The deck below was drenched in cascades of water that had been caught in the furls. The Englishman was glad he was wearing his sou'wester and oilskin. Complaints went up from the affected crew but were ignored.

Tangle shivered and staggered as the water hit him like a blow. Sodden and cold, his teeth chattered and he clamped them together, but there was no concealing the shivering of his frame.

"Are you all right, sir?" Thorton asked.

Tangle squeezed words through clenched teeth. "A chill, Mr. Thorton. Nothing more." He forced himself to stand up straight and wring out his shirt. He turned to walk back towards the poop, swaying unevenly as the galley rolled beneath his feet. Although the wind had moderated, the sea was still quite active. Thorton saw bloodstains on the back of his white shirt.

Thorton ran up beside him, "Sir—"

Tangle suddenly grabbed his arm and Thorton had to brace himself to take part of the man's weight. Before he could speak, Tangle's eyes went glassy and rolled up in his head. He sprawled on the deck in a faint. Thorton knelt beside him and shook his shoulder.

"Captain Tangle!" The man's flesh was burning hot through the wet linen. Thorton laid his hand on his brow and felt the fever there. "Bring a bucket! Douse him!"

The joy of being an officer was to give orders and have them miraculously carried out. Thorton had been a foredeck hand—he knew the work involved. The petty officers would pass the order for a bucket and a line, somebody would have to fetch the requested items, then the bucket would be lowered over the side and hauled up full, which was a heavy load, then carried to the lieutenant to be thrown on the head and shoulders of the supine rover.

Tangle spluttered and blinked. He looked up querulously at Thorton and said something in Turkish.

"You swooned, sir. You have a fever."

Tangle replied crossly, "I know I have a fever. Help me up."

Thorton pulled him to his feet. Tangle stood shivering in his wet clothes. The pale linen was nearly transparent with water and clung to his chest and shoulders. His dark skin showed through it. It wasn't decent at all.

The Turkish captain was a little disoriented, so he snapped, "Report, Mr. Thorton."

"All sails are set, heading northeast, sir."

"Very good. You may join me on the poop. I believe you will find the afternoon instructive. Have the hands dressed and dined?"

"We gave them clothes, but I had no orders about dinner, sir." The crew was wearing what was found in the Spanish sea chests. They were all provided with breeches and shirts but none of them were wearing shoes. Shoes hurt feet that had been naked for so very long.

"Give them rice and peas with a biscuit each and a little cheese. Give them wine watered four to one." Thorton passed the word and the mood lightened perceptibly.

Tangle climbed slowly to the poop. With a shock Thorton realized that the man was exhausted. Force of will had carried him through the crisis but his emaciated frame could bear only so much. He took up his usual stance on the windward side with his hands behind his back and his legs braced wide. He shivered uncontrollably. He alone among the crew was not warmed by the sun. He stood his post and studied the galley, the sea and the English frigate, now visible from deck level.

Thorton dared to speak. "Sir, the English are not your enemy."

"Mr. Thorton. You are a seaman. You know as well as I that any nations that do not have a treaty are not friends. Their vessels are lawful prizes."

"For a corsair, perhaps, but an English warship cannot make a prize of a neutral ship."

"We are not the ship of a neutral nation, Mr. Thorton. In the eyes of the Spanish, we are mutineers and pirates who have stolen their vessel. That they abandoned it in no way contravenes their title; ships lost at sea belong to their owners unless and until the rights of salvage are given elsewhere." He paused to give Thorton a wolfish grin. "By surrendering command to me, you are complicit in our crimes. There will be a court martial for you if we're caught, Mr. Thorton."

Thorton's eyes went wide with horror. "I did not! I acted for the safety of the ship! I never thought—"

Tangle shrugged. "I doubt a lack of foresight on your part will be an acceptable defense to the Admiralty."

It certainly wouldn't be to Bishop. Thorton's teeth ground together in fury. He should have stood his ground and not yielded command to the rover. The man knew exactly what he was doing. He had thought out all the implications while Thorton the dunderheaded fool had not seen beyond his own nose. He cursed himself silently.

The wind was out of the north, fitful and gusty. The waves were running from the west to east; the *Bart* was on a close reach and sailing well in spite of the repaired bow. The frigate was running from the north with the wind behind her, just off her quarter, which was her best point of sail. The two vessels charged towards each other. At some point their courses would cross. The question was, would the galley pass ahead of the frigate and so escape, or would the frigate pass ahead of the galley and intercept her?

"Mr. Thorton. What speed is the *Ajax* capable of making?"

"Eleven knots or better, I suppose. We never had her full out, sir. She's new to us."

"Her crew is not seasoned?"

"No, sir. Captain Bishop and the officers came aboard just three weeks ago. She's got seamen in her; we had the pick of the press, but many landsmen too."

"How does she tack and wear?"

"Slowly."

Tangle nodded, absorbing that information. "Cast the log."

Thorton translated the order from Spanish to English for Maynard's benefit. The blond boy was very familiar with the task from tending the log on the *Ajax*. He tossed the log over and the seconds were counted.

"Seven knots, sir," Thorton reported.

Tangle grunted. He estimated the distance between them, laid out their courses in his mind, and came to his conclusion. "'Twill be close."

Thorton, who had a head for figures, agreed. Tangle looked over the sea thoughtfully. He considered his options. "Make a point north," he told the helm.

That would bring them closer to the frigate. "I thought you wanted to avoid them, sir."

"I do." The corsair was sweating and shaking with fever but his eyes were preternaturally bright. "Tell me why this will work, Mr. Thorton."

Thorton looked over the rail but did not really see the other vessel. He was plotting the courses in his head. "If you can cross ahead of her, you can run on the galley's best point of sail, but the frigate will have to beat after you on her worst point of sail."

"Just so, Mr. Thorton."

"But sir, making a point north you will bring yourself closer to her and quicker."

"Very true, if we had a round hull. However, we have a galley. We will make as much leeway as way. Thus I must aim high in order to pass low. If I made straight ahead, the leeway would blow me far south and I would wind up covering a long leg while letting the frigate run on her best course even longer."

"I see, sir." He was uneasy. He was an Englishman, his duty was to rejoin the frigate. He was disturbed by the possibility that he might be found at fault—fatal fault—for his part aboard the runaway galley. He turned to look at the crew below. None of them would submit meekly to having their chains replaced. "Perhaps you could negotiate, sir."

Tangle shook his head. "Eel Buff is out there and I know where it is, Mr. Thorton. Sadly, I haven't enough water to make it. I'll head for the French coast to replenish my supplies, but then I'm going home."

It would have never occurred to an English naval officer to seek refuge in a nest of pirates and French corruption, but for a rover like Tangle it made perfect sense.

"I see, sir. But still, the Sallee envoy is on the *Ajax*. Surely some sort of amicable arrangement can be made to return you home, sir."

"Is he? Why is that?"

Thorton had already told him, but he could see that Tangle was not entirely in command of himself, even though he had perfect command of the galley. "Mr. Achmed was negotiating in England. Our job was to convey him to France. I'm sure he'll help you, sir."

"I prefer to negotiate from a position of strength, Mr. Thorton. As you have pointed out, a galley is at a disadvantage with a frigate. Such a factor would weigh heavily in the negotiations. No, I will make for Eel Buff."

Thorton stared out across the sea towards the *Ajax* slowly growing larger. Perry was over there, and his old life, too. He touched the gold lace on his uniform. He had finally made lieutenant and could hope in time to rise higher. He would not be a lieutenant for life, not if there was any justice in the world.

Tangle had other things on his mind. "Go through the Spanish signals. Find the ones that the English will understand. I want to be able to signal 'Enemy sail to south.'"

"Aye aye, sir." He saw the plan. English signals would lead the *Ajax* to believe the galley was under Thorton's command. A false signal would draw them off to meet the enemy, letting the galley escape. He felt disquiet about participating in such a subterfuge.

"Thorton?" Tangle had noticed his inaction.

"Aye aye, sir," he replied reluctantly. "Pass the word for a man who can sew." The word was passed. Shortly thereafter a man was brought forward who looked quite timid.

"Your name, sailor?" Thorton asked him.

"Pedro de Palma. I was a tailor in Barcelona before I was sentenced to the galleys, sir."

"Your crime?"

With a soft but dignified voice, Palma replied, "I am a Jew."

Thorton had never met a Jew and he did a double-take. The man was an inoffensive looking person with curly hair that had been badly cut to a short length. He wore a white shirt and tan breeches as did many of the crew. His clothes had formerly belonged to a Spanish sailor. Thorton explained what was wanted. Palma listened, then went to hunt for the sailmaker's kit and loot sea chests for the colored cloths he would need.

Tangle spoke. "Have you made a quarter bill, Lieutenant?"

"No, I don't even have a muster roll, sir. I've been busy."

"Make a muster roll, Mr. Thorton. Bring it to my cabin. We'll make the quarter bill together. Along with the usual name, age, and occupation, please record nationality and religion."

"Aye aye, sir."

"I'm going below. Call me if anything changes."

CHAPTER 13 : INTERCEPTION

The wind was fitful and the sails luffed like thunder. They filled again, but the wind was not steady. The frigate loomed large and Thorton watched it creeping closer. Again the galley's sails luffed. He consulted the binnacle in its case. He looked at the sails, then the helm.

"I think the wind is veering a little northeast. What do you think?" Thorton said to Hizir, the renegade Swede who was burned as brown as a Turk. His hair had been shaved close to his scalp but not entirely removed. A red cloth was tied over his pate and he wore a white shirt and red Spanish uniform breeches. He was the same height as Thorton, even in his bare feet, and had the wiry, muscular build of a galleyslave.

"Yes, I think so, too."

"Give us a point east. Keep her full and by." The helm obliged and the sails filled properly and stopped their racket.

Thorton sent word to Tangle and the man appeared on deck a little later. He was bleary-eyed and unsteady on his feet. When he stood near Thorton, the lieutenant could smell the sweaty, sickly smell of him. The officers on the poop saluted.

Tangle saluted in return, then said, "Glass?"

Thorton produced the spyglass from his coat pocket.

Tangle studied the frigate through the glass. "She's making good time. How many knots for us?"

"Eight last time we heaved the log, sir."

"Throw it again. This galley is capable of at least nine with a wind like this. She's not making the speed I'd like. Are you keeping her bow pumped out?"

"Aye, sir. We are. Maynard! Make ready the log!" Thorton stood by with his watch. "Out log!"

Maynard tossed it over the tafferel. It splashed into the water and the knots ran out.

"Time!" Thorton barked.

"Seven and a quarter, sir," Maynard replied.

Tangle nodded. "I thought we'd lost speed. Set a course southwest, please."

The helm responded. Thorton frowned. The new course would take them out to sea, away from the French coast, away from the frigate, and if they ran long enough, towards Spain. They dared not run that direction for long, both for the peril of the Spaniards and their own want of water. It was now obvious to the frigate that they were trying to avoid a meeting. The news must be causing considerable consternation on the *Ajax's* quarterdeck.

Tangle spoke. "Make a signal, 'Enemy sail sighted southwest,' Mr. Thorton." It was not implausible. The rest of the Spanish squadron was out there somewhere.

Thorton hesitated. To participate in a deliberate deceit was a step toward the hangman's noose. "I cannot, sir. I am an English officer and duty-bound to Captain Bishop. " He stood rigidly at attention.

Tangle shot him a look, but called Foster instead. The renegade ran the signal up. On the frigate's deck glasses strained to make out the signals. Even if they could not read them at this distance, there was only one explanation that would make any sense to them: an enemy in sight the galley could see but not the frigate.

One by one the *Ajax*'s studding sails bloomed. She gathered speed as she raced southwest to meet the enemy. It was a glorious sight to see, and if he hadn't been the object of their chase, Thorton would have enjoyed it a great deal. As it was, it frightened him. If ever the frigate caught the galley, they were doomed. He envied Perry who had only to obey his commanding officer and do what his heart wanted to do: fly before the wind as he raced to give battle to the enemy!

The crew of the galley was all watching the frigate and speculating. With both vessels running southwest the galley would be the loser. It was the frigate's best point of sail and their worst. The distances shifted as the frigate ran on towards destiny and the galley fled it. How angry Bishop would be when he discovered the deceit! Thorton was mortified. How would he explain himself? No one had put a pistol to his head. He had no excuse. He had meekly handed over command of a neutral vessel to a Sallee rover. And not just any rover! The Captain of the Corsairs of Zokhara.

Zokhara. Capital of the Sallee Republic. Each port of the Sallee Republic sent out galleys, xebecs, barques, galiots, frigates, polacres, feluccas, and brigantines, to raid and harass Christian shipping. They were always at war with Spain, and often with the Italian republics, and from time to time with France, England, the Dutch Republic, Denmark, Russia, and Sweden. Any country that wasn't Muslim took a turn filling the corsair galleys with slaves and loot. Occasionally they even went to war against their fellow Muslims, but these differences were put down by the Sublime Porte, as the sultan in Istanbul was called.

Maybe it would be all right. Achmed was negotiating an arrangement. He was not an ambassador and it would not be a treaty because the Sublime Porte reserved diplomatic rights to himself, but still, an envoy would come, and an agreement would be made. Perhaps Thorton would not be condemned for helping them. He prayed fervently to God to watch over him and keep him safe from harm. There was no one else he could ask for help.

The afternoon wore on with the frigate gaining on them as they ran. The wind turned colder and more clouds piled up overhead. It could have been exciting, but it wasn't. It was an endless afternoon of 'hurry up and wait' as the frigate steadily gained on them.

"They're making a signal," Thorton informed Tangle. "*Ajax* to galley, 'Query?'"

"Send the reply, 'four sail south.'"

Thorton wouldn't send it. Another man had to do it, one with fewer scruples than the blond lieutenant. In other words, Foster, the renegade. He was perfectly pleased to deceive the navy of his homeland.

Tangle swore in Turkish. In Spanish he told Thorton, "We made too much leeway. I wanted to be to windward of her. She is going to weather us."

Thorton replied, "Bishop is a competent captain when it comes to handling the ship." His voice was a little grudging.

Tangle asked, "Is he?" in a neutral voice.

Thorton shrugged a little. "Adequate. Lacking in imagination."

Tangle nodded and added that to his store of knowledge he needed to win this race. Then he croaked, "Water. I need water."

Thorton passed the word and a skin was fetched. Tangle drank. Thorton watched. The wind blew. The sun shone. The clouds piled up. The frigate and the galley raced on. Half an hour passed tensely. The frigate was overhauling the galley and would soon come up on her.

MacDonald ran up. "Begging your pardon, sir, but we're leaking." Not knowing Spanish, he spoke English. Much to everyone's surprise, Tangle replied in the same language.

"Man the pumps, MacDonald."

The Scot and the Englishman looked at him in astonishment.

"Foster and I were bench mates for more than a year. I taught him Arabic and he taught me English. I can swear and talk about the ship and the weather, but nothing more."

"Aye aye, sir," replied MacDonald. He went below.

Thorton looked at Tangle in amazement. A galleyslave improving his education while chained to an oar? He did not think he could have done the same. It bespoke an uncommonly developed mind.

The frigate kept her course. She was going to meet the enemy she thought was out there, so continued to close in spite of the opposition of all the hearts aboard the galley except for three of the four Britons.

To make matters worse, a squall was sweeping towards them. Thorton spoke. "Mr. Maynard, my oilskin and sou'wester please. I left them in the master's cabin."

"Mr. Maynard," Tangle said in Spanish. "Get me an oilskin and hat from the Spanish stores, if you please."

"Aye aye, sir." The blond boy scampered away.

The temperature dropped and the wind veered more easterly and freshened. Every change in the wind conspired to bring her closer to her ruin. "Mr. Thorton, take in two reefs. We're going to receive a gale."

"Aye aye, sir." Personally he thought they could stand it a little longer, but then again, the big lateen sails were hard to handle. He gave the necessary orders and men swarmed up the antennas. Hauling the big sail to the mast and tying it with the knittles was a long and laborious process. They must wrap their legs around the antenna and lean down to grab the sail and haul it up. Up there the motion was far more exaggerated than on deck. In ordinary circumstances the vessel would be brought dead into the wind to ease the burden of making reefs, but not today.

Tangle spoke. "Keep those men up. The instant that squall engulfs us I want to make all sail. I wanted the weather gauge, but I'll take what I can get. As soon as we disappear in the rain, we'll run east." With the wind from the northeast, it would be an ideal course for the galley but not the frigate. Ideal if the galley could withstand the weather. The squall would not bother the frigate. Still, Thorton knew that Bishop was conservative in the extreme with foul weather. It might work.

"Aye aye, sir." Would the rain or the frigate arrive first? There were murmurs in the waist as the crew saw the frigate come up. Tangle waited still. The curtain of rain swept across the seas and the waves were rougher. The galley bobbed like a cork and waves broke against her poop.

"Dammit, Thorton, I need a steward! Were the storm shutters set in my cabin?"

Thorton paled. "I don't know." He passed the word and received the reply. "No, sir. A hand is setting them now."

Tangle's brow was dark and angry, but before he could say anything, Thorton spoke again. "She's making a signal. 'Take position two cables off my larboard.'" The frigate reduced sail to pace the galley.

"Damn square-riggers. They think the world revolves around them," Tangle replied. Then he said, "Send the affirmative. The rain isn't going to cover us. Prepare to spill a little wind from the foresail. When the frigate overshoots us, we'll turn south. As soon as we disappear in the rain, I want to run east with all sail." If he succeeded, the frigate would think they were running slowly south before the gale but in reality they would be racing east.

Thorton didn't know if he planned to obey or not. He was in a stew, but his hesitation was overleaped by Foster who made the signal in spite of his doubts. The frigate was coming closer, within long range for her guns, but her guns were still inside their ports. They watched tensely. At just the moment that the frigate was coming along their starboard side, Tangle gave his order.

"Loose the sheets."

Thorton bellowed, "Loose the sheets!" The foresail flapped noisily and the galley lost perceptible headway. The frigate shot ahead.

Tangle said, "Every man to the windward rail. Prepare to wear ship. The moment the galley comes around on her new tack, send them to the other side. Make sure you do not foul your lines!"

Thorton shouted his orders. "All hands prepare to wear! Idlers to the windward rail! Main and foremast hands to the halyards!" The men tensed and readied themselves. They all knew the risk. A bungled evolution would leave them sitting dead in the water for the frigate to run up on.

Tangle glanced over his shoulder at the English frigate. She had backed sails and was wallowing in consternation. She had lost her way. Bishop was confused by their maneuver and had not started his turn.

"Helm hard over!" Tangle snapped.

The helmsman threw his weight onto the tiller. The *Bart* turned her stern across the wind. The wind blew over her larboard rail.

"Flatten sail," Tangle ordered. With the sails running fore-and-aft into the wind it eased the burden as the sails no longer filled. "Ease the antennas. Shift the tacks."

"Ease the antennas! Shift the tacks!" Thorton bellowed to the crew. This was the hard thing about a lateen-rigged craft: her antennas must be eased, the tack dragged around the mast, and raised again. The main antenna dropped so fast that for a moment Thorton thought it was going to pierce the deck like a giant javelin, but it caught up short. The ends of the antennas were heaved bodily around the mast.

"Keep those lines sorted!" Thorton bellowed. "Idlers to the larboard rail!"

The men ran across to the other side. Running the hands back and forth was something a frigate would never, ever do, but Thorton had caught the sense of it. The galley, being so light and shallow, was very sensitive to the placement of weight aboard. The weight of a hundred and fifty men was eleven or twelve tons. Where they stood mattered at moments like this.

"Make all sail!" Tangle bellowed in Spanish and Arabic. "Haul the topping lifts! High peaks!"

Up went both sails, and quickly, too, as the men hauled with gusto. The petty officers shouted the heave-ho, then the sails bellied out and flapped like thunder. The hands on the sheets kept them bent them around the belay points to control the sail. She was drawing hard before her sails even reached the peak. She heeled so far over so that the foaming waves were frothing over her lee benches. Had there been any slaves in the benches they would have been drenched to the waist. Thorton had not timed it, but he thought they had accomplished it all in about eight or nine minutes.

"Ease the helm a point," Tangle said calmly. She reduced her heel but still was running hard over. The Turk watched the storm and sea. Waves crashed against her larboard side and sent up huge sprays. The men clinging to her rail were thoroughly wetted.

The sudden change of course caused considerable consternation on the frigate. Thorton could imagine the scene. The Spanish screaming that the galley had turned pirate and must be pursued, the doubts about the signals, the accusations of deceit and disloyalty. His name was black now. He was the very opposite of what he'd ever thought he would be. Against his will he had become a pirate.

The frigate slowly turned. She had lubberly hands with not much experience; not only did she have to make the turn, she had to haul in her studding sails. That was a maneuver her crew had little training in. Thorton timed them.

"Eighteen minutes to get the studding sails in. They need practice." Only then was the *Ajax* able to wear ship to follow the galley—Bishop was not a man who cared to explain to the Admiralty why he had snapped his stuns'l booms. They also had to gather enough way to be sure of making stays and coming around on their new course.

"God, they're bad," Thorton moaned. It was no consolation to him that with all the training he and the other lieutenants had given them, they had halved their time. They had only been to sea a few weeks after all.

The *Ajax* was eight points off the wind on a beam reach while the galley was five points off, running close-hauled. The frigate trimmed her sails and came a point closer.

Tangle snorted. "If it was me, I would have left the studding sails. They'll need every stitch of canvas they've got to chase us now." The

Saint Bart had a half hour head start and was gaining headway on the frigate.

"Bishop is no daredevil." *But you are,* Thorton added silently. It frightened and thrilled him. The men continued to cling to the windward rail. The wind freshened and the first spatters of rain came down.

"Toss the log."

Twenty-eight seconds later, Thorton said, "Nine knots less a quarter, sir."

Tangle smiled. The rain swept across them at last screened them from each other. "Take in one reef."

Thorton heaved a sigh of relief. "One reef!" he bellowed, passing along the captain's order.

Tangle had tempted fate and gotten away with it. He'd known he would. He knew exactly what he was doing, how to press his vessel for everything she could give, how to balance her between disaster and victory. Thorton had to admire his skill—and his nerve. He'd grabbed all speed he could to make the turn and get out of gunshot, but dared not keep so much canvas aloft in the wind and rain. The making of the reef was painfully slow with such wet and heavy sails, but the reefs eased the wildness of the ride a bit. She heeled a little less, but she still cut through the water at a breakneck speed. Tangle watched the frigate, but she was a wavering grey shadow in the rain. He could not determine her sail set in the dimness of the squall, but their courses were diverging.

MacDonald came up and saluted, "Begging your pardon sir, but the patches are out and we're taking water. We've got a foot and a half forward already. I've kept the bulkhead sealed and went down through the fore hatch."

"Thank you, MacDonald. Pump and mend. As much as it pains me, I'll have another reef in those sails, Mr. Thorton," Tangled replied.

Thorton bawled the order. The sodden hands went up the antennas and took another reef in the waterlogged sail. As the sail area reduced, the heeling eased further. They had no carpenter, so MacDonald must do the job himself. He mustered some hands from among the idlers on the rail and went below.

Tangle spoke conversationally as if the slant of the deck beneath his feet and the sheets of spray breaking over the bow were routine to him. "Ordinarily we'd bring the antennas to the deck to put the reefs in, but now is not the time. Toss the log again please."

The log was tossed. Thorton reported, "Seven and a half knots, sir."

The galley pitched and rolled as the waves broke over her foredeck and sent up great sprays as she buried her head in the sea. Low as she was she could not help shipping water, but the buoyancy of her compartmentalized hull sent her bobbing to the surface like a cork. The bow came up and the concave deck shed water in great streams. Each scupper was a cataract.

The sun still shone on the waters south of them. It was a glorious scene and Thorton thought that he might like to paint it, if he had had any skill at painting. The rain came down in sheets and ran off their oilskins and hats. The men working on deck were soaked.

They ran for almost an hour, until MacDonald came back and reported. "Mended, sir." The frigate was well out of sight in the driving rain.

Tangle gave another order. "Prepare to tack. We'll put the third reef in while we've got the spars down, Mr. Thorton."

The great antennas were lowered to the deck, the last reef tied in, then hauled around to the other side of the mast, and raised up. The new course was north, on her best point of sail, under treble reefs. She clipped along and the log gave six knots. The frigate would have to beat about on the last known course to find her, but not until the rain cleared would she discover her mistake. Bishop lacked imagination. It would not occur to him that the galley would run back the way she had come.

"Will we have enough water, sir?" Thorton asked.

"Harvest the rainwater. We will make do with what we have."

"Aye aye, sir."

CHAPTER 14 : NIGHT WATCH

If the cabins of the frigate were small, those of the galley were strait indeed. However, they were better furnished thanks to the personal effects the Spanish had left behind. Thorton's bunk had a mattress stuffed with horse hair three inches thick, along with sheets, blankets, a coverlet, and other niceties belonging to a gentleman of comfortable resources. He found the bed luxurious compared to his own straw stuffed pallet on the *Ajax*. Thorton liked being the first lieutenant on a galley—if he hadn't been flying toward a hangman's noose for the crimes of desertion and piracy with every mile. How that tormented him! To fly away from duty and punishment, to run towards freedom and guilt. He did not have time to brood because Foster came knocking at his door.

"Captain Tangle asks you to join him in his cabin, sir."

Thorton presented himself. The crystal chandelier above the table had one of its lamps lit. It cast rolling shadows over the room as it swayed. Tangle sat sprawled in a chair. He said, "Peter. Thank you for joining me," thereby signaling that the visit was an informal one. The conversation was in Spanish as the mutually intelligible language.

Thorton stepped in and shut the door behind him. He waited for instructions. Tangle's eyes were sunken as he watched Thorton. "At ease, Lieutenant. This is not an official call."

"Aye aye, sir." He stepped forward and waited.

"I am not well."

"Aye, sir." Thorton nodded.

"You have assigned me a steward, but I am uncomfortable asking him to attend me as closely as I need tonight. If he sees me as I am, he will gossip to the crew and that will undermine their confidence in me. My reputation and my presence heartens them. As long as they think the great corsair is their commander they will obey and that will carry us through difficulties. You heard them murmur about the frigate, did you not?"

"I did, sir."

"Damn it, Peter. Don't you ever unbend? Sit down. Here's cider. Have some. And give me some."

Thorton found another cup in the cupboard. The crystal was very fine and delicately etched with someone's coat of arms. He rejoined Tangle at the table and poured for them both. As the captain drank

Thorton attempted to take a seat but found it occupied by the ship's cat. After a brief stare down (which Thorton lost), he selected another chair. He studied the haggard corsair as he sipped his cider.

After they had drunk, Tangle said, "If the men know how ill I am, they will start to wonder if I am fit to command. That will encourage the mutineers among them."

Thorton knew an officer's charisma could make men work in spite of trying circumstances. Perry had it. Forsythe, Bishop, and Thorton did not. Tangle had it more than any two men combined. "Aye, sir. You have a wonderful effect on the men. You are an excellent captain, even if you are a corsair."

Tangle gave him a skeleton-like grin and said, "I am a corsair because I am an excellent captain. 'Tis a rewarding career, albeit one with dangers. Not even Spanish cruelty can make me regret my fate." He waved his sparkling goblet full of cider. "However, I am pleased that you regard me as well as your English scruples permit. I rely on you, Peter. You're a good officer."

Thorton was surprised to receive such a compliment. "I have an obligation to the safety of the ship first and foremost. That is uppermost in my mind, sir."

"As well it should be. You are an able officer and I admire it. Even though you are a stiff-necked Englishman, I like you."

Thorton sat up straighter in his chair as he stiffened without thinking.

Tangle smiled a little. "Even now, when it makes you swell up like a cockerel. I pray you, do not crow at me, I am paying you a compliment!"

Thorton blinked and realized the man was teasing him. He could not remember ever being teased by a captain. He didn't know what to make of it. "Aye aye, sir," he finally said.

Tangle's head swayed as the galley rolled through a particularly rough gyration. Her timbers groaned and the Turk cocked his head to listen. Satisfied, he slumped in his chair and put an elbow on the table and his head in his hand.

"I am distracted, Mr. Thorton," he said wearily. "I know I had a point to make, but I can't remember it. Pray remind me."

Thorton could not bring himself to remind the man that he had been attempting to compliment him, so he returned to the prior subject. "You were talking about the men's morale, sir."

Tangle's eyes glazed. "Morale? If you say so. I am beating about the point, and I think I had better drive straight at it before I lose the wind completely. I know you will forgive a sick man."

"Aye, sir," Thorton agreed.

"I want to be clean and have my wounds attended. I don't want to ask the steward because he will gossip. I am asking you to help me because you are an excellent officer. You will not fraternize with the men nor spread tales about your captain. I know it is beneath the dignity of a gentleman to act the part of a body servant, but I hope you understand my reasoning." The speech came out in a rush. Tangle did not look at him; it pained him to ask for help.

"I will do it, sir." Thorton had been a sailor on the spar deck, a prisoner, a midshipman, and finally a lieutenant. His best coat was another man's castoff and he hadn't a penny in his pocket. He found it hard to think of himself as a 'gentleman' in such circumstances.

Tangle relaxed. "I am in your debt." He gave Thorton a grateful look.

Thorton rose and came around to his side of the table. "What are your wounds, sir?"

Tangle leaned forward. "Pull up my shirt and see for yourself." He laid his head on his arms.

The Turk's shirt was damp with an unpleasant smell and was smeared with red and brown. Each bump of his spine could be seen beneath the fabric where it pulled tight against his back. The terrain of the neck, back, and shoulder muscles was clearly limned against the thin shirt. Two years of rowing had built him up and whittled him away, leaving behind only bone and muscle. Thorton eased the shirt out of the waistband and pulled it up. The evidence of Spanish cruelty lay exposed: Tangle's back was lashed with fresh, recent, old, older, and very old cuts, welts, and bruises.

"When a galleyslave faints, they lash him to see if he is feigning. If he starts up again, they put a bit of bread and wine in his mouth to revive him. If he doesn't wake, they throw him overboard. I am near death, Peter. I confess, hope flickered in me when you came aboard and turned the key in my chain, but I am too weak to recover. I am determined to survive long enough to see these men safely to freedom. What happens to me doesn't matter."

Thorton called the steward for water and soap. "The captain wants a bath," he told the man. "Give us a bucket of fresh water." That sounded luxurious, not febrile. Ordinarily the potable water was reserved for drinking. Washing was done with salt water. Pretty soon the water came. It was even warm. Thorton put a cloth in it and began to gently bathe the lacerated back. Tangle flinched but held still for it.

"Cinnamon," Tangle said. "See if there is any cinnamon in the officers' stores. That will mend me best of all. And I want garlic in my food every meal if we've got it." His sentences were disjointed and made little sense to Thorton, but it was simple enough to humor a dying man, so he agreed.

"You must mix one part cinnamon to three parts flour, apply it to my wet back, and bind it up with bandages. 'Tis a powerful poultice," Tangle instructed him.

Thorton passed the word for cinnamon. While they waited he told the corsair, "Come, sir. Let us undress you and put you to bed."

Tangle staggered to his feet and banged his head on the roof of the cabin. He nearly fell, but Thorton grabbed his arm and steadied him. Thorton was tall enough he had to mind his head on the beams, but Tangle was taller than he by several inches. The Sallee captain slumped down to sit on the edge of his predecessor's bunk and looked up at Thorton. The lieutenant took a deep breath to steady himself. To see a powerful man reduced to such a state moved him to pity, even more because he found himself liking the man even though he shouldn't. The galley continued her corkscrewing rolls and he braced his feet, then dropped to his knees before the man. It was easier to steady himself with a lower center of balance. He reached out to take hold of a button. Tangle's half-hooded eyes gazed down at him.

Thorton was transfixed. Grey eyes met brown and they stared into each other's souls. He recognized something in the corsair that made his pulse leap. Tangle saw it too because he lowered his head to brush his lips against Thorton's. Thorton thought the galley must have capsized because he felt the world turn upside down. He was frightened —he dared not accept such an advance—even though he was lonely. Not with the noose for sailors who offended God and King. He ought not feel such things for a corsair. He ought not feel such things at all. It must be the appetites of his body wanting surcease after a long and difficult day. He should not prolong this kiss. It was a trick by the wily Turk. It was a sin, an abomination. Such were the thoughts that whirled in the maelstrom of his mind.

Tangle felt his response and cupped Thorton's face in his hands. He kissed harder. He had been reduced to the most bestial of conditions aboard the galley and now that he had been released, all of him wanted release. Yet he was in no condition to perform the virile act. He wanted to, but his blood did not quicken. For the first time in his life his flesh did not answer his desires. He raised his mouth to stare down at Thorton.

Thorton was breathing hard and the yearning showed in his face. Yet he pulled away and batted Tangle's hands off of him. "This is not the duty of an officer!" he rasped out.

Tangle shook his head. "Forgive me. I am not myself."

Thorton gulped a deep breath and steadied himself. Externally at least. Internally his stomach was all a-sea and rolling contrary to the motions of the ship. "You are delirious," he announced. That explained everything: Tangle was out of his mind. "Let's get you to bed. Now off with this shirt."

Tangle stretched out on his stomach on the too short bunk. Thorton washed the captain's wounded back with businesslike motions. His hands were gentle, but they shook. Once this had been a handsome man, intelligent and full of vigor. It would be a pity for him to die.

"This one is infected, sir. I'll have to lance it."

"Do so," Tangle mumbled into the featherbed. His back tensed.

Thorton pulled out his pocket knife. He lanced open the wound and it oozed pus. He squeezed more out and mopped it up with the cloth. He cut away some of the hardened yellow encrustations that lined the wound and it bled. He mopped the captain's back again. It was not the only infected wound; the Turk had others on his back, as well as his buttocks and the backs of his thighs. Thorton treated them all. Tangle grimaced and bit the pillow but made no cry. When the English lieutenant patted the cinnamon powder onto the wounds he gasped but held still. Thorton wound the linen bandages around the captain's body to hold the powder in place.

"By Allah, it stings," Tangle breathed. "But I'll be the better for it." With his wounds bound, he rolled onto his side. He shivered. "Cold, too."

Thorton pulled the covers up. He was glad to cover up the gaunt form that excited his pity. It also relieved him to conceal the dark masculine body that was making his blood simmer. He did not understand how he could feel such opposing things at the same time.

"Thank you, Peter. Mr. Thorton, I will have your promise on something." Tangle was wandering back and forth between formal and informal address—it was symptomatic of the disordered condition of his mind.

"Sir?"

"I am going to sleep, perchance not to wake. I want you to promise me that you will carry these men to freedom and not hand them over to the Spanish."

"I cannot determine their fate, sir. That right belongs to a higher power."

"Promise me that you will do everything humanly possible to give them their freedom."

It was a dying man's request and Thorton felt bound to honor it, yet he could not. He was an English officer. "Don't ask me such things!" he whispered.

Tangle sighed deeply. "Then you must rouse me if anything changes. Make me get up, no matter how ill I am. I am exhausted, Mr. Thorton. If you will not conn this vessel, I must."

Thorton flushed at the rebuke. "I will conn it, sir, but I must do so in accordance with mine honor."

"Does your honor permit you to return these men to Spanish chains? They don't deserve it. You came aboard. You know how cruelly they were treated. I am dying of it. They will die if they are taken again. To be condemned to the galleys is to be condemned to death by means of slow torture."

Thorton had once thought he would become a minister. His conscience pricked him now to think of the miserable souls he had released and had yet the power to succor. "Some of them deserve it," he said desperately.

"A whipping or a hanging to be sure, but to be compelled to sit in their own excrement for months on end? I think not, Mr. Thorton. And you don't either."

"Not that, no. But if it were humanely done. With food and clothing . . ."

"It is not humanely done, Mr. Thorton. Not on a Spanish galley."

"No . . ."

"A Sallee rover is different. The slaves keep their clothes and their religion. They can use the head and the galley is kept clean because Allah loves purity. They even earn a half share of the booty. For these reasons they know they are better off on our ships than their countrymen's, and they row willingly."

Thorton was sworn to God and King, and God came first. However, King would be most displeased if Thorton's divine duty interfered with his naval duties. "I am an Englishman. I will do my duty as an officer of His Majesty's Navy." He felt quite noble and virtuous for having made his stand.

"And a damn stubborn one, too," Tangle muttered. "Very well, Mr. Thorton. You are dismissed. Go to your cabin and stay there until called for."

"Aye aye, sir." It never crossed Thorton's mind to disobey, and that was a measure of both his character and the effect Tangle had on other men.

CHAPTER 15 : MOONLIGHT MANEUVERS

Thorton was exhausted. He napped in the master's cabin as the galley lay hove to in the rough seas. He had the sailor's ability to sleep through anything. Hizir stood watch overhead. A Sallee rover, a Swede, a renegade, and a converted Muslim, his loyalty was to the captain sleeping in the berth beneath his feet. He paced softly so that his footfalls on the planks over the captain's head would not disturb the sleeping man. Sometime after sunset the wind abated and word was passed for the captain. They could not rouse him and came to Thorton instead.

Thorton dressed and went first to the captain's cabin. Tangle was incoherent. His respirations came in shallow pants. Thorton was no doctor, but he could tell that Tangle was a very sick man. He went out and called for a loblolly boy. There was neither surgeon nor surgeon's mate on board the galley. Someone would need to attend the sick captain whether he wanted to be seen that way or not.

Coming up on the poop deck Thorton said quietly, "The captain is unfit for duty. I am taking command."

Hizir and Bellini, a small dark man serving as a midshipman, gathered around him with sober looks. The tall Swede grunted, "He seemed well enough on deck."

"You may inspect him for yourself, Mr. Hizir. I will wait for you."

Hizir went below. He was gone a long time.

Thorton studied the sea and sky. It was still rough, but there, breaking through the clouds, was moonlight. "Raise the antennas and prepare to make sail." He did not know what course he would choose. West, to rendezvous with the frigate? He had three days water. "Three-quarter rations water for the crew." He must make for land and attempt to find water. He had no other choice.

The men were tired and there was no emergency. Getting the sails up took time—time enough for Hizir to return. He had Tangle with him. The captain was dressed in an unbuttoned shirt hanging open and brown velvet breeches, both of which were too short for him. He shivered in the night air; it was very chill on a spring night after a rain. He climbed the steps to the poop deck with Hizir's help. Thorton's jaw tightened. He said nothing.

Tangle let go of Hizir's shoulder and stood swaying on his own feet. "I am fit, Mr. Thorton." His voice was carefully controlled. "You have contravened an order I gave you earlier today. I am displeased."

Thorton made a simple response. "I did what I thought necessary, sir."

Tangle looked around the deck, checked the sky and the sea, then the binnacle. "You have not changed our course?"

"No, sir." Thorton did not see any point in adding that he was confused in his mind about what course he should take. He had attended to the things that needed attending while mulling it over.

"It was well to make sail," Tangle conceded grudgingly. "Any sign of the frigate?"

"No, sir."

"Anything else, Lieutenant?"

"I ordered the water ration reduced to three-quarters, sir," Thorton replied.

Tangle scowled. "That order was mine to give, Mr. Thorton."

"You could not be roused, so I took command, sir. I gave the order in my capacity as Acting Captain of the vessel." Thorton was stiffer than he had ever been. Whatever the corsair captain might do to him would be easier to bear than whatever the British navy might do. It crossed his mind that his attempting to take command of the vessel when he had the chance might help him in a court martial, although that was not why he had done it.

Tangle muttered something in his own language, then said, "You break my sleep and vex me sore, Mr. Thorton."

"'Twas not I who broke your sleep, sir. The watch sent for you, but you would not rouse, so they fetched me instead."

"What? Is this true?"

Hizir was forced to admit that it was. He explained, "When you didn't answer no matter how Mr. Bellini knocked, he came and told me and I told him to fetch Mr. Thorton. You made him first lieutenant, sir. Thorton came up and said you were unfit."

Tangle was not at all pleased with this news. He turned on Thorton. "Did you try to rouse me, Mr. Thorton?"

"I did, sir. I would not have taken command if you had risen or spoken something coherent."

"What did I say?"

"You mumbled something in Turkish. It was nothing that I could understand, and you struck me. You would not get up, sir."

Tangle digested this news. Thorton remained wooden. Bishop would have never heard him out. Most officers of the English navy wouldn't have heard him out either. Thorton stood rigidly with his hands at his side and his eyes forward.

"I apologize for striking you. I was not myself."

Thorton was stunned to receive a public apology. He stared at the man in disbelief.

Tangle continued speaking. "I believe you acted in good faith. No blame will attach to you. Next time you find me so fast asleep, douse me with cold water. Make me get up. 'Tis my duty."

"Aye aye, sir."

"Keep this course. Mr. Thorton, my cabin please."

Tangle went down and Thorton followed. Just as his foot touched the weather deck, the cry of "A sail!" came down from the masthead. Tangle swore peevishly. "One night's sleep, just one night's uninterrupted sleep in that feather bed. Is that too much to ask, Allah?" Then he squared his shoulders and dragged himself up to the poop again.

"What kind of sail?" he asked the officers.

"Lateen," was the answer. "South by east."

That sent a jolt through them all. "The Spanish squadron, I'll wager," Tangle said grimly. "They can run as well as we can, and they haven't got a hole in their bow." He shivered and wrapped his arms around himself. His eyes were intensely weary. He racked his brains as he tried to think how to dodge both the English and the Spanish.

"If worse comes to worst, I'd rather risk my lot with your English frigate. Douse the lamps."

Hizir opened the ornate bronze lanthorn. It was very large and depicted the martyrdom of Saint Bartholomew, complete with flayed skin. He extinguished the light and darkness engulfed the deck. The moon continued playing peek-a-boo with the clouds. He told Kaashifa, "Pass the word. Douse all lights."

Kaashifa trotted off to take the message to the watchmen. One by one their lanterns blinked out. The moon came out from behind a cloud and the sails glowed ghostly white, but a few minutes later disappeared again. The sails became a dim grey fog hanging over their heads.

Thorton entreated Tangle, "Sir, you could run into Correaux. France is at war with Spain so they will probably receive you well. Once your men are dispersed there won't be any way to round them up again."

"The French won't release the Spanish. They'll be made prisoners of war."

"That's better than the galleys, isn't it?"

"I suppose it is. I can make Sallee rovers of the moriscos. The criminals can stay in prison with the French instead of the Spanish. I like your plan, Mr. Thorton. I need a latitude and longitude. Do you know where we are?"

Tangle had been sailing blind. That he was in the Bay of Biscay, he knew, but he was not privy to the Spanish navigation records. The captain's papers had gone with the captain. Tangle had only a vague idea of where he was.

"I have an inkling, sir. I've been keeping the traverse boards. I can give you a general course in a moment. Tomorrow at noon I can shoot the sun and give you a better course."

"Excellent. What course, Lt. Thorton?"

Thorton considered his reply. He had known where the frigate was, but there had been an interruption of more than an hour while the galley battled the storm. After that he had kept the traverse boards. He consulted the chart in his head. He felt he was likely to be correct within twenty miles. "East northeast will do for tonight, sir. We will strike the French coast tomorrow morning, God willing."

Tangle was impressed. "Thank you, Mr. Thorton. Let us go to the chartroom."

The chartroom was the sailing master's office. It was a small room crammed with a desk, charts and instruments. A curtain screened off the sleeping quarters. They squeezed in side by side with a chair brought from the captain's cabin. Thorton went to the other side of the curtain and brought back a coverlet to wrap the Sallee rover. Tangle was intensely weary and cold. He gave Thorton a grateful look and murmured thanks. Thorton lit the lamp and it warmed the room a little. He worked his figures and rechecked them. He had recourse to a Spanish slide rule and other devices.

Tangle watched him. "You've forgotten to carry the one, Mr. Thorton," he said.

"I find it difficult to concentrate when you are leaning over my shoulder, sir."

"Sorry." Tangle moved back a little.

Thorton was amazed at the difference between Tangle and other captains. He felt warm and easy in his presence, yet there was no doubt he was the captain. There was a sort of camaraderie between them, but it did not diminish the respect he had for the man. On the contrary, it increased it. He was felt he could trust Tangle, as strange as it seemed to trust a corsair who had stolen a galley out from under the nose of an English frigate. He was also relieved that he had agreed to run into Correaux. Correaux was the *Ajax's* next port of call; it was the logical place to rendezvous. To get the *San Bartolomelo* to rendezvous with the frigate he felt would remove the stain of piracy he feared was attaching to his person. He felt slightly guilty about not revealing this key piece of information to Tangle, but he was afraid the corsair would be frightened off if he knew.

"By Allah, I could use some coffee. I'll see if we can get a pot. Supper, too. Have the hands eaten? What hour of the clock is it? You keep working." He patted Thorton's shoulder as he rose and stuck his head out the door.

There was a marine posted outside the captain's cabin door now: one of the Salletines that Tangle trusted. Other Sallee men were guarding what needed to be guarded, such as the powder room, wine stores, and bread room. He was pleased at the improving order on the galley. Exhausted men were sleeping below in the crew's hammocks. Hands on watch but not needed at the moment were huddled in the coach.

It seemed to Thorton it must be the middle of blackest night, but the action had occurred about midday. They had slept some and night had fallen; his inner sense of time was disturbed by the perturbations of his schedule. Was it only this morning he had boarded the deck of a sinking galley? It seemed an eternity ago.

Coffee arrived. The bitter stuff was strange to Thorton, but it was hot and he was cold. He gulped it down. Sugar made it even better. The sweet black concoction woke him up.

Tangle joined him. "By Allah, that's good! The coffee is even decent."

The corsair's stomach rumbled loud enough for Thorton to hear it. Half an hour later the steward shuffled in. He was an obsequious man with a shaved head and a blue Spanish marine's coat over the black and white checked shirt and black breeches he had scavenged. Another Salletine. The captain favored them. The steward bore a tray with roast yams and a tiny slice of beef, a cabbage salad with some sort of vinegary dressing on it and a few shredded carrots among its limp leaves, and watered cider. He placed it on the desk between Thorton and Tangle and withdrew.

"Well, the cider must be made to last," Tangle said philosophically as he drank. He dug into his food like the starved man he was.

Thorton was hungry too. He ate neatly but without ceremony as he worked his position out.

Tangle's color improved with the food. He sat back in his chair and patted his full stomach. "That's much better. An hour ago I was so faint I was thinking about relinquishing command to you, but food has restored me. Well, perhaps not restored me, but saved me from perishing on the spot as I thought I surely must."

This news caused Thorton considerable surprise. "Sir?" he asked. He was still eating his yams.

"I need sleep, food, and water. If you would be so good as to change my dressings and apply the cinnamon, I'd appreciate it."

"I will do it after supper, if it pleases you, sir."

Tangle nodded. "Tell me, Peter. Have you ever been to Correaux?" His voice was artless.

Thorton finished chewing his current mouthful and dabbed his lips with his napkin. "Never, sir."

"Then why Correaux?" In the close confines of the chartroom the rover felt easy with the English lieutenant and was more direct than he might have been otherwise.

"'Tis the headquarters of the Atlantic Fleet of France," Thorton replied truthfully but evasively.

"There isn't much left of the French Atlantic Fleet, thanks to the British. Yet while galleys have their virtues, 'tis admittedly unusual for the Spanish to haul them out of ordinary and use them for coastguards, don't you think?"

"Aye, sir. 'Tis passing strange and I wondered at it."

"It is because the French have been successful against Spanish possessions in the Mediterranean and menace the Balearic Islands. Since there is little threat on the Atlantic side, thanks to the damage wrought on the French fleet by the British, they have diverted most of their round ships to the Middle Sea. They have left a skeleton fleet fitted out with old galleys to patrol the coast and raid the French."

Thorton wondered if the Admiralty knew about the French successes in the Mediterranean. They probably did, but that did not mean they saw fit to inform a very junior officer like Thorton. He soaked up the news.

Tangle mused, "And the British have sent an old French frigate to wander the Bay of Biscay with a lieutenant who happens to speak fluent Spanish on board. Why is that, I wonder?"

Thorton blushed a little. "Oh, that is nothing. They wanted men who spoke French."

"Parlez-vous français, monsieur?" Tangle was adding up the French frigate, French-speaking officers, and a landfall in Correaux. He kept his guess to himself and continued to question Thorton.

"Un petit peu," Thorton replied. He turned the topic back to Tangle's concerns in an attempt to avoid too close an examination of

his own. "Correaux will have a prize court. With the war between the France and Spain, I'm sure they'll look favorably upon your success."

"'Tis kind of you to be concerned for my well-being," Tangle replied drily. "But also unlike you. Where is that stubborn dedication to your English duty?"

Thorton lost his smile. He sat very still.

Tangle said, "I have been giving considerable thought to Correaux while you've been working out our position. You've done a very nice job of it, too, Peter. I'm glad to know that we do not need to depend entirely upon my addled brain for navigation. But I digress. Correaux."

Life had been cheap in both money and compliments to Peter Thorton. That Tangle was sincere he never doubted. He was a cunning rogue, but he had a streak of honesty in him. His praise gave the younger man a warm glow. Curiosity mixed with dread prompted him to ask, "Correaux?"

"Aye, Correaux. I ask myself, why is an English captain nosing about in the Bay of Biscay in an old French corvette with officers who speak French? I conclude he must be attempting to get intelligence. What would he want to know about? Why, the fleet in Correaux, of course. So I ask myself, why does an English lieutenant seem unconcerned about bearding the lion in his den? I conclude that while I was chained to a galley bench, a truce must have been declared between England and France." He looked to Thorton for confirmation.

Thorton was crestfallen. "You have it, sir. A treaty was signed last fall. I'm sorry I did not think to tell you."

Tangle tipped his chair back on two legs, but the rolling of the deck tipped him forward again and the chair legs thumped down. "I am in the dark, Peter. So many things have changed. I have tried to hear what I could, but that's little enough. New slaves bring new stories and rumors. 'Tis a poor way to be informed."

"If you had met the *Ajax*, I'm sure Mr. Achmed would have explained it all to you. He's charming and will talk to anyone, but since you are his countryman, I expect he would have told you something useful."

They sat smiling at each other. The silence grew intimate as they realized they enjoyed one another's company. Thorton jumped up and gathered the plates. He opened the door and put the tray out. He turned back and started putting away his quills and instruments.

"Peter."

Thorton turned. "Sir?"

"We're going to Correaux. I'm going to sleep. Wake me for an emergency. I trust you. If anything happens, use your best judgment. I'll tell Hizir you have command until I reappear."

"Sir!"

Tangle rose. "Make sure you rest this evening. You have the night watch."

"Aye aye, sir." Thorton saluted.

CHAPTER 16 : PROOF OF COURAGE

Thorton stood his watch in the cold dark night. It was still damp but the wind had dropped and the log showed only three knots. He had discovered coffee and ordered a cup be brought to him to keep him warm and awake through his watch. The Salletines loved the stuff and kept a pot going at all hours. He watched the sky, the sea, the ship, the moon, and his thoughts. Presently he roused himself. Was she head down again? He went and looked over the side. He thought she was. He checked the position of the lateen sail they had spotted earlier. It was growing larger in the moonlight. Thanks to their loss of speed the strange sail was gaining again. He snapped to work.

"Dangle the lantern over the side," he directed the man. He had noted a scar on the galley's red paint when looking over the side before; the lantern showed that the scar had slipped below the waterline. The *Bart's* head had sunk again. Ordinarily he should notify the captain, but Tangle needed his rest. This did not qualify as an 'emergency.' An exigency, perhaps, but not an emergency. It was his to solve. He had hours before the strange sail would overtake him.

"Wafor! Man the pumps."

Most of the crew were below in their hammocks. A few were gathered in the coach to share gossip and rumors while others stared out into the wine dark sea. They started up when called and went to the pumps with sighs and wherefores, but the black mate silenced them with a sarcastic, "Because there's water below, that's what for, you imbecilic offspring of a midget whore!"

MacDonald was sent for, and also the man who had been appointed carpenter's mate, there being no proper carpenter. Daymen, they were getting precious sleep, but they roused up quickly enough. They knew why they were being called in the middle of the night. They gathered their men and tools and hurried forward. A short conference was held in which it was decided to heel her over and patch the hull again.

"If you can get her patched, then we'll open this hatch and pump her out. If not, we'll reinforce the hatch and pray it doesn't burst."

"Aye aye, sir," MacDonald replied.

"Oui, Lieutenant," the acting carpenter replied. They got busy.

Thorton went to the poop and changed her heading to a close-haul so that she heeled well over, lifting the hole out of the water.

MacDonald came and reported. "She's holed all right, about ten inches by two feet, sir. The plank and patch are both gone. The carpenter is patching now."

"Very well, MacDonald. Carry on."

Thorton was relieved the forward section of the galley could be sealed so well; they would have sunk long ago otherwise. Even with her head full of water she would still float. It was a delicate position, crank and lumpen, vulnerable to storm and mishap, but still, it was far better to be afloat than not. He was developing an almost superstitious faith in the watertight bulkheads and thought English vessels could be greatly improved by the adoption of the same. Not that anyone was going to ask the advice of a mere lieutenant.

The bells were struck, the log was tossed. Speed was two and a half knots. The wind dropped further. At the next bell they were down to two knots, but the bow was higher. MacDonald made a new report. "We've patched her, but the oakum is out of her seams aft the break for a couple fathoms. 'Tis working loose and I expect it'll run all the way to the middle hold if we let it."

Oakum was made of long strings of fiber; once the sea got hold of it, it would rip out of the seams like knitting unraveling. Thorton's faith in the inviolability of the middle hold was now destroyed. She was going to leak amidships before the night was over.

"Can you do anything?"

"Well, sir, if you keep her heeled over I can go over the side and bend some nails over it. That should keep the oakum from running until we can make a proper fix."

"Make it so."

Thorton fretted. Should he call Tangle? He'd want to know about this. He glanced at the other sail. It had gained. Still, the task was within his ability to handle. Yet if it got away from him Tangle would want to know why he hadn't been called sooner. He found himself frightened by the responsibility. It was up to him to do the right thing. Still, he had able warrant officers and specialists to take care of the matter. All they really needed from him was permission to do so. He found it nerve-wracking to be in charge. Slowly, he settled. The men were doing their duty. The challenge was worrisome, but not severe. The weather was mild.

"Land ho!" the lookout cried.

Thorton took the night glass and trained it east. The image in the glass was upside down making it harder to discern—day glasses had an extra lens to turn the image right side up, but doing so removed part of the light. Night glasses needed all available light, so only one lens was used. He watched a long while, then slowly a low dark line that was neither sky nor water made itself vaguely apparent across the northeastern horizon. Just then the moon set and the darkness was absolute. Land disappeared.

"Keep a sharp ear out for breakers," he told the quartermaster.

MacDonald climbed up to the poop. His legs and coat were wetted from the waist down. He reported, "Staples in, sir. We bent quite a few nails over her seams and hope they'll hold until we can fix 'em proper, sir."

"Very good, MacDonald."

He gave orders to fall off the wind a little and the ship eased her heel. MacDonald went below to check the leaking. Thorton went with him. They moved among men in their hammocks as quietly as they could in the dark. MacDonald's bull's-eye lantern cast a narrow beam of light that helped them find their way. Wafor opened the aft hatch and they climbed into the middle hold. They crouched under the very low deckhead in water up to their knees. Water sloshed among the casks and crates. When the galley's head rose to a wave, it sloshed aft, and when her head went down and her stern rose, it ran forward.

"Are the stores spoiled?"

"I don't think so, sir. The water isn't sitting so it hasn't soaked the wood yet."

"All the same, we've got to get it out of here."

"I was going to do that after we pumped out the forward hold, sir."

"Pump this first, then the forward hold. The damage is done forward. We must save as much as we can from the middle hold. We're short on water as it is. I don't want it contaminated."

Thorton went forward to check the hatch between the forward section and the middle section. Water was leaking around it as high as his waist. Watermarks showed that the water on the other side had been a foot higher, but the clanking of the pump forward let him know the men were at work to lower the water.

"I would nae open that, sir," MacDonald said in his Scotch burr.

"No, I shouldn't," Thorton agreed.

They climbed back to the weather deck.

"Our cable's gang to rot if we can't get it dried out soon," the boatswain said.

"I know. But all I really care about is staying afloat until we reach the coast of France. What happens after that is not our worry. We'll be back with the *Ajax*, God willing."

"Aye aye, sir."

Thorton went back to the poop. Another bell sounded. The faintest decrease in the darkness of the east made the stars a little paler. Dawn in an hour. He looked around the sea but could see nothing. The lateen sail was out of sight. Just because of the dark, or had she changed course?

At dawn Foster and Maynard came on watch. Thorton stayed on the poop and talked to Maynard in a lecturing tone. He explained the holds of galleys and their lovely watertight bulkheads and the way her head rode down or up depending on the leak. He took him to look at the marks himself so he too could reckon how her bow was riding. He impressed the boy with the grave need to be attentive to all details. Maynard was duly intimidated.

The sun came up in a rosy aurora that circled the horizon in a faint blush. It grew bright in the east. By the time the sun rose, the wind died completely. The *Bart* lay becalmed amid the gentle swells. How unlike the heaving, foam-torn waves of the day before! Thorton ordered the lead out.

"No bottom with this line."

"No bottom here."

He kept them casting because the dark smudge of the coast of France was looming larger as the swells pushed them nearer. She had no steerage as she drifted in the calm. The only consolation was that the strange lateen sail was likewise becalmed. They could see her south of them. With the glass on her he could see motion at her sides; she had ordered out her sweeps.

"A sail!" sounded from the masthead.

Thorton looked over the side and saw only the one. "Where?" he shouted up to the lookout.

"Another lateen to the south southeast, beyond the first sail."

Thorton swore. "Douse the sails. Out twelve oars." The new watch was fresh from their breakfast and their first night's sleep as free men. They were eager to work. The sails were taken in and the oars were run out. As the oars bit the rudder gained steerage way.

He checked the binnacle. "Southeast by south," he told the helm. The galley turned and cruised parallel to the French coast. He would need to shoot the sun at noon. That would tell him his precise latitude. When he knew that, he could trace that line of latitude to the coast and know exactly where he was and how far it was to Correaux. His stomach growled, but Tangle still did not appear.

"Mr. Foster, if those breakers sound louder you're too close. Send for me if anything changes."

What to do? He decided to update the log. He hadn't many officers and even fewer who could write. Half the Muslims could write in their own languages, but that didn't do him any good. Only about one in three of the Europeans could write their own tongues. He transferred the details of the traverse board to the log and made other relevant notes. Whoever came after him would be able to understand exactly what had happened to the ship and where she was during his watch. Finally he and Hizir were called to attend the captain in his cabin.

Thorton saluted and said, "You're looking well this morning, Captain."

Tangle was stooping to look out one of the two small stern windows. He was dressed in nothing but a robe of blue and yellow brocade he had looted from the Spanish captain's sea chest. He turned and smiled.

"I feel much improved. I do believe I will live. Yesterday I had my doubts. Sleep is a powerful restorative."

"Your fever, sir?"

"Broken. I feel a trace of vigor this morning. How fares the ship?"

"We lost our patch and the broken board too. We mended her and put in staples to keep the oakum from running. Land is in the offing and we are paralleling the shore on a course southeast by south at one knot. We have twelve sweeps out. A second lateen sail has appeared beyond the first, which has gained on us during the night. They are south by east of us, sir."

Tangle grimaced. One lateen sail could have been anything from a fisherman to a Spanish scout. Two was looking more and more like the Spanish squadron.

"My compliments, Mr. Thorton. It sounds like you had a quiet evening." He twitched a little as he restrained himself from running up on deck immediately.

Hizir arrived. He'd been asleep and was still pulling on his shirt. He saluted blearily. "Rais," he greeted the man without saluting.

Tangle replied, "*Salaam*." He gave Hizir a look but said nothing about his appearance. Instead he addressed himself to something he very much wanted to do before immersing himself in the duties of command. "I want my ears pierced. Gentlemen, will you oblige me?"

The announcement took Thorton by surprise, but Hizir nodded. "As you please."

Thorton replied belatedly, "Aye aye, sir."

Tangle pulled one of the chairs from the table and took a seat. He put a hand to his ear. "You'll find holes closed up where I had them before." His steward had a needle and four earrings ready on the table with a cloth and a small basin of water. A looking glass was by them.

Thorton had never pierced anyone's ears before, but Hizir had. Thorton stepped behind the seated man and held Tangle's bald head steady as Hizir jabbed the needle in. Tangle's nostrils flared, but with Thorton holding his head still, the twitch caused no damage. The earring went in. Hizir waited a moment for Tangle to catch his breath, then said, "Turn his head so I can reach the other one."

Thorton turned the captain's head to bring the left ear into reach. The other earring was set. Hizir daubed at the blood, then looked critically at his work. Thorton let go and stepped back. The new gold hoops added luster to Tangle's weathered countenance. He looked more alive and less like a skeleton. Or a slave. Tangle picked up the hand mirror and had a look.

"Yes, that is more like my old self," he said approvingly. He stood up and untied his belt. "Now the hafada."

Hizir nodded and waited while the captain opened his robe and slipped it off. Thorton could not imagine where a man might possibly wear earrings other than his ears. When Hizir knelt before Tangle and motioned him over, he was at a loss.

"Hold his testicles for me," Hizir explained.

"I beg your pardon?" Thorton replied in considerable astonishment.

Tangle laughed. "The hafada is a Muslim custom—a rite of passage. I had them done when I was a boy, but the Spaniards took all my jewelry, the rotters. They weren't very nice about it, either. Losing them hurt worse than acquiring them."

Thorton gaped at him. "But—but—but—whyever would you pierce *that?*" He couldn't help glancing down at the captain's shaved groin. He swiftly jerked his eyes up again but was confronted by the powerful chest and lean abdominals. He looked away.

Hizir grunted, "To prove his courage. A boy undergoes it to prove that he is a man. If he has it done, then in the future he cannot turn coward. The rings prevent it. Perhaps you have experienced the feeling of your bollocks attempting to crawl back up inside your body in a situation of great dread? The rings prevent it from happening. Thus you maintain your courage when other men are losing theirs due to the natural operations of the body."

"We don't do that in my country." Thorton's amazement knew no bounds.

Tangle grinned at him. "There is a reason why the Sallee rovers have a reputation for great daring and peerless courage, Mr. Thorton.

Now, if you would oblige me, I'd like them to go in a little easier than the Spanish took them out." He braced his legs wide.

So Thorton knelt and had the very peculiar experience of lifting the captain's virile organ in his hands. He diverted his eyes and attempted to hold completely still as Hizir brought the needle near. The ship rolled gently through a swell and Tangle put his hand on the back of the chair to steady himself.

"Stretch them a little," Hizir said.

Thorton pulled gently so that the skin was taut. He had to look to make certain he didn't hurt the man and color flooded his face.

Tangle watched in amusement. "Ready," he announced.

Hizir jabbed. Thorton winced. It was neatly done; the needle went through the skin between the bulge of the right testicle and the base of the penis. The ring was placed and the gold gleamed darkly against the manly portion. Since Tangle was devoid of hair the gold ring was displayed to good effect.

Hizir glanced up. "All right, rais?"

Tangle sucked in a deep breath. "Excellent. That didn't hurt nearly as much as having my sores lanced last night. Pray continue. I prefer a matched set."

Hizir chose his location and Thorton held his breath, eyes wide. *'Twas a barbaric proof of physical courage,* he thought. The Muslim crew members would be most impressed. Hell, Thorton was impressed. But nothing would induce him to undergo such an operation himself.

"Ready?" Hizir asked.

"Carry on." A tightening of the captain's muscles, a twitch of the warm cullions that Thorton held firmly in his hands, and the needle was through. Hizir left it there while he picked up the other ring and threaded it into place. The deed done he stepped back to admire his handiwork. Thorton rose on shaky knees. He felt quite peculiar.

"The glass, Mr. Thorton."

Thorton handed Tangle the looking glass and the Turk admired both sets of earrings. He turned his tall lean form before the mirror and smiled. Finally he set the mirror down. "My pantaloons, if you please, Mr. Thorton."

Thorton lifted the white pantaloons off the sea chest and handed them over. Tangle gingerly tucked the family jewels back into their proper place and did up his buttons. "I am obliged to you, gentlemen."

Thorton felt a little pale, but murmured, "Not at all, sir."

"My pleasure, sir," Hizir replied with a saucy grin.

"I'll meet you on deck, Mr. Thorton." Tangle continued dressing.

"Aye aye, sir." Thorton fled.

CHAPTER 17 : BEAT TO QUARTERS

Tangle stared through the spyglass at the two lateen sails. He glanced up at the sky. The weather was clearing nicely and the breeze had backed around to the northwest. The morning was cool, but the sun was warm. The gentle breeze felt good.

He sighed. "I wish it would keep raining, or perhaps a lovely fog. A magic spell to render us invisible would come in handy as long as I'm yearning for the impossible. How I wish I were the sorcerer they claim I am!" He lowered the glass. "Bring us closer to shore, right to where you can see the waves breaking but not in the breakers. Out all sail. Do you think we are north or south of Correaux, Mr. Thorton?"

"North," Thorton replied promptly. "We had cleared Finistère and were well into the Bay of Biscay when we made our run. That line of shore runs northwest to southeast by east, more or less. See that headland, and that one?" He pointed to distant landmarks. The northwestern one was hazy with distance but the other was plain enough. "The shore will turn south and run that way about eighty miles, and there in the estuary of the Caronne River we will find Correaux."

"How long?"

"Two days. Maybe more. It depends how far south we are. I'll know for sure when I take the noon sighting."

"They're south of us, in place to intercept us before Correaux. They're faster, too. They don't have a hole in their bows. Has the French fleet come out yet?"

"I don't know about Correaux, but in Brest they were no where near coming out."

"Here's hoping they're cruising for the Spaniards on their door step, but I doubt it. The English War cost them dearly and the Spaniards have wrought havoc in the Bay of Biscay. The Atlantic coast of France is effectively closed to French shipping. How far are we from Brest?"

Thorton consulted the map in his head. "With this wind, at least four days. You'd have to beat hard to make it back up the coast."

Tangle eyed the shore and the lateen sails. "By Allah, if we didn't have company, I'd run on the nearest beach and take on take on three or four tons of water. That would give us three more days. However, it would be a disaster if they caught us with our bow on the beach and our stern exposed. Which is why galleys work in packs, Mr. Thorton. One is vulnerable, but five together is a hedgehog bristling with spines in every direction."

"If you say so, sir."

Tangle stood meditating. This morning he was well-dressed; Palma the tailor had sacrificed a pair of good white damask tablecloths so that the captain could have proper clothes. Tangle wore pantaloons of the Turkish sort: loose around the thighs and tapering close to the lower leg. A tunic was worn over them, square cut at the bottom and short-sleeved, no collar and a slit down the front laced with a leather thong. With a blue-checked kerchief over his head and earrings in his ears he looked the very picture of a pirate. Although most likely no pirate before or since had ever gone to sea dressed in a pair of Spanish tablecloths.

"A sail!" cried the lookout.

"Damn it, this sea is beginning to feel as trafficked as the path between a French whore's legs!" Tangle swore.

Thorton ignored his comment and shouted back, "What sail?"

"Lateen, sir!"

"I conclude we have found the rest of the Spanish squadron, Mr. Thorton. Do you know anything that would indicate otherwise?"

Thorton shook his head.

"What about the *Ajax?*"

The *Ajax* would run very well on this course and was probably heading to Correaux as well, but she was overloaded with her Spanish castaways on board. Although her capacious hold could supply water and food for months, even with the additional mouths on board, she would be packed to the beams. Tempers would be short. Bishop was not the kind of man who would willingly withstand such things. With her studding sails out the *Ajax* could fly before the wind while the galleys were on courses that were not to their advantage. Sooner or later she would overtake them. Would that be before or after the rest of the Spanish squadron caught up to the runaway galley? Or the injured galley limped into a (hopefully) friendly French port?

"I don't expect to see her for a while."

"We are going up, Mr. Thorton. Bring me the tack!"

Tangle went up like a monkey. Thorton followed more slowly. He wrapped his legs around the antenna and grabbed the wooldings to pull himself up. He felt very insecure about making his first climb up a lateen yard. The antenna was made of two great spars overlapping one another and the whole lashed together with wooldings. It was these lashings of thick hempen cords that they grabbed to pull themselves up.

Thorton mused to himself that it was a clever solution to the problem of finding timbers large enough to do the job. The British navy had laid claim to the best timber in all of England, but still had to import masts from the Baltic countries and even as far away as the American colonies. More than one English vessel had gone to sea with a mast or other spar fished together for want of sound timber during the last war.

The breeze was stronger up here. The antenna creaked and swayed. The pair of lines at each corner of the triangular sail drew it taught, but the long antenna flexed more than a square yard would. Thorton made the mistake of looking down. The galley's deck seemed very far below. His stomach felt a little uneasy. The rocking of the galley as she climbed and slid down the swells was amplified; the men at the peak were swaying through great spiraling circles that were only mildly felt down below.

Tangle looked down and grinned at him. "You'll have to go faster than that, Mr. Thorton! I want you to climb the mast every day until you can mount it like a monkey."

"Aye aye, sir," Thorton replied as he schooled his face to remain expressionless. He'd served under English captains that had done the same. They'd made their landlubbers do it on the *Ajax*. God pity the weary or frightened man who lost his grip. Still, it had to be done. An officer needed to be able to go anywhere on his vessel without the slightest hesitation or fear.

Tangle wrapped his legs tightly around the antenna and pulled his glass out of the pocket in the seam of his pantaloons. "Damn me if I don't think there's another lateen sail out there. See? On the other side of the second one. She masks it, but there seems to be an extra peak where there ought not be one. They aren't spaced properly to be a three-masted vessel, so it isn't a xebec. I don't know whether to be happy or disappointed. I'd love to take a xebec. I could give your frigate as good as I got if I had one." He continued watching through the glass.

"They must be desperate for water if they are the Spanish squadron. We have half the men that they do, and we're thirsty. They must be parched," Thorton replied.

Tangle made no answer. His mind was busy working out a plan. Presently he remembered to answer Thorton. "I think you're right, Mr. Thorton. If we are lucky they have not spoke the English frigate and don't know we are their enemy."

Thorton calculated the frigate's last known course and speed, the speed and courses of the galleys, and ventured, "I doubt they've met, sir. I bet they ran for land once they lost contact with the *Bart*."

They clambered down and orders were given. The foresail was furled and the fore antenna used to sway a pair of small guns out of the hold. Her nose sank a little. All water casks, provisions, cable, sail — anything the vessel had — were shifted to the aft portion of the hold. The galley adjusted her trim and rode well enough with the small guns in place. Next they raised the big guns and placed them upon her foredeck. Her head sank.

"What else can we move?" Tangle racked his brain. With very little provision in her, there wasn't much weight that could be moved. He kept his hands clasped behind his back as he stood at the rail of the poop deck and studied the galley's waist. "Everything is aft, even the crew who are not working!"

The bad trim was causing them not only to lose a knot or two of speed, it made them less handy and reduced the range of the guns — they would have to be elevated to compensate, but they could only be elevated so far.

Suddenly Thorton said, "Water, sir."

"We've moved all the water casks, empty and full."

"Aye, sir. What if we filled the empty ones with sea water?"

Tangle's eyes widened. "By Allah, you are a thinking man! Make it so! After that we will drill the gun crews with empty guns. If we are to take them by assault, it would be well to have a chance of hitting what we shoot at."

Thorton replied, "Aye aye, sir."

"Tell Hizir to drill his marines as well. We'll need sharpshooters."

"Aye aye, sir."

They pumped casks full of sea water. Thorton used a piece of charcoal to mark a large X on their lids to keep them from getting mixed up with the potable water. Another gang rigged a hoist from a pair of sweeps and the aft antenna gallows. They rolled water casks aft from the pump then lowered them into the hold below. It was slow work, but they had time. Little by little the heel of the galley sank until she had a decent trim. Meanwhile, Maynard and Foster went to the foredeck and drilled the gun crews.

Thorton went to the poop. "Salt water stowed, sir. Mr. Maynard sends word he thinks they might be able to fire the guns without killing themselves, but he has no confidence in being able to hit their marks."

Tangle made a moue of displeasure. "Bad gunnery loses battles. Tell him that, Mr. Thorton."

"We have already talked. His men need live fire practice, sir."

Tangle grunted because it was true, but he didn't want to alarm his quarry by firing the guns, nor waste his powder and shot. A galley carried a limited amount of everything, including munitions.

"We have done as much as we can." If he had doubts about going into battle with a gun crew that couldn't shoot their way out of a barn, he did not voice them. "Break out the Spanish colors. If we see anything that looks French and threatening we will strike them immediately."

"Your plan, sir?"

"To take the first galley while she is helpless on the beach, after she has loaded several casks of water, before the others come up, then run for our lives."

It was a daring plan. It would net him another prize, and more importantly, several days of water without him having to run the risk of getting it on his own. Done deftly, he could sail away with his prize before the other galleys came up. If arriving at Correaux with one captured Spanish galley would be good, arriving with two would be very grand indeed. Success was its own justification.

Thorton would have to sit out the action and accept no prize money. He was an officer of a neutral nation. Even as he thought it, his palms itched, and he knew he would not be able to resist the temptation to take part in the battle. His conscience twinged; he must not turn pirate. He must return to the *Ajax* with a clean record. The life of a pirate was not for him—look how they ran and worried with no trust in any port and very short provisions! Yet how very tempting to throw off the English uniform and sail under the redoubtable Captain Tangle, serving as a lieutenant to one of the ablest and most notorious captains of the age! Thus his desires warred with his sense of duty. Duty won.

"Sir. I will go below during the action. I cannot take part in a battle against a vessel belonging to a neutral nation."

Tangle folded his arms over his chest and stared at Thorton.

Thorton stood straight and tense, but he knew his action was the right one. "I am a British officer, sir. My position upon your vessel has not changed that. I will not compromise mine honor."

"I had counted upon you to captain the prize, Mr. Thorton."

"Mr. Hizir will serve very well, sir."

"What of Mr. Maynard? Will he work the guns for me?"

"I don't know, sir. I have not mentioned the matter to him. He is very young and I don't think he has thought of the *Articles of War* at all. I will address the matter with him."

"No, I will. MacDonald, too. And Foster, he's an Englishman as well."

The English were gathered on the poop deck and Tangle addressed them in awkward English. "Gentlemen of England. Until now you are saving a ship that was sinking and thirsty. Your King may forgive you. However, I am going to take that Spanish galley. She is mine enemy, not yours. If you help me your King will hang you for pirates. If you don't help me you will be my prisoners. You must choose."

Foster spoke instantly, "I am with you, sir. I've no wish to go home to England."

Maynard and MacDonald looked at Thorton. He answered, "I have already informed Captain Tangle that I will not participate in an attack upon a neutral nation."

MacDonald looked at his feet. Then he said, "Nor will I. I'll keep this boat afloat as well as I can, but that's only because I don't fancy sinkin'."

Maynard fidgeted. He wouldn't look at Thorton and gave a sidelong peek at Tangle. He stewed a while longer, then said, "Will I be a lieutenant if I fight, sir?"

Tangle nearly smiled. "If you hit what you aim for, I'll make you a lieutenant afterwards."

Maynard nearly bounced with excitement. "I'll stick with you, sir!"

MacDonald growled, "That's desertion, boy."

Maynard smiled broadly. "Only if they catch me, MacDonald. I don't think they will. Not with Tangle as our captain. Bishop is too slow and stupid."

"The Spaniards will hang you if they catch you, too," Thorton warned him.

Maynard grinned. "They won't catch me. Will they, sir?" He looked to Tangle for confirmation.

"No boy, they will not catch us. I will sink before I surrender." Tangle looked over the rail toward the headland where the first of the Spanish vessels would soon disappear.

"Pass the word to clear for action quietly, Mr. Maynard. Rowers into the benches without shirts or kerchiefs. Officers and marines into Spanish uniforms. We do not want to alarm the enemy; we want them to think we are their lost consort. Rig the preventers. MacDonald, Thorton, you are relieved of duty. You may go below."

Thorton and MacDonald replied, "Aye aye, sir," and made their way down the ladder. Thorton went to his cabin. He had very little in it, but he made it up as neatly as he could. He sat down cross-legged on his bunk like a Turk. There was nothing to do but wait and hope for the best. He thought this a good time to renew the prayers he had neglected for a very long time.

CHAPTER 18 : FOX AMONG THE HENS

Tangle donned the coat and hat of his Spanish predecessor. The coat was too small and he could hardly move his arms, but it was blue and the scarlet reverses and cuffs could be easily seen. The other officers were ordered into Spanish uniforms as well. Thus it appeared that Spanish officers had their slaves at their benches. Her guns were hauled up and placed under her *arrumbada*. A tub with slow matches was lit alongside as back up in case the flintlocks failed, as one or more surely would during an extended encounter.

Maynard, being a fair-haired boy, climbed onto the *arrumbada* and started capering and waving his hat as skylarking boys were wont to do. The wind blew his curls out. That angelic blond head could not possibly belong to the savage visage of a Sallee rover, yet Sallee rover was what he had become. How he had thrilled to the tales of adventure on the Narrow Seas! Soon it would all be his. He grinned into the wind and watched the enemy approach with the keenest delight. Some of the men climbed onto the *arrumbada* next to him and waved wildly to the newcomer.

Ahead of them the Spanish galley made signals. Tangle read them; he had watched and learned every facet of the operation of the galley in which he was a prisoner. "'Tis the *Santa María de Madeira*. Make our private signal: No. 121. Send 'need water'." Foster jumped to do his bidding.

Tangle kept back. He knew glasses would be trained upon the *Bart's* deck and he did not want to be recognized as not being the lawful captain. He kept the tricorn hat well down, which was understandable with the brilliant sun reflecting diamonds of light on the surface of the sea. The wind eddied behind the headland and the great lateen sails flapped and thundered. He ordered sail reduced. Men in Spanish clothes went up; they were a mixed lot of Frenchmen, Spaniards, Moors, Italians, and Turks. It didn't matter. The Spaniards pressed men wherever they could find them and their crews were as motley as any. It was the Spanish clothes that marked them as being Spanish crewmen. Not that the men had a uniform; only the officers wore uniforms. The ordinary seamen wore what ever they had. The slop chest contained tan duck and white linen that was sold to the sailors to make clothes, so they were generally attired in white shirts and tan breeches, but with odds and ends of other clothes as well. Here and there among them were the blue coats of Spanish marines, muskets at their sides. The marines were all Salletines, but since half the Sallee rovers were European renegades, they passed tolerably well. At a distance, at least. Tangle did not intend to close. Not yet.

Soon enough the *Santa María* found a fishing village and a stream coming down to the water. The fishboats were all out and nothing but aged people, women, and children were left behind. At the sight of the Spanish galleys they fled into the hills. The *María* signaled them to cover her while she ran upon the beach. Tangle was pleased to obey; it was the perfect position from which to ambush her.

The wind carried the other galley's stench to them. That smell more than anything hardened the hearts of the men on board the *Bart*. Even Thorton in his cabin could smell it. It smelled like shit, filth, illness, rot, brimstone, death and despair. It smelled like tyranny. Thorton gagged and covered his face with his handkerchief. Had the *Bart* really smelled that bad? She must have, but in the rain and wind and panic of sinking the stench had not seemed important. After the *Bart* had been scrubbed out they had all rapidly become accustomed to the better air. Being chained in such foulness was a fate none of them could stomach. They would die rather than surrender to the Spanish.

The *María* ran her bow onto the beach. The sails hung limp as men jumped over the side to slosh through the water to the beach. They ran and drank from the stream in general disorder. Their officers shouted at them, but the thirsty men ignored them to laugh and cavort and drink greedily from the stream. Meanwhile, her holds opened and both antennas were used to haul up empty water casks and set them on the deck. The empty casks were thrown over the side to splash into the shallows. Some of the shore party fished them up onto the beach. Full of fresh water, they were rolled back and wrapped into a cargo net to be hauled on board.

Tangle turned to watch the headland behind him. It would not be long before the other galley rounded the point. "Back sails. Oars out." He knew exactly where he wanted to be.

The captain of the *María* was very glad to see the *San Bartolomeo* was not lost as he feared, so he ordered his boat over the side. With a lieutenant and midshipman to attend him, his gig rowed out to meet the *Bart*.

"Prepare to render honors," Tangle called. "Sideboys line up!"

The Spanish captain and his officers came aboard to the sound of a ragged drum roll. The *María's* captain was a short man with iron-grey hair and a leather face. He had a barrel chest confined in a blue coat with plenty of gold lace and a fine white linen shirt and red breeches.

His buttons were real gold while his stockings were perfectly white silk, leading down to high-heeled shoes with golden buckles. His garters were gold braid. His hat had gold braid going around the brim and very fine white ostrich feathers for extra panache. Mr. Hizir saluted him. The Spaniard didn't recognize the rawboned Swede and puzzled at him. There was no time for chitchat, not with the other captain approaching.

"Renaldo! We are very glad you are not sunk!" he greeted him enthusiastically.

Tangle stepped out from behind Hizir and said in a pleasant baritone, "Allow me to introduce myself. I am Isam Rais Tangueli, Captain of the Corsairs of Zokhara. You are my prisoner."

The Spaniard's jaw dropped and he turned absolutely white as he confronted that dark Turkish face above a Spanish uniform. "Mutiny!" he growled.

"A lawful prize. The Sallee Republic and Spain are at war and I am a duly commissioned privateer. Your sword, please." The Muslim marines pointed their muskets at the captain. The rowers aboard the *Bart* had already brought her head around so that her guns were aimed at the *María's* exposed stern. "Run out the guns, Maynard!"

Young Maynard leaped off the *arrumbada* and his guns ran out with a sound like thunder. Aboard the *María* all was confusion and distress. Their captain taken, the galley aground, half their crew ashore, and the bow battery of the *Saint Bart* aimed right up their poop! The first lieutenant hung over the tafferel and shouted, "Captain Ximénes! Your orders, sir!"

Tangle spoke smoothly. "We can blow you to pieces where you lie, sir. I suggest you order the surrender. You will be treated honorably. We are Muslims and hence civilized. We are not like you Spaniards. We will not lower ourselves to your level."

Captain Ximénes was not in a mood to die. His brain worked frantically to solve the tactical problem, but while he could see possible success for his galley should he give the order to fight, he did not see any possibilities in which he himself would not die. He stalled. That was his best bet: delay until the other galleys came up and gave him a fighting chance.

"What have you done with Captain Renaldo and the rest?"

"They saved their hides by climbing aboard an English frigate, the cowards. They left us chained to the benches of a sinking ship, so we are not in a mood to humor you." Tangle pulled a pistol out of his left coat pocket and cocked it with his thumb. He aimed it at Ximénes' face. "Please do not inconvenience me by further delay. You can die if you wish, but I don't want to swab the decks again."

The Spanish captain stared into Tangle's pistol barrel. He was positive that Tangle would shoot him dead if he annoyed him any further. Sweat broke out on his brow. "Let us have water and we will surrender. We have drunk up all our vinegar and everything else. We are near to perishing for want of water."

"Granted. Your sword and name, please."

"Don Alfonso Ximénes y Floridablanca, captain of the *Santa María de Madeira*." As if in a dream he handed over the sword.

"Order the surrender."

He shouted across, "Strike the colors! We are taken!"

The Spanish colors were struck and the crew waited nervously to discover their fate.

"Mr. Hizir, kindly take your prize crew aboard the *María*. Release the slaves and put the Spanish crew ashore. Captain Ximénes, your men will fill the water casks under our guns and load water into the *María*. When that is done we will sail away and leave you on the shore. Hizir, get that galley off the beach and turn her around. Make ready her guns. Put her stern on the beach and receive the water with the main antenna for hoist."

Hizir moved to obey.

"You will understand, Captain Ximénes, if I detain you aboard my vessel until all the conditions have been satisfied. You and your men will be given water. Put them in the third lieutenant's cabin and guard them well." The last order was directed to his marines.

"Aye aye, sir." There was nothing else Captain Ximénes could say. He was not pleased at the prospect of being marooned on a French beach with the villagers no doubt running to fetch the nearest coastguard, but it was infinitely preferable to being shot or sold into servitude in the Sallee Republic.

All was done as Tangle ordered. The Sallee rovers—for that was what they all were now—made haste. They were greatly elated at taking the *María* without a shot being fired. Aboard the *María*, the galleyslaves were jubilant and disorderly. The rovers bashed a few heads and informed them they must row but would be freed if they did as they were told. They would even be granted a share of the prize money. The filthy naked men did as they were bid and the *María* got off the beach. The galley was absolutely dry. She had run out of water the day before and men were fainting for the lack of it. They rowed and hoped for the best.

"A sail!" came the excited shout. The cry was taken up on the *María*. The marines standing guard over the water party on shore ran for the boats and pulled hard for the galleys. They left a dozen casks on the beach.

"Turn!" Tangle shouted. Half the oars pulled and half backed, spinning the *Saint Bart* majestically in the calm waters of the cove. Her prow very nearly raked the chain-wale of the *María*.

"Fend off! Fend off!" men on both galleys shouted. Boathooks pushed and prodded and the *Bart* cleared the *María's* rigging without catching.

Tangle held his breath, but she was free. "Get us clear. We need to let the *María's* guns bear. Take position to her starboard."

Both galleys were facing the newcomer, their oars holding them in place and Spanish flags flying. The private signal was still up on the *Bart*. Maynard climbed onto the *arrumbada* and waved his hat. "Wave!" he ordered the men around him. They started waving and cheering. When the arriving galley saw that it was the missing *San Bartolomeo* with her blue-coated officers on deck, they cheered and waved back. They were glad to rendezvous with their missing consort.

They were still jubilant as the galleys glided closer. The new vessel's name could be read: the *San Antonio de Padua*. Her captain frowned as he swept his glass over the poop and did not recognize any of the men standing there. "Something's not right. I don't know those men," he told his lieutenant.

"A mutiny, sir? The men are restive from lack of water," his first lieutenant replied.

"Load guns. We'll soon quell 'em."

Tangle saw the fourth galley rounding the headland a mile away. "No time. Out guns! Hoist the Sallee colors! Charge!"

Tangle's voice carried across the short space between the two galleys. Hizir echoed his commands. The two galleys charged forward and the bow batteries ran out as the ensigns came down. Hizir's battery ran slow and ragged, but Maynard's battery shot forward like they knew what they were doing. The purple ensign with its three silver stars and crescents fluttered from the flagstaff of the *Bart*, and the former galleyslaves put their backs into it and rowed with a good will. They outpaced the *María*.

The sound of the drums from the *San Antonio* came loud and clear. Tangle watched her gunners through his glass. They moved smartly, but *Bart* was already loaded and had a brief but precious advantage. The Sallee galley raced towards her intended victim at eight knots, crossing the glossy water at a blistering speed. The *María* came on slower, but she came.

"Aim to sheer off their larboard oars!" Tangle called. "Fire!"

Maynard screamed, "FIRE!" and the cry of 'fire' echoed across the water. His bow guns boomed out within a half second of each other. They were a little beyond musket shot range and the arc of fire nearly level. He had the great satisfaction of seeing two balls strike, one blowing the *arrumbada* to pieces and the other blowing a hole in her gunwale. The shriek of wounded men came clearly across the short expanse of water. Half a minute later the guns of the *María* fired raggedly. They sprayed a great deal of water with one shot coming near the *Antonio's* bows without striking.

"Take her starboard oars!" Tangle bellowed across to the *María*.

The *San Antonio* fired her guns in answer. The Spanish gunners knew their job; the *Bart* took balls in her bow and *arrumbada*. Number Three gun was blown off its carriage and all of its crew wounded. A third ball skimmed over the gunwale and killed one of the rowers instantly. A fourth ball sailed through her rigging with no obvious damage.

"Fire as she bears! Grapeshot! Clear her quarterdeck!" Tangle bellowed. He wasn't worried about the bow hits—the forward hold was already sealed off. "Damage report!"

Thorton in his cabin was practically under Tangle's feet. He heard the shouted orders. He gripped the edge of the bunk tightly as he listened and felt the timbers shiver.

Maynard was busy supervising his gun crews. They scampered and hurried, but the guns were not ready at the same time. It was easier to load the smaller guns than the larger ones. He had the smaller remaining guns and one of the larger guns loaded by the time the prow of the *Bart* ran up on the *San Antonio*. "Fire!" he bellowed.

His guns were practically aboard the *Antonio*. The grape rained hell on them. Men died. Others shrieked or shouted orders. The *Antonio's* surviving guns were nearly loaded. As they struggled to get their balls in, the *Bart's* prow thumped hard and scraped along her side, snapping off oars and knocking standing men off their feet. The butt ends of the oars flipped and swatted their rowers, breaking arms and skulls as the paddle ends were sheered off or knocked askew by the sharp prow of the *Bart*. All down her side the *Bart* ran, neatly pulling in her own oars to save them. Nearly every oar on the *Antonio's* larboard was broken or lost. Half the galleyslaves were hurt by the sweeps. They were thirsty, angry, bruised, and broken. They mutinied. There was little they could do, but they could refuse to follow orders. They stabbed at their tormenters with the ends of broken sweeps.

A minute later the *María* sheered along the starboard side. She did not strike as hard or as well, but she took out the forward oars. The Spanish guns spoke: one, two, three. The *Bart* received the shots, but down in his cabin Thorton could not tell what damage they did.

"Damage report!" Tangle howled in Turkish. He repeated the call in Arabic and Spanish.

Their victim was desperately trying to fend them off to prevent being boarded. To be taken nearly simultaneously on both sides was too much to be born. The officers on the defender's poop were cool, and the swivels were swiftly loaded and fired. The poops of the *Bart* and *María* each received small arms fire at point blank range, but their own swivels were already at work and a deadly crossfire of grape sprayed the *Antonio's* poop deck as they passed along side. The *Bart* received a rake of Spanish grape, but it was poorly aimed and she was little hurt. Thorton heard it peppering the quartering and the small light in his cabin shattered. He ducked instinctively as broken glass fell on his bunk.

Tangle felt the wind of a bullet through his coat and the sharp bite of something in his thigh. He gritted his teeth and remained standing. "Row as soon as your oars are clear! Full speed ahead! We'll do the same to the next galley!" He looked around and saw that the tillerman was wounded. "Mr. Bellini, take the tiller." The Italian midshipman was wounded too, but he limped over and grabbed the iron bar and leaned on it to steady it.

They left the disabled *Antonio* behind and charged to meet the galley coming to her sister's aid. The newcomer dared not fire her bow guns for fear of hitting the wounded *Antonio*. Maynard was screaming invective like a true officer and his five remaining guns reloaded and fired in ragged order. The *Santa Teresa de Ávila* received their fire, and then the *María* was popping out from behind the *Antonio* to let loose her guns. The *Terry* fired on the *María* but aimed a little too wide in their effort to clear the wounded *Antonio*. The boatswains on the wounded vessel whipped the slaves liberally but could not quell the general mutiny among the chained men. The *Antonio* drifted helplessly. Her guns were pointed towards shore and no use to support the *Teresa*. The poop deck was a bloody shambles.

Aboard the *Terry* all was not well. The chained slaves, well perceiving that two supposedly Spanish galleys had turned on them, had no desire to experience the punishment inflicted on the *Antonio*. Those in the larboard benches refused to row because they had a good view of the carnage wrought by the *Bart*. The slaves on the starboard side continued rowing, causing the *Terry* to begin to turn, swinging her bow towards the *Bart*.

Tangle shouted, "Grape shot! Clear the poop!" Overhead the marines on the antennas kept up a sharp chatter of musket fire. The *Terry's* marines were scrambling up the antennas to answer in kind.

The guns traversed as far as they would bear and let fly again at very short range. The rain of small balls left a bloody trail on the *Terry's* poop deck. The *María* came up slowly and fired raggedly at the bow of the *Terry*. One of the smaller balls hit and bounced off, but the rest scattered uselessly in the sea. Tangle swore violently about it, but there was nothing he could do about their marksmanship.

Maynard had his men whipped to the very pitch of excitement and they loaded in less than three minutes. "Grape, Mr. Maynard, grape!" Tangle bellowed. With that, two guns fired and a few seconds later, the third. Half a minute later the fourth and then the fifth. They raced to reload.

The *Bart* changed her course slightly to come at an angle against the oars. The slaves on the *Terry's* larboard side pulled the oars in to save themselves from being battered like the unhappy souls aboard the *Antonio*. Once again the guns spoke. The Spanish boatswains flogged their rowers and screamed invective at them. On each side commands were shouted in Spanish. More small arms crackled and a grenade was thrown from the *Terry* to the *Bart*. Someone scooped it up and flung it overboard. It exploded just before it hit the water.

The *Terry* fired her bow guns as they were ready, and a ball blew through the gunwale and went skipping along the bridge, leaving a trail of destruction behind it. It caromed into the coach and Thorton threw himself on the floor in instinctive reaction to the sound of the ball slamming against wood very near at hand. The guns of the *Bart* replied in kind, giving as good as they got. On the *Teresa's* deck the captain fell mortally wounded. The *María* fired again. A ball skimmed just above the gunwales at head height, killing one and shattering the halyard tackles. The great antenna plunged to the deck with a mighty crash. Taken by surprise, the *Terry* had not had time to rig her preventers. Sailcloth billowed and covered the benches and made it impossible to traverse the bridge.

Tangle shouted orders and the *Bart* began to pivot in place. "Hold your fire! Wait for orders!" The *María* maneuvered along the other side and the slaves on the starboard clawed out from under the fallen sail and screamed for mercy. They threw their sweeps overboard. Wounded and helpless, the *Santa Teresa* struck her colors. A cheer went up from the *María* and the *Bartolomeo*.

There was one more galley out there. At the sound of the gunnery, she made all haste and charged into the cove. The carnage left her in disbelief, but worse, the purple flag of the Sallee Republic was flying over it. The *María* saw her and fired. Her shots fell short and scattered in the sea between her and the *Santiago de Compostela*. Tangle swore mightily and his rowers worked to aim the *Bart's* bow. The *Santiago* dumped her wind and ran out her oars to back frantically away. Galleys could row almost as well to the rear as forward; the retrograde motion allowed her to keep her guns on the Sallee rovers. She fired in answer to the *María's* blast and one of the balls struck the *María's* beak-head. The shattered remains dangled at the front. Another ball struck the hull obliquely where it veered from bow to midships and left a long scar in her red paint. Maynard was strangely silent, but the bow guns of the *Bart* spoke again and they did some damage. The enemy backed further and further way, then turned and ran out to sea. Tangle did not pursue.

The captain of the *San Antonio* swore prodigiously about the stupidity that had placed *María* in the hands of the pirates, the furious attack which had deprived him of the ability to control his own vessel, the ease with which the *Teresa* had been taken, and the cowardice that had sent the *Santiago* running without giving a fight. With the few oars he had he was slowly, painfully, turning his vessel around to bring her guns to bear on the *Bart's* stern.

Tangle had not forgotten about the *Antonio*. Glancing over his shoulder, he saw her. "About face!" he bellowed.

The rowers spun the *Bart* around to bring her guns to bear on the *Antonio*. With a full and able crew, she made the turn faster than the Spanish. The *Antonio* was caught broadside to the *Bart*, still spinning slowly.

"Fire!" Tangle shouted. Grape sprayed across her waist and there were more casualties. The few slaves who could row threw their oars overboard and raised their hands, begging for mercy. The Spanish captain shouted his own orders. His swivels spun to menace the rowers as he barked at them, "Row or die!"

The slaves desperately yanked their chains to no avail. "Fire!" A swivel discharged into the rowing gang, killing or wounding six. Some of the slaves grabbed oars and tried to row, but most did not.

Tangle bellowed, "Prepare to board!" The marines were in the tops as sharpshooters, but they came flying down response to the order. "Ram her! Put the prow aft the mainmast!"

The helmsmen turned the tiller accordingly and the rovers pulled hard and dashed across the short space. The smaller bow guns were already reloaded and fired again, but the big guns were still loading. The beak-head ran over the gunwale and blue-coated marines charged onto the *Antonio*. On the other side Hizir did not have a sufficient force of free men to assault, but he brought his guns to bear. Choosing his angle carefully to avoid the *Bart* and her marines, he raked her poop deck.

The *Antonio* could not hold off both the *Bart* and the *María*, but she tried. The marines had to fight their way onto the poop deck. When they reached it, not one of the Spanish officers surrendered. With cutlasses and pistols, swords and pikes, the two forces struggled in blood and death. Given the odds, the end was inevitable. The colors came down and lay soaking in Spanish blood upon the deck.

CHAPTER 19 : HOSPITAL SHIP

When the guns fell silent Thorton dared to stick his head out of his cabin. There were wounded men in the coach. "What happened?"

"We won!" exulted a short man with blood running down his face into his white collar. Several other sailors were carefully lowering a stretcher down the companionway to the lower deck. Thorton spotted blond hair.

"Oh no! Maynard! Archie, my lad! What happened?" He ran out of the cabin and met the stretcher at the companionhead. Maynard's left leg was a bloody ruin from the knee down. Blood stained the thighs of his blue breeches and his blond hair was plastered to his face in wet ringlets. A piece of rope was between his teeth and he bit it hard to keep from crying out as they jostled him getting him down the ladder.

"Careful with him!" Thorton cried.

Somebody else replied, "They got us good in the bow, sir. The foredeck's all tore up. The gammon knee is shot, and poor Maynard, too."

Thorton gave Maynard's disappearing stretcher a last agonized look. "The boy's only fourteen!" The men murmured agreement. What of it? Most of them had gone to sea at an equal age, if not younger.

Thorton hurried out onto the deck. He saw the damage in the waist and the dismounted gun on the foredeck. A stretcher was going up to the poop. He ran up after it. To his relief Tangle was still standing. He had shed his Spanish coat and cut a long strip from it that he was tying about his thigh for a bandage. The tillerman was carried away in the stretcher. Looking around, Thorton saw four galleys in the possession of the Sallee rovers. He was amazed.

Tangle spotted him. "Mr. Thorton. Good of you to come on deck. I have something to ask of you."

"What is it, Captain?"

"I would count it a very great favor if you were to go over to the *San Antonio* and take possession of her."

Thorton stiffened.

Tangle raised his hand. "I know your English scruples prevent you from serving as a prizemaster. My favor is something different. I would like you to make a hospital ship of her. She has a great number of wounded on board and stinks abominably. We will load all of the casualties into her where they can be tended together. You will fly a white flag in token of your status as a noncombatant. Will you do it?" He tightened the bandage on his thigh, tied it off and straightened up.

"It will be my privilege, sir."

"Take twenty men over. Don't beach her, but draw in close enough able-bodied men can jump over and swim ashore. I promised Captain Ximénes water and they shall have it." He grinned with wolfish humor. "Then pick up the wounded from the *Bart*, *María*, and *Terry*. They managed to get some water into the *María* before we caught her, so get as much as you need from them. Be quick about it; we aren't going to linger here."

Thorton ordered a boat and his dunnage along with the requisite sailors and marines. He transferred to the *Antonio*. Her surviving officers did not pipe him aboard; in their eyes he came as a conqueror. He sent the man he'd selected as boatswain to inspect, sent the marines to secure the powder room, spirits, bread, armory, chartroom, and captain's cabin. Then he mounted to the poop deck with Midshipman Kaashifa in tow. A pair of swarthy marines came along as bodyguards.

The Spanish captain received them with a morose face and his arm in a sling. He was sitting on the deck with both of his bloody legs stretched out before him as a loblolly boy tied bandages around them. The first lieutenant was dead on deck. All the other men on the poop were dead or wounded, including several rovers from the boarding party.

Thorton addressed him in Spanish, "I am Lt. Peter Thorton of His Britannic Majesty's frigate *Ajax*. As a neutral, I have been asked to take charge of this vessel and turn it into a hospital ship. Your able-bodied men will be allowed to go ashore. You may carry your wounded with you, or your wounded may stay here where they will be treated with kindness."

The captain's eyebrows shot up, but he handed over his sword and said, "I'm Captain Alfredo Guerrero y Alvarado, captain of the *San Antonio de Padua*. I accept your terms."

Thorton said, "If you will be so kind as to direct your men to bring the galley close to shore but not beach her, I would be obliged."

That was done. The Spaniards leaped into the sea and swam or waded ashore if they could. The Spanish captain elected to remain aboard with the rest of his wounded. He did not fancy being stranded on a French shore without supplies and himself unable to walk. Thorton issued orders. The wounded to the cockpit, marines to their posts, the officers' cabins searched, the slaves freed and put to work. Thorton wished he had a good lieutenant. Kaashifa was willing but didn't know the job. He had to tell him everything. He decided to leave him in charge of ship operations; he knew how to make the galley move at least. Thorton started making a tour of the vessel. He assigned freed slaves to various tasks as their chains were removed. Unfortunately, many of them were ill with the bloody flux. He held a handkerchief over his face on account of the stench.

So much work! So many ill and injured! The *Teresa* was requesting permission to come along side and discharge her wounded into the *Antonio*, but he was not ready to receive them. He needed six of himself to do everything that needed doing. Now that he needed a good lieutenant of his own, he realized how valuable an able officer was. No wonder Tangle tolerated his stiff-necked English pride. If only he had had an officer like himself, he would have indulged his every whim to keep him working.

At last his tour brought him below. He found the Spanish surgeon at work sewing up gashes in the chest of a wounded man. The doctor looked up as Thorton came through the canvas screen that separated the operating area from the sickbay.

Thorton introduced himself. "I'm Lt. Peter Thorton, master of this vessel. We are now a hospital ship."

The doctor nodded. "Dr. Álvaro Menéndez y Delgado. Who is my replacement?" He kept sewing but glanced at the aides Thorton had with him. The doctor had curly black hair, sideburns, mustache and goatee. His coat was off and a blood-stained leather apron covered his white shirt. His sleeves were rolled up above his elbows. His mates were at work on their own patients—broken bones and stitches and other easy cases.

Thorton looked chagrined. "We have no surgeon. We have only loblolly boys."

"What about surgeon's mates?"

"None, I'm afraid. The *San Bartolomeo* is manned by her freed slaves. There is no doctor among them. There is a tailor though. He can cut and stitch. I'll send him to you."

Dr. Menéndez shuddered. "If the muscles are cut the wrong way the man will be crippled for life. No, this is no game, Lt. Thorton. Send me a qualified replacement. I will not go until he comes."

"You will wait a long time because there is no one."

Dr. Menéndez gave him a level look. "You'd best move aside then. I have much work to do."

Thorton stepped back and let the curtain fall. Menéndez called out sharply, "Lieutenant!"

He lifted the curtain. "Yes?"

"You will find eight water casks that have been marked with charcoal. They are foul and have been condemned. The slaves, ordinary sailors and marines have been drinking it for several days. Most of them are ill with dysentery as a result. Some of them have died of it. Do not let them get into it. They are desperate for water."

"Thank you, doctor. I'll attend to it." He called his sergeant of marines and put a guard on it.

Thorton climbed out of the hold with heavy steps. He called up to Kaashifa, "Let the *Teresa* come alongside. We will accept her casualties."

Next Thorton collected a party of slaves and assigned them to man the pumps and start scrubbing out the galley. They were not pleased to do it, but he snapped at them, "Do it, or I'll whip you as hard as any Spaniard! I will have a clean ship!"

The *Terry* was safely under a prize crew and her Spaniards ashore. She reported three tons of water, which was enough for her diminished complement for three days. The *María* had enough for one day on three-quarter rations. The *Antonio* was dry. The officers had drunk up all the cider, spirits, and vinegar to avoid drinking the fouled water. The sick and wounded suffered terribly because of thirst. The *Terry* transferred one ton of water to the *Antonio* along with her wounded.

Thorton spoke across the poop deck rail to Tangle. "We need to take on water. These men are desperate, sir!"

"No. If we send a party ashore, the Spaniards will capture them. We make sail now."

"Sir!"

"I understand, Thorton. But if our shore detail is captured it will not provide water to the men. We must find another place. The coast is green here; it can't be far."

"Aye aye, sir." He wasn't happy, but he obeyed.

Tangle stayed with the *Bart* in spite of her damage. He knew her and it would only cause confusion to transfer the crew that was used to her to another vessel. She nosed her way carefully out of the cove with her consorts following in a line. Tangle feared an ambush (that is what he would have done), but all they saw was the last Spanish galley at a great distance, flying away as fast as she could go. For a moment he had the urge to leap after her—had he been alone, he would have, and damn the water.

The escapee had a terrible tale to tell: Sallee rovers loose in the Bay of Biscay! It would take several days for her to make the nearest friendly port, but after that, the sea would swarm with vengeful Spaniards searching for him. Tangle needed to repair his bow and re-rig the *Terry's* halyards. He needed water. He needed rest—his own strength was giving out. He couldn't fly after the *Santiago* even if he wanted to. He looked back at the squadron following him. Maybe if he took the *María* . . . He could have left Thorton to shepherd the prizes to port, but Thorton would not. Damn him for a righteous man.

Tangle ordered Sallee colors for all the galleys. The men who could sew stitched them up. Thorton had one made but did not display it; the *Antonio* kept her white flag. The *Bart* lurched along, her bow patched again and her forward hold pumped out repeatedly. The carpenter jury-rigged the gammon knee and rebuilt the carriage for the dismounted gun. Tangle had to do the work of three officers, and him with his wounded leg still untreated. He missed Thorton and Maynard.

As for Thorton, he found himself in possession of a captain's cabin. He politely provided the first lieutenant's cabin to the wounded captain and sent his personal things to it. He kept the captain's furniture for himself because he had none of his own. Everything in the *Antonio's* great cabin was neat, orderly, and well made of plain but of pleasant design. The carpet on the floor was a sturdy canvas painted in a checkerboard pattern of navy blue and beige. The other furnishings were similar. Thorton thought he might have liked Captain Guerrero had they met under other circumstances.

For a few minutes he stood and looked around the room. It was his first command. His heart could not help but thrill to that. Then the burdens of the position weighed on him. He took a deep breath, gathered his composure, and went back out on deck. This time when the call "Captain on deck!" rang through the ship, it rang for him. That was the moment when he knew he would never give up his naval career, no matter what it cost him.

CHAPTER 20 : CORREAUX

When the watchtowers of Correaux spotted a squadron of four galleys approaching they sounded the alarm. Tales of Spanish raids on the French coast had been coming in for several weeks. Now the raiders were on their very doorstep. Two French frigates were not quite finished taking on their stores and did not have full complements, but they came out to meet the attack anyhow. Word ran swiftly through the city and people lined the shore to witness the encounter. Peering from a distance, they could not see what the frigates saw: the broad purple pennant of a Sallee commodore flying at the masthead of the capitana. Much to everyone's surprise, the frigates rendered passing honors with their guns booming a salute. Three of the galleys replied in kind, but the galley under a white flag did not fire her guns.

The two frigates escorted the Sallee squadron into the harbor. Their signals sent the story ahead of them, "Sallee rovers with prizes."

It had been a long time since Sallee rovers had been seen on their shores and in their ports; one of the effects of the war with Spain had been the squelching of a great deal of Moorish and Sallee activity on the Atlantic coast, to the point that when mothers scolded their children, "Behave, or the Sallee rovers will get you," the children had to ask, "What's a Sallee rover?"

One frigate passed between the towers, then the *San Bartolomeo* with a tall, dark-faced Turk, complete with turban, dressed all in white on her poop deck. As she cleared the towers, the people lined up on the mole could see the Spanish colors dragging in the water behind her. Although it was the custom of the Mediterranean Sea to humiliate the enemy in this way, it was not done in northern waters. Yet for the Atlantic French who had long suffered at the hands of the Spanish and had no victories yet this season, the sight of their allies bringing Spanish prizes into harbor was glorious indeed. The vermilion of the galley hulls and the purple flags above them dazzled their eyes and lifted the doldrums in which they had suffered through all the winter and most of the spring. They shouted and cheered and waved as one by one the galleys filed in.

Thorton, standing his poop in his British uniform, felt the elation of victory. Never had he played such a prominent role in such a dashing and daring victory; never before had he been the master of a vessel receiving the crowd's accolades. Hats and flowers were thrown.

Women waved their aprons. Crewmen hung over the sides of the galleys to shout and wave. Some of the French on board recognized some of the people they saw on land. On the mole, in the bumboats, and on the quay, shrieks of joy greeted the return of remembered faces.

The official boats came out. The harbormaster, the health inspector, the lord governor of the port and the mayor, too, came out to meet the victorious heroes. The Sallee consul was hard on their heels and just as astonished as the rest of them. The health inspector spent an especially long time on board the *Antonio* before clearing her to land.

A French pilot was put aboard the *Bart* and he lead them into a side channel and from there into a cove. It contained a sloping beach perfect for beaching galleys. A fresh broad stream ran down from the hills above it. The cove was separated from the main harbor by a marshy point of land. As soon as the galleys were in shallow water the French started leaping off and swimming and wading to land. Thorton shouted at them to stand, but there was no holding them. Many of the neutrals, Hollanders, Swedes, Germans, Irish, Italians, and so forth, leaped overboard as well. Even some Spanish galley slaves, dreading the reception they might get from the French officials, leapt for freedom.

A flood tide of humanity raced onto the shore. They capered and shouted, kissed the ground and kicked up sand. The French officials who came out of the buildings in the cove shouted for order but were ignored. The freed men started streaming along the road towards town. They met horsemen and runners coming out of town. Women and children begged for husbands, fathers, sons and brothers, but most of the names they asked for were unknown. Here and there unhappy news was given and the women fell on the grass to weep. In other places, families embraced. Few, true, but more would trudge the roads to their own homes and in the next few days or weeks would arrive dusty and footsore to be welcomed by glad arms. They were going home.

That afternoon the French officially released all those who had originally been prisoners in the galleys, which was well since they were already gone. The French did not release those convicted of crimes. Some of those fled anyhow, or passed themselves off as Italians or even Turks. The sick and wounded were taken off to a French hospital, but not all of them wanted to go. An exhausted Dr. Menéndez and his mates and loblolly boys completed the task of conveying two hundred stretchers on deck. They were carefully lowered down into the wagons that were drawn into the water as deep as the horses' breasts to receive the wounded. Captain Guerrero was dead of his wounds; Maynard was alive and well enough to refuse to go. Such were the fates of war.

Tangle surveyed four galleys pulled up side by side on the beach with great satisfaction. A prize court would be held on the following Monday, but the French assured him it was mere formality. The *Teresa* lay awkwardly, canted to the larboard due to her deadrise, but the other three sat level on the sands. The *Terry* was beamier than the other three and her keel was raked so that she was deeper at the heel than the toe. Her two masts carried more sail than her galley consorts, but she had a full complement of oars with which to row. With her greater beam and draft she was not as quick under oars as a true galley, but anything was fast compared to a becalmed merchantman with no wind in her sails.

The *Teresa's* ancient hull was made of shiplap construction, which was something like lapstrake, except the strakes were routed where they overlapped so that they formed a single thickness. They needed no caulk: the swelling of the wet wood sealed the seams. With no caulk, there was no oakum to work out in heavy seas. Thus she kept drier than other vessels. Such vessels were too expensive to build anymore—she was a relic of an older age. Her transom was decorated with a handsome sculpture depicting the religious ecstasy of Saint Teresa (complete with seraph and arrows), but the gilding was chipped and faded. She had been mended but not restored.

Tangle handed over the *María, Bart,* and *Antonio* to the French to be sold at auction when the prize court ruled, but kept the *Terry* for his own use. That required all the remaining supplies and personnel to be transferred to the *Terry*. She was biggest and best equipped; she had been the flagship of the Spanish squadron. Tangle needed to circumnavigate halfway round an Iberian peninsula swarming with vengeful Spaniards to get home; the *Terry* would give him the best chance of doing so.

Thorton came on board the *Terry* last. He found Tangle settled in his new cabin with his wounded leg propped on a chair. He was talking to Ortíz, who had been Thorton's clerk but was now his. With more than half the galleyslaves gone, Tangle was going through the muster roll to pick out staff he needed. Hizir was there and Foster and even Maynard was carried in on his stretcher.

"Put him on the bed," Tangle directed the stretcher-bearers. "Gently! Lieutenant Maynard is a fine officer and worthy of your respect."

Maynard heard the title 'lieutenant' attach to his name and grinned at it. He was weak and drawn but alive. His stump was well-bandaged.

Thorton saluted Tangle and received a salute in reply and a warm smile from the victorious rover. Thorton nodded to Foster and Hizir, but went directly to Maynard's side. "How are you, Archie?" he asked in a kindly tone.

Maynard smiled back. "I'm better, sir."

"Oh, you needn't call me 'sir,' anymore, Lieutenant! My name is Peter."

"I'm better, Peter."

Thorton ruffled the matted blond curls. "Nobody has dragged a comb through this mop in a few days, I think." He turned to Tangle. "May I borrow your brushes?"

Tangle rubbed his own bald head where the hair had grown to a length that could be described as 'new beard' if it had been on his chin instead of his head. "I don't have one, Mr. Thorton."

The *Terry* had been Foster's command, so Foster dug into the Spanish captain's sea chest. "I have brushes."

Maynard sat up in the cot and Thorton began to gently brush the long locks. The boy did not normally wear his hair pulled back in a queue like most sailors—he knew what a sight his mop of blond curls was, and how it made older men smile kindly at him. This time he was exhausted by pain and unable to attend his own needs.

Tangle spotted a stranger hanging back of the various officers. His eyes fixed on the Spaniard who reluctantly came forward. "Who are you?" the Turk demanded.

"Dr. Álvaro Menéndez y Delgado, surgeon of the *San Antonio*. I presume I have the honor of addressing Isam Rais Tangueli?" His voice was wooden.

"You do." Tangle looked a question at Thorton.

Thorton left off brushing Maynard's hair and came to the table. "Forgive me, Captain. I was so pleased to see Archie sitting up I forgot myself. Dr. Menéndez has come to take the ball out of your leg, sir."

Tangle relaxed a little. He leaned back in his chair and said, "'Twas good of you to stay, doctor. We are in your debt." His brown eyes studied the man thoughtfully, much like a naturalist might examine a strange beetle in the effort to identify its place in the Linnaean scheme of the world.

Dr. Menéndez gave a little bow. His manners were stiff but correct. "It was my duty to care for the sick and wounded, rais." He could not bring himself to address the dreadful corsair by any Spanish honorific. "If you wish, I shall examine your wound."

Tangle nodded. "Please."

Menéndez approached. He set his bag on the table and unbound the azure bandage made from the coat of a Spanish officer. He took an instrument and probed the wound. Tangle grimaced, but he made no sound.

Thorton spoke, "You gave me orders to run the hospital ship as I saw fit. Therefore I promised Dr. Menéndez that he would not be a prisoner and would be released wherever convenient and provided with some money so he could return to Spain, sir."

Tangle breathed a little easier when the probing stopped. He gave Thorton a slight smile. "If that is what you have promised, that is what you must do. Welcome aboard, Dr. Menéndez. You are our guest. I hope you will join me and the other officers for dinner tonight."

Menéndez did not expect a blackhearted rover to keep faith with him. He had trouble believing the offer. He looked to Thorton to see if a knowing half smile might be on his face, but Thorton's expression was entirely natural. Menéndez had to make an answer, so he bowed slightly and said, "Only if you command it, rais." His voice was cool. The doctor selected another instrument. "Please hold still. I am going to remove the ball."

He had a loblolly man with him; the fellow came forward in his stained leather apron to clamp powerful hands firmly to Tangle's leg.

Tangle continued studying Menéndez. The other men kept quiet and let the doctor and captain handle their respective businesses. Thorton was never certain of Tangle's temper, but he hoped the corsair would not take offense. Tangle spoke pleasantly. "Carry on, doctor. We can offer you the surgeon's cabin on the *Santa Teresa* for your berth. You will have a little privacy and can pick a steward from the loblolly boys until your return home is arranged."

Again a cool little bow. "Thank you, rais." Then the forceps plunged into the wound. Tangle stiffened and his chair creaked. His head went back and his eyes went wide. Two bony brown hands grabbed the edge of the table.

Menéndez said, "Swab," and the loblolly man mopped the blood leaking around the instrument. Menéndez wiggled it a bit and Tangle gasped. "Hold very still, rais." The loblolly braced the Turk's leg hard.

Tangle grunted and his face went grey beneath his tan. After a moment the forceps emerged from the wound and the ball with it. The doctor laid the ball on the bandage on the table and examined it. "No fabric. I shall have to probe the wound. I need more light. I recommend a second pair of hands to hold the leg."

Thorton, who had forgotten Maynard's hair during the extraction, laid the brush on the bed next to the boy and came over. He clamped his hands to Tangle's thigh above the wound while the loblolly man held his knee. The doctor told Tangle, "This will be unpleasant. Do you want a piece of leather to bite on?"

Tangle's eyes darkened and he snapped, "I have suffered worse at Spanish hands."

The doctor's eyes met his with equal anger and his nostrils flared. "Not from my hands, rais. I am a doctor."

Tangle grunted an acknowledgment, then said, "I have ill feelings about my treatment, but you are right. It was not at your hands. Pray continue."

Menéndez put an instrument into the wound and remarked, "This is going to hurt." Then he spread the wound. Tangle's back arched and he gasped and nearly cried out. He grabbed tight to the table and ground his teeth together to keep silent. Thorton turned his face away as blood and pus oozed from the spread wound.

"You should have had this taken care of sooner, rais," the doctor rebuked him. "Have you been running a fever?"

Tangle was having difficulty breathing. His chest rose and fell in harsh pants. He rasped out, "I was busy, and yes, I have been afflicted with galley fever."

"Angle the light—yes, right there." Foster was holding the chandelier in a convenient position. "I see it."

The clamp held the wound open and the doctor reached in with a pair of tweezers. He pulled out something that looked like a bloody scab. He laid it on the bandage and examined it carefully. "Blue wool, red satin and a layer of red wool. Looks like a uniform coat with its lining and breeches. Is that all you were wearing, no drawers, rais?"

"Yes," Tangle grunted.

"We have got it then." He laid aside the tweezers and closed the clamp. He pressed around the wound to evict the pus, then packed it with medicine and wrapped a linen bandage around it. When that was done, he wiped off his instruments on the old bandage. "If you run a high fever or the bleeding won't stop, let me know."

Tangle said, "Thank you, doctor. I appreciate your services. Gentlemen, show Dr. Menéndez to his quarters and get his dunnage aboard."

That was a dismissal. Menéndez left the cabin. Thorton got up off his knees and stretched his back. Foster put the chandelier to rights. They gave Tangle time to catch his breath and to rub his sleeve across his sweaty face. He bumped his elbow against Thorton's thigh. When Thorton looked down at him, Tangle gave him an amused look.

"You and Menéndez are quite alike. You must hate each other."

Thorton stiffened. "Sir!"

"Stand down, Thorton. And finish Lt. Maynard's hair. He looks a fright." Tangle's voice was gruffly affectionate even though his face was strained. Thorton gave Tangle a reproachful look, but he went back to brushing Maynard's hair.

Tangle took a deep breath to steady himself. "All right. Report. Mr. Foster, how much money do we have?"

"Three hundred and forty-three Spanish *reales*. That's all of it, out of every galley."

"Crew, Mr. Hizir?"

"Three hundred and twenty hands, sir."

"Casualties, Mr. Thorton?"

"Sixty-three sick and wounded. I put two hundred and one ashore, sir."

"Powder and shot?"

"A little over two tons, sir," Maynard replied. Much to his annoyance, his voice cracked.

"Water?"

Foster replied, "Eleven tons, sir."

Tangle sighed. "Not much with this complement. Seven days at most. I want the *Terry* filled to capacity with water. We'll need provisions as well, but I'll wait until after the prize court to get them. We can't afford food, not with a mere three hundred and forty-three Spanish dollars. How much food have we got?"

"Six tons, sir," Foster replied. "Rice, peas, potatoes, yams, vegetables, dried apples, a little salt beef and pork. Nothing fresh, no eggs, no cheese. No cider, beer, wine or rum. No spirits of any sort."

"Firewood?"

"Half a ton."

"One hot meal a day then. No wasting! See that the trash is all burnt for fuel. See if we can get some firewood. If not, we'll have to cut green stuff."

"Aye aye, sir."

"Now for officers. I'm confirming Padilla as a midshipman. Pity Cloutier went over the side. I could have used him. What's the name of that lad you had on the *María*, Hizir?"

"Hanash, sir."

"Hanash. I confirm him as a midshipman as well. Have we got a sailing master?"

"Thorton and you are the best qualified."

"Thorton, I'm putting you up as sailing master and first lieutenant. You can have the sailing master's cabin. I'm sorry to double you up, but that's the way it has to be. Should I put Kassmeyer or Yazid as the acting fourth lieutenant?"

The *Ajax* had not come in, so Thorton did not know what to do but serve on board the *Terry* as he was assigned. It was either that or be left ashore with the clothes on his back and no money. He did not care to ask the French for charity. Less than a year before Britain had been at war with France.

The blond lieutenant replied, "Kassmeyer is adequate in ship operations. I think he'd make a better boatswain. Bellini would be a better choice for an officer. He can read and write."

"Yazid?"

"Vigorous and brave, sir. An experienced corsair, but hot tempered," Hizir replied.

"I can cool his temper for him. Make him a sergeant of marines. Very well. Acting Lieutenant Bellini is our fourth." Ortíz wrote out the necessary commissions and Tangle signed them.

So it went. Damage reports, reshuffled staff, new officers made, supplies needed, French requirements. At last they were done.

"Mr. Hizir, you will be in charge while I go ashore. No shore leave for anyone still aboard. Mr. Thorton, you'll accompany me. Send for Palma. I'll need a pair of marines and our stewards, too."

The Sallee captain's first stop was at a moneylender. The man was happy to extend him credit against the galleys' value at auction. Tangle used that to establish a line of credit for the supply of the *Terry*. He also drew a private loan of 100 livres, to be paid by his accountant and brother-in-law, Shakil bin Nakih of Zokhara. He sent a letter.

> *Dear Shakil,*
> *When this letter arrives you will know that I am free. Pray tell Jamila that I am well and that her loving husband is coming home as soon as Allah allows. Do not let her come to meet me! I know her heart, but the seas are very dangerous right now. Tell her that I love her and miss her and want nothing more than to see her again. Tell the children that I love them and will bring them presents. Please remit 100 livres in either Spanish reales or Genovese ducats as the moneylender tells me he cannot easily change Sallee sequins here. I will be home by midsummer, inshallah.*
> *By my hand, this 19th day of Shawwal, aboard the Santa Teresa de Ávila, Correaux, France,*
> *Your loving brother-in-law,*
> *Isam Rais al-Tangueli*

The bill for the money was bound up with the letter and the two entrusted to the Sallee consul's diplomatic packet.

Tangle went shopping. The limp from his wound didn't slow him down at all. First he bought a bolt of French blue wool, brass buttons, gold braid, a bolt of white linen, a sewing kit, thread, and other necessary items, then sent Palma back to the ship with the chore of making him a new uniform. He bought shoes and boots, silk stockings, a belt and knife, a purse for his coins, a baldric and saber (there being no scimitars in Correaux), a black peacoat, a pair of fine knitted undershirts (one cotton, one wool, both white) imported from the English island of Jersey, an oilskin and sou'wester, a shoe polish kit, a shaving kit ("I cannot abide shaving with another man's razor any longer"), quills, paper, ink, and sealing wax. He bought a sextant, spyglass, slide rule and compass (good ones), tide books, a portolan for the Atlantic coast of France and Spain, thermometer, thunder glass, and other navigational instruments. He bought a bag of winter oranges (very dear), a bag of new potatoes, turnips, carrots, garlic, onions, leeks, cabbage, eggs, dried apples and pears, almonds, cinnamon sticks and spice grater, a couple of jugs of cherry cider, wheels of cheese, soft white bread, a she-goat and a pair of lambs. He bought string bags to hold them all. The two stewards, Thorton, and a marine staggered under their loads. They lead the livestock on ropes. Tangle bought two wicker crates of pullets and hoisted them onto his shoulders.

They were on their way out of the market when they passed a booth selling musical instruments. Tangle put down the chickens. His human packhorses waited. The fearsome corsair cupped his hands around a small blue ocarina and blew into it. His long fingers covered the holes and struck an ill note. He tried again. On his third attempt he played a passable scale. Thorton stood with a bag of books hanging from one shoulder and a bag of navigational instruments from the other. A wheel of cheese was tucked under his left arm and half a dozen long baguettes under the other. He watched in amusement as the corsair played with the instruments. Tangle bought the blue ocarina and a red one painted with flowers, a pair of tambourines, and three tin whistles.

"I must find some tin soldiers and a pair of French dolls," he informed Thorton.

Thorton, being a gentleman, had not read over Tangle's shoulder when he wrote his letter home and couldn't read Arabic anyhow. He stared at him in surprise. "Why?"

Tangle smiled at him. "For my children, Mr. Thorton. I always bring them presents when I come home. Don't you?"

Thorton gaped. He replied, "I'm not married, sir."

"That doesn't prevent a man from having children, does it?" Tangle grinned at him. The golden earrings gleamed against his mahogany skin.

The part of Thorton that had expected to become a preacher was scandalized. "I do not have children," he replied primly. "I have no intention of marrying. I am happy as a bachelor."

"I recommend marriage, Mr. Thorton. 'Tis a very happy institution. I say that as a man who was as staunch a bachelor as you. I never looked at women and never even lay with one until I married."

Tangle married? Thorton could not picture it. Tangle enjoying the soft tittering of empty-headed women? Tangle pillowing his head on generous bosoms? Impossible!

"How many children do you have?" he asked reluctantly.

"Six, by Allah! Four boys and two girls and every one of them a fine and likely child. The oldest is Tahirah, who . . ." He stopped suddenly to count up the missing years in his daughter's life. "She will be nine now. I have been gone for a quarter of her life. Hamet is seven. The triplets will be five this winter. They might not remember me. Alexander will be walking and talking. He was a baby when I left . . ."

His eyes misted over and he walked blindly ahead without his hens. Thorton touched his elbow and kept him on course, otherwise he would have walked right into a portly woman with a brown bonnet.

Tangle stopped and faced Thorton with a woebegone face. "I am homesick, Mr. Thorton." He was safe ashore, his health was recovering, he would have money for his prizes, he could go home. "I wish I could fly! I would wing south like a stork in autumn!" He turned and faced that direction and longed for the magic power to see all the way to Zokhara.

Thorton was jealous. It simply wasn't fair that the wild corsair should have a home and family he longed to see when Thorton had nothing. The only person he wanted to see was Perry. He turned to the west, wondering if the frigate would be coming into Correaux any time soon. Why was he carrying the corsair's purchases like some kind of lackey? Somehow, through a magical means he didn't understand, Tangle spoke and men obeyed.

He wanted to turn to the man and take a step closer to him, but he didn't. His feelings troubled him. He remembered when the delirious captain had tried to kiss him. And he a married man! Well, he had been ill. He didn't know what he was doing. He must be forgiven. Why now when Thorton knew the man was not available did he admit to himself that he found him attractive? Why this awkward habit of wanting things he couldn't and shouldn't have? He sighed heavily. He was an unlucky person. God must be punishing him for the unnatural desires he harbored. He had been neglecting his prayers, too. He must make amends.

"We had better return to the ship, sir." Naval discipline was the thorn Thorton pricked himself with to avoid thinking too much.

Tangle recollected himself and gathered up his chickens. "I must have dolls, Mr. Thorton. French dolls with porcelain heads and velvet dresses. The very best!" So the human pack train followed him further into the market until he found the dolls he wanted. Big ones with lace bonnets and real hair—very expensive. They were packed into boxes lined with tissue for transport. Tangle was worn out with shopping, broke, and limping hard by the time they returned to the *Terry*.

CHAPTER 21 : PRIZE COURT

The prize court was perfunctory. The Spanish consul's protests were duly noted and ignored. The galleys were condemned, and one was bought on the spot by the French navy for use as a dispatch runner. The other two would be auctioned later. All together they brought fourteen thousand livres—a fraction of their value—but it pleased Tangle to have it. Ten percent of the proceeds went to the French government, ten percent to Tangle as the owner of the vessels, and the rest was divided out in prize money to the crew. A single share was worth twelve livres, or about six weeks wages for a working man. Officers got several shares and Thorton found seventy-eight livres awarded to himself. It was a stupendous sum. Were he drummed out of the British navy he would have enough funds to live until the end of the year.

The Sallee rovers milled about in front of the naval offices after the prize court. Admirals and lords, captains and commoners plied them with questions, invitations, and even a hip flask. Tangle smiled agreeably and replied, "I do hope to see you at the dinner the Sallee consul is hosting tomorrow," to the offers that were made.

The triumphant rover was resplendent in his new coat that Palma had labored all night to produce. It was a Turkish coat with full skirts and narrow sleeves with no cuffs. There was enough gold braid on the collar and sleeves to suggest his rank, and the patch pockets in the skirt were likewise decorated. Insignia in the form of a pair of crossed scimitars and a star decorated his collar, cuffs, and the pockets of his coat. A triple row of brass buttons ran down the front and bars of gold braid ran across the chest connecting them. Wool pantaloons of the same French blue tucked into black Hessian boots that came up to his knees. His saber hung on his right hip from a plain black baldric with a brass buckle—Tangle was a left-handed man. He was topped off with a snowy white turban and golden earrings.

Thorton received his share of questions and comments, but his French was not equal to the task. He wished Perry were here. Perry spoke the language with easy grace. He was racking his brains to try to think how to explain himself to some French naval officers when his eyes went past them. The square yards of a frigate could be seen coming in. He knew those spars. "The *Ajax!*" he exclaimed.

Heads turned. There was some curiosity and confusion. The vessel looked French . . . but they did not know her. The British ensign flew from her stern and a signal gun sounded from the towers. The French officers startled badly—with the treaty less than a year old, they were not comfortable with the entrance of a British warship.

Tangle bumped elbows with Thorton. "You must tell me what kind of person your Captain Bishop is," he said jovially.

Thorton had a knot in the pit of his stomach. "You will despise him and he will hate you." Tangle gave him a questioning look. Thorton's face turned to wood as he prepared himself for the ordeal ahead. "I must report immediately."

He started forward, but Tangle put a hand on his arm. "I have not released you from service, Mr. Thorton. You have duties to attend."

"Sir, my duties are to God and King. Captain Bishop, their representative, is receiving the French harbormaster even as we speak. I must go."

Tangle tightened his grip on his arm. "I will not allow it."

Thorton turned and faced him. "Am I your prisoner, sir?" Their conversation was in low Spanish so the Frenchmen around them could not understand.

Tangle released his arm. "No, Mr. Thorton. You are my lieutenant and a damn fine one. I am offering you a commission with the Sallee rovers. You shall be first lieutenant on any vessel I command. In good time, you will be a captain in your own right. There will be prize money and honors for you, Mr. Thorton. All you have to do is turn Turk."

Thorton schooled himself to impassivity. "I have sworn an oath, Captain Tangle. I must decline your offer."

"Let me meet with your Captain Bishop. I will prevail upon him to release you from that oath."

"He will not do it, sir."

"Do you want to return to him? I don't think you do."

Thorton hesitated, "No, I don't. But—duty."

Tangle waited, but there was nothing else to be said. Finally he replied, "I will see you at dinner tomorrow. You have been invited by name and the officials will be offended if your captain denies you leave to do it."

"Aye aye, sir."

"Very well. I'll send your dunnage. Godspeed, Mr. Thorton."

"Peace be upon you, Isam Rais." Thorton saluted the corsair for the last time.

Tangle returned the salute. "And also upon you, Lt. Thorton."

Thorton squared his shoulders and walked down to the docks. He stood at the end of one and waved his handkerchief. He had no hat since he had refused loot from the Spanish chests. He was wearing the same shirt and coat he'd had on beneath the oilskin that fateful day. He had no cash—Tangle had no cash for his prizes, only letters of credit to draw against.

MacDonald came up next to him. "'Tis a pity Mr. Maynard won't be coming with us, sir."

"He's happier where he is."

"So sad he didn't survive having his leg blown off, sir."

Thorton turned and looked sharply at him. He replied thoughtfully, "Aye, 'twas a grievous wound, MacDonald. Would you be so kind as to request Captain Tangle to send the deceased's personal effects aboard the *Ajax?*"

"I don't think he had any, sir. Just the oilskin and sou'wester he was wearin' when we went aboard."

"But do request it of Captain Tangle."

MacDonald snapped a salute. "Aye aye, sir."

MacDonald ran back and spoke to Tangle, who grinned even while he said, "A very sad thing it was, too, to lose him just when we thought he might survive the amputation. He perished this very morning."

MacDonald had a hard time keeping the smile off his face when he climbed into the jollyboat with Thorton, but Thorton, preoccupied with his own worries, had an appropriately long face. How he dreaded to set foot on the *Ajax*. How free and useful he had felt aboard the galleys under the Sallee flag! The pipes called and he climbed up the side and onto the deck.

Perry was there to grin at him. He clapped his hands on Thorton's upper arms and said, "By God, Peter, I think I could kiss you! Whatever have you been up to?"

Thorton smiled at the welcome. "Lt. Peter Thorton, reporting for duty, sir," he replied, mindful of the proprieties. He managed to salute in spite of the impediment that Perry was posing.

Perry let go of him and returned the salute. "Welcome home, Mr. Thorton."

Home. Someone's home, but not his. Thorton's smile faded.

The bluff-faced boatswain came over the side and Perry greeted him, "MacDonald. Good to see you back." He returned the boatswain's salute.

"Where's Maynard?" Perry looked over the side, but there were no blond curls in the boat.

Thorton had difficulty speaking through his great emotion. "His leg was blown off during the battle with the Spanish squadron. He succumbed and this morning was written off the muster roll, sir."

Perry's face fell. "By God, that's a hard thing! I liked the lad."

"We all did. He was a gallant officer and he handled the guns very bravely."

"A battle? Wherefore were you fighting?"

"That's a long story. Bishop will need to hear it."

"Of course!"

Achmed and his blackamoor were among the spectators. Once the officers started to break up, he stepped forward to bow. "Peace be upon you, Mr. Thorton. Tell me, is true that Isam Rais al-Tangueli was on that galley? The Spanish officers tell me that he was, but they claim he is broken in body and spirit. They have been praying to God to hasten his death all the time they have been aboard. Tell me, who commanded the *San Bartolomeo?*"

Thorton responded, "Aye, sir, he was, but he has transferred his flag to the *Santa Teresa*. Captain Tangle is recovering his health and is in good condition. He was wounded in the thigh so he limps, but he hasn't slowed down. He's in high spirits."

Achmed's face split into a splendid grin. "By Allah, that's good news! Two galleys? He took another of the Spaniards? I can't wait to see him!"

Thorton smiled a little. "More than that. He took four of the five. They're all laid up in Galley Cove. You should see it! The French are absolutely wild. He is the darling of the moment. The Sallee consul is hosting a dinner tomorrow to celebrate, so I'm sure you'll want to pay a call on him. If you'll pardon me, I have to report to Captain Bishop."

Achmed's eyes went wide, then he chortled in glee and slapped his thigh. "By Allah, we've missed him! The Spaniards must be pissing in their boots! The great corsair loose in the Bay of Biscay!"

The frigate was very crowded with nearly two hundred Spaniards on board. They were huddled in groups to stare at the French shore. Captivity had seemed better than sinking, but now that they were to be captives, they wished they had sunk. They transferred their glares to Thorton as someone among them translated his remarks for them. Some of them spit on the deck and made rude gestures in his direction. It was all his fault. If he hadn't demanded the key, the galleyslaves would all be drowned and Thorton with them. The young lieutenant fancied he could feel the prick of a Spanish poignard between his shoulder-blades already. He must watch his back.

Thorton climbed the ladder and presented himself on the quarterdeck. Captain Bishop was looking both grim and pompous. He wore his dress coat complete with powdered wig as was his habit in fair weather. His portly form had gained no additional weight in the intervening days, but he looked torpid and lumpen to the returning to lieutenant. Likewise his personality seemed irascible rather than authoritative. Thorton had gotten used to the dark leanness and lively demeanor of the Turkish corsair.

Thorton stood to attention, saluted, and said, "Lt. Peter Thorton reporting, sir." He was crisp and erect. Strangely, Bishop no longer intimidated him. Thorton didn't like the man, but he seemed a stuffed shirt strutting about his deck. The last few days had given the young lieutenant a great deal of seasoning.

"You have a great deal to account for, mister."

"Aye aye, sir. May I begin with the prize court? The French government has made its ruling, sir."

"What?"

"They ruled on several points. First, that Isam Rais Tangueli, being a captain of an allied nation, was entitled to use the French court to adjudicate his prizes; second, that he was a privateer of the Sallee Republic, duly commissioned with a letter of marque and reprisal; third, that although he had been seized in the body and condemned to the galleys of Spain it did not invalidate his commission; fourth, because a condition of war existed between the Sallee Republic and the Kingdom of Spain, his seizure of four Spanish galleys was both lawful and admirable. Therefore they have sent the galleys to auction and awarded prize money. The Sallee consul is hosting a dinner for him tomorrow night, to be attended by all the local dignitaries. I have been informed that my attendance is compulsory, sir."

Bishop gaped. "The man is a pirate! A mutineer! A barbarian!"

Thorton continued, "A privateer, sir. You may be interested to know, we liberated eleven Englishmen from the Spanish galleys, including the surviving members of the *Rebecca* of Landsea. They have requested permission to come aboard because they'd like to go home. What answer shall I make them, sir?"

"The *Rebecca*? What business is that?"

"She was a sloop hauling rice from Garonne to Plymouth. A Spanish galley stopped her, declared her cargo contraband and enslaved them in the galley."

"What! Send for Captain Renaldo!"

The argument that ensued went on for a long while in French and Spanish. Thorton stood next to Perry and watched the fireworks.

Forsythe, milquetoast that he was, ventured to share an opinion with his fellow lieutenants. "Damned arrogant Spaniards!" He kept his voice very low. "You can't trust them."

Perry asked out of the side of his mouth, "Four galleys? However did he do that?"

So Thorton recited the pertinent events in a low voice. He had been below while it all happened, but he had heard about it in great detail from every viewpoint afterwards. Not to mention, the French prize court had wanted to hear all about it, too. "The French savored each and every detail of the Spanish defeat, I can assure you," he concluded.

"Damn me if they wouldn't. But it was an unfortunate business about Maynard, turning corsair and all," Perry replied.

"He's better off where he is," Thorton replied with a pious look.

Perry and Forsythe uncovered their heads out of respect for the dead boy.

The crew of the *Rebecca* was brought and questioned along with the other Englishmen men rescued from the galleys—except Foster, who had thrown in his lot with the rovers. Thorton saw fit not to mention him. Let Bishop do as he pleased since he insisted on doing so anyhow. If he never thought to inquire beyond what was in front of his nose, so be it. It was his prerogative to be stupid.

At last Thorton was dismissed without any hurt. "But I will want a full written report!" Bishop roared at him.

"Aye aye, sir," said Thorton. He went below.

Perry followed him into the cabin they were to share again. Out of sight of prying eyes, he took hold of Thorton's shoulders and didn't let go. "I was worried about you."

Thorton smiled happily. He hugged Perry cautiously. He was flush with relief—it seemed he was going to escape a court martial. Everybody was terribly busy with events more important than one wayward English lieutenant. Perry was holding him and looking happy.

The silence grew a little awkward. Perry cleared his throat. "Uh, Peter. I have thought about things a great deal, and there's something I'm sorry about."

Thorton gave him a worried look. "What is it?"

"Well, when you were caught on the galley, and we all thought it was going down, I thought to myself, 'Damn it, Roger. He's the best friend you ever had. You could have at least kissed him before he died.'" He let go of Thorton and rubbed his hands on the skirt of his frock coat.

"Roger . . . do you mean it? Um . . . " Thorton blushed.

Perry blushed in his turn. "Hell, I've kissed girls for less reason. Do you want me to kiss you?"

Thorton nodded.

"All right. Just once, in Christian fellowship. But don't tell anyone, right?"

Thorton nodded again. His heart was beating faster, wondering if Perry would really do it. The other lieutenant leaned in brushed his lips lightly against Thorton's. It was little more than a peck. Disappointment coursed through Thorton. That was it?

Perry patted him awkwardly on the shoulder. "All right. Let's get your gear stowed," he said in a business-like fashion.

"Roger . . . wouldn't you like to kiss me properly?" Thorton asked a little desperately.

Perry turned his back. "No, I wouldn't, Peter. Please don't mention it again." His voice was cold.

Thorton stared at Perry's rigid back. He had pressed his friend too hard. If he wanted to stay friends, he would have to keep himself in hand. He swallowed hard. "I'm sorry, I overstepped my bounds. It won't happen again."

He reached deep inside himself for the strength needed to stuff his feelings into a small dark place and lock the lid on them. He was a British officer. Nothing more. God and King had their laws and he must obey. "I'll see if I can bunk with the midshipmen. With Maynard gone they'll have a berth down there."

Perry turned around and gave him a relieved look. "If Achmed goes ashore you can have your own cabin back."

"It hardly seems like mine."

"What in the hell were you doing on the galley anyhow, Peter? We thought it was under your command at first, making English signals like that. I wondered if you were running away. I could hardly blame you. Then we got close enough to see the tall dark fellow with the spyglass. Was that Tangle?"

"Aye, it was. And a damn fine captain he is. He was in charge of the vessel as soon as the Spaniards left her. I never did have command. The men obeyed him not me."

"You could be in trouble for that."

"Possibly. The French court found no fault with me, so I'm hoping the Admiralty won't either."

Perry balled up his fists and gave Thorton an exasperated look. "You're damned difficult at times, do you know that?"

"I do. Captain Tangle remarked upon it."

Perry laughed in spite of himself. "That's the Peter Thorton I know. A pox on everyone around him. Even the Turks."

Thorton's feelings were hurt by the remark, but he didn't show it. It was Perry's way to make jests at another's expense. He didn't mean anything by it. He sighed inside. He must get used to the English way of doing things again. How easily he had fallen into the routine aboard the galley!

"I must see to my dunnage," he replied.

"Aye," said Perry. "I won't get in your way."

"Aye," Thorton replied. Neither had anything further to say.

CHAPTER 22 : APERITIF

Thorton shaved, brushed his good coat, selected his best linen shirt and wool stockings (he didn't own any silk), polished his shoes, got his good hat out of the storage tin, wore his best breeches (that were not very good at all), and studied himself in the mirror. He made a presentable figure. Perry remained with the ship. Thorton was secretly relieved that he would not have to sit through dinner with him. Forsythe got the honor of accompanying Bishop and Thorton. MacDonald, being a mere boatswain, had not been invited.

They took the captain's gig and rowed ashore. That is to say, a dozen sailors and a cockswain rowed them ashore. From there they walked half a mile to the inn that had been hired for the event. A pair of marines accompanied them to guard against footpads. The British arrived at the inn at the stroke of seven—they were naval officers, they were punctual. Captain Tangle was also a naval officer with an equally well developed sense of punctuality. He limped up with Foster and a pair of Sallee marines as escorts. Midshipman Kaashifa carried the lantern. Sadly, the Frenchmen who made up the majority of the guests manifested the usual dilatory nature of the French naval service. Not one of them arrived on time. Accordingly, the Englishmen and the Sallee rovers stood in the yard staring at each other for a while.

Bishop was very well dressed in his best wig and dress uniform (he had more than one). His hat was fresh and adorned with gold lace and a bit of ostrich feather around the brim. His white gloves were neat. He looked quite distinguished. Tangle was tall and lean in his Turkish coat of French blue and a white turban. His boots came up to his knees and he didn't have any gloves. The white collar of his shirt was buttoned up in a simple standing collar without any stock or ornament. He stood with his weight on the right leg to spare the wounded one. He looked like a peacock in his blue and gold.

Tangle spoke first. "Peace be upon you. Captain Bishop, yes?" His English was accented, but understandable.

"Captain Horace Bishop of His Britannic Majesty's frigate *Ajax*, if you please," Bishop replied. He did not bow.

Tangle tilted his head in acknowledgment and by that small gesture claimed the superior status. "Isam Rais Tangueli, *Kapitan Pasha* of the Corsairs of Zokhara. I know already Mr. Thorton, but I do not know the other lieutenant."

"This is Mr. Albert Forsythe, second lieutenant," Bishop replied unwillingly.

Forsythe didn't know whether to salute, bow, or stand to attention. He chose the latter. "Your servant, sir," he replied.

Tangle continued, "This is Lt. Joshua Foster, of the *Santa Teresa*."

Bishop's eyes drilled into the redheaded man. "An Englishman!"

Foster touched his turban in salute. "Formerly. A Sallee rover now."

"Renegade." Bishop spat out the word.

Foster sulked at him, but Tangle said, "Let us go to dinner and insult each other over the foie gras like civilized men." He swept through the door first and his party followed him. Bishop fumed and came in second.

Inside the Sallee consul came to greet Tangle. He was a man of average height with a soft middle but a still powerful build. The short hair below his turban was grey. His full-skirted coat was brown and worn open over an embroidered waistcoat in pink and buff, thereby combining Turkish and European fashions. His turban was white. Achmed was with him and resplendent in a silver and midnight blue coat with a jeweled broach in the front of his turban. The three Salletines smiled and kissed each other on the cheek like Frenchmen. They spoke warmly in Turkish.

The consul switched to French so they could all understand him. "I am Fudaid bin Rabah, the Sallee consul for the Atlantic coast of France, and I am delighted to meet you all. Isam Rais, your men can refresh themselves in the common room. It is through that door over there. Let me show you the way to the salon." He lead Tangle and Foster to the right. Bishop fumed more as he was left behind again.

Fudaid returned and greeted them. He gave Bishop a polite enough welcome but didn't kiss him. He turned his attention to Thorton. He gave the English lieutenant a single peck on the cheek. "Isam Rais has spoken very highly of you, Lt. Thorton. The British navy is lucky to have such a fine officer." He spoke better French than Thorton.

It was bad enough coming in second to a Turkish corsair, but Bishop did not care to be upstaged by his most junior lieutenant. He broke in, "Mr. Thorton is the least of my lieutenants."

The consul kept a politically necessary smile on his face. "Then your lieutenants must be paragons. How fortunate for you. May I show you to the salon?"

So Bishop had to go. Thorton trailed after. He reflected sadly that he had not said a word but was already in trouble.

A few French officers were resident in the inn and so were on time, if only because it gave them first chance at the wine and appetizers. They pounced on Tangle to give their compliments and ply him with questions. They ignored Bishop. Thorton and Forsythe remained silently by Bishop's side.

"Wine, sir?" A waiter brought a tray over to Bishop. Bishop took a glass of red.

"Where are the rest of the guests?" Bishop asked.

"You're early, sir," the waiter replied.

Bishop pulled out a gold watch. "Early! 'Tis fourteen minutes after the hour already!"

The waiter shrugged and offered the tray to Thorton, but the lieutenant shook his head. He looked around the room in search of distraction. "Oh say, that's a fine portrait." It featured a beautiful woman in a low cut gown. Bishop turned to look and the waiter explained who it was. Thorton slipped away.

A carriage pulled up outside and a middle-aged woman in a pale blue gown and diamonds was handed down. She wore a high white wig and fur wrap. She too entered the salon. She was introduced to Tangle and gave him her compliments in French, but Tangle, with a glass of wine in his hand, smiled and bowed politely. The officers around him were polite enough, but she was wise to them.

"I see I am interrupting you, gentlemen. You are no doubt discussing arcane matters like double jammed jibs or some such thing."

She moved away and the consul brought her over to meet Captain Bishop. She was Lady Somebody-or-Other, but Thorton's French was not good enough to catch it. Bishop and the Lady both wanted somebody to talk to, so wound up talking to each other. Bishop had an excellent command of French and was soon engaged in a voluble conversation. More guests arrived. Forsythe abandoned his countrymen to get wine and canapés. Thorton slipped away. He did not like fine affairs of this sort, and not just because he had rarely been invited to them. It was one thing to talk to his fellow officers, but what could he say to the upper crust?

The inn was built in a U-shape around a courtyard. It was not much of a courtyard, but it had a stone well and a pear tree that was losing the last of its blossoms. Their sweet mild scent hung in the evening air. It was dark and pleasant under the tree and he found a pair of wooden benches there. He settled on one and watched the lights of the inn. More carriages arrived and the volume of conversation grew louder inside. Nobody missed him. It was developing into a very full house and it became obvious why the consul had hired the inn to accommodate his dinner party. There must be more than fifty people there. The common room was equally full with their attendants. He could see French naval uniforms, gowns, and once in a while, a turban go past the windows. It was like a puppet show without any words.

Tangle had a rosy view of the world after drinking several glasses of good red wine, but it was very warm inside and he was getting tired of answering the same questions each time somebody new arrived. He slipped out to the courtyard. It was so dark under the pear tree that he didn't know anyone was there until he had ducked under a low branch.

Thorton could see him quite clearly as he approached. He rose and said, "Good evening, rais."

Tangle startled and peered. "Peter?"

"Aye, sir."

Tangle settled on the bench next to him. He patted it for Thorton to sit down. He addressed him in Spanish. "So this is where you've run off to. You should be inside letting the French lionize you. They are hungry for heroes since they don't have any of their own. I've been offered a commission in the French navy. Admiral Renaud seems a decent old man."

Thorton gave him a startled look. "Are you going to take it?"

Tangle shook his head. "Of course not." Casually he wrapped his arm around Thorton's waist.

Thorton froze and his eyes went wide. He said nothing.

Tangle smiled and said, "But I am going to kiss you, Peter. I've wanted to for a very long time."

He proceeded to do so. Right on the mouth. Thorton sat paralyzed with disbelief. He trembled. What if somebody looked out the window and saw them? He wanted to say something but his throat was dry and words were impossible. He found himself responding to the kiss with more ardor than was seemly. Tangle's arm pulled him closer and he squeezed his eyes shut. This could not be happening. Did he want it to happen? He wanted something to happen to be sure. He was tired of being alone and lonely. Other men had sweethearts or harlots to occupy them, but Thorton had no one.

He had the navy, his captain, his reputation, and his life. It should be enough. He turned his face away. Tangle continued kissing his neck. Flushed with triumph and wine, the corsair felt entitled to receive whatever delights Fate might bestow upon him. Finally, after two years of privation and misery he would have his reward. It took him a few moments to realize Thorton was no longer cooperating. Puzzled, he looked up to see if somebody had come out to interrupt them, but nobody had.

"Is something wrong?"

Thorton sat very stiffly. "I cannot kiss you, sir."

"Why not?"

Thorton shot him a look of disbelief. So many reasons! All of them obvious. He started with a simple one. "You're married!"

Tangle shrugged. "I'm a Muslim. I'm allowed more than one as long as I treat them all fairly."

Thorton gaped, then replied, "I am not a Muslim. Besides, 'tis a sin."

"A sin? No. A temptation, perhaps, but not a sin."

"'Tis a felony punished by death, sir."

It was Tangle's turn to gape. "Kissing is a felony? What a benighted country you come from, Peter." His wine-soaked brain could not comprehend the enormity of such barbarism.

"Not kissing. Buggery!" Thorton was exasperated by the captain's amorous advances and drunken stupidity.

"No worse a sin than fornication or drunkenness. I do believe the average English seaman regards those as entitlements, not reasons for censure."

"'Tis not a crime where you come from?"

Tangle shook his head and gave him a disbelieving look. "Only a minor one. Unless you force yourself on someone, or practice it with an animal or child. Besides, even then it takes four witnesses to prove it, which is nearly impossible."

Thorton stared in astonishment. A country where he could live without fear of being hanged? "Is there not public censure?"

"I suppose there is. I've never worried about it. You shouldn't either." He waggled a finger at Thorton.

Thorton resorted to his initial objection. "But you're married!"

"My wife is a marvelous woman. She tolerates it. She knows my love affairs with men never last." He sighed at that. Because he'd been drinking and because he liked and trusted Thorton, he said, "I've been lonely for someone, you know. In spite of my reputation as a very great sodomite, I haven't had very many lovers. Finding a man who shares my proclivities is hard. But you do, don't you, Peter?" His arm squeezed Thorton's waist.

Thorton's mind was topsy turvy. These were matters he had never discussed with anyone. The subject was closed with Perry. He yearned to speak and to be heard with understanding instead of condemnation or embarrassed silence. He looked away to conceal his expression. "I do, sir. But I am an English officer. The *Articles of War* punish it with death. We must never speak of it."

Tangle hugged his waist again. "I want to speak of it, Peter. I have wanted you ever since I first laid eyes on you. You're handsome." He took Thorton's hat off and set it aside in preparation for kissing him again.

Thorton leaned away in alarm.

"Don't you like me? I think you do. I've seen your eyes following me. I've seen how your face softens when we are alone. I like you, Peter. I want to be your lover."

Thorton couldn't believe what he was hearing. "You're drunk, sir. You won't remember any of this tomorrow."

"I'm not drunk, although I admit my tongue has gotten a little loose and my lips are numb. But I will remember because I've been thinking about you for days. I've been waiting for you to admit that you feel the same, but you're too proud to do it. So I have decided to set my course and make chase. You won't get away this time, Peter."

Thorton shook his head. "No thank you, Captain."

Tangle was not used to being refused. Although durance vile in the galleys had humbled him compared to his previous state, he had retained a good opinion of himself. He searched himself to discover some fault that might explain the Englishman's resistance.

"Have I lost my looks? I was accounted a handsome man before I went into the galleys."

Thorton shook his head.

"You find me handsome then?"

"You're rather dark and thin," Thorton replied.

Tangle began to shrivel. He had come to the party very full of himself, but Thorton's coldness was reducing his swelled head to something less than its usual dimensions. Not handsome? Too dark and thin? If a seaman, who was accustomed to some very homely faces, found him disagreeable to look at, what would his wife think when she saw him?

He had always counted on certain things being constant: his looks, the attraction others felt for him, the passion of his wife. He swallowed hard. He let go of Peter and looked at the back of his hands, but they were so dark he could barely discern them in the night shadows. What if she didn't want him anymore? What if they'd given him up for dead and his wife had remarried? It was wine that let him plunge from such heights to such a low. Usually such thoughts would never cross his mind. He stared bitterly at the lights of the inn where he should be celebrating his freedom and victories.

Finally he asked, "Do you even like me, Peter?"

"Yes, sir. I do. You are a fine captain. You are very brave and skilled. It has been a pleasure to serve under you."

Tangle felt a little better. "Is that all you feel? A professional esteem, nothing more?"

Thorton hesitated, then added, "I like you as a person. You're very easy company."

Tangle cheered up a bit. "We're friends, then?"

"I think we might be," Thorton replied cautiously.

Tangle smiled. "I could use a friend, Peter. I don't have many of them."

Thorton found himself smiling too. "I don't either."

"Then you should not be so standoffish with me!" Once again Tangle leaned in. He caught Thorton's chin in his hand so that he could not turn away. "All I want is a kiss. I promise I won't take any liberties you don't want me to take." His face was very close to Thorton's.

Thorton tried to shake his head. "No, sir. I have a weak will and I'm afraid I'll do what I'd regret."

Tangle was losing patience. He did not like the self-doubt he had experienced, and he did not like Thorton being coy with him. "I could force you," he threatened.

Thorton replied bitterly, "You wouldn't be the first."

The words hung between them like a poison veil. They shocked Tangle out of his peevishness. "Peter, I'm sorry. I am sorry, Peter. I shouldn't have said that. It was wrong of me. I'm sorry!"

Thorton's jaw set and he pulled away from the corsair's grasp. He replied flatly, "It was a long time ago. So you see, I understand why such an unnatural vice is forbidden to men of the British navy. I am in perfect agreement with the *Articles of War.*"

Tangle shook his head. "It doesn't have to be that way, Peter. It shouldn't be that way. When two men want to do it, it is quite pleasurable. I would never hurt you. You have my word on it."

Thorton shrugged. "I can see why a man who perpetrates such a deed might enjoy it, but his victim never can. 'Tis too painful, too humiliating, too harmful to his health. It shames him forever and he must collude with his abuser to keep the secret or be ruined. That makes him vulnerable to blackmail and worse."

"No, Peter. You're talking about rape. That's completely different."

Thorton was getting stubborn. He folded his arms across his chest. "I won't do it. Not for you or anyone."

Tangle tried to pry one of his hands loose, but Thorton clamped his arms tight against his chest. Tangle wheedled, "You don't have to. There are other ways to make love. I can show you."

Thorton looked at him in sullen surprise. "What? Oh, you mean the French vice. That's disgusting."

Tangle said in exasperation. "Kissing, Peter. That's all I have proposed to you. I do recall mentioning it."

Thorton blushed. "Oh, well, that's true. You did."

"Will you kiss me?"

"Kissing leads to other things."

"Upon my honor, I swear it won't."

Thorton knew Tangle well enough to know that he was a man who kept his word, and more importantly, that he was a man strong enough to keep his word when tempted otherwise. "Ye-esss . . ."

The corsair kissed him and this time Thorton let it happen even though he trembled in fear. He eyes closed and his lips pressed back. He lingered in the kiss; he wanted to savor every moment and make it last as long as he could. His arms went around the rover. Tangle's shoulders were broad and strong and the corsair smelled clean and male. How good it felt to kiss and be kissed! All these years he had been forced to keep himself under control with his deepest desires hidden and his natural urges locked in darkness never to be released.

Tangle gave a little groan. He desperately wanted to do much more than just kiss, but he'd given a promise. He felt the way Thorton's body inclined to his and knew that if he broke his word, Thorton would let him do what he pleased. His hands tightened on the Englishman's body. Oh, the temptation! But he had given his word. Thorton would never forgive him if he didn't keep it. He broke the kiss at last.

Thorton was flushed and flustered and entirely at a loss for words. He rubbed his hand over his face and pulled at his collar. His body ached for more, but he was afraid. He had better go before he caved in entirely. Yes, he had better get up. Right now . . . just as soon as he could make his legs move. He was about as miserable as a man could be, almost as miserable as the time he had blurted out his secret to Perry. It was acutely uncomfortable to be flushed with concupiscence and racked with guilt at the same time. He was lonely and wanted someone, anyone, to make him feel better. And there was Tangle, willing to do it. He pushed him away.

CHAPTER 23 : DINNER

"Lieutenant Thorton?" Coming from the bright lamplight into the dark of the courtyard Forsythe couldn't see anything. He did see a pale blur that he thought might be Tangle's turban. Tangle jumped to his feet while Thorton turned away and grabbed his hat and crammed it on his head to hide his face. Tangle walked swiftly forward to forestall Forsythe's advance. He deliberately slapped a tree branch out of his way so that it made a rain of white petals that screened whatever was behind him. Thorton could not see Forsythe because Tangle was directly between them. He darted around behind the tree. His heart hammered in his chest. So nearly caught! Thank God Forsythe was deficient in wits.

"Mr. Forsythe, is it not?" Tangle's baritone French was smooth.

"Aye, sir. I'm looking for Mr. Thorton. They're going in to dinner. Have you seen him?"

"I did. We were discussing the relative merits of Islam and Christianity while we took the air earlier. He isn't here anymore, though. I'm sure we will find him in the dining room." He took Forsythe's arm and steered him toward the lights. Everything he said was the exact truth, and yet, it was pure deceit.

Forsythe looked over his shoulder at the pear tree. "Was someone with you?"

Tangle chuckled. "I already told you. I was talking to Mr. Thorton, but he's gone."

"I thought I saw . . ."

Tangle kept a tight grip on Forsythe's arm and propelled him through the door. "A gentleman does not pry into another gentleman's affairs. If you persist, I will be forced to think you do not regard me as a gentleman."

Forsythe flushed and tugged his coat straight when Tangle released him. "Oh no, sir, I never meant to imply any such thing!"

Tangle smiled warmly but falsely at him. "Of course you didn't. Shall we go in to dinner?"

Better men than Forsythe had bent to the corsair's will. He had no option but to do as Tangle wished. "If you please, sir," he replied. At least he knew how to capitulate gracefully. That might be the secret of his success in the British navy: he had a habit of doing as he was told.

Everyone was there except Thorton. They were waiting for the guest of honor. Bishop glared at Forsythe and the lieutenant swiftly disentangled himself and darted around to the other side of the table to join his captain.

Tangle smiled and bowed to accept their felicitations and salutations. He made his way around to the head of the table. He had the old Admiral Renaud on his left and the elderly Lady Choisy on his right. Bishop was located at the other end, next to the consul. Forsythe, being a nobody, had a seat near the middle of the long table. Thorton managed to slip in and find his place midway along the table opposite Forsythe.

Dinner was excellent with a salad of spring greens in a rich sauce, boulli of broth with its meat, Rouen duck in orange juice stuffed with shallots, pepper and parsley, a roasted roebuck, salmy partridges, and a dessert of fruit tarts and cheese, accompanied by a cherry cordial. Side dishes included couscous served with spices and butter, which baffled the English but delighted Tangle, artichokes, eggs in partridge gravy, and various small dishes made with the leftovers from the larger meats, such as ducks' feet in sauce. It was served on blue and white faience porcelain dishes made in France, better than anything the English had. Better than anything had by the English with whom Thorton was acquainted, anyhow.

The wine was very excellent and flowed freely. Sadly, Thorton was no judge of wine and knew only that it was wet and intoxicating. He merely sipped it. As for Tangle, he drank heartily and was well on his way to being drunk under the table by Lady Choisy, but he had not yet succumbed. In fact, thanks to the darkness of his complexion, the flush of wine was not obvious. He grew loquacious with drink and his voice grew louder, but as he had not yet stood up, he did not realize he was sailing with three sheets loose to the wind.

The dinner guests were happy to be regaled with tales from his career. He was busy explaining his miraculous escape when bottled up in Djerba harbor some years earlier.

"The peninsula is almost an island, and around the port it is low and marshy. The harbor has several coves, but only one entrance which is so narrow that only one vessel may come out at a time. So the Spanish ranged a dozen galleys around the entrance with their guns trained on the only exit, waiting to blow us to pieces one by one."

He commandeered several pieces of silver and a gravy boat to represent the situation. "I had my xebec, the *Sea Leopard,* and a very fine and well armed vessel she was, but in my train I had a pair of galiots and half a dozen galleys. The passage out winds like a snake so it is impossible to make a charge out of the harbor. I was sure I could bowl my way through with the xebec, but not so the other vessels. Being a small place, we had no more than a month of supplies. The Spanish settled in to wait us out.

"I mentioned that the land is low and marshy. There was a creek that lead across part of it. It came to within a mile of the shore in back of the point. This was when it proved most beneficial to be an educated man. In the *History* of Ibn Fadhlan the Traveller he told about how the Northmen would make a portage by picking up their galleys and carrying them on their shoulders. I thought that if the pagans could do it, we could, too. Our galleys are bigger than theirs, but we are a civilized people and they were not, so we had the benefit of engineering.

"I took everything out of the galleys, rigged their tackle to the trees, and dragged them across land on greased skids. We launched them on the beach and put their guns back in them but nothing else. Time was everything. I went back to my xebec, and exactly at dawn, just before the sky lightens in the east, we crept to the mouth of the harbor. At that moment the six galleys swept upon the Spanish flank and threw them into confusion. The xebec charged out, the galiots after us. We sank three, captured six, and three got away. Including Admiral Doria, who showed us a very clean pair of heels."

Applause greeted his story—except for Bishop who thought the whole thing poppycock. He had also had enough wine to say what he thought. "Dragging ships over land? Balderdash! You're nothing but a lying pirate!"

Tangle leaped to his feet and slammed his hand down on the table. The crystal jumped and rattled. "I am no pirate, ye damned dog! I am a corsair!"

"These Frenchmen are licking your thieving boots while Spanish gentlemen rot in prison. The frogs haven't the bollocks to fight so they hire a knave like you! They don't know how you ran from me with your tail between your legs. You left that out of your story, didn't you!"

"Ha! You cut your grapples to save your own hide and left me to drown! You advanced very rapidly to the rear that day!"

"The Spanish should have stretched your filthy, piratical neck when they had the chance!"

The Admiral stood up and shouted, "Gentlemen!"

Fudaid cried, "Peace be upon you! Let's have no quarrels at the table!"

Tangle had the wind in his sails and there was no stopping him. His teeth bared in a fierce snarl. "You have made me an insult that can only be wiped out in blood! I demand satisfaction upon the field of honor!"

Bishop jumped to his feet and his chair pitched over backwards. One of the liveried footmen grabbed it and set it up again. "Pistols at dawn, sirrah! I'll drill you like the gutless whoreson you are!"

Tangle drew himself up to his full height, but he had a definite list to starboard thanks to the heavy ballast of wine he was carrying. "Choose your second! I accept your terms!"

"Mr. Forsythe will second me." It was an order, not a request. Forsythe turned unusually pale as he got up and hurried to his captain.

Tangle's head swung heavily around the table until he spotted his quarry. "Thorton will second me!"

Thorton was suddenly oppressed by the weight of eyes upon him. He sat very stiffly and replied, "Gentlemen, I implore you. 'Tis the wine talking. Let it go."

There were nods and further remonstrations from the guests. Somebody patted Bishop's arm and the Admiral tried to reason with Tangle. The two captains ignored them.

Tangle persisted. "I asked you a question, Mr. Thorton. Will you be my second?"

There was no escaping it. Thorton rose quietly and said, "I will, sir. But my advice is to set this quarrel aside."

"I'll have none of your stubborn English ways, Thorton! Mark this: I'll nail him between the eyes."

"The Devil you will! 'Twill be my pleasure to plug you where it will do the most good, in the mouth!" Bishop stormed.

Forsythe gave Thorton a beseeching look. Thorton spread his hands helplessly. There was nothing the two lieutenants could do. Bishop pushed his way to the door with Forsythe in his wake. "*Ajax!*" he bellowed, and the men roused from their drinks in the common room to accompany him back to the ship.

Thorton came around the table to Tangle. "Come, sir. We must get you to your bed if you are to be fresh for the morrow. Please excuse us everyone, but I know you will understand."

Thorton had to take Tangle by the arm and pull him out of there. The corsair rolled as he walked, bounced off the door frame, and stumbled outside. His marines and Mr. Foster caught up to them. Kaashifa came running after with the lantern. It was a good thing there was not much traffic in the street at that hour because Tangle was meandering like a rudderless ship. He tripped and nearly fell into the gutter. Thorton had to haul him clear. Tangle had no idea what peril he had been in. He grinned at Thorton.

"There's a good friend, Peter. Let us walk arm and arm together like brothers." He hooked his elbow with Thorton's. Thorton sighed but endured it. "Have you got a pistol, Mr. Thorton?"

"Not with me, sir."

"I have. I think." Tangle patted the two patch pockets in the skirt of his coat, but came up empty. He turned to the marine. "May I borrow your pistol, please? I want to practice shooting tonight."

The notion of a drunk Tangle shooting up the town was more than Thorton could bear. He rounded on him. "How dare you utter such a reckless and foolish thing! You who are supposed to be the greatest corsair of the age! You're stinking drunk! You've been chained in a galley for two years. You couldn't hit the broad side of a barn if you were in it!"

Tangle was not angry at this speech. He tried to reason with Thorton. "That is why I must practice. I intend to plug Bishop. I don't want him to drill me." He swayed very gently from side to side as he spoke.

Thorton grabbed his arm and started dragging him along the road in the direction of Galley Cove. "Help me get him home," he told the others.

Foster came along the other side, but Tangle forgot what they had been arguing about and began to sing in Turkish, his left hand waving in time to the music. His baritone was loud and on key. Thorton might have enjoyed it at another time, but not now. Somebody threw open a window and yelled out into the chilly evening, "Stop your filthy foreign caterwauling!"

Tangle made a rude gesture in that general direction. He tripped over a loose stone and fell. He tried to get up, but he couldn't. Instead he puked on the cobblestones. Thorton and Foster pulled him up again. It took an hour and he threw up twice more, but they eventually reached the galley. He had to be hauled aboard in a bosun's chair because he couldn't climb the ladder. Thorton dumped the captain into his bed, pulled off his boots and turban, stowed his sword well out of reach, stripped him to the skin, and washed him. The rover was snoring before he was half undressed. Thorton sighed but finished the chore. He wrapped up in a blanket and slept on the floor, just in case the drunk corsair woke up and did something foolish.

CHAPTER 24 : DUEL AT DAWN

Thorton woke Tangle painfully early, before the false dawn, with a single lantern lit in the cabin. The captain groaned and held his aching head, but Thorton had no sympathy for him. He mercilessly jerked the covers off to expose him to the chilly air, then rolled him out of bed. Tangle fell on the floor with a thump. He moaned and crawled onto his hands and knees. Thorton grabbed the naked corsair by the back of his neck and dunked his head into a tub of cold water.

Tangle came up sputtering. "I'm awake! Damn you! I'm awake!"

"You left standing orders to douse you if you didn't rise when you were needed. Your soap, sir." He handed it over.

Tangle grumbled in Turkish, but scrubbed himself in the cold seawater. Thorton served him breakfast: cherry cider, oatmeal, a boiled egg, and a mashed yam. Tangle drank a great deal of water and cider, then went to the roundhouse to relieve himself. He shaved in sullen silence, then got dressed in his good clothes. They had been brushed and pressed overnight. The boots were freshly shined. Apart from his aching head and cottonmouth, the corsair was quite presentable. Thorton had slept in his shirt and breeches and looked a little rumpled. He dragged a comb through his hair, re-braided the long blond queue, folded it up and tied it in a club with the black ribbon. That was about the best he could do without his sea chest. While Tangle was pulling himself together, Thorton prepared the pistol, cartouche, and shot case. Finally they stepped out on deck.

The habit of command carried Tangle through. "Mr. Bellini. Turn the ship around. I want her stern lightly on the sand. Her business end should always point to the sea. It had better be done by the time I get back. I want everything shipshape. We're leaving today. Probably in a hurry. I plan to kill a man."

"Aye aye, sir," Bellini replied.

Mist lingered everywhere. It was cold and damp and made a halo around the lantern that Thorton carried. The white facings of his dress uniform were ghostly in the crepuscular light. He wished he could change, but he was obliged to wear what he had worn to dinner the night before. He did not care to borrow a shirt from the lanky corsair. They walked briskly along the road, encountering a few woodcutters and farmers, but no one else. Thorton hailed a wagon loaded with cabbages, and they were allowed to sit on the tailgate. In this way they saved their energy and Tangle spared his wounded leg.

They arrived at the appointed place. The quay was at the edge of the harbor next to the marsh. The lanterns of ships in the harbor glowed like fox fires in the fog. The chiming of harbor bells could be heard, then the ringing of ship's bells. Six am. The ships themselves were vague hulking shadows in the dim light. The opposite side of the harbor was impossible to see. There was no wind, just a damp chill that worked its way through clothes in a thoroughly unpleasant manner. Thorton set the lantern on top of a piling and waited. He checked the pistol again. Eventually they heard the quiet splash of oars and Bishop's gig loomed out of the fog. It bumped gently against the quay and the sailors tied up.

The neighborhood was desolate: the warehouses were inactive. French commerce had suffered greatly due to the depredations of the English during the last war and the ongoing raids by the Spanish in the current one. The lanterns carried by the dueling party were the only lights.

"Good morning, sir," Thorton said, saluting Bishop properly.

Bishop scowled at him and made a vague gesture intended to pass as an acknowledgment of the junior officer's salute. Having been as drunk as Tangle the night before, only now did it dawn on Bishop that Thorton had been missing. It displeased him mightily. "You were absent without leave last night, Mr. Thorton."

"I beg your pardon, sir. I was under the impression that you consented to Captain Tangle's request for me to serve as his second. You did not refuse your permission, sir."

"You are impertinent, Mr. Thorton. I shall make a note of it."

Tangle's aching head had no patience for this kind of talk. "Let's go over there and kill each other quietly," he said in French.

They walked past the warehouses. Heels rang hollowly on stone, then thudded onto grass. Weeds swished around their ankles. The three Englishmen momentarily envied Tangle the tall boots that kept his feet dry. None of them were in the habit of dueling and had not thought about proper footwear for the exercise.

Forsythe was worried. "Gentlemen, I beg you. Let us make apologies and settle this business without recourse to blood."

Having been trundled out of bed earlier than he wanted in a state somewhere between drunk and hungover, Bishop was not in a good mood. He was sober enough to apprehend the gravity of the situation and experience certain doubts, but too sulky, proud, and stubborn to apologize.

For his part, Tangle had been considering the matter with something approaching his usual intellect. Cottonmouth not withstanding, he decided make a fair speech. "I apologize for my behavior last night. I was drunk and spoke too freely."

Unfortunately, Tangle's apology made Bishop bold. "Ha! What did I say! You *are* a coward!"

"I can admit when I have done wrong. Are you big enough to do the same? If you are, we can part on friendly terms."

"I haven't done anything wrong!"

"It was wrong of you to insult me, as it was wrong of me to insult you. Come, let us apologize and be done with the matter."

Bishop roared, "Never! I demand satisfaction!"

"Sir, 'tis a fair apology. I beg you reconsider," Forsythe said anxiously.

"I will not!"

Thorton had never thought the corsair would apologize, not when Bishop had insulted him so thoroughly. He spoke up, "Let's settle the matter peacefully. The Turk has apologized."

"Never!"

Tangle spoke coolly, "Very well. The pistols, gentlemen." He had apologized three times and been rebuffed. He would not apologize again.

With a heavy heart Thorton went over to Forsythe. The two conferred, inspected the weapons, then loaded them. Satisfied, they carried the pistols to their respective duelists. Bishop's face was florid and puffy with drink and insufficient sleep, Tangle's was thin and angular and his jaw was set in a stubborn line. Thorton and Forsythe moved onto a hillock overlooking the scene while Tangle and Bishop stepped up to face each other.

"Turn and count off ten paces, if you please, Captains," Thorton said. He had never been a second in a duel before, but Perry had fought one and told him all about it. Tangle and Bishop gave each other final glares, then turned back to back. At Thorton's nudging, Forsythe began to count. Bishop and Tangle paced away from each other, then turned to face each other again. Tangle held his pistol casually by his side in his left hand.

Bishop raised his gun and squeezed the trigger as fast as he could. His ball went wide and buried itself in the mud and weeds. Forsythe and Thorton looked at each other; they had heard only one shot. Tangle was still standing there with his pistol hanging down by his side. As they watched, he slowly lifted it until he held it before his face. He sighted carefully down the barrel and used both hands to steady it.

Bishop went white. He must stand and receive fire. Anything less would be cowardice. Sweat ran under his wig and into his collar. His adam's apple bobbed as he swallowed and his eyes were wide with fear. In spite of his terror, he neither ran nor spoke.

Tangle's gun pointed directly at his heart. "I suggest you accept my apology, Captain Bishop."

Bishop squeaked, "I accept!" His legs shook beneath him and the fear was plain in his face.

"Very well. I am satisfied." Tangle lowered the gun and discharged the ball harmlessly into the earth at his feet.

Bishop nearly fainted with relief. Forsythe hurried down the hill to be with Bishop, but Tangle walked up the hill to be with Thorton.

"Very gallant, sir. You're lucky he didn't hit you," Thorton congratulated him.

Tangle laughed a little at that. "I had no idea whether I could hit him, but I was pretty sure he couldn't hit me. He does not have the look of a man given to the shooting sports."

Just then figures came moving along the quay. The mist was brightening enough to show light blue uniforms with silver epaulettes on their left shoulders. A voice cried out in French, "Halt! You're under arrest for the crime of dueling!"

Tangle grabbed Thorton's hand and pulled him down the far side of the hillock. "Run, Peter! I'll not go to gaol and neither will you!"

They ran across the grass and among the trees. The ground turned soft and they went squishing along. Tangle's boots served him well in spite of his limp, but Thorton nearly lost his shoes. "Where are we going?" the lieutenant gasped out.

Tangle grinned and replied, "Back to the galley! Keep running!"

He kept the aurora of the rising sun on his right and eventually, after they had fouled themselves with mud and water up to the knees, saw the grey ghost of the *Santa Teresa* rising through the mist. The galley's bow pointed out to sea and her great stern lanthorn was a column of light in the mist.

Thorton suddenly perceived what Tangle had planned. "I can't go with you, Isam."

Tangle stopped and faced him. "Yes, you can. You'll be honored in Zokhara. You can live in peace, rise through the ranks, become a captain in your own right, and find a lover. 'Tis your future, Peter."

Thorton trembled. He glanced back into the fog where the French were busy arresting Forsythe and Bishop. "Do you think they'll release them? If they don't, Perry will be the acting captain."

Tangle started limping again and pulled Thorton along. "Don't stop now. You don't know for sure the French didn't follow us. Or maybe ran around by the road. Let's get to the safety of the ship before we have this discussion."

That spurred Thorton to keep up with him. They scrambled aboard. The boatswain's pipe called, but they were on deck before the sideboys were lined up properly.

Tangle bellowed, "All hands on deck! Out sweeps! Get us off the beach, Mr. Foster!"

The pipes shrilled and the hands ran to their places. They had plenty of men and rowed with a good will.

"Will you drop me at the *Ajax?*" Thorton asked.

"No."

They had gone to the poop deck. Tangle was grimacing about his leg. He could feel the blood trickling under the bandage and running down inside his new blue pantaloons and into his boot.

"I'm not going with you!" Thorton retorted.

"I've already made up my mind. I'm kidnapping you, Peter."

"Wha-at?"

Tangle smiled warmly at him. "You are my prisoner. But yes, we will stop by the *Ajax*. You can fetch your dunnage."

Thorton fumed and paced the poop deck. The *Terry* crept around the point and came into the harbor. Tendrils of mist were still swathing the port as the sun's edge rose above the housetops. The frigate was riding at anchor. Perry was on the quarterdeck when they came along side.

Tangle ordered, "In port sweeps." The two vessels slowly drifted together. "Ahoy the *Ajax*! Is Bishop aboard?" Tangle called in English. The two vessels gently bumped together.

Perry called back, "He's been arrested. Forsythe, too. Peter, are you all right?"

Before Thorton could answer, Tangle spoke. "We are. I'm leaving and I'm taking Thorton with me. Send his dunnage over."

Thorton grabbed Tangle's sleeve and begged, "Don't do this. Please. Don't. I am an Englishman. I can't go with you, I love Roger!"

There was only a few feet between the *Terry's* poop and the *Ajax's* quarterdeck. Perry was at the rail. Men on both vessels heard his confession. Tangle stared across at Perry. Perry stared at Thorton in horror. Thorton turned a brilliant shade of red as he realized how he'd betrayed himself. He wanted to sink like a stone to the bottom of the sea never to be seen again. He stood frozen in place.

Perry turned away and snapped an order to Midshipman Chambers. "Get Thorton's dunnage up."

Tangle ordered, "Grapples."

The two vessels clung together. A moment later Thorton's sea chest was being passed over. It thumped on the *Terry's* deck with a sound like finality. The tin with his good hat rattled down next to it.

"Good bye, Peter," Perry said. "Cast off grapples."

Thorton stared at his former friend. "Good bye, Roger."

"You just weren't cut out for the British navy," Perry said as the two vessels started drifting apart.

Thorton shook his head in wordless agreement.

Tangle ordered, "Fend off." Boathooks came out and pushed the two apart. "Out sweeps." The oars walked along the side of the *Ajax* for purchase, then *Terry* began to draw ahead of the anchored frigate.

"What a waste," Perry said to Chambers. "He could have been something." His words came faintly through the thinning fog.

Tangle spoke again. "Head for the towers. We're going to sea." The quartermaster nodded and repeated his orders to the helm.

Thorton turned away. He stared straight ahead and neither spoke nor moved. His shoes were full of water and mud. He felt like he was sinking. Around him the men moved on the poop deck and orders were passed. Most of them didn't speak English, but Foster did. He remained bland and avoided looking at Thorton. As the galley eased away, Tangle stepped up beside Thorton and put his hand on his shoulder.

"So that's my rival." Tangle's voice was matter of fact.

Thorton colored again. He pulled away from Tangle's hand. "He is not! By your leave, I will go to my cabin. Sir." He added the last word as a bitter afterthought.

Tangle let go of him. "All right. Stow your dunnage."

Thorton blindly descended the stairs to the weather deck. He avoided looking at anyone and started dragging his sea chest. A couple of men came forward to catch the other end and help him carry it. A proper sea chest, it was the size of a coffin. It contained all his worldly possessions. He blundered into the sailing master's cabin and stowed it. He shut himself in the cabin and stayed there.

CHAPTER 25 : THE EEL'S GAUNTLET

The sun rose and burned the fog away, developing into a very warm spring day. Thorton lay on his bunk dressed in nothing but his drawers and a thin sleeveless jersey. He stared at the planks over his head and brooded. Every misstep of his past was laid clear to him. He should have been stronger and wiser. He should have shut his mouth more frequently. He had been lacking in fortitude and grace.

His first mistake had been fooling around with Charlie Scruggs when they were both lads. If it hadn't been for that, he would have never run away to sea. He had been an intelligent youth and he had soon learned to handle the dowdy little schooner he'd signed onto. He did that for two years, then got caught by the press gang while drunk one night. He'd stayed away from strong drink ever since. He had been pressed into a victualing ship, the *Marigold*. He was young and fair and there had been a particularly cruel—no, he would not think of that. Crossing the Atlantic Ocean without their bawds, and that man (he would not even name him to himself) and his friends—no. He must turn his mind to something else. He viewed his body from a distant vantage as if it were any other piece of dunnage and a not particularly important piece at that.

Yes, the *Marigold*. Bad luck and worse to him. They'd been captured by a Spanish ship, their cargo declared contraband, and all the ordinary sailors, himself included, pressed into the Spanish navy. He'd learned Spanish the hard way. After four years he had escaped back to England, which sounded heroic, but all it really meant was that he'd jumped over board and swum to a French merchantman in Sint Maarten's harbor. He'd served with the French vessel for some months, finally making his way to Jersey, and from there returning to the English navy to become a midshipman. Finally he got his promotion to lieutenant, just in time for peace to be declared. He'd met Roger Perry along the way, who had become his best and only friend.

Now Perry had put him off the *Ajax*. Thorton knew Perry had done it to save him (or maybe it was to save himself) after he had blurted out such a ruinous thing, but it rankled all the same. Thorton could have been court-martialed for such an indiscreet remark and Perry along with him. They'd bunked together from Pool to Brest; who would believe that nothing had happened? Not after that suspicion had been raised. Perry had spurned him to save both them.

"He could have kissed me properly so that at least we'd be guilty of something. Surely 'tis better to be hanged as a wolf than a lamb," Thorton grumbled. "How do you defend yourself from suspicion? No matter how many times you say nothing happened, no one will believe you. How much easier to say, 'We kissed, and that was all. Even Jesus kissed John. There is no sin in it.' There was certainly no sin in the way he kissed me, damn him."

He sighed. Now he was a deserter from the British navy. If he was caught, he'd be hanged. The heady triumph over four Spanish galleys would mean nothing to the Admiralty; they would find him derelict in his duty. He should not have given up command to Tangle. Just because the French had ruled him never to have been the master of the *San Bartolomeo* did not mean that the Admiralty would see it that way. He was complicit in mutiny: he had run off with the chief of the mutineers himself. He had not gone willingly, but he had gone all the same.

A knock sounded at the door. "What is it?" he called in Spanish.

"Captain Tangle wants you in his cabin, sir," Foster called.

"Send the captain my compliments, but his passenger is staying right where he is."

A minute later a more authoritative knock rapped against his door.

"What?" he barked.

The door opened and Tangle stuck his head in. A captain had the right to put his head in anywhere he pleased on his ship. He saw Thorton lying on the bunk and came in, shutting the door behind him. "What's this, Lt. Thorton?"

"I'm not a lieutenant anymore. I'm a passenger." It felt wonderfully wicked and selfish to lie there in the presence of the captain. He was courting the corsair's temper, but he didn't care. He might even like to be upbraided or beaten for his insolence—he was in that bad a humor.

Tangle could not glare intimidatingly while stooping under the beams, so he pulled the chair out from the built-in desk and sat on it. That allowed him to hold his head and shoulders erect. He folded his arms over his chest and stared at the recalcitrant lieutenant. Thorton felt uneasy. Tangle said nothing, merely waited. Thorton had seen him waiting before. His expression was stern but silent. Under the pressure of that gaze, Thorton had to say and do something. He sat up.

"Uh, I'm not feeling well, sir," he said in an apologetic tone.

"Maynard's stump is healing, but he's still weak. He's not fit for duty. I need another lieutenant. A first lieutenant. A damned good first lieutenant. We have to run the gauntlet to Eel Buff."

Thorton's brain was starting to absorb nautical matters whether he willed it or not. "Eel Buff, sir?"

"I think you know it, Lieutenant," Tangle said drily. "An island about a hundred and fifty miles off the northwest coat of Spain. A veritable den of pirates, nominally under French control. They took it from Spain—one of their few successes. A perfect base from which to raid Spanish shipping. Does that sound familiar to you?"

Thorton admitted that it did. "Why are we going there, sir?"

"Because we've got a French letter of marque and passport as well as new Sallee papers issued by Consul Fudaid. As long as Eel Buff is in French or piratical hands, we can take on supplies there. If the weather cooperates, we can run south past Spain and make landfall at Tanguel in Africa."

Thorton sat up and crossed his legs like a Turk. He was considering the nautical situation but not with his usual sharpness. He still had a great empty hollow in the pit of his stomach. His eyes were sad and far away. Tangle watched. It irked him that Thorton was mooning over Perry like that. In his own mind Tangle was certain that Thorton had rebuffed his advances because he preferred Perry. It galled him to come off second best in any contest, but he was big enough to leave Thorton alone about it. For now. However, he was also the captain and he would not allow his most valuable officer to waste himself like this.

He spoke sharply. "You are first lieutenant of the Sallee rover *Santa Teresa de Ávila* whether you like it or not. You are free to consider yourself pressed into Sallee service against your will if you like, but you *will* work." Tangle rose. "I have been too kind and indulgent with you, Mr. Thorton, and you have given me cause to regret it. You will do your duty or I will have you flogged."

Thorton winced. "Aye aye, sir. May I look in on Lt. Maynard first, please?"

Tangle's dark eyes flicked over him. "No, you may not. It is not the ship's fault you've been sulking in your berth all morning. I will not excuse you from your required duties to make a social call. You should have seen Lt. Maynard when you were off watch."

Thorton was crestfallen. "I'm sorry, sir."

"Plot me a course for Eel Buff."

"Aye aye, sir."

Tangle stepped out and shut the door with a thump.

Thorton brooded as he dug in his sea chest for his clothes. Tangle was treating him with the professional exactness he accorded all the officers and hands. Not until he was treated the same as the others did Thorton realize how very much he'd been in Tangle's good graces before. Now that he had lost the favor he hadn't known he'd had, he was melancholy. Depression piled on depression. He sat at the chart desk and started his calculations. He found it hard to concentrate and it took a long time to mope his way through them.

He stared at the charts, then brightened because he realized he had something very good indeed. He had Spanish charts. He ran his finger over the ink of the northern coast of Spain. There were the ordinary ports and naval ports marked, not to mention, the Arsenal at Coruña. And the signal towers . . . He dug through the papers and came up with the Spanish signal book. That was an excellent prize! He must memorize it. He opened it and studied the private signals and other useful items. Invigorated by this discovery, he plotted the desired course, then put his head out.

"Messenger!"

Midshipman Kaashifa appeared. He was one of the Moors only recently taken into the galleys and still had a good physique. "Inform Captain Tangle that his sailing master has something to show him, if he is at leisure."

Kaashifa nodded and hurried to the poop deck.

Tangle knew Thorton would not call him for a trivial reason, but he was not ready to give in and be reconciled. He would appear spineless if he allowed the moody Englishman back into his good graces too easily. He waited a full twenty minutes.

Hizir had the conn, so Tangle took a stroll about the ship and inspected her and the men. Many of them he did not know personally, so he stopped to smile and chat with them, asking their names and occupations. They touched their foreheads respectfully and murmured, "*Salaam, rais.*" It felt good to speak Arabic openly and freely, so he chatted with them about their duties, the ship, the weather, and other items of personal interest.

The *Terry* was tight and dry below and he was as pleased with her. The falling antenna had damaged her weather deck, but fortunately, she was an old-fashioned vessel with a double deck in the old style. The watertight concave deck supported a false deck that provided a level surface to work the guns. Some of her weather planks had been stove in, but she had taken little damage to the concave deck beneath. She was deeper in draft and carried larger sails than an ordinary galley, too. In consequence, she was more seaworthy and weatherly than the *Bart* in spite of being shorter. She could carry more stores. If he had had enough firewood and food, he could have stayed at sea for five or six weeks, instead of the usual two to three weeks for a galley. In other words, she was a galiot.

Finally he stopped by the chartroom. He rapped firmly and Thorton knew it was him by the authoritativeness of his knock.

"Enter," he called. He rose from his chair to meet the man. Tangle ducked through the door and stood crouched under the beams. The chartroom ceiling was the deck of the poop, and it was exactly six feet above the floor. Even in his bare feet Tangle could not stand up straight.

The corsair returned Thorton's salute. "You had something you wanted to show me?"

Thorton showed him the map of Spain. "Look at this."

Tangle peered at the symbol Thorton showed him. "Yes?" he asked, not grasping what the thing was.

Thorton pointed. "'Tis the Spanish mark for a signal tower. Here at La Coruña, sir."

"Yes, they often have signal towers in harbor. 'Tis easier and quicker than trying to run boats back and forth with dispatches."

Thorton nodded. "Notice this."

Tangle looked. Another signal tower was half an inch away from the first. His eyes followed Thorton's finger to the next symbol. And the next, and the next, and the next, until his eyes walked all the way to the center of the country.

"By Allah! They've built a line of signal towers all the way to Madrid!"

Thorton walked his fingers to the northeast corner of the squarish Iberian peninsula. "Barcelona, too. But not their southern shores. Madrid knows what happens on her northern coasts in a matter of hours."

Tangle apprehended the usefulness of such a system immediately. He sat down in the only chair. "Why none to the southern coasts? We harry them immensely."

Thorton replied, "I doubt they fear an invasion by the Sallee rovers. What can you do but raid their coasts and inconvenience their shipping? They are at war with France, a war in which real gains in power and territory might be won or lost. The rovers are gnats biting at their rumps while the bulls charge each other."

Tangle, who had considered himself a very great corsair of a very great naval power, suddenly had his perspective dwindle. "Is there a chart of the Sallee coast?"

Thorton shuffled papers and found it. There on the shores of the Sallee Republic were the cities of Tanger and Sebta, Abizir and Djo, all in Spanish hands. Tangle sat back in his chair. He was greatly dissatisfied with the change of view, but for Thorton it was nothing new and he did not apprehend the cause of the captain's silence. The English lieutenant continued the thought that he had hatched.

"Sir, if we disguise ourselves with Spanish uniforms, we could creep close enough to deliver a false message. We could tell them, 'Tangle in *San Bartolomeo* on course for England. Last seen 47 N 4 W.'"

Tangle smiled. "You're devious, Peter. I like that. But no, 'tis too dangerous. I'd rather head straight to Eel Buff. The Bay of Biscay is large. Hopefully we will not meet a Spanish patrol, but if we do, we have plenty of room to run. I like the *Terry* better than the *Bart*. If we get a gale she will handle it better. Mind you, I don't care to ride a hurricane with her, but I feel secure enough to stay off the coast."

"Very well, sir."

Tangle put the matter of Spanish superiority from his mind. He had something of more immediate interest to consider: the companionable intimacy had returned. He liked Thorton this way, relaxed and unguarded and speaking to him freely about matters of mutual concern. He longed to reach out and touch the man, but he knew it was too early to renew his suit. He must feign nonchalance. He racked his brain for a topic of conversation that would not trouble his mind or Thorton's.

"How did you become a sailor if you were intended for a minister?" he inquired. He knew that much at least about the man.

Thorton straightened up. In his shoes his blond hair just brushed the deckhead. His hat hung on a hook on the wall nearby. Tangle had the only seat.

"Oh." He blushed. He had never ever told anyone how he had come to run away to sea, but strange as it was, he felt Tangle was a trustworthy confidant. He fidgeted, then admitted, "My stepfather's housekeeper caught Charlie Scruggs and me fondling each other in the parlor one day. She started shrieking like all the devils in Hell were loose. We ran out of there. We ran all the way to the waterfront and I signed on with the first vessel that would have me. I've never been back."

"That's the terrible dark secret you've been keeping all these years? That you *fondled* another boy, you vile libertine!" Tangle laughed. He couldn't help it. He had been more than two years in the cruel clutches of a Spanish galley, and Thorton's *moment terrible* consisted of boyish antics? He laughed and laughed. He knew he was laughing too much, but thinking that only made him laugh again.

Thorton cringed at the laughter. Then he grew annoyed, then positively indignant. "'Tis no jest! My stepfather would have taken his belt to my backside if he'd caught me!"

Tangle laughed even louder. "A belt!" he gasped. His back was scarred by many floggings. "You're afraid of a belt? What? Do you think he'll turn you over his knee and spank you if you go home now?"

Thorton scowled. "You don't have to laugh so much."

Tangle tried to control himself. He gulped in a great breath and held it, but then he looked at Thorton's face and started laughing again.

"Stop it! Just stop!"

Tangle tried again. "All right. I'm stopping." He grinned wildly for no good reason and his brown eyes sparkled.

Thorton's pride was wounded. He felt he must do something to even the matter to his satisfaction. He asked slyly, "Are you ticklish?"

"I'm very ticklish," Tangle replied. Then he shot Thorton a look. "Oh, no, you don't!"

Thorton said very seriously, "Lt. Thorton would never lay hands on his captain, sir." Tangle relaxed. No. Of course not. This was Lieutenant Peter Thorton, prim and proper Englishman. Thorton said, "But Peter might tickle Isam."

He didn't know why he did it, but he did it anyhow. His hand darted to the captain's ribs. Tangle yelped and squirmed. He was at a disadvantage with his bandaged leg, but even so he leaped to his feet, smacking his head on the beam above and nearly falling on his butt. The initiative lay with Thorton and he used it to tickle the captain madly in both sets of ribs. Tangle got trapped in a corner. He whimpered and laughed as he tried to protect himself.

"Mercy! Quarter! Enough, Peter, enough!"

Thorton stopped. There was a moment of flushed excitement when he realized that the mighty corsair had yielded to him. He stared at the man and Tangle caught his breath. The moment grew taut with meaning. Victory had rarely belonged to Thorton and it excited him. He wanted to—well, he was not sure exactly what he wanted to do. He had the urge to do something bold, like sling the rover over his shoulder and carry him off, but that was hardly practical. Tangle was much too big for that, and even if he did, where would he take him?

Thorton's heart pounded in his throat as he stepped in close and pressed his mouth slowly and experimentally against Tangle's. He was giddy. Who was Peter Thorton? What had happened to that frightened, repressed boy who had been glad to don the King's coat and wrap himself in the protective cocoon of protocol and etiquette, duty and danger that was naval service?

He was that man no longer. He'd lost the right to wear the uniform and it grieved him. He'd lost his best friend. He'd lost his reputation. What did he have left? Nothing. Who was he, if he was not who he used to be? He didn't know. He pulled back. Confusion was written in his face. Always someone else had told him his place. Never before had he been allowed to decide for himself who he was and where he belonged.

Tangle's heart heeled heavily to starboard, then rolled around the other way and shipped water over the larboard rail. He was sinking in place. He wanted to pull up anchor and sail away, but his heart was snagged on something and he couldn't get it loose. He was in love. Of all the horrible inconvenient things that could have happened to a newly liberated galleyslave, it was hard to imagine anything worse, short of being returned to the captivity. He didn't need or want to be in love. He had a wife and family and he was going home to them.

"Your course, Mr. Thorton?" Tangle's baritone was unsteady.

Thorton blinked. Oh, he meant the charts. He turned to them. The two men sought refuge in the comforting armor of naval duty. Thorton laid out the course. Tangle nodded and answered him. Their voices seemed strangely far away.

When Tangle left Thorton put away his papers and moped. Everything had changed. Anything was possible. He was a pirate now. His heart hammered and he felt the heat stirring in his veins. Why hold back? He had nothing left to lose. Still he held onto—something. Habit, if nothing else. He thought about Perry. How he yearned to lay with him and press him skin to skin! He would have let Perry do whatever he wanted, if only he had wanted to do it. But he didn't. Tangle wanted Thorton and would have gladly done what Perry would not, but Thorton didn't want Tangle. Or more correctly, he didn't want to want Tangle. His face reddened and he buried it in his arms on the table.

The bold rover had kissed him. That made him skittish. He would have found it easier to kiss a pale-faced clerk, or maybe even a ruddy carpenter's mate. Someone who was not so tall and dark and unnerving as the Captain of the Corsairs of Zokhara. Yet how good it felt to kiss a man and feel him kissing back!

Thorton rubbed a hand over his inflamed face. Maybe when he got to shore he should spend some of his prize money and pay a whore to let him do as he pleased. That was what other randy sailors did. There must be a male whore somewhere. He groaned as he realized how low he was sinking. Tangle had put lustful thoughts into his head and nothing would dislodge them.

CHAPTER 26 : SWEET FIFTEEN

Duties finally done, Thorton paid a call on the youngest lieutenant. He found Maynard sitting up in his own bed and dreadfully bored.

"Will you help me go out on deck, Peter? I want to see the sun!"

"Of course, Archie." He felt rather like an indulgent older brother where Maynard was concerned. He supported Maynard on one side while the boy used a crutch on the other. They hobbled out.

"Oh, they're sewing! I want new clothes, too!" Maynard exclaimed. "I need a lieutenant's uniform and my new insignia!"

Thorton had no idea what the uniform of a Sallee rover should look like. Did they even wear uniforms? He could not help but imagine them as some sort of ragged, piratical lot. Yet that did not describe the men who were busy making decent shirts and pantaloons for themselves. Rough and foreign, perhaps, but not quite like the stories he had heard. He settled Maynard on an overturned washtub and mounted the steps to the poop. Tangle was always there when he wasn't in his cabin.

Thorton was very crisp and correct as he saluted. "Begging your pardon, sir, but Mr. Maynard inquires about uniforms and insignia for the officers."

Tangle returned his salute. "French blue coats and pantaloons. You'll find it in the slop chest. Plain gold braid for a midshipman, braid and gold star for a lieutenant. A scimitar for a commander. Crossed scimitars for a captain. Brass buttons down the front, as many as you like. The coats and pants may be of any style you please. Any undress may be worn while working, but when battle stations are called, we enter port, receive guests, or engage in any other activity for which rank is important, you will wear your uniform coat with the insignia showing. By the way, give all the men a piece of the blue and white check to make a kerchief. My gift to them."

Thorton paid close attention. He was relieved to learn there was something approximating a uniform on board the vessel. He could not stand a slovenly appearance. "Aye aye, sir. What of the crossed scimitars and star?" That was the insignia on Tangle's blue coat.

Tangle smiled. "*Kapitan Pasha*, of course."

"Aye aye, sir." He was not sure if that was equal to a commodore or an admiral but did not inquire further. It was enough to know that

Tangle was an officer of high rank among the corsairs of the Barbary coast.

Thorton and Maynard bought blue duck out of the slop chest for jackets. Thorton talked Maynard out of half the gold braid he wanted—the boy was quite pleased with his new rank and wanted to flaunt it. He even decided to make a short jacket like many of the rovers because he was enamored of all things Sallee. Thorton decided to make a short jacket because it would be cheaper. Thorton finished his jacket first and tried it on. Because he was lean for his height the hip-length jacket looked good him. He quickly learned a drawback: with no coattails to protect his backside the breeches would get dirty quick. He made a pair of blue duck petticoat breeches. The loose fitting garment hung down to the top of his calves and looked like skirts at a distance, but required little fitting and gave freedom of movement. Maynard bought a straw hat and tied a scrap of the blue and white check around it for a ribbon. He must have petticoat breeches, too, so they made them up. He hopped around on his one good foot to show off his new clothes.

Maynard was unstoppable: he had go up to the foredeck. He was quite wedded to his position with the bow guns and regarded them as his personal fiefdom. He had a knack for gunnery; he had quickly grasped the essentials of aiming, calculating nicely for the pressure of the winds and the rocking of the ship in the waves. He beamed at the men and they beamed back. Thorton chased after him, worrying that he was overdoing himself charging about on his crutches like that.

"Good to see you on your feet, sir. Begging your pardon, sir! A figure of speech, sir!" the gunner's mate greeted him. He was an Englishman who had stayed with them and served as Maynard's intermediary with the men.

Maynard waved it off. "No matter, Patterson." To Thorton he said, "I want all these men to have a cup of good wine in my honor tomorrow. None of that watered stuff. 'Tis my birthday and they will drink my health!"

Patterson translated. The men cheered and congratulated him.

"How old, sir?" Thorton asked.

"Fifteen." Maynard's voice cracked as he said it. He blushed with chagrin.

The men were coarse fellows made more brutish by their Spanish captivity, but they adored their boy officer. His blond curls shone in the sun, the ribbon fluttered from his straw hat, his brass buttons gleamed, and his coat was fresh and new. His courage and competence had been proven in a terrible contest, yet here he was, cheerfully up and about and not feeling sorry for himself and his lost leg.

The gunner's mate said, "Three cheers for Lieutenant Maynard! Hip hip, huzzah!"

"Huzzah!" the men roared back.

Thorton said, "It will be a pleasure to host a birthday party in your honor in the wardroom tomorrow night, Lt. Maynard."

Maynard grinned. "I'd like that!"

Now Thorton had to organize a party amongst his other duties, but he was happy to do it. First he put Maynard back to bed and scolded him for doing too much. Maynard protested, but he was tired and let Thorton win the scolding.

Thorton went next to the wardroom. He found Foster there. "Hey Foster, Maynard's birthday is tomorrow!"

"What? Jolly good. Are we going to celebrate?"

"Of course we are. I'm thinking about trying to buy one of the captain's lambs. Will you go in a share if everyone else does?"

"Of course I will. Rack of lamb is mighty tasty. Especially if we've got some mint jam to go along with it."

"I don't think there's any mint jam, but I'll negotiate with Tangle about the lamb if you'll get the rest of the wardroom to go shares. Ask the warrant officers if they want in too. If they buy in, they're invited to the party."

"Aye aye, sir."

Tangle was more than willing to let them have the lamb for such a good reason. It pleased him to honor Maynard and even more to see Thorton ingratiating himself with the men. The birthday party developed into a very grand affair. Marines in their new jackets and pantaloons served as footmen at the mess, and any man who thought he could cook contributed something to the feast.

By the time of the dinner party all the crew had new clothes. Even those who did not know Maynard had caught the fever and wanted to look sharp. The new clothes were not intended as uniforms (ordinary sailors and men-at-arms wore whatever they had), but given the limited sartorial opportunities aboard the vessel, they wound up looking uniform all the same. Some men wore pantaloons and others breeches, some wore culottes or dungarees, but they were all French blue duck. They wore white shirts and blue jackets in the evening coolness. Dark blue-checked kerchiefs were around their necks or on their heads. Parties of men kept trooping up to deliver presents. Maynard acquired a heap of things: scrimshaw and new shirts, a small wooden box artfully carved, a ditty bag, a pair of sandals made from rope and leather, and other such items as the men could make or loot from what was at hand. The officers gave him gifts as well, but they were hard pressed to find something suitable. Tangle gave him three oranges and several sticks of cinnamon, Thorton made him a nightshirt, Midshipman Kaashifa gave him a checkerboard with black and brown pieces, and Hizir sang to him in Swedish. Even Menéndez emerged from his self-imposed exile in the cockpit to join the festivities.

Those who knew English sang, "For he's a jolly good fellow," then the rovers sang something in Arabic that was equally rousing. Thorton didn't understand a word of it but presumed it must be their version of a birthday song.

They had a baker but not the supplies necessary for a cake; the baker made a rum custard instead that was very well appreciated. They had good bottles of wine but Tangle and Thorton drank sparingly. Maynard got tipsy and sang in his cracking boy voice. Tangle had his ocarina and piped along—it was the only musical instrument on board. Song followed song and glass followed glass. When they got into a bawdy French tune of innumerable verses, Tangle put the ocarina into the capacious pocket of his Turkish coat and just listened.

Thorton supposed he ought to be scandalized that a boy of tender years knew such naughty verses, but Maynard was a battle-hardened veteran who had gone to sea at the age of nine. Thorton leaned back against his chair. He froze as his shoulder encountered Tangle's hand. The captain's blue-clad arm rested casually along the back of his chair.

For a long time neither man said anything. Then Thorton said quietly enough only Tangle could hear it, "The party's too merry for me. We need our sleep—we'll be doing half their work while they nurse their aching heads tomorrow."

Tangle replied equally quietly, "I'll walk you to your door."

The door would hardly take a minute to reach, but Thorton said, "I'd like that."

They rose and said their good nights. The others waved at them and begged them to stay, but privately they were happy the senior officers were leaving. Now the party could really start. Once the captain and first lieutenant disappeared up the ladder they became extremely boisterous.

Thorton opened the door to the chartroom. His bunk was behind a curtain. "Do you want to come in for a moment?" he asked.

Tangle smiled and nodded. "I do."

They stepped across the dark room and fumbled through the curtain into the tiny sleeping berth. A small square sidelight admitted the evening's dimness. Thorton waited breathlessly as Tangle stepped up close enough to him to feel his body's heat. When he bent his mouth to Thorton's, Thorton wrapped his arms around his neck and kissed him back.

It was very warm in the little room and their coats were quickly shed. Shirts were unbuttoned and hands slid across skin. Pants dropped and shoes were kicked aside. Thorton's heart was hammering violently in his chest. He clung hard to Tangle and kept kissing him. He was afraid to do anything else. Skin to skin contact made him groan, but he kept remembering what had happened to him so long ago. This was different, he wanted Tangle. He was still afraid. He told himself that it was enough to simply slide his bare hands over another man's naked body and feel the strength of his arms and the broadness of his back, the curve of his rump, the stiffness of—No, it was not enough. He climbed into the bunk with Tangle.

Tangle kept his promise, a promise Thorton had forgotten he had given. He proved that it was possible for two men to enjoy each other without resorting to buggery. Thorton was relieved to discover it. He had been afraid at first, but grew ardent when he realized that Tangle wouldn't hurt him. The pleasure was intense—for Thorton it was the first time he had voluntarily become intimate with a man, and also the first time his partner was determined he should enjoy himself. He fumbled back, trying to do everything that his bold Turkish lover did. Never had he felt such a fire in his flesh.

Eventually they slept together in the narrow bunk.

CHAPTER 27 : THE LOW BLACK SCHOONER

Thorton woke to find himself on the very edge of his bunk and in danger of falling out through the gap in the cradle board as the ship rolled. Sleepily he thought the pillow must have gotten between himself and the wall and he gave it a hard shove to make room for himself.

Tangle grunted and said, "What?" a little crossly at being squashed in the stomach.

Thorton jerked to full wakefulness and the horror of his situation. "Sir!" he exclaimed. He sat bolt upright in bed, but the rolling of the *Terry* as she slid down the wave toppled him toward the wall. He put a hand out to brace himself before he fell onto the naked corsair. His brain was reeling. "Oh God, what have I done?"

Tangle scowled. "That's not a very nice thing to say to your lover," he replied in exasperation.

Thorton panicked. "But—I didn't mean—I'm sorry—oh my God!" He was as naked as the captain and the sheets were stained with something more than sweat.

"Avast that prattling, Mr. Thorton, and come down here and kiss me." A strong dark arm wrapped around Thorton and pulled him down.

Thorton was drawn in diametrically opposed directions. His body was very happy to provide a harbor for the amorous corsair, but his conscience was fluttering like a mainsail that has come unsheeted and blows and flaps while the hands leap for it. Deep inside he was lonely and desperate and clung to the only comfort to be had: Tangle. He was lost to the old world, lost and utterly dependent upon the foreign captain. He quieted and settled against him. His course was set; there was no changing his mind and going back now. The inevitability of it settled him. They were getting on tolerably well when there was a knock on the captain's door. The captain wasn't in his cabin, but the sound came faintly through to them. They ignored it.

The thumping sounded louder and a voice called out, "Captain Tangle, a sail!"

So. He must get up. Tangle sighed, climbed over Thorton, found his pantaloons and pulled them on. He was still buttoning them up when he opened the door and asked, "What is it?"

The messenger, Midshipman Bellini, a curly-haired Italian of thirty years, turned around in surprise. The sight of the captain doing up his buttons in the chartroom nonplussed him, but he made an intelligible answer. "A low black schooner out of the sou-sou'west. She was right there when the sun came up, sir."

"What flag?"

"Spain."

"I'll come." He stuck his head back into the cabin. "Peter! Schooner on the horizon."

"Oh no, sir. She's not on the horizon; she's about two miles off and closing," Bellini replied. "She made no lights last night, that's why we didn't see her until the sun came up."

That galvanized Tangle. "Spanish uniforms and every hand to quarters, quietly! Run up the Spanish flag. We don't want them to think they've spooked us. Rowers to the benches with their shirts and kerchiefs off. We must look like a Spanish galley."

Moments later all the officers were on deck—even the dreadfully hung over ones—with the sole exception of Maynard. He was still passed out in his bunk. With his amputated leg he was not expected to take a battle station anyhow. Tangle had crammed himself into a too small Spanish uniform again and could hardly move his arms. Thorton came up wearing a brown coat, there not being any uniform among the sailing master's effects. Hizir, the quartermaster, and midshipmen were in blue coats with red reverses.

"By Allah, how she flies! I want that vessel!" Tangle announced. He was staring through the glass. All the hands were at their stations and craned to see across the sea. The schooner was smaller than their galley, but she had topsails and topgallants set over her gaff-rigged lugs and three headsails. No guns poked out from her sides and a modest number of men were visible on deck. "Make the Spanish private signal. Let's see what she answers."

So the signal flags were run up. A moment later there was an answer, "Need doctor."

"That is not a proper answer," Thorton replied. He had the Spanish signal book in his hands.

Tangle nodded. "So it isn't. But it suits me to pretend that we believe her. I want to get close enough to run the prow over their decks and deliver a boarding party. We will take her by storm because it would pain me greatly to put holes in my new vessel. Make whatever answer you please, Mr. Thorton, as long as it leads them to believe we want to close with them on friendly terms."

Thorton replied, "Send boat."

The schooner had her own ploy to play and was slow to answer. When the signals went up, Thorton thumbed through the signal book.

"Apparently, the bubonic plague is hull down to our north, sir," he replied with a certain amount of amusement.

Laughter went around the poop deck and was just as abruptly cut off. The vermilion and azure figure of Maynard thumped along on his crutches to take up his post on the foredeck. His men hastened to overturn a tub for him to sit on while he leaned his back against the bulwark. They fussed over him and took every care of their darling lieutenant.

"Pass the word to Mr. Hizir to have a party ready to board over the prow as soon as possible. Grenadiers and musketeers to the tops. Tell Mr. Maynard to keep his guns and swivels in readiness. Grape, if you please. When they fire on us he is not to return fire. He is to save his shot to clear a path for the boarding party. We will take them abaft the mainmast."

That would place the boarding party as close as possible to the quarterdeck. If they carried it they could use the schooner's own swivels against the waist and strike her colors.

"Gun ports still closed, sir," Thorton reported.

"Good. They think they have us fooled. They'll wait until they are alongside before letting us have it."

Thorton grimaced. To take a broadside at point blank would wreak havoc upon the galiot. The officers of the poop deck would be prime targets. Men would die this day. He was still peering at the schooner through his glass. "She looks American, sir. Some of their smugglers like a raked rig like that."

Tangle chewed his lip. The American colonies were protected by the treaties of Mother England. A treaty did not yet exist between the Sallee Republic and England, but Achmed was carrying those dispatches across France to a port on the Mediterranean, and from there to home. He was also carrying Tangle's letter to his wife.

"I think she is a pirate. Anyhow, as long as she's flying Spanish colors we are right to treat her so. Make ready the Sallee colors. Keep those men well down. She can't be carrying too much weight of metal. What sort of guns do your colonists use, Mr. Thorton?"

"Four pounders, sixes, and eights, maybe nines. I doubt they have nine-pounders on a little schooner like that."

"She's got room on her deck for no more than eight in her broadside. So, no more than seventy-two pounds a shot. Probably not more than sixty-four. Our two big guns are a match for her broadside all by themselves. That would explain why they're trying to sneak up on us. They're afraid of our long guns."

Thorton cheered up. The *Santa Teresa* had two thirty-two pounders on her center line, flanked by a pair of eighteens and eights, for a total weight of a hundred and sixteen pounds. The real difference was the caliber of her guns; a thirty-two pound ball could punch a hole where an eight pound ball would bounce off. Provided the gunners could hit the target. With a large broadside luck was on the gunner's side; with so many guns surely somebody would hit something. The fewer number of guns on a galley required precision; not for nothing were the Spanish galleys famous for their marksmanship. Or had been, in an earlier age.

Closer and closer they came. The sight was a glorious one: two vessels racing towards each other as the sun lifted above the rim of the world. Brilliant streaks of color illuminated the sky and the schooner's upper sails shone a golden pink. It only took ten minutes for the two vessels to close. The schooner backed sails and presented her broadside as if to invite a grapple. Her gun ports were still closed. How many did she have? With her faded black paint it was impossible to know. Fifty yards apart. Thorton trembled with anticipation. Still she did not fire.

"Hoist the Sallee flag. Out oars. Charge!"

The rowers ran out their oars. Suddenly she was racing to crash against the schooner's side at an oblique angle. Shouts were heard on the schooner and her crew of cutthroats appeared above the gunwale. The ports flew open: one, two, three, four, five, six. Maynard screamed, "Fire!" The *Terry's* guns crashed out and grapeshot swept across the schooner's deck. The schooner gave them her broadside as a yellow flag with a snake on it shook out.

The *Terry* took a shot in the bow but it bounced off—galleys had very strong prows. Another shot passed over her deck at head level, harming nothing. A shattering crash told them that a ball had passed through the captain's cabin sidelight. Where the other balls went Thorton didn't know. The galley shuddered as they rammed the schooner. Her long prow shot over the schooner's deck and the swivels barked and wrought havoc among the pirates (for that was what they were) as they tried to fend off. Hizir and his marines leaped up from behind the rembate that protected the foredeck guns and ran along the prow to leap onto the schooner. The smaller vessel's bowsprit was at an angle to the galley's poop; they could read her name clearly: *Carolina Belle*.

Tangle gave up his pretense of being a mere tillerman and jumped forward to bark, "Damage report!"

They were receiving small arms fire from the schooner and Thorton lost his hat to it. He felt a trickle of sweat run down his neck and put up his hand to rub it away. His hand came away red. The swivels on the *Terry's* poop were busy firing upon the pesky Americans. The first wave of marines took casualties, but a second wave was running after them. The schooner threw grappling hooks and attempted to pull the galiot alongside. They were reloading their cannons.

Tangle roared, "Port side, back oars! Starboard side, forward oars!" Thus the galley resisted, slowly rotating to become more perpendicular to the schooner. She received several ragged shots, holing her above the waterline yet again, but she was nearly perpendicular to the trajectory of the guns, so two shots caromed off like billiard ball striking a bank and bouncing. The tillerman dropped on the *Terry's* deck and the quartermaster howled for a replacement while he held the tiller himself.

The schooner was not as well manned as the galiot. The marines fought their way to the quarterdeck and took it in a shower of blood. The desperate men there would not surrender; being pirates they knew they would be hanged if taken. (It was well for Tangle that he had been recognized a privateer by his captors. His letter of marque had kept him from the hangman's noose.) Thorton looked up. Somewhere in all the excitement, Midshipman Bellini had done his job and raised the purple and argent ensign of the Sallee Republic. The star and scimitar flew over the scene and his heart leaped. Pirates were a legitimate target for a vessel of any nation. He could fight this battle with honor.

The Sallee marines seized the schooner's quarterdeck swivels and turned upon her waist. The pirates rushed the quarterdeck and were beaten back by the bloody crossfire from quarterdeck and the *Terry's* guns; Maynard was firing onto the schooner's deck in support. The fighting broke off and men raised their hands or fell to their knees. Hizir fired again.

Tangle bellowed, "Avast firing!"

Hizir was taken with battle lust and his men fired again and again into the desperate prisoners. The Americans fled below decks to escape the killing and some tried to leap to the *Santa Teresa,* but were beaten back as the rowers rose from their benches and struck them with oars.

"Thorton! Get over there! Take command!" Tangle bellowed.

Thorton flew down the steps and ran the length of the bridge. He ran along the prow until he could leap to the deck of the schooner. He nearly got his head blown off by trigger happy marines. By the time he got to the quarterdeck the massacre was over. Nobody was left upright on the schooner's deck.

"You are relieved of duty!" Thorton shouted into Hizir's red face.

Hizir glared back at him like a wild beast, then he struck Thorton full in the face with his closed fist. Thorton sprawled on the deck. Tangle saw it and cursed. He looked around the shambles of his own quarterdeck. Midshipman Bellini was wounded and sitting on the deck. The timoneer was dead and the quartermaster was bleeding from both arms. By a miracle Tangle and Midshipman Kaashifa had no wounds. "Mr. Kaashifa, you have the conn!"

"Aye aye, sir. I have the conn," the younger man replied. The color drained from his face as the weight of command fell on his shoulders.

On the quarterdeck of the *Carolina Belle* Thorton swept his legs around and toppled Hizir. He sprang on the big Swede's back, seized his throat in a choke hold and held it. Hizir flailed about and tried to break his grip; he elbowed Thorton in the stomach and made him grunt. He attempted to throw himself over on his back, but Thorton kept his grip and did not allow it. He had learnt to wrestle from his cousins, the Shawnah Indians, when he was a boy in Maryland. He choked Hizir until the renegade's vision blurred and his struggles grew faint. The rest of the men, bloody and full of battle lust, formed a circle. Thorton looked up.

"You!" Thorton was still busy choking Hizir, so he had to use his chin to point at the man, "Take a crew and go below. Find the survivors. Assure them they are safe. There will be no more shooting."

Startled, the man looked at Thorton like he was insane, but saluted and replied, "Aye aye, sir." He took several of his blood-splattered cohorts and went below.

By the time Tangle got to the schooner's quarterdeck, Hizir was unconscious and Thorton had command. Thorton saluted crisply. "Quarterdeck secure. A party is searching for survivors now, sir."

Tangle returned the salute. "Bring me the schooner's papers and the surviving officers."

The surviving officers proved to be a master's mate, purser, and midshipman. The midshipman was a boy only a little older than Maynard but considerably less experienced. Tangle addressed him in English.

"Name?"

"J-oshua H-hamilton, sir." He was terrified. He was a redhead and freckles blotched his sunburned complexion.

"Rank?"

"M-mmidshipman, sir."

"You are now the commanding officer of the *Carolina Belle*, Mr. Hamilton. I am Isam Rais Tangueli, known as 'Captain Tangle' to the English. I am a Sallee rover, master of the *Santa Teresa*." His English was tolerably good on nautical subjects. "You have my deep and sincere apologies. Mr. Hizir behaved contrary to the rules of conduct expected of a corsair. We will give any aid you require, but we will not take you as a prize. I will not profit by murder."

Midshipman-Acting Captain Hamilton blinked blankly at him. "Yessir," he replied, having no idea what he agreed to.

Thorton touched Tangle's elbow. "If you please sir, I have had experience with hospital ships."

Tangle indicated Thorton with a gesture of his chin. "This is Lt. Peter Thorton, a fine and honorable gentleman. I will leave him here to assist you."

Tangle returned to the *Terry* with Hizir under arrest. Right then and there he held a drumhead trial on the aft deck. The men who had obeyed Hizir he did not charge, even though they were as guilty as he. It was too difficult to sort out which of them had done what and when, who had fired the fatal shots, whether they had heard the order to desist, and all the other details. The thing that was absolutely clear was that Hizir was in charge, and he had not only failed to stop the slaughter but actively participated in gunning down men who had surrendered.

The noose was made and put around his neck, and with the roll of a drum, the men hauled the lines and the peak of the fore antenna rose high. Hizir dangled above their heads. His legs kicked and danced for several minutes before he finally went limp. The survivors aboard the *Carolina Belle* cheered to see their murderer dead before their decks were even cleared. The grisly thing was left there for the rest of the day and night.

CHAPTER 28 : TAKING THE TURBAN

Tangle sat alone in the dimness of his shattered cabin. The broken glass was cleaned up and the window boarded over. The rover wore his loose white damask clothes with his wounded leg propped up on the opposite chair. His dinner was untouched before him. Thorton knocked once, then twice, but received no answer. The marine on duty assured him that the captain was in there, so Thorton opened the door and stuck his head in. Tangle did not move.

Thorton came all the way in and shut the door behind him. He crossed quietly and stood next to the brooding captain. Tangle stirred a little and looked up at him with bitter eyes. "Never before have I presided over a massacre, Peter."

Thorton bent and kissed the top of his short-haired skull softly. "I know, Isam. You are an honorable man." Oddly, he felt an urge to protect the redoubtable corsair.

"'Tis an ill thing and will tarnish my name."

Thorton said softly, "So it will. Many things diminish us in the eyes of others that are no fault of our own."

"What will my wife think when she hears it?"

It hurt Thorton to think about his wife, and it hurt him that Tangle was thinking about his wife, too. He forced himself to say, "If she loves you, she won't believe it."

Tangle gave him a weak smile. "She will think it a Spanish lie." He sighed. "The men of this crew are not the men I would have chosen. They were condemned to the galleys for their crimes after all. There are some men of quality among them, but in general they are ruffians and knaves."

Thorton rested his hand on Tangle's shoulder. "That they are."

"We must review the muster roll. The men who participated in Hizir's slaughter are to get a black mark. I cannot tell the innocent from the guilty, so we will let them go at Eel Buff. The rogues will find employment there. We must recruit some decent men to replace them, if any can be found in that den of thieves. If not, we must run as fast as we can south past the Iberian coast. We should be able to raise Sallee within a week of leaving Eel Buff. I will put in at Tanguel, disband the crew, and sell the ship. I have cousins there who can be my agents for the sale. We will go overland to Zokhara."

"You will not keep her for yourself? You can hire a new crew."

Tangle shook his head. "I want a xebec, Peter. I want a hand-picked crew. But not soon. I want to spend time with my wife and children."

Thorton's hand tightened reflexively on Tangle's shoulder. Tangle felt it. "By Allah, you have been a help to me, Peter. I love your stiff English neck and righteousness. You have self-control. You would not have let bloodlust overwhelm you." He put his arm around Thorton's waist. Thorton stood stiffly in the circle of his arm.

"What about me? Will you cast me off with the rest of them?"

Tangle looked up. "Is that why you've gotten cold with me? No, of course not. I plan to take you and Maynard and Kaashifa and Foster and some of the others with me to Zokhara. Traveling the interior is not safe. We'll go together. You'll be my guest at my home just outside of Zokhara. If you want go to sea, I'll help you find a berth. However, I was hoping you'd wait for me to acquire a vessel of my own. With my reputation I ought to be able to find investors willing to advance me the money to get a new vessel. I can rebuild my fortune from there."

Thorton sighed. His future was not under his control, but then, ever since he'd gone to sea, it hadn't been. He owed it first to God and King, and now to this corsair. Only if he obtained a vessel of his own would he be able to set an independent course. But what course? Raiding the enemies of the Sallee rovers, bringing home loot and captives for ransom?

"Is that what you will do, go back to being a corsair, Isam?" There was a note of disapproval in his voice.

"Don't tell me the lapsed minister is trying to reform me!"

Thorton pulled out a chair and sat in it. He looked very earnestly at Tangle. "Isam Rais Tangueli, you are better than that. You could be a great admiral in a mighty navy. You should consider enlisting. Join the French if it pleases you to fight the Spanish."

Tangle shook his head. "Sallee is my country and Islam is my religion. I fight for Allah and the Dey. 'Tis what I believe in." He knitted his fingers together. "I will propose to the Dey that we should mount an expedition and drive the Spaniards from our shores. We have tried before and lost, but not since I have been a grown man. My father was killed the last time we tried to take Sebta. His death was for nothing. I want to set that right."

"How old were you?"

"Twelve. He performed my circumcision and confirmed me in submission to Allah the day before. I went to battle as a man that day and saw my father torn to pieces by Spanish grape. He died with his guts on the quarterdeck beside him and there was nothing I could do could stop it. I want to take Sebta for my father's sake."

Thorton wrapped his hands around Tangle's. He held them tightly. "I will stay, but not to turn corsair. Driving the enemy from the shores of your homeland is an honorable thing. If Sallee is to be my home, then I will serve Allah and the Dey as I have served God and King."

"You will take the turban then?"

Thorton squared his shoulders and sat upright. "I will."

Tangle spoke softly. "Then repeat after me, *Allahu Akbar; Ash-hado allaa Ila-ha illallah; Wa Ash-hadu anna Muhammader Rasoolullah.* Allah is the greatest; I testify that there is none worthy of worship but Allah, and Mohammed is His messenger."

This was the greatest step that Thorton had ever taken. With it he severed all connections to the old world and committed himself to the new. He had no doubts at all about it. He spoke the Arabic words in a rolling voice that rang in his ears.

Tangle's dark face split into a broad grin and he wrapped Thorton in a bear hug. He pounded him on the back and said, "Well done!"

Thorton felt light-headed but happy. The terrible torment was over. He had become a new man on a new course. "I believe Mr. Maynard may wish to convert as well. He is enamored of everything Sallee."

"Well then. We shall ask him. Let's go to him. I will not make him get up when he is still convalescing."

Maynard had overdone it and was back in bed. He was grey and drawn but happy to have visitors. He smiled at them.

Tangle gestured to Thorton. "Mr. Thorton has some news to share with you."

Thorton took a deep breath. "I have converted to Islam, Archie. When we get to Sallee I shall apply for citizenship. I hope to acquire a post with the Sallee navy. Not a corsair."

Maynard listened to this with a quizzical expression. "Are you going to wear a turban?"

Tangle replied, "That he will. 'Tis the symbol of our faith. No more of that Christian tricorn, Mr. Thorton! It symbolizes the Trinity and that is polytheism."

"I want to take the turban too," Maynard announced. "You have a much better way of doing things than the British navy, sir."

Tangle administered the profession of faith to Maynard. The lad recited it in his piping voice, then Tangle taught them how to wrap a turban. Wrapping it was easy, wrapping it so that it held together and looked good was difficult. As they practiced, Tangle instructed them in the five pillars of Islam.

"The profession of faith, that there is no God worthy of worship but Allah, that Mohammed is his messenger; prayer; charity; fasting during Ramadan; and the pilgrimage to Mecca once in your life if you are able. Everything else flows from that."

It was simple enough at the root. Tangle's baritone continued. "I have been remiss about the prayers," he said. "If a prayer is missed it can be made up, or substituted with some other meritorious deed, such as freeing captives, feeding the hungry, or donations to charity. The Qur'an permits us to omit prayers entirely while traveling, if necessary, but we can fit them in as long as there is no emergency. You two must learn your prayers. You will add Arabic lessons and instruction in the Qur'an to your duties. I will tutor you."

The next morning the crew as awakened by Tangle's sonorous baritone. *"Allahu Akbar. Allahu Akbar. Allahu Akbar. Allahu Akbar."* Allah is great. Allah is great. Allah is great. Allah is great.

The ululating cry, never before heard on the deck of the *Santa Teresa de Ávila,* caused heads to turn in astonishment. The Christians aboard shivered at the strange melody, but Muslim hearts were glad.

Tangle continued to sing out, *"Ash-hadu alla ilaha illallah. Ash-hadu alla ilaha illallah."* I bear witness that there is none worthy of worship except Allah. I bear witness that there is none worthy of worship except Allah.

The Muslim hands started hurrying, swiftly hauling up buckets of salt water to wash and purify themselves before prayer.

"Ash-hadu anna Muhammadar Rasulullah. Ash-hadu anna Muhammadar Rasulullah." I bear witness that Muhammad is the Messenger of Allah. I bear witness that Muhammad is the Messenger of Allah.

Tangle smiled as he watched them scrambling to get clean. Some of them had already bathed and could come directly aft to stand on the deck below him. Checking the sun, they made their best guess as to the direction of Mecca and formed a line diagonally on the deck at the foot of the stairs. The men arriving later filed into orderly rows behind them. There was not much space. Some entered the coach while others filled up the bridge as far as the foredeck.

Maynard and Thorton in their turbans were first in line to form the congregational prayer. Maynard had difficulty; with only one good leg he could not easily perform the changes in positions required. Thorton helped, but Maynard decided to stay seated for most of it. He bowed and turned his upper body in an approximation of the motions.

Afterwards, Tangle sat on the bottom step of the leeward stair and spoke to them about the divine revelations received by Mohammed and the absoluteness of the One. Thorton and Maynard were surprised to discover that Islam accepted the authority of the ancient prophets

Abraham, Moses, and Adam, and that they likewise accepted Jesus as a prophet born of an immaculate conception. What Muslims did not accept was the divinity of Jesus and the Holy Ghost. Thorton was glad; he had never been able to understand how there could be such a thing as a 'three-personed God' when the First Commandment said, 'Thou shalt have no other God before me.'

Tangle quoted some verses from the Qur'an (he was especially fond of verses having to do with the sea) and his melodious voice rolled over them, "He it is Who enables you to journey through land and sea until when you are on board the ships and they sail them with a fair breeze and they rejoice in it, there overtakes them a violent wind and the waves come on them from every side and they think that they are encompassed, then they call upon Allah, in sincere submission to Him, saying, 'If thou deliver us from this, we will surely be of the thankful.'"

He paused for a moment overcome by emotion, then said softly, "And so we worship Him who has delivered us from the hands of our enemies, the Spaniards, and sent us a fair wind to speed us home."

To that there was no argument. Thorton and Maynard joined the crew in saying, "*Ameen.*"

CHAPTER 29 : EEL BUFF

The *Santa Teresa de Ávila* was on the latitude of Eel Buff. All they had to do was sail due west and hope they wouldn't meet any Spanish patrols. The wind grew faint and fitful. They ran out the oars and swept; when the wind improved they sailed. So it went. Sweeping and sailing, sailing and sweeping. They crawled along the line of latitude making very slow progress. When not rowing they made and mended, scrubbed and drilled. The mood was somber after the massacre and the men were given to quarrels among themselves. The morning prayers helped, and the novelty of the Englishmen in their inexpert turbans was a source of amusement, but the mood was cross and changeable.

They were keyed up in expectation of meeting Spanish patrols or even an invasion force sent to retake the island, but they met no Spanish vessels at all. Once a three-masted ship sailed past them to the north, but she was hull down and they could not make her out. She did not alter course to either meet or avoid them. On the fifth day out of Correaux the wind switched around to the south and they made four knots. They had plenty of water and food but very little meat.

On the sixth day the wind strengthened and became gusty. The *Terry* behaved well. The waves got rowdy and she shipped water over the bows, but she did not drench herself the way a true galley would. It rained and there was thunder and lightning and even a bit of hail. They gathered rain water to replenish their casks.

In the middle of the rain they spotted a strange sail. It broke out the black hourglass: a pirate flag. Tangle broke out the purple ensign. After a brief pause the other vessel ran down the black flag and ran up the French flag. The two vessels approached one another warily. All hands were at battle stations, but the other vessel, a quick little brig, shouted to them through a speaking trumpet.

"*Quoi vaisseau?*"

Tangle grinned. "I wonder if they've heard? Make them a proper answer, Mr. Thorton."

Thorton shouted through his own trumpet, "*Santa Teresa de Ávila, Capitaine Isam Tangueli du République Salé. Quoi vaisseau?*" His French was passable, but he spoke it with a Spanish accent.

The Frenchman replied, "*La Belle Fille, Capitaine Maurice Thibault. Où saut?*"

"Eel Buff," Thorton replied. "What news?"

"Barcelona has fallen to the French! Catalonia is ours!" Pirate that he was, he still had some national feeling.

They were cold and damp in their oilskins, but the news made them warm indeed. The French on the Atlantic coast might be laggardly, but their colleagues in the Mediterranean had been busy.

Tangle elevated his opinion of the French. "Damn me. This is the year to sweep the Spanish from African shores! If the French can take an entire province, surely we can take a few cities!"

"What news?" The pirate asked them in reply.

"English cruising the Bay of Biscay."

"Have they declared?"

"Not yet! How far to Eel Buff?"

"Twenty-five miles. Just over the horizon."

Arriving in Eel Buff was something of an anti-climax. The French forts commanded the bluffs over the entrance and a ragged mud brick town ringed the harbor. The galiot glided into it easily and never mind the shoals. The purple flag of Sallee excited a certain amount of interest as they came in, but not many people wanted to brave the drizzle to take a closer look. Half a dozen vessels of ill repute occupied the harbor along with several honest ones that wanted water badly enough to risk their company.

A Moorish galley was pulled up on the beach not far away, and there were a couple of schooners, a brig, a saettia, a galley, and a lugger under pirate, privateer, or corsair command careening or taking on water. A pair of French guard galleys were present, and they learned that four were stationed here to run patrols, backed up by a resident frigate. The frigate could only get in and out at high tide. It had the unkempt look of a vessel that never went anywhere.

The *Terry* needed powder and shot, and the corrupt French officials were pleased to sell them a ton of powder out of the fort. Sadly, the balls were not the right size to fit the larger guns, being French measure not Spanish. They spent part of their time making up cartridges for the big guns under Foster's supervision. Other gangs went ashore to cut firewood. Menéndez was put ashore with some cash and the appropriate bribes to let him remain unmolested in spite of the war. He hoped to find a ship for Madeira, and from there, passage home.

Next they passed a couple days careening the hull. Although she had not been at sea long, green growth was starting to attach itself to the bottom. Tangle wanted a clean and greased hull when he made the run past Spain. He was parsimonious with the prize money to keep the men working on the vessel, but they had a habit of sneaking off anyhow. By the time they were done the townsfolk were going to be increasing in number and diversity of bloodlines.

As long as they were making and mending and resupplying, Tangle had the carpenter build him a bigger bed. He was tired of curling up in a six foot long bed; he wanted to stretch out. The carpenter made him a solid wood cot—no rope netting to sag. It was seven feet long by four feet wide and hung from chains so that it would sway as the ship rolled and not dump him out of bed in a squall. Tangle bought a mattress three inches thick stuffed with horsehair. He would have liked to have had a down bed but that was a luxury beyond his means. As it was, the bed held two men quite comfortably. Thorton spent every night there.

That's where he was when Tangle's steward, a ferret-faced Arab, burst in one morning before dawn. "Rais, the *Ajax* is here!" He screeched to a dead halt as he stared at the two sleeping men.

Thorton sat bolt upright in bed before he was even awake, but Tangle groaned, cracked one eye open and said, "What?"

Thorton turned and shook his shoulder. "The *Ajax!* And . . . your steward." His face was quite red to have been caught like that. He wasn't even wearing a nightshirt. He whispered, "We are ruined."

"Never mind that. We already have reputations. What are the English up to? That's what I want to know." Tangle yawned and climbed out of bed. He walked stark naked to the roundhouse. "Get our wash water and quit ogling us like you've never seen a naked man before," he told the steward as he passed.

The man fled.

Thorton climbed gingerly out of bed. "What do you mean, we already have reputations?"

"You did blurt out that unfortunate declaration to Perry in front of the men. I am not the only one aboard who speaks English. Perhaps they have taken it to mean brotherly love, but I doubt it." His voice came from the roundhouse.

Thorton donned his shirt and pants before the steward returned with a bucket of fresh water for washing. Being in port, they could afford to use fresh water.

Tangle yawned and scratched. "Bishop must be out of gaol if the *Ajax* is here."

"But why is she here?" Thorton wanted to know.

"We'll have to ask, won't we? He must not have any dastardly plans or something would have happened while we slept. Besides, we're in a French port and he's a neutral. There's only so much he can do. Now get washed and dressed. I have to call prayers shortly."

They washed and shaved. This daily bathing struck Thorton as excessive, but Tangle insisted that as long as they were washing the prescribed parts for prayer, they might as well wash all the parts. Especially since they'd rendered themselves impure the night before. Tangle also insisted on shaving. Since they were run up on the beach with no motion in the ship there was no better time to shave the sensitive male anatomy.

"Why shave *there?*" Thorton asked.

"Because cleanliness is purity and Allah loves purity. Besides, you'll smell better if you shave your crotch and armpits. You barbarians may love the smell of stinky men, but I don't."

Thorton spluttered. "I am not a barbarian!"

"Then shave."

Thorton shaved himself very gingerly indeed. "I don't have to wear that jewelry, do I?" he asked, indicating Tangle's hafada.

Tangle smiled at him. "Not unless you want to, but you will have to undergo circumcision."

Thorton jumped and nearly cut himself in a painful location. "Circumcision!" He gave Tangle an alarmed look.

Tangle was highly amused. "All Muslim men undergo circumcision when they're old enough, about ten or twelve years old. At that age they're old enough to profess Islam and know what they do. No one will believe you're a Muslim if you aren't cut. If you are ever captured by the Spaniards, 'tis proof positive you are not a Christian. It is more than a commitment, Peter. It may even be a matter of life and death." He became serious as he spoke.

Thorton swallowed hard. "If you think it is absolutely necessary."

Tangle swatted his shoulder. "Don't worry, we won't do it until we get to Zokhara and can have it done properly. Now get dressed."

With the *Terry* drawn up on the beach, her prow pointed to the southeast towards Mecca. Tangle went to the foredeck to call the congregation to prayer. "Prayer is better than sleep! Come to Allah! Come to success!"

Other men were already washing and dressing in the faint light of dawn. They heard his call and hurried to finish and present themselves. Maynard hobbled up from the wardroom and took his place next to Thorton, and the other men filled in behind in neat rows. Not all of the men were observant and Tangle did not make anyone attend. He simply called the prayer and those who came, came. The Christians and Jews were in the minority and they stayed well away. The prayers had at first excited their attention, but the novelty had since worn off.

Next to them the *Great Moor* lay sleeping. Gabir Rais was an impious rogue who never called prayers, not even before battle, but some of his men came on deck when they heard Tangle's baritone floating pure and piercing through the mist. Gabir groaned and rolled over and buried his head in his pillows. Muslims were like any men: they varied in their qualities. Beyond them the *Ajax* lay at anchor. Being a converted French corvette with a shallow draft, she had skimmed over the shoals. Perry finished dressing and came on deck to watch the scene through his spyglass.

"Damn me! That one in the short jacket is Thorton!"

MacDonald stood next to him. "So he's turned Turk, has he? A pity. He was a good officer."

"We have to give him the news. Order out my gig."

"Aye aye, sir."

CHAPTER 30 : THE AJAX

Perry stood on the damp sand in his silk stockings and frock coat with his cocked hat firmly on his head. His hair was queued and tied with a black velvet ribbon. The white lace of his cravat spilled over the top of his waistcoat and lace showed beneath his coat cuffs. His white facings were crisp and the gold lace and brass buttons gleamed in the sun. The bottom of his white waistcoat could be seen where the frock coat cut away. A gold watch chain ran across the front of the waistcoat. His breeches were perfectly blue and made of good stuff. His naval sword hung at his hip. He was as fine a figure of a British naval officer as anyone could hope to see. Thorton's heart did a slow roll when he saw him.

"Acting Captain Roger Perry of His Britannic Majesty's frigate *Ajax*," he announced. "Permission to come aboard?"

"Yes, of course. Pipe him aboard." Thorton held up four fingers to indicate the correct number of sideboys. The ragtag Sallee marines quickly lined up and presented their muskets.

In his cabin Tangle heard the drum and pipe. Recognizing that a captain was coming aboard, he bolted the rest of his breakfast and grabbed his good coat. He came out in time to see Perry climbing over the galiot's gunwale.

Perry and Thorton stared at one another without speaking. Their eyes raked one another's clothing to take in the changed circumstances. Slowly, as if in a dream, Thorton raised his hand and saluted. Perry returned it.

Tangle stepped forward.

"Sir, I have the honor to present Lieutenant Roger Perry, acting captain of the *Ajax*," Thorton said. To Perry he said, "Captain Isam bin Hamet al-Tangueli, Captain of the Corsairs of Zokhara."

"Welcome aboard, Captain Perry. Peace be upon you." Tangle's voice was bland.

Perry stood to attention. "Thank you, sir." They were speaking English as the mutually intelligible language. "I have news to impart that I believe may be of considerable interest to Mr. Thorton and perhaps also yourself."

Maynard came on deck just then, hopping along with his crutches and turban. He stopped short as he saw Perry.

Perry stared at him. "Maynard! My god! You're alive! What, have you turned Turk too?"

"Aye, sir, and gladly. I'm a lieutenant now." He held up his hand to display the gold star on his cuff. He hobbled over to join them.

Perry turned on Thorton. "You told me he was dead!"

Thorton should have been embarrassed at having been caught in a lie, but he wasn't. He said softly, "He very nearly was. We thought it best that he pass out of the Service in an honorable fashion. Mr. Maynard has been keen in his new career."

Perry looked at the empty space below the bottom of Maynard's breeches. "What happened?"

"'Tis a long story," said Thorton.

"I want to hear it," said Perry.

So Tangle, Thorton, Perry, and Maynard went to the captain's cabin. They gathered around the table and coffee was served. The tale was told with interruptions and questions. They told Perry all of it—except for the part about Thorton sleeping with Tangle. Perry in turn told them that Bishop had had a heart attack and was laid up in a French hospital.

"He never should have gone dueling. The wine, his age, the excitement, the indignity of a French gaol . . . He collapsed. So, with the captain unfit for duty and Forsythe in gaol, I opened the secret orders." Perry's eyes danced wildly.

"Go on, you must tell us!" Thorton said.

"Oh, I was to look in on Isle Boeuf and if it was not in French hands, to take it." He pronounced the name properly thanks to his excellent command of French.

"Damn. Hard luck that. The French have got it," Maynard put in.

Perry's eyes twinkled. "There's more."

"Yes?"

"The French have taken Barcelona."

"We knew that," Maynard put in.

"You did?"

They all nodded. "Well," said Perry a bit testily. "Did you know that England has declared war against Spain?"

Thorton and Maynard sat bolt upright around the table. "My God!" Thorton exclaimed.

Tangle smiled and nodded, but his mind was busy calculating how that would affect his own plans.

Perry was explaining. "The taking of the *Rebecca* is the official cause, but it was not the first time the Spaniards have done something like it. You remember the *Marigold?*"

"I was on the *Marigold,*" Thorton replied. "That's why I speak Spanish."

"Oh, that's right. I remember. 'Twas long before we met."

Thorton inclined his head in agreement, but it pained him that Perry had forgotten such an important thing.

Maynard and Tangle looked at Thorton in surprise. Tangle asked, "What is the *Marigold?*"

Perry explained, "A British supply ship. She was carrying victuals for the resupply of the Jamaica squadron. The Spaniards apprehended her in the West Indies and claimed she was carrying contraband. They made prisoners of the officers and pressed all the ordinary seamen."

"I was a foretop hand at the time, so I was pressed," Thorton explained.

Perry went on, "If you ask me, the real reason for the war is that the Spaniards have closed the Strait of Gibraltar to neutral traffic. You have to apply for a permit and they take the devil's own time about it and want a tremendous bribe. Our ships can't get in or out of the Mediterranean, and neither can anyone else. Gibraltar is in desperate want of supplies."

Maynard bounced in his chair. "Are we going to run the blockade, rais?" He gave the Turk an eager look.

Tangle shook his head. "I plan to land at Tanguel before I make a decision. Maybe there will be a letter for me—I have relatives there. What about you, Captain Perry. What are your plans?"

"I'm to scout Isle Boeuf and make a report about it, then go to Plymouth for further orders. They'll put somebody else on as captain, I'm sure. Merely looking into Eel Buff is hardly exciting enough to get a promotion. I think I'll cruise the coast of Spain all the way to the French frontier, then run up to Correaux. I may be able to get some prizes. They won't know I'm there."

"Yes, they will. They've got signal lines from the French border to Madrid, and another one from Coruña to Madrid," Thorton replied.

"How do you know that?"

"Spanish charts. You won't have the element of surprise," Thorton explained.

"Damme. Well, 'tis worth doing anyhow. The heavy fighting has been on the Mediterranean coast. They've moved most of their ships east. They've only got galley coastguards up here in the north. You couldn't ask for a sweeter set up for a little prize-taking." For a frigate the prospect of making some prizes of Spanish galleys and cabotage was very likely.

"What about you? Any prizes?"

"Not since Correaux," Tangle replied.

"We could cruise together."

Tangle shook his head. "I'm going home. I want to see my wife and children. And I want to get my ship back."

Thorton winced at the mention of his wife. He kept silent.

Perry reached across the table to grasp Thorton's hand. "I need you back, Peter. I need another lieutenant, a good one."

Thorton made no answer. His head was spinning.

Perry kept talking, "Bishop's gone. There will be no punishment. Maynard, too. Forsythe's all right now that Bishop isn't scaring him silly. Chambers is a nincompoop. I need you both. You're the best officers the *Ajax* had. Come back."

Maynard frowned and set his jaw stubbornly. If he had been a little younger it would have qualified as a pout. Thorton stared at Perry's hand on his.

Maynard spoke first. "I don't want to go back. I've made lieutenant and I like serving under Captain Tangle. I want to run the blockade and see Africa and the Mediterranean."

Perry gave Maynard a beseeching look, but the boy-lieutenant folded his arms over his chest and stared him down. Perry looked to Tangle, but Tangle would not overrule one of his officers on such a personal matter, especially when it was better for him if Maynard stayed. Perry looked to Thorton.

"All right. I'll do it," Thorton said.

Tangle slammed his fist down. "No, you won't. I forbid it. I'll hold you here at pistol point if I have to."

"I have a duty."

"Dammit! You converted. You submitted to Allah. And I believed you." His voice was bitter. He pushed his chair away from the table. "The only valid conversion is a freely made one, a conversion for no other reason than the love of God. A conversion made for gain is not a valid conversion. A conversion made to spite someone is even less valid. Tell me which it was, Thorton. Did you or did you not make a sincere conversion?"

"I . . . don't know."

Tangle slammed his fist again and the table jumped. "Damn you, Peter Thorton! Damn you for a perfidious Englishman."

Perry cleared his throat. "May I speak to Peter in private, sir?"

"Go. Use his cabin." Tangle gestured a dismissal.

Thorton and Perry rose and slipped over to the chartroom. Thorton pulled back the curtain and let Perry into his sleeping cabin.

"I wish I knew what was going through that head of yours," Perry said.

Thorton sat on the edge of the bunk. He wished he knew what was going through his head, too. Perry had thrown him over, Perry wanted him back. Bishop would flay him, Bishop was in hospital. He might escape a court martial after all. How could he explain himself?

"Captain Tangle is my lover." It sounded quite peculiar to his ears.

Perry's jaw dropped. "What?" It was not a very charming or articulate thing to say, but Perry was at an unusual loss for words.

Thorton nodded. "I'm not really sure how it happened, but he is fond of me."

Perry sat down on the edge of the bed next to him. "Hell's bells. I never really thought you'd do it. I suppose I knew you would, someday, somehow, but a Turk! He's practically a blackamoor."

"He's not. The galley sun has burned him dark. Besides, he's a normal male in all other regards. He's very brave and strong and fair. He's stern, but friendly, too. He's a fine officer. You would like him. I've learned a lot this month."

Perry listened to this. "His taking of the galleys was well-played, I give you that. I heard about it from some French officers. I don't doubt his tactical ability, just your wisdom for getting mixed up with him. He's a pirate, Peter. A pirate!"

"A privateer," Thorton corrected. "An honorable man. There are few better."

"Maybe we should entice him to enlist. I could use a midshipman like that," Perry remarked drily.

Thorton missed the joke and answered him seriously. "He wants to go home to his wife and children. He is the *Kapitan Pasha* of Zokhara. He won't give it up to be a junior officer in the English service."

"No, I didn't think so. And you, Peter Thorton, are having an affair with a married man. Shame on you! And shame on you for all the times you wagged your finger and clucked at me!" He wagged his finger and clucked at Thorton.

Thorton turned bright red. He wanted to sink through the decks and disappear into the bilge. "Well, that was before this happened. I promise I won't say anything about your affairs ever again."

Perry scuffed a shoe on the floor and tried to school his face to a neutral expression. "'Tis an awful vice, Peter. I feel sorry for you. I know you'd change it if you could. I don't know why God would do such a thing to a man. It must be the Devil's work."

Thorton stiffened. "You don't know anything about me. I haven't committed the unnatural sin you allude to, either, so I'd appreciate it if you'd wipe that filthy thought from your mind!"

"You haven't?"

"I have not," Thorton said very firmly. "We are . . ." He searched for words to describe it. "Ardent friends. I cannot feel there has been any dishonor in our conduct. Did not Achilles and Patroclus cleave to each other? They loved each other and nobody thought the less of them."

"That was in ancient times before Our Lord Jesus Christ came to lead us out of sin."

"I have read my Bible, Perry. Christ does not mention the subject. He does mention adultery. His response to the people who wanted to stone the woman taken in adultery was, 'Let he who is without sin cast the first stone.' If God forgives all sins, then He forgives any I might have committed. I should not be judged more harshly than an adulteress."

"Well, you are an adulterer."

Thorton laughed suddenly. "No, I'm Muslim now. Muslim men are allowed more than one wife, provided they treat them all fairly and can support them. The Qur'an does not mention male lovers, but it does mention dealings with women to whom one is not married. In short, fornication is not a mortal sin. I'm not sure that what we do qualifies as 'fornication' anyhow."

Perry was mystified. "How could it not?"

"Well, it involves a great deal of kissing and hugging, which is not fornication," Thorton said with a blush.

"That's true. Kissing and hugging are not sins, although they certainly pave the way for sin."

"So . . . generally speaking, if done passionately enough, they are 'enough.'" Thorton was bright red.

Perry considered that. He held his hat in his hands and worried the cockade. "You know people will think you're doing something else. They won't believe you. I do, because I know you, but they won't. The Admiralty won't."

"I don't want to go back, Roger."

"You said you would!"

"I thought it was my duty, but I'm happy here. I didn't even know it until we talked and I realized how different things are for me now. Honor, love, happiness. I have them now. I can't go back, Roger."

"Robbery and kidnapping. You left those out, Peter. Kidnapping Christian souls and selling them into slavery if they can't pay the ransom. That's what corsairs do, and your lover is the king of them!"

"The English do the same to the Africans, but with no chance of ransom. They are bound into servitude forever."

"'Tis not the same thing. Blacks are inferior people. Without the guidance of civilized men they consort themselves as animals. They have no culture but what we give them. Therefore when we enslave them, we improve their condition and that pleases God. But we are a civilized people, so it degrades us to be made slaves by a people inferior to ourselves."

Thorton had served with men of many colors, races, nations, and religions in the past month. His jaw tightened. "I don't think the color of a man's skin determines his qualifications. Isam is proof of that."

"You said yourself 'twas not his natural color."

"Men on this vessel are judged by their merits. Complexion never enters in. Ability, courage, intelligence, fortitude, honor—these are the things that matter here."

"It sounds very noble, I admit it. But it doesn't change things. Your paragon is a robber at sea and a despoiler of villages. And to what purpose? Profit! Profit and nothing more. He's not even trying to win a kingdom for himself. If the damn rovers ever tried to take and hold a piece of land, I could countenance it. But their holy war is only an excuse to pillage. Look at the *Great Moor* beside you. That's what they're generally like. Sloppy, cullion-faced, impious thieves."

Thorton's face fell. "I admit it bothers me. However, I have decided that when we reach Zokhara I will enlist in the Sallee navy. Then it will be my duty to guard against Spanish raids. That's an honorable thing."

Perry gave him a disgusted look. "That's your ambition? To be the coastguard of a thieving nation? The Spaniards are right to raid them. If such a plague of vipers molested England, we'd do the same. We did it to the French. One day Christendom will unite against thieves and robbers and make war on them instead of each other."

Thorton was silent for a long time. Presently he said, "No doubt you are right. But I know that England will never change. She can never be any better than she is. Look at our own navy. Corrupt, mediocre, and moribund. Influence determines the promotions, not merit. The Spaniards have been molesting our shipping for years and what did we do about it? 'Tis only now with the Mediterranean trade interrupted that we are suddenly concerned about the *Rebecca* and the *Marigold* and all the others. Maybe the men of the south have a chance we pale skinned races don't. They are willing to take the risk. We aren't."

"You're a fool. Your brain is making excuses to justify your prick. Or whatever part you're sharing with the pirate."

Thorton set his jaw. "I never talked about your mistresses like that. Don't talk about my lover that way."

Perry sighed. "Peter, I'm trying to get you to come to your senses. I admit I've committed some peccadilloes of my own, but not on such a grand scale! I'll do what I can to keep you out of trouble. I'm sure I can fix up the reports to make it all right. I'll report what Tangle said, that he carried you off by force. If we take some prizes it really won't matter what you've done. Success justifies everything."

"No."

"If you won't come back, I must report you for desertion. If you're ever caught, they'll kill you. You know the *Articles of War.*"

Thorton paled. "I do. But I've violated the very first. It requires all officers to establish the Church of England and see that its rites are followed. Now that I've converted to Islam, how could I return?"

"Then you must resign. Cite religion if you must."

Thorton rubbed a hand over his face, then nodded shortly. He went to the chartroom desk and trimmed a quill. He began to write, *I have the honor of addressing* . . . His pen continued scratching and dipping in the ink, . . . *since being convinced that Islam has the most correct understanding of the commandment, "Thou shalt have no other god before Me," I cannot support the Trinity, nor any Christian sect which promotes the Divinity of Jesus and the Holy Ghost* . . . He laid down his quill and reread the letter. Yes, it said what it needed to be said. He finished it, *Therefore I must respectfully tender my resignation from the naval Service.* He signed it. He pushed the paper over for Perry to read.

"That will do. Copy it into your book and let me have it. I'll write my acceptance."

That was the end of the discussion and their friendship. Perry's gig carried him back to the *Ajax.* Thorton watched him climb aboard the frigate to the sound of the drum and boatswain's whistle. He finally turned back. When he let himself into the Tangle's cabin, he found the corsair sitting in his chair and brooding. He glanced up when Thorton came in.

"Well?"

Thorton bowed deeply in the Muslim way with his hand pressed to his forehead to show great respect. "I resigned my commission. I'm staying with you."

A great smile broke across Tangle's face. "Excellent. I'm glad to hear it. Come join me in a cup of wine. We'll celebrate."

"'Tis a not a thing to celebrate," Thorton replied with great feeling.

Tangle stared at him for a long moment. Then he held out his arm. "Then come and sit with me, Peter, because I am glad to have you by my side."

Thorton settled in the circle of his arm. He leaned against the man who was his lover, captain, and kidnapper. The tumult in his heart was hard to bear, but bear it he must. "Tell me about your wife. Is she fat and ugly?"

"Not at all. Jamila is young and beautiful and clever. She tried to ransom me. I know, because they beat me for it. She sent her brother, Shakil, with two thousand *reales*, but they refused to accept it and raised the ransom to three thousand. She raised the money and Shakil came again. Again they refused him and demanded five. They thrashed me within an inch of my life that time. It took my family a long time to raise five thousand *reales*, but they did. The Spaniards refused them outright. For three days I was chained to the deck, beaten, whipped, starved, and parched, a target for any assault and insult they cared to heap on me. I thought I was going to die, but they doused me with water, put some bread soaked in wine in my mouth, and dragged me back to my bench."

Thorton listened. "Did your wife and her brother see you like that?"

"No. They had to work through agents. It was too dangerous. They don't know what happened to me. I won't tell them, either. Shakil is a good man and it would bother him. My wife . . . doesn't need to know. It would trouble her too much."

Thorton had no family. He could not imagine anyone being troubled over his fate. "They must love you," he said at last.

Tangle smiled. "They do. Shakil is like my own brother. He gives much and asks little. If he ever asked me a favor, I would not refuse him, no matter what it was. Jamila is like no other woman in the world. She is as kind and wise as she is beautiful. You will like them."

But would they like Thorton? He doubted it. He dreaded arriving in Sallee as much as Tangle yearned for it. Once he had longed for a man who would understand his secret desires. Now he longed for an understanding man who was also a bachelor. The word 'adulterer' did not lie easily on his conscience.

He sighed. "If you say so."

Chapter 31 : Prizes

They paralleled the coast of Iberia at a distance of a hundred miles. Sometimes they saw fishboats, then finally crossed the latitude of Lisbon and saw sails heading for that great port. Here they picked up a fat little brig returning from the West Indies. She was loaded with cane sugar, rum, and molasses. It was a sticky sweet cargo, but she'd fetch a good price in the market.

"Take a crew and board her, Mr. Bellini. Send over a hundred weight each of sugar and molasses, and two barrels of rum."

Bellini's mouth hung open. "Me, sir?"

"Aye, you, mister. She's a choice brig and we're far off the Spanish coast. If you keep to sea until you reach the latitude of Tanguel, you should be fine. We'll rendezvous at Tanguel. You won't be able to get her over the sandbar without lightering her load off, so don't go in. Wait for me. I want to investigate the town before I bring a prize in. If weather turns against you or you run into trouble, go on to Fezakh in Morocco. They've got a fine deep harbor. My cousin Wafiq bin Edip is a caulker there. Look him up, he'll be my agent. I'll give you a letter."

Bellini's' expression was growing alarmed as he heard his instructions. "But I've never had a command before, sir!"

"About time, isn't it? We'll run with you a little ways, but then our ways must part for we are a lateen rig and yon brig is a square-rigger. Send all the prisoners over, they're seasoned hands and I need the sailors."

Bellini gulped. "Aye aye, sir. Rendezvous at Tanguel?"

"Aye, Mr. Bellini. Mind you sound the approach well. They haven't dredged in thirty years."

Bellini took twenty men with him. They got into the rum and six of them got roaring drunk before he established order. He shipped the six back to the *Terry* and rather shamefacedly asked for sober hands. Tangle gave them to him without comment. Bellini fumbled his way into mastery of the vessel, put guards on the rum and stores, sent over the requested supplies, sent over the prisoners, and set everything in order.

Thorton asked, "Do you think it wise, sir?"

"I need competent officers, Mr. Thorton. They become competent through experience. 'Tis an easy command; I wouldn't waste you or Foster on it. I need you on the poop deck and him on the guns."

Thorton cleared his throat self-consciously, keenly aware of his very limited experience of command. He'd been given a sloop to master once when he was a midshipman, but no other prize until Tangle had made him the master of the hospital ship. He sent a yearning glance after the brig. Such a command would have done a great deal to enhance his experience and bolster his confidence.

"I don't think I have as much experience with prizes as you believe I do, sir." His cheeks were pink as he said it, but it had to be said. Tangle must have a realistic appraisal of his officers' capabilities.

Tangle studied him. "That may be so, Mr. Thorton. But you've got natural gifts that exceed those of other men. I'm confident you will handle whatever assignment I give you. Now let's examine the prisoners."

Tangle and Thorton went down to the waist to look at the captives. They were sixteen in number. The officers were Spanish for the most part, but the hands were colonials and some of them had the sallow look of mestizos. Tangle addressed them in Spanish. "I am Isam Rais Tangueli, Captain of the Corsairs of Zokhara. Which one of you is the captain?"

A man stepped forward. He was a thin man of average height with a thin mustache. He replied, "I am Captain Guillermo García y Navarro, of the brig *Dulcinea*. What are our ransoms?"

Tangle smiled without warmth. "The usual. If you can't afford to pay it or your families and friends won't pay it, you shall be sold at auction in Sallee, to labor until they do pay, or until you die, however it shall please Allah to arrange your fates." They all looked unhappy about that. "Or, you can swear your fealty to me and remain free men. I need serviceable men who know something about sailing. I also need a surgeon and a carpenter's mate. If you're inclined to join us you'll have a full and equal share of the prize money and all the privileges of free men, including your own religion. If you'd like to enlist, step forward now."

There was some looking back and forth, nervous shuffling and clearing of throats. Two men came forward. "Very good. Mr. Thorton, read them in. Mr. Wafor, chain the rest of them to the benches."

As Thorton and the black boatswain started forward, another man moved with alacrity to join the renegades. One of the officers, a younger man with sandy brown hair, asked, "Please sir, can we get an officer's post if we join?"

"If you're willing to take the turban, yes. If you're not, you'll have to serve before the mast as an ordinary seaman."

The Spanish captain gave his junior officer a contemptuous glare. That made up his mind. He'd lost the respect of the men around him; it would be intolerable to stay with them. He swiftly joined the renegades.

"Carry on, Mr. Thorton, Mr. Wafor."

Wafor gave them an evil, yellow, snaggle-toothed grin. He and they both knew the horrors of the sugar plantations. If there was a fate worse than being a galleyslave, it was being a sugar slave. In addition to being worked fourteen hours a day, beaten and starved, kept naked or nearly so in conditions of extreme squalor, they were often burned when boiling sugar in the refineries. While outright deaths were rare, it was not unusual for a slave to be burned so badly that he was willing to cut off his own limb, counting the amputation less excruciating than the burn. Even less severe burns were certain to become infected. Slaves died slow, agonizing deaths because of it. The survivors were often maimed and disfigured. Thorton knew none of this. Wafor took great pleasure in chaining the captives and gave them three lashes each to start them off right.

The daily routine of life went on. The *Terry* kept running south. That miffed the men a little. If they'd cut closer to the Spanish coast while rounding Cape Surprise, they could have picked up prizes in the Gulf of Cadiz as they entered or left the Guadalquivir. However, they would have run into a Spanish fleet, too. Spain was calling out all her forces and sending them to the Mediterranean.

The following day they spotted sails to the south, and the sails spotted them. As they closed to investigate, a Spanish frigate broke away from her convoy and menaced them. They fled and the frigate went back to shepherding her charges. The *Terry* hung back, but as soon as night fell, she ghosted up without lights. There were stragglers in the convoy in spite of their brush with the strange lateener. One of them was taken silently by boatloads of men who climbed up her ornate stern, in through the stern windows, and surprised the captain in his bed. They seized control without a sound. They extinguished her lights and left the convoy.

After twenty minutes or so, the lookout on the next vessel noticed that her lights were gone. That vessel flashed the message to the next with lantern lights, and so it was passed along the line. By the time the message reached the frigate and the frigate reached the rear of the convoy, the *Terry* had run to windward. It was an easy and bloodless prize. Foster was made prizemaster.

From her vantage point to windward the *Terry* swooped on the middle of the line and fired her bow guns into a fat snow. The merchants who had guns sent a few shots her way, then scattered, leaving the snow to her fate. The snow promptly struck.

Tangle gave Maynard special orders. "Once the frigate is hull down, haul down your tophamper and change course to diverge from the other prize. Maintain absolute silence and darkness. I want you to disappear in the night. Once you are far enough away your tops will not be seen, you may set them as you please. In fact, you may do almost anything you please, if only you make rendezvous at Tanguel. Do you understand me?"

An excited Lt. Maynard snapped a salute. "Aye aye, sir!" The young officer could do it; he had the nerve, even if he had to be carried on board in a boatswain's chair. The men would do it because they loved him. The little snow slipped away in the night.

Thorton was passed over in the matter of prizes. Although he thought Maynard and Foster suited to their charges, he was the senior lieutenant. One of the prizes should have been his. He stiffened as he generally did when distressed in his mind, but he did not question Tangle, not with the frigate clawing to windward in pursuit of them.

Tangle gave another order. "Pursue that Indiaman."

The helm responded and the galley went skipping after the great merchant ship. She was fat, tall and heavy, laden with goods from the New World. She was worth more than five snows and brigs put together.

Tangle spoke quietly. "You have two good legs, Mr. Thorton. You will need them if the frigate overtakes us. You can work the bow battery even better than Maynard; you taught him. I know it is a glorious thing to be a prizemaster, but it is even better to survive. We must play a game of iron nerves with yon frigate as long as we can stand it while our prizes escape. That is the duty I know you will perform better than Foster or Maynard."

Thorton didn't answer. He watched the Indiaman running through the night like a leviathan, her stern windows and massive lanthorn lit up like a ballroom. Red flashes spoke from her sternchasers. The splash was well short of the galiot's bow. He glanced back at the frigate laboring to come up on them. Then he looked west to where the ghostly apparitions of the prizes were running away. The merchantmen of the convoy were breaking up, each running as best he could to escape the sea-wolf among them. The bold corsair had scattered the orderly convoy. They might be able to pick off several more prizes over the night and day. It would take at least twenty-four hours for the frigate to get them all rounded up and under its protection again.

Thorton nodded. He had no choice, but he trusted that the man was right even if he didn't like it. "Aye aye, sir."

"If Allah should see fit to deliver us the Indiaman, you shall have her as your prize. Now work those bow guns. Topple their mainmast."

"Aye aye, sir." Thorton ran to the foredeck.

The frigate was fast enough to run down the prizes, but the *Terry* was swooping down on the Indiaman on a good point of sail, her bowchasers blazing. Allowing Tangle to carry off a nice fat Indiaman right under their noses was a provocation not to be born. To lose the Indiaman while saving the snow was a bad bargain. The frigate came after them.

The galiot ran with all sail set and phosphorescent water foaming over the lee rail. Thorton had no time to admire the eerie luminosity; the Indiaman was turning onto her best point of sail and abandoning the convoy. She must be making seven knots—very nearly her best speed. To run before the wind on a broad reach was not the *Terry's* best point of sail, so she ran on beam reach and would tack over. If Tangle calculated right, they would hook over to grab the Indiaman before the frigate came up. If not . . . The frigate was overhauling the Indiaman, choosing a course that split the difference between the rover and the Indiaman. She was trying to put herself between the two.

The galiot could not fire on the Indiaman unless her bow was pointing at her, but the Indiaman could give them her broadside. It was long range and poorly pointed, but still, she outgunned the *Terry*. It was worth it to try. She had plenty of shot and powder in her capacious hull. Tangle let her waste her powder. Yet he dared not run too long on this tack; the frigate might decide the Indiaman could take care of herself and pursue the prizes. Tangle tacked sooner than he wished and charged the Indiaman, long guns blazing.

Thorton pointed the guns himself and they scored some hits. One square in the bow, and a short shot ricocheting across the water to smack into her side. Thorton yelled at his men and they sponged, loaded, and ran out the guns as fast as they could. He sent two more balls whizzing towards the Indiaman, but did not have a good enough range to do her mainmast any damage. The Indiaman answered with her broadside and something that sounded like a gigantic bee went whizzing over his head. The galiot took damage amidships and a hole appeared in her foresail.

Tangle ran out to the extreme of her range. He consulted the hourglass and his pocketwatch, then turned back to charge the Indiaman again. He must attack aggressively enough for the Indiaman and the frigate to believe she carried a sufficient body of troops to take the prize by boarding. The frigate must defend her. The convoy was left behind as the three vessels raced each other. Every minute counted to buy time for the prizes to slip away.

Thorton searched the horizon. The prizes were hull down in the darkness. As he watched, the snow's topsails came down so that she was a mere smudge of white on the horizon instead of the usual pyramid. In a few minutes even that vanished below the horizon. Foster's ship was already out of sight. The *Terry* abandoned the Indiaman and ran back to windward.

Tangle picked a new target: a trim little brig that would make a handsome corsair if he could get her into port. When the brig saw the *Terry* swooping for her, she struck immediately. That was unexpected. Did he have time? He glanced over the tafferel. He thought he did, even with the emboldened Indiaman in pursuit.

"Thorton, the brig is yours. Take a crew." Thorton and his men went over the side in a boat. Tangle left them there. He must dodge the frigate and torment the Indiaman to cover the taking of the brig.

Thorton's men rowed hard towards the brig, but when the boat was nearly over, she took to her heels. She could outrun a jollyboat easily enough. Thorton swore mightily. He was now at sea with the *Terry* and the brig diverging on opposite courses and the Indiaman coming up. He had no way to catch the brig. He glanced over and saw the frigate beating hard to come up to meet the lateener. He swore again. He must think like Tangle and put his boat where he needed to get picked up. *The brig is my prize, therefore I must cover it. The Indiaman isn't fast enough to close with me when I really run. Therefore, it is only the frigate I must worry about. My course is—*

Thorton pointed. "That way." The men rowed.

Tangle did not intend to get close to either the frigate or the Indiaman. He glanced over his shoulder at the brig. "Douse the lights, damn you, Thorton," he muttered.

The fire from the Indiaman grew hotter as she closed. No more time to play with her. Tangle swooped around to chase after the brig and cover her. Then he spotted a flash of lantern light where there was no ship: two long, two short—the private signal. Thorton's boat! He slowed to pick up his men. The Indiaman was wild with excitement. Not being able to see the boat in the galiot's lee, they thought she was stopping because she had suffered some hurt. More shots flew across the water and tore through her sails. Thorton and the men came scrambling on board like monkeys.

"Row! Full speed ahead! Dead into the wind!" Tangle roared. The men leapt for the sweeps and hauled them out and began to row like madmen. No ship can sail into the wind; that direction is the galley's prerogative. The Indiaman struggled through a tack to cross their wake and rake them, but it took time. Precious time. The men rowed like the demons of Hell were after them. The *Terry* sprinted across the water at nine knots. Tangle watched the sea and ships behind him.

Thorton raced to the poop to report. "The brig ran away from us, sir! She never intended to surrender—she was playing with us!"

"Damn her black eyes. She was delaying us so the Indiaman and frigate could come up. I knew it was too easy. Why are you all wet?"

"Near miss from the Indiaman." He was drenched.

"Move the big guns into my cabin and keep them hot, Mr. Thorton. I want to thump her nose and make her shy off."

"Aye aye, sir." Thorton stepped briskly down to the weather deck. Soon the big guns rumbled as they were hauled aft. The thirty-two pounders boomed out with a deafening roar in the confined space under the deckhead.

The men of the *Terry* bent their back to the sweeps until they were spent and gasping. Some of them vomited from the strain. From there she ran close-hauled on her best point of sail while the Indiaman and frigate wore after her on their worst point of sail. The Indiaman gave up the chase and turned back to find her consorts in the scattered convoy. The frigate followed her back. Thorton didn't get his prize after all, but the rovers got away with only minor damage.

CHAPTER 32 : THE SEA LEOPARD

The wind rose and blew a half-gale from out of the northwest. The *Terry* shipped water and had to be pumped, but compared to the *Bart*, she was as buoyant as a cork in a washtub. The wind blew itself out in the wee hours. When dawn lightened the sky, the coast of Africa was a large smudge on the horizon. At noon Thorton shot the sun. Tangle didn't wait for him to plot a course; once he knew his latitude he knew exactly where he was and adjusted his course southwards. He soon spotted landmarks that he knew. "We'll be in Tanguel by sunset!" he said joyously.

It was a glorious day, warm and windy, and perfect for a victorious corsair to stand dreaming about prize money waiting for him ashore. Thorton was gaining a first hand appreciation for what a pest Tangle had been to the Spaniards. If the Turk could do what he did with a mere galiot, how much more damage could he do with a xebec and a pack of sea wolves running with him? An empire lived by its ships; they brought her the materials she needed to build her machines of war and feed her populace while pampering her aristocrats with the luxuries they craved.

Thorton and Tangle were on the poop deck as usual. Tangle had unbuttoned his new linen shirt to the waist and it blew open to show his muscular chest. His body hair was growing to form swirls on his chest with a line leading to his waist. With sufficient food and rest he was filling out well. He was a manly specimen with little trace of Spanish captivity left upon his skin, and he was in an expansive mood, regaling them with tales of his exploits.

Thorton found the sight of the captain's undress terribly distracting, so he kept peering through his spyglass at the coast of a continent he had never seen before. Part of him was listening; he was absorbing knowledge of xebec tactics which he was certain would prove useful in the course of his career. But it left him feeling uncomfortable as well. Prizes for profit, that's what Tangle was talking about. There was a state of war between Spain and the Sallee Republic but was it really anything more than waving a flag over piracy? That's what the European powers called it. Larceny, with a shiny veneer of religion and patriotism.

Thorton was dressed in his jacket and petticoat breeches. The loose pants were cooler than ordinary breeches. The fourth time he slapped his hand against his head to keep the straw hat in place he was too late. The hat blew across the poop deck, dodged all hands grabbing for it, and blew over the lee rail. His blond hair was left exposed to shine in the golden sun. He took his dark blue-checked kerchief out of his pocket and tied it over his head to keep his brains from broiling.

"A sail! Fine on the starboard bow!"

They all moved to the windward side to have a look. The vessel was hull down and too far away to make out more than a bit of white that might not be a wave.

"What kind?"

"Xebec!" the lookout replied.

Thorton's attention sharpened. He'd heard enough about them by now to be eager to see one. Glasses clapped more eagerly to eyes. Eventually they saw her rising above the waves. She was traveling an oblique course that would cause their paths to cross, but who would cross whose wake was not yet certain. Her big lateens were much larger than those on the *Terry*. Her mainmast was straight enough, but her foremast leaned toward the prow and her mizzenmast leaned aft. Thorton had never seen such a cockamamie contraption.

"What on earth is wrong with her?" he exclaimed.

Tangle gave him a curious look. "What do you mean?"

"Look at how crazy her masts are! She looks like a drunk put her together."

Tangle laughed out loud and so did the other men on the poop deck. "They're supposed to rake like that. Here I thought you had noticed something wrong with her mainsail."

Thorton looked around at the grinning men. He harbored a suspicion they were amusing themselves at his expense. "What's wrong with her mains'l?" he asked.

"Too small. If you laid it down on deck, the antenna wouldn't reach from her lazyboard to her prow," Tangle pointed out.

"What's a lazyboard?"

"A grated platform that extends aft the transom. It provides footing for the sailors working the mizzen."

Thorton looked where the poop ended at the tafferel and wondered why you'd need anything aft the transom. He studied the newcomer and measured her main antenna against her deck. "I see what you say. But neither does ours. Why would you want it to?"

"We're a galiot. Our sails are bigger than a galley because our hull is a deeper and broader, but not by much. With a xebec we belay the foresail well forward on her prow and her mizzensail well aft on the boom-kin. We get a good spread of canvas on her; twice as much as a

European vessel of the same size. We can do that because she's deep enough to bite and beamy amidship, but her floor is narrow and raked so she's fast. She's stable enough to carry broadside guns. She's like a fast, agile frigate. Yon xebec has got a timid master or a man who doesn't know how to sail." His brow knit in concentration as he put the glass back to his eye.

Thorton studied the vessel through his own glass. She was blistering along at an excellent rate of speed—fast enough to have a creamy white bow wave giving her a mustache that was visible even at this distance. She was enlarging noticeably as she approached. Her ensign was a blue flag with something yellow on it and a narrow private commission pennant was streaming from her masthead. She looked a very brave sight in spite of Tangle's criticism.

"By Allah! The *Sea Leopard!*" The sight of his own vessel flying towards them was astonishing beyond belief. "It must be Kasim." A moment later he erupted in fury. "What in the Hell did he do to my ship!"

"Who's Kasim?"

"My brother-in-law. A disagreeable fellow who fancies himself a corsair, the damned butcher. That's what he was, a butcher, before I married his sister. He made a few cruises with me, but he wasn't the sort of man I wanted. He only sailed when he needed money to pay his debts and I wouldn't let my wife lend it to him. He cut down the main antenna, the rat bastard! I had seven thousand square feet in that big lateen! Damn him for a cheapskate and a coward! He sails like a Spaniard!" He writhed in fury.

Thorton lowered his glass and stared speechlessly at the rover. He must not have heard him right. "Did you say seven thousand in the mainsail, sir? Surely you meant seven thousand all told."

"Aye, seven thousand in the mains'l. He can't have more than five thousand in that pitiful little thing. She's slow." Tangle was grieving like he'd had his arm cut off.

Thorton swiftly worked the numbers in his head and determined that the *Santa Teresa's* mainsail was about thirty-six hundred square feet. A lateen sail was a right triangle, so its dimensions were easily worked out with the Pythagorean theorem. The Indiaman, hulking great beast that she was, carried about as much sail as the slim little xebec but had more than four times the volume of hull. The xebec was scooning along at ten or eleven knots. That was slow?!

"Good God, you'd dismast yourself or capsize!"

Tangle grinned broadly at him. "Not with a lateen rig. But yes, I advise you to keep to the windward rail when we are flying. Two hundred men on the high side is a necessary counterbalance."

Thorton thought Tangle might be exaggerating, but he'd already experienced the man's daredevil tactics and was obliged to think he might be serious.

He raised his glass and studied the xebec again—there on the foredeck was something blue and gold. As he watched, the blur of color resolved itself into the form of a woman with her silks blowing about her. A sky blue veil was fastened to her head with a cap of gold coins and ornaments. The delicate piece of silk could not confine her hair and brown curls blew wildly with it. Her sky blue gown had bell-shaped sleeves that billowed and fluttered. They winked in the light, proving that they too were ornamented with gold. The skirt blew around her legs. It was slit up the sides so that it streamed out nearly horizontal and snapped and fluttered like a flag. Her legs were clad in matching blue pantaloons. Her hands carried rings of gold, her wrists wore bracelets of gold, her skirt was spangled with gold. She stood by the rembate with her hand upon the stem-post for support. Her other hand she held to her forehead to shield her eyes as she searched the galiot.

Tangle lowered his glass. He could not speak.

"What? Who is it?" Thorton demanded.

"My wife," Tangle replied. A smile grew on his face as he gazed at the lovely apparition. "Jamila bint Nakih, the most beautiful woman in the world."

Thorton was appalled to see the audacious corsair mooning over a woman. His wife, no less! Maybe if she had been an opera singer or countess or something equally impossible he could understand it. But a wife? Thorton lifted his glass and gazed at the woman. She must be beautiful, he supposed, although from this distance it was impossible to judge her features.

The xebec coursed across their bow and white plumes of spray were thrown up as she cut through the waves. Tangle came to life. "Heave to! Prepare to render honors!"

"What honors, sir?" Midshipman Kaashifa asked.

"The honors due the wife of the *Kapitan Pasha* of Zokhara, damn it! I need my coat and turban!"

The word was passed and the items supplied. Tangle put his turban on and donned his coat. The xebec hove along side the *Santa Teresa* and husband and wife gazed across at each other. Tangle was still shoving his arm into his coat sleeve and grinning like a lunatic when she cried out, "Isam!" and stretched her arms out to him.

"Habibi!" Beloved, he called back.

Thorton's mouth turned down. He walked to the far side of the poop deck as if to give them privacy, but in reality to hide his own expression. He was berating himself for succumbing to Tangle's seductive wiles when he had known all along the man was married. He clasped his hands behind his back and stared at the blank and empty sea. All attention was on the happy reunion. Sweeps on both vessels splashed and stroked, easing them close enough together that grapples could be thrown.

"Jamila, get back from there! The ships will bump!" Tangle called to her in Arabic.

Thorton turned around and looked in spite of himself. The woman clambered back inside the rembate but would not leave the foredeck. The two vessels clashed together with a solid thump and were lashed bow to stern, each pointing in the opposite direction. Thus the xebec's foredeck and galiot's poop deck were side by side.

The xebec was a bit longer than the galiot and her gunwale a little higher. Her quarterdeck was a proper quarterdeck of good height and length above her waist. The foredeck carried a rembate with small bowchasers, but she had twelve ports cut in each of her sides with twelve-pounders behind them. The guns were on the weather deck. Her crew in motley clothes worked leisurely to brail the sails. Their tacks flapped loosely. It was a sloppy, casual way of handling the vessel, not at all like the taut ship Tangle ran. If it miffed Thorton, it must gall Tangle.

Tangle barely said, "You have the conn, Mr. Thorton," before he flew down to the waist and scrambled over the railings onto the xebec. Jamila flew to meet him and threw herself into his arms. He picked her up and whirled her around and around and she squealed in delight. The silk sleeves fell back to expose her caramel-colored arms, arms that hung around the corsair's neck and would never let go. Thorton hated her on sight.

The happy husband kissed her in front of everyone. She melted in his arms and kissed him back. The crews of two vessels cheered. All except Thorton. He had the conn or he would have gone below to his cabin to sulk. He felt a terrible ache in his chest—and also parts lower. How easily he had attached himself to that which he had resisted for so long! The more fool he. He folded his arms and turned away.

Midshipman Kaashifa was looking expectantly at him. "What orders, sir?"

"Find out if the captain wants his dunnage moved to the *Sea Leopard*. I expect he does." So Kaashifa ran down to the deck and scrambled over to the xebec. He had to wait until Tangle noticed him. There was a happy nod from the dark head, then Kaashifa was running back with the message.

"Make it so," Thorton replied.

Thorton must be a topic of conversation because Tangle was talking animatedly and his wife was looking in wonder towards the poop deck of the galiot. Thorton turned pink. Surely the captain would not be so indiscreet as to mention his affair to his wife at a moment like this. No, he must be explaining about Thorton's role in his rescue. Glumly he waited for the horrible scene to end.

Tangle was calling to him. He went to the forward edge of the poop and leaned over the rail, "Sir?" he called.

"We're going into Tanguel. Follow us."

So Thorton watched Tangle mount the xebec's quarterdeck like he owned it. His wife clung to him. Thorton wondered if she could feel his eyes drilling into her back. The galiot was now his to command. He barked his orders and steeled his heart against the man he knew he should never have accepted as his lover.

CHAPTER 33 : FAMILY QUARREL

On board the *Sea Leopard* things were not going as well as Thorton imagined. Oh, Captain and Mistress Tangle were certainly pleased to see each other. Happy, delighted, thrilled, ecstatic, radiant—no words were sufficient to describe the joy of their reunion. In spite of anything that might be inferred about his character from his amours, Tangle truly loved his wife and she loved him. However, there was another person who was even less happy to see Tangle than Thorton had been to see Jamila, and that was his brother-in-law, Kasim bin Nakih.

It began civilly enough when Tangle and Jamila mounted the quarterdeck and Kasim Rais said, "Peace be upon you, Isam. Welcome aboard."

Kasim looked something like his sister, but his wavy hair was plain brown while hers was auburn. He kept it short under the turban. It was a black turban, worn above a black shirt embroidered with silver and gold and very costly. He wore a red sash with a scimitar hanging from it, black pantaloons, and red shoes. He wore a gold chain around his neck that supported a medallion set with rubies and diamonds. Rings adorned his hands. He wore a short curly beard and mustache trimmed close to his face. He was a handsome man but there was something hard and dissolute in his face. He was getting thick in the body and his face was fleshy, but he looked healthy and prosperous. He was ten years younger than Tangle and glowing with vitality.

Tangle looked like a gangly and half-dead stick next to him. Had he let his beard grow there would have been a white streak down the middle (which was why he kept it shaved). His arms and legs were long, lean and ropy. A month of freedom had put meat on his bones, but his waist was still many inches narrower than it had been when he left Zokhara.

Tangle replied, "Peace be upon you as well. I thank you for bringing my wife to meet me. I have missed her." His arm hugged tightly around Jamila's waist and he kissed her brow. "Although I wish she had stayed home where it was safe, I am sure she would not. You pestered him, didn't you, Ami?" His tone was affectionate.

Kasim shrugged. "Jamila has gone to sea before, as you well know." There was a sting hidden in his words.

Tangle forced himself to be polite. "How are your wives and children?"

"They are well. I have married again and had another son while you were gone."

"Congratulations. I hope mother and child are well."

"They are."

"Congratulations on your marriage. How many wives is that for you now?"

"Three. Not counting the worthless one I divorced." His eyes blazed defiance.

Tangle's jaw worked, but he turned to his wife and asked politely, "Are Shadha and the children well?"

Jamila replied softly, "Yes, she has been very kind to me in your absence. Ruwaydah and Thaqib are old enough to be a real help around the house now."

Kasim spoke angrily, "It was wrong of you to make servants of them. People speak ill of me and claim I wasn't supporting them."

"That's because you weren't supporting them," Tangle shot back.

"When I gave her money, she spent it on herself instead of the children!"

Tangle would have answered, but Jamila intervened. "Kasim, Isam! That is old business. Let it lie, I beg you." She took her brother and the husband by the arms and tugged on them, giving them each pleading looks.

Tangle took a deep breath and exerted some self-control. "You are right, *habibi*. All right. Let's go into Tanguel. I need to arrange for a prize agent. We took a ship and a snow last night, and a rum runner a few days before that." He gave his wife a peck on the cheek, then released her and took a step forward to look over the ship. "Loose grapples," he ordered.

Kasim snapped, "Belay that." The men on the quarterdeck hesitated. "I'm captain here. I give the orders. You and your wife may retire to her cabin. I'm sure you have much to catch up on."

"Kasim," said Jamila in a placating voice.

"Don't 'Kasim' me, Jamila! I'm the captain. He is my guest and he will do well to remember it."

"The ship is mine," Tangle pointed out.

"No, she's *my* ship. I paid her price. Not you. Once she was yours, but you were foolhardy and you lost her. I bought her. She's mine now."

Tangle gave his wife a look like a thunderstorm about to break. "Did he?"

"We organized a corporation of investors. I didn't have enough to buy it back by myself," she explained apologetically.

"How many?"

"Twelve shares, nine investors. I own two shares and Shakil owns two. Kasim and Nakih each own one, then there are the other investors. They are friends of Kasim." She looked nervous. "I'm sorry, Isam, but I couldn't afford to buy her without help. When the Spanish wouldn't release you, we bought the ship back and hoped that somehow you would come home to us."

Tangle's eyes grew hard and angry. He set his jaw. Several impulses went through his head, not the least of which was that it would feel eminently gratifying to punch the usurping Kasim right in the nose.

"You take advantage of my misfortune to advance your own? You don't even know how to use it. Look at those stubby little antennas! You cut them down like a cowardly Christian!" he accused his brother-in-law.

Kasim's face went white. "I'm a better corsair than you give me credit for. Haven't I brought in prizes while you were gone? Tell him I have, Jamila. You know I have. Haven't I supported your family in your absence? You owe me, Isam."

A vein throbbed in Tangle's temple. Jamila squeezed his biceps frantically. "He didn't cut it down, the Spaniards did. We can talk about this when we get back to port. Please don't quarrel. What matters is that you are back safe and sound!"

Tangle longed to leap at his brother-in-law, but he couldn't with his wife standing right there. "I am Captain of the Corsairs of Zokhara, so you must obey me. You won't take my ship out from under me, no matter what you try."

Kasim gave him an evil smile. "You aren't the Captain of Corsairs and haven't been since your ransom failed. Murad Rais was made *Kapitan Pasha* when you were taken. When the news came that you were free, he hastened to the Dey to have his position confirmed. You aren't *Kapitan Pasha* anymore. Murad is. He doesn't like you."

Tangle's face was white with fury beneath the mahogany tan. He bared his teeth in a snarl. He turned to his wife. "Is this true?"

She gave him an apologetic look so that he knew that it was, even before the words were out of her mouth. "I'm sorry, dear."

Kasim gloated with his arms folded over his chest. "You're the lord of nothing, Isam. You're in debt. You own nothing. You are nothing. Your career is over. A new generation of men will rule the seas."

Tangle was in the most furious rage of his life, but he had the self-control to refrain from doing anything violent. When he had mastered himself, he said, "We will transfer to the *Santa Teresa*."

Tangle exited the quarterdeck and stormed over to the rail. His wife was nearly pulled off her feet as she ran to keep up with him. His dunnage was sitting on deck waiting for him, never having been stowed.

"Make ready a boat to carry Isam bin Hamet and Jamila bint Nakih to the galiot," Kasim ordered with great satisfaction. He deliberately omitted 'rais.'

Thorton was astonished when Tangle, his wife and their luggage, or more correctly the vast heap of Jamila's luggage and the captain's sea chest, went over the xebec's side into the ship's boat. The sailors rowed strongly and the *Leopard's Whelp* bobbed over the waves toward the galiot.

"Prepare to receive boat. Prepare to render captain's honors," he ordered.

They piped Captain and Mistress Tangle aboard. Tangle hoisted Jamila up and she clambered onto the aft deck of the galley and looked around uncertainly. She wrinkled her nose. Was it the vinegar they'd used to wash the decks or had they failed to entirely eradicate the galley's infamous stink? The wrinkled nose gave Thorton another reason to dislike her. Tangle climbed aboard and the hands began hauling up the luggage. Ladies didn't have 'dunnage,' they had far too many clothes for that. Tangle lead his wife to the captain's cabin.

A few minutes later Thorton was knocking on the door.

"Enter," Tangle called.

Her luggage was heaped all along the side next to the captain's desk. She was sitting in his lap and had her arms around his neck. Thorton politely averted his eyes. Tangle made introductions with the woman still in his lap.

"Mr. Peter Thorton, Jamila bint Nakih, my wife. You must forgive our informality. We haven't seen each other in a long time." He spoke Spanish then Arabic to make certain they both understood.

"Enchanted, madame," Thorton replied with formal correctness. He gave a little bow. "*Salaam*. Peace be upon you," he added in Arabic.

"And also upon you. I'm delighted to meet you, Mr. Thorton." Her Arabic flowed beautifully for several more sentences, but he could only understand her greeting. Up close he saw that she was indeed beautiful, although her eyes and cheeks were hollow. She did not veil her face so he could see her features quite clearly: luminous large dark eyes, a slim straight nose, small rose lips. He had not paid much attention to women himself, but he was sure Perry or any Englishman but himself would have been enthralled by the creature.

Tangle smiled indulgently at her, then translated. "She says she's grateful to you for helping to bring me home. Achmed has arrived in Zokhara and so have my letters. The little minx—" his tone was fond in the extreme, "persuaded Kasim to bring her to meet me. They guessed that we would come in to Tanguel, what with the blockade and us with a shoal draft vessel."

"My pleasure, I'm sure." Thorton gave another bow. "You ran the blockade of the Straits?" He opted for Spanish as the common tongue.

"We did," she replied. "We flew a Spanish flag. Kasim said that with her shorter spars they would believe we were Spanish, and he was right."

The rage was swift to return. Tangle thundered, "That damn Kasim has stolen my ship and made a trollop of her! I never saw such an ill-favored lot of snivelers and look at the trim on those sails! She sails like a pig!"

Jamila had been studying Spanish ever since her husband was captured, but she could not keep up with his outburst. Between her conciliatory explanations in halting Spanish and Tangle's fluent rants in Arabic, Turkish and Spanish, the story was transmitted to Thorton. He thought the financial arrangements were nothing that the corsair should complain about; his wife and relatives had accomplished something quite remarkable in getting his ship back. His wife's other brother, Shakil, had even risked his life to go to Sebta and find agents that could help them. Being acquainted with Tangle's daredevil ways at sea, he harbored the theory that Kasim was a reasonably competent mariner, in spite of being rude to his brother-in-law. He wisely refrained from saying so.

Tangle put Jamila in a chair and paced around the cabin. He had to keep his head ducked in order to pace. He put his hand against a beam. "Damn it, I had the *Sea Leopard* built with a seven foot deckhead so that I could stand up straight in my boots and turban! I'm tired of waddling around like a toad!"

Thorton ventured, "The Spaniards lawfully condemned and sold her. All you can do is buy her back. You're lucky she's in Sallee hands."

"Kasim won't sell," Jamila said anxiously. "I've already spoken to him. He likes being captain."

Tangle fumed. "When Jamila and I were first married, he had only one wife. He was a butcher by trade. He was still paying his wife's dower. Kind-hearted, foolish man that I was, I gave him the money to finish paying her dower. GAVE it to him! See how he repays me?"

Jamila bit her lip again. She did not like to see her husband so angry, especially not now, and especially not at her brother. "Isam, *habibi,* you are free! That is what matters! We will go to Zokhara and you will see the children. They've grown so much since you've been gone!"

Tangle bent and kissed her cheek. There was still fire in his eye, but he banked it for the sake of his wife. "You are right. I have missed the children something fierce. Do you think they will remember me?"

"Tahirah does and Hamet too. The triplets . . . recognize your picture. Little Alexander has no idea who that man is, but he repeats, 'Baba' when I prompt him. Tahirah has told them that Baba will bring them presents, so they are all looking forward to your return." She smiled tremulously at him.

Tangle smiled at that. "Fortunately, I went shopping at Correaux. I have all manner of trinkets for them."

Thorton began easing towards the door, but Tangle noticed the movement. He straightened up and accidentally smacked his head on the deckhead. He grunted and rubbed his turban. "Mr. Thorton, will you dine with us tonight?"

Thorton shook his head. "I think your wife has a better claim to you, rais." He escaped before Tangle could call him back.

Safe on the poop deck, Thorton paced. His pacing was an agitated stroll from the front rail to the tafferel, stepping up next to one of the sternchasers, then back again. The other men left him alone. He was given the windward side as was customary for the commanding officer. He thought about Tangle's situation and was pleased that he himself had no such family entanglements. He was a bachelor and half an orphan; his father had died in Maryland and his widowed mother had returned to England and remarried. There was a large span of years between Thorton and his half-siblings, both of whom had died in infancy. He wondered if his mother missed him, her only surviving child, and felt a pang of guilt. He had not seen her in ten years and written only a few times. It had been years since he had had a letter from her. He wondered if she were still alive. He supposed he ought to write her and find out. For some reason he was feeling homesick, but not for her husband's parsonage in England. He missed Maryland and the cabins of the Shawnah Indians.

CHAPTER 34 : TANGUEL

Thorton suddenly paused his pacing. Beneath his feet the sound of female pleasure drifted up through the planks. Captain Tangle was making love to his wife in the bed where only this morning Peter Thorton had lain. Did she know it? Did she guess? Would some member of the crew tell her, just to spite him? What would she do when she knew? They were agonizing questions. They made his face white and his heart black with jealousy. He paced and paced, like a lion in his cage. Or maybe only a leopard. He was not great enough to qualify as the 'king of the beasts.' No, it was Tangle who qualified for such a title. Pace, pace.

The marine turned the hourglass and struck the bell. "Six bells and all's well!" he called. From various corners of the ship the men on watch called back, "All's well!" Thorton counted them with half a mind. All the lookouts were accounted for.

The noise below died away, was quiet for a little while, then began again. The quartermaster grinned. "He's a right lusty man, our captain."

Thorton glared at him. "That is an improper remark, Mr. Vendabal."

"Aye aye, sir." The quartermaster stopped smirking and pretended to see and hear nothing further.

Thorton's face turned red to think that maybe he and Tangle had been overheard, even though he had always bitten back his cries and smothered his face in the pillow. He thought they had been quiet enough, yet how could he be sure?

He turned to the rail and stared at the land. It was a green and pleasant land full of rolling hills. Behind it rose the great brown bulk of the Atlas Mountains. In myth it was the place where Atlas held the sky on his shoulders. Thorton felt as if the burden had been shifted to his own shoulders. So. This was the country that had given birth to the mighty corsair. It was deceptively placid. Perhaps it was boredom that had driven the men of Tanguel to the sea. He took his spyglass out of his pocket and studied the land. He could make out the white dots of sheep, brown cottages, and the occasional brilliant costumes of peasants.

The xebec ran ahead of them. No matter how much Tangle had cursed her loose ways, she was still faster than the galiot. On her quarterdeck Kasim Rais was of no mind to set a speed the galiot could keep. He began to skylark, tacking back and forth across the wind. Each tack required his men to ease the antennas, heave the tacks around the mast, and raise them up again. He was showing off. Thorton pulled his watch out and timed them. They took between thirteen and twenty-one minutes for each tack. How Tangle would rage at their ill work. He was displeased that his crew could barely get their own sails around in ten. His goal was five.

Thorton did not know the area, but some of his men did. Midshipman Kaashifa said, "Should I get the lead out, sir?"

Thorton turned around. The expression on his face made the other man step back half a pace. The renegade lieutenant schooled himself to civility. "Do you think it necessary?"

"Aye, sir. We're coming up on Tanguel. That's the Shepherd's Rock there. There are shoals here." The xebec wasn't zipping along any more. She was a mile ahead and slowing.

"Very well. Get the lead out."

The carpenter's mates went forward and sent their lines over. Their calls were passed back and Thorton paid close attention. There was little enough water here as he discovered. Fortunately, the *Terry* was a shoal draft vessel. Slowly they gained on the *Sea Leopard*. Tangle came out of his cabin, glanced over the side, and mounted to the poop deck. "Shepherd Rock Shoals," he commented.

"Aye, sir. We're casting the lead," Thorton replied.

"Carry on. The *Sea Leopard* is waiting for us?"

"Aye, sir." He did not mention that Kasim had been showboating for his benefit. How chagrined the other captain would be to learn Tangle had seen none of it. He had been busy below attempting to beget offspring number seven. For his part, Thorton was about to choke on a great ball of spite. He stood very stiffly in his turban and short jacket. They came up quickly on the *Sea Leopard's* stern.

"Damn him, she's aground!" Tangle growled. He swore some vile Turkish oaths.

Indeed she was. The *Sea Leopard* sent her boats over with tow cables. No matter how hard the men bent their backs, she did not move. Tangle was about to eat nails and spit grape. He paced violently, whirled around, and said, "Mr. Thorton. I'm promoting you to captain. The *Santa Teresa* is your command now. Do as you think fit. I'm going below."

Thorton was quite astonished. His jaw dropped. He stood with his mouth hanging open while he tried to make sense of the situation. Tangle was the owner of the *Santa Teresa*, he could appoint whom he pleased as her captain. As the owner, he was the ultimate source of orders and the captain was his agent. Generally speaking, owners did not travel with their ships, but when they did, they could, if they chose, exercise command. Or they might leave the operation of the vessel to the master they had hired. Perhaps making him captain of the *Terry* was his way of compensating Thorton for not having given him a prize. Or maybe it was just a furious Tangle speaking out of spite for his brother-in-law. He might change his mind when he calmed down. Thorton had a moment of nostalgia for the soul-deadening bureaucracy of the British navy where everything was certain because it was done according to protocol, signed and countersigned, and written down in the copybooks.

He gave his first command as captain, "Mr. Kaashifa, make a signal, 'Query.'"

Kaashifa ran the signal up. There was no answer from the *Sea Leopard*. Thorton scowled and wondered if Kasim was refusing to acknowledge, so unseamanly he hadn't seen the signal, or just an idiot.

"Make a signal, 'Send boat.'"

Once more the signal was run up and got no answer.

"Damn them for the misbegotten offspring of a poxy whore," Thorton muttered in English.

Kaashifa didn't understand. In Spanish he asked, "Sir?"

"Send them a boat with some good stout fellows in it. Ask them if they want a tow."

The boat was sent, but the offer was rudely refused. The boat came back. The *Sea Leopard's* captain was too proud to accept help. Kasim tried kedging next. The boats came in and fetched her anchor and hauled it away and let it drop. The sound of the Arab chant came to them as the fife and drum set the tune for hauling the line.

Thorton tilted his head in curiosity. "Is their capstan broken? That sounds like a line-hauling chantey."

Kaashifa gave him an odd look. "There are no capstans on xebecs, sir."

Thorton gave him an astonished look. "How do they haul their anchors?"

"The same way we do. By hand."

Thorton watched dumfounded. A galley had the benefit of its two hundred slaves to haul anchors, but xebecs were crewed by freemen. It was one thing to haul a ship by the brute labor of bondsmen, but quite another to warp a ship with the proud backs of free men. The *Sea Leopard* kedged and sweated, sweated and kedged, until at last with a great sucking sound, she came off the mud. She ran out her sweeps a few at a time and began to stroke raggedly. It took a long time to get into cadence as they rowed backwards towards the *Terry*.

Kasim was at the tafferel shouting in Turkish. What he said Thorton didn't know. Turkish might be the familial language of the Tangueli clan, but Thorton was ignorant of it. "What's he saying?" he asked Kaashifa.

Kaashifa gave him a sideways look, then edged away from the English captain. "He says, 'Move your stinking galley, you goddamn sodomite.' An exact quote, sir." His voice was apologetic.

Thorton scowled. That the words were in Turkish meant that they were addressed to Tangle not himself, but he did not take them kindly. Tangle knew his brother-in-law and had removed himself from command before he flew into a rage and did something stupid. Now Thorton had to control his own temper and deal with the son of a bitch himself.

"Thank you, Mr. Kaashifa. No blame attaches to you for making an accurate translation. Come forward with me, please. Mr. Vendabal, you have the conn. Maintain position." The quartermaster murmured his acknowledgment.

Thorton walked briskly to the bow. Standing at the rembate, he swept his eyes across the water. There was plenty of room to pull off; the *Terry* had stopped well short when they realized the *Sea Leopard* was aground. Kasim hopped up on the lazyboard that extended aft the transom and made a rude gesture when he saw Thorton. He shouted something in Turkish that did not sound friendly.

"Back up, or I'll ram you!" Kaashifa translated for him.

Thorton said, "I'll have the long gun loaded and run out, if you please, Patterson."

The gun captain gave him a long look, then replied, "Aye aye, sir." He called for his crew and they swabbed the cannon while their boy ran for a cartridge.

"Touch my ship and I'll blow you a new asshole!" Thorton bellowed at Kasim. "Translate that, Mr. Kaashifa." Kaashifa reluctantly came to the rembate and shouted in Turkish.

Kasim was a swarthy man, but he turned a little pale when he found himself staring down the barrel of a thirty-two pounder at short range. "Are you mad?" he shouted. Kaashifa did his best to turn invisible while continuing to translate.

The *Sea Leopard's* sweeps were slack and she drifted. Her momentum continued to carry her toward the *Terry*. Thorton stepped through the gate in the rembate and walked out to the end of the bowsprit. It was a dangerous gambit. With his limited Arabic, he bellowed, "I am Peter Rais Thorton of the *Santa Teresa*. Stand off or die!"

Two thoughts simultaneously crossed Thorton's mind: first, that Tangle would probably be delighted if Thorton blew away his execrable brother-in-law, and second, that Tangle would be furious if he put a hole in his precious xebec. Both thoughts were immediately followed by the conclusion that they were irrelevant. What mattered was that he had no intention of giving way to an oafish nincompoop. Having threatened death he was bloody well determined that he would fire the gun if necessary. Was it Tangle who had told him, 'I never bluff'? Perhaps it had been. He was not about to begin his career as captain by letting some swine who thought he was a seaman tell him what to do.

Kasim turned and gave orders. The sweeps were flustered, but they started pulling instead of backing. Kasim went forward on his quarterdeck to bellow and swear. His rowers pulled and his rudder turned. He pulled along side the mudbank, backed, turned, and with another rude gesture for Thorton, pulled into the deeper water. They crept along towards Tanguel, then stopped.

The tide had gone out. The *Sea Leopard* could not get over the sandbar into the harbor. Thorton walked the prow back to the foredeck to listen to the call of his own leads. "Three fathoms and rising bottom." A moment later, "Two and a half fathoms and sandy mud."

Thorton directed, "Send out a boat and take soundings ahead."

The galiot's boat went into the water. The gang sounded the way for a couple of pistol shots ahead. The report came back, "Minimum depth, two fathoms and a quarter. Three fathoms on the other side of the bar, sir."

"Pass the word to Mr. Vendabal. Slowly and carefully pass the *Sea Leopard* on her larboard. We're going over the sandbar. Out sweeps. Brail sails."

The commands were echoed in Spanish, Arabic, and Turkish. The fore and mainmast hands went to their posts and brailed up the sails while the unskilled seamen fetched the sweeps from where they were carried in outriggers along the quarters.

Thorton called loudly in Spanish, "Let's show them how real sailors handle a ship! Handsomely, lads, handsomely!"

The drum beat and the oars dipped in unison into the water. Slowly, majestically, with each oar in perfect time, they eased around the *Sea Leopard*. Thorton smiled to see how well the men comported themselves and how gracefully the *Terry* moved. Until then the men had not taken any particular pride in their skills; rowing was something they did because they must. Now as they passed the clumsy xebec they became aware of themselves not just as rogues who happened to work a ship, but as seamen, by Allah.

Somewhere in the ranks a man began to sing. His song was taken up by the other men, the lusty male chorus keeping time with the sweeping of the oars and the beat of the drum. The song thrummed in Thorton's veins and he fancied the deck itself served as a great sounding board to magnify the voices and project them across the sea. The *Terry* swept past the *Sea Leopard* like a monarch of the seas passing a peasant. On board the xebec sailors in their motley colors stood at the rail and watched with sulky eyes.

Thorton on his poop deck felt like the king of the world. His heart was bursting with pride and pleasure at the beauty of his vessel. However, being the master of such a vessel carried heavy responsibilities and he must attend them. He turned away from the *Sea Leopard* and considered his own situation.

It was a very bad place for an invader. A narrow channel meandered among mud flats aplenty; to be stuck there was to be stuck under the guns of the stone fort that commanded the headland. Three guns saluted them with puffs of smoke. No wonder it had once been a thriving base for the Sallee rovers. It had excellent natural protection and was not far from the Pinch, as the rovers called the Strait of Gibraltar. Round ships had surpassed the galleys of the Middle Sea and nations that clung to such an antiquated way of going to sea were being left behind. Still, with her entrance silted up like that, Tanguel had no choice. She was a relic of the past.

The galiot made it safely into harbor. "Pass the word to Isam Rais. We have arrived."

Tangle and his wife came up to the poop deck. He was dressed in his French blue uniform and pantaloons, boots and sword, with a white turban on his head. His buttons and gold lace gleamed. The sky blue of his wife's silks fluttered around him. She clung to his elbow as if she would never let him go. He smiled at Thorton.

"I admit my curiosity got the better of me. I stood in the coach and watched. My compliments, rais." Tangle's baritone was warm and approving.

Thorton flushed a little. Had Tangle ventured onto the deck, he would have seen him—and so would the men. The older captain had kept out of sight on purpose.

"Thank you, sir," Thorton replied.

Tangle looked back. "Is the *Sea Leopard* aground again?"

"No, sir. She hasn't enough tide to get over the sandbar."

Tangle nodded. "It could be a good harbor if they'd ever dredge the damn thing. I'd love to strike at the Spanish Plate Fleet. Tanguel would be an excellent base. Tanger's a good one too, but 'tis in Spanish hands." He sighed.

Thorton looked at the town with its mud brick houses and faded whitewash. The fishing fleet was out and a pair of rotting galleys were dying on the beach. Two more were drawn up in good order, but they seemed deserted. He did not see any watches on them. The beach itself was a beautiful half-circle of tan sand. A small river carried fresh water down from the mountains. The land was high enough to be dry in most seasons, but there were marshes to the north where it became difficult to tell land from sea and channels might shift with a storm or even a good hard surf.

The biggest building was an old mosque. Its blue dome and minarets loomed over the town. Beside it was a library and a bathhouse. Other important buildings ranged about the square. The main road ran straight and broad from the harbor to the mosque. The biggest dock ran out from the foot of the road into the harbor. There were many empty places along the dock. The vessels were various small craft: feluccas and brigantines, demi-galleys, barques, and sloops. Off to the side was a dockyard where a galiot was up on stocks.

A crowd in dusty and faded colors lined the waterfront to see the strange vessel come in. The *Sea Leopard* had touched there before cruising the coast in search of Tangle; the people of the town had an air of suppressed excitement. When they recognized the blue figures on the poop deck, they burst out cheering. Tangle smiled and waved his hand, and his wife waved her hand, too. Sunlight flashed and glinted on her jewelry.

A man with a very large white turban, black vest and long white shirt was waiting at the end of the dock. He was flanked by soldiers and clerks. Thorton brought the galiot's larboard side along the end of the dock. Mooring lines were made fast. Thorton was the captain now, so he went to the weather deck and spoke to them over the rail. He had Kaashifa along to translate. It was a welcoming committee. No harbor fees would be charged; Isam Rais was a hometown boy and entitled to dock his vessel for free. There would be a banquet in his honor at the governor's palace on the morrow. The entire crew was invited. The man addressed Thorton very civilly but kept looking past him to the poop deck where Tangle and his wife were resplendent in blue and gold.

Thorton at last sent Kaashifa to fetch them. Now the official was truly delighted. There was a great deal of salaaming and bowing with his hand pressed to his turban to keep it from falling off when he bowed so low. Tangle smiled and accepted the honors with a gracious inclination of his head. Thorton had never seen a king, but he thought Tangle acted like one. The Tanguelis spoke Turkish mixed with Arabic; he heard 'Peter Rais' but very little else that he understood.

Tangle turned to him and explained. "This is my cousin Rahmat bin Sahm. He's the harbormaster here. He and his wife will host me and my wife. I expect you will want to stay with your vessel, Captain. I'll have our dunnage removed from your cabin as soon as the wagon arrives."

He made other introductions, but Thorton did not remember any of the names. Besides the harbormaster, there was his deputy, a health inspector, officers of the local militia, a representative from the palace, an imam, representatives from the merchants' and mariners' associations, and other functionaries, along with a number of Tangle's kinsmen and curiosity seekers.

Thorton stood erect and replied, "*Salaam*," whenever someone addressed him.

Tangle touched his sleeve. "Change that insignia before the banquet. 'Twill be a formal affair."

"Aye aye, sir. Shall we ask the harbormaster to send help to Kasim Rais?"

Tangle sucked his teeth thoughtfully. Then his eyes twinkled. "Aye. 'Twould be the gracious thing to do." Not to mention, it would infuriate Kasim.

The harbormaster nodded. "I will send lighters to take off part of his load. We will tow him over the sand bar."

That done Tangle and his wife went ashore. The harbormaster's deputy remained behind to loiter and gaze upon the sight of the victorious galiot. He addressed Thorton in polite Arabic, but Thorton understood only part of it. Kaashifa had to translate into Spanish for him.

"He wants to know if you took many prizes."

"Tell him Isam Rais took three. They are supposed to rendezvous with us here. A brig, a ship, and a snow." The harbormaster's deputy was burning with curiosity, but he maintained his dignity and conversed in slow Arabic with the midshipman. "You may talk to him as much as you please. I must tend the ship." Thorton stepped away.

The new captain was at something of a loss. He had helped a ship to get ready for sea without her captain on board, but never had he been responsible to bed her down. A momentary panic stitched through his breast. He took a deep breath to steady himself. What did Tangle want done with the crew? He had promised them liberty when they saved the galley in the Bay of Biscay, but Thorton was loathe to let any man go ashore; they needed the crew.

"Deputy harbormaster. I need to unload my captives. What shall we do with them?"

"We will take them to the prison," he replied.

That required a detachment of soldiers to be brought from the fort. The receipt for the prisoners had to be signed, which meant their roll had to be called. None of this was done with anything resembling speed. The soldiers strolled around the harbor from the fort to the dock and Thorton nearly went mad with waiting. They ported their arms sloppily—sloppily in the eyes of a naval officer accustomed to the brisk exactness of the British Marines. At last the prisoners were dispatched. Meanwhile, lighters unloaded what they could from the xebec, then towed her in. She came to the dock and took a berth near the shore. She had to back up, twist and turn, and try again. Kasim Rais used the 'bump and fidget' method of docking. Thorton wanted to strangle the man.

Turning his back on the *Sea Leopard,* he saw square sails beyond the headland. The stranger fired a single gun in acknowledgment of the fort's flag and received a single gun in response.

Thorton pulled out his glass and studied the vessel a while. "Maynard! He can't get that snow in here!"

As they watched, the snow slowed and stopped. Twenty minutes later, it crept forward about a fathom and stopped again. The harbormaster's deputy called to his boats and they went out to meet her. A few minutes later they returned empty handed. They explained that the boy captain was heaving casks over the side to lighten the load. His boats were shepherding them into a group and lashing them together to form rafts. It took all afternoon for enough of the hogsheads to be jettisoned to raise the vessel. When at last she was light enough, she glided slowly over the sandbar. She towed the rafts behind her. Her boats tended the rafts to keep them from fouling.

Slowly she came into Tanguel's harbor with her men straining at her sweeps. The sun was sinking in the west behind her and turned her topsails to orange. Maynard released his rafts, then neatly put his snow into the dock. He moved slowly and carefully. The snow had only four sweeps, but he used them to turn her until she was properly lined up. He eased into her berth and her sailors leaped to the dock to secure her mooring lines. Her crew finished by flemishing the lines. Tangle preferred the lines on his vessel to be off the deck with their coils neatly pinned, but either way was a seamanly way. By contrast, the *Sea*

Leopard's lines were whichever way they happened to be left. Some coiled, some not, some on deck, some in a heap, some lashed to the pinrail. Thus the personalities of the various captains could be read at a glance.

Thorton sent his own people to help break up the rafts and haul the casks out of the water. They needed to use the yardarms and antennas as cranes to lift the hogsheads. Leaving Kaashifa on the quarterdeck, he descended to the dock and went over to look up at the boy officer on the snow's quarterdeck. The snow was a high-sided vessel compared to the lateeners, so Thorton had to strain his neck.

"What on earth have you got in there anyhow?" he called in English.

"Tobacco," Maynard replied. He was very tired and his face was ashen. He leaned heavily on his crutches.

"That will sell," Thorton replied. It was not an especially valuable commodity, but it was certainly marketable. "I'll send word to Tangle that you're here. He's at his cousin's house. There's a fancy dinner for us at the palace tomorrow, so get a good rest and wear your best uniform."

Maynard raised his hand wearily in an approximation of a salute. "Aye aye, sir."

"Maynard. Well done." Thorton returned the salute smartly.

"Thank you, sir." A smile crossed the boy's weary face.

CHAPTER 35 : MAP OF GLORY

The whole palace was very grand but in a state of decay. It had been built in the heyday of the corsairs when fleets of galleys brought home argosies of wealth. Now they were living in their own shadow. It was not that they had diminished, but that the nations of Europe had grown past them. The Sallee Republic didn't know that it was in decline; the increasing wealth of Europe meant that the prizes the corsairs brought home were big and rich. Thus the elite lived in wealth, oblivious to their own inferiority. By Sallee standards Tanguel was a large and prosperous town of at least ten thousand people, but it was divided between rich and poor, and the rich were not as rich as they imagined themselves to be, in spite of their opulence.

Life moved at a slower cadence, even compared to the sluggish French of the Atlantic coast. It was not due to the greater heat. It was early summer and the stultifying heat had not yet come to oppress them. Thorton recognized the feeling. He had had it himself. It was the sluggish despair of people who were aware that somehow they did not belong in the world which they inhabited, and that their best efforts were insufficient to bring them the rewards they ardently desired. They had no idea how to slip the bonds of tradition, traditions that had once served them well but which now held them back. This was the country of which he would become a citizen, the country for which he would fight and perhaps give his life. No wonder they fought for money and religion. Home failed to inspire.

For Tangle, the miasma was even more pronounced. When he was a boy Tanguel was in decline, but it had not been obvious to a child. Now Fezakh just over the border in Morocco was prospering and Tanguel was becoming a sleepy byway. Zokhara had long been the capital of the nation, gifted as it was with a good, deep harbor and an easy strike at the wealth of the Middle Sea. Yet Tangle had rowed a Spanish galley along the western coast of Europe for two years and he had seen that the Atlantic traffic was very great. America across the sea was sending her riches to England, France, and Spain. The *Santa Teresa de Ávila's* fleet number had been 121, and she was neither first nor last in the Spanish navy. The entire coast of Sallee could not raise even a third that number of warships.

As for Thorton, even the Spanish coast seemed quaintly backwards compared to the densely populated towns and coasts of southern

England. Had Tanguel been in England, there would have been mills all along the riverbank with bustling barges hauling raw materials to feed them. Coal fires would have sent dark smudges of smoke to hang in a pall over the city and the pace of life would have hummed with energy. Perhaps he would invest his prize money in a woolen mill with machinery imported from England. There was a spot above the old Roman bridge that might be suitable. With plenty of sheep in the country a small woolen mill would be just the thing to make a small fortune. So he daydreamed because he could not understand most of the speeches and toasts even when they were in his honor. He simply smiled and raised his glass when everyone else did.

Tangle was given the post of honor, a seat on a divan in the courtyard opposite the Bey of Tanguel, an aging gentleman with snow white hair and beard, a large belly, very rich robes and a large white turban. He was flanked by a dozen or more sons, viziers, and officers. Tangle was flanked by Thorton, Foster, and Maynard. Other officers were seated on cushions nearby. Kasim Rais and several local captains were the centers of their own coteries of officers and attendants. Black and white eunuchs waited on them. The food was never-ending and dancing boys entertained them to the sound of Arab lutes and flutes. Tangle was obliged to regale them with the tale of his escape, the capture of the galleys, and the capture of the prizes. The crowd was very pleased to hear that two more prizes would rendezvous at Tanguel.

Eventually Tangle got off his divan and excused himself for the trip to the necessary. He was gone a very long time. Thorton began to wonder what had happened to him. He was also tired of trying to converse in a language of which he had little knowledge. Some of the corsairs spoke Spanish or French, but mostly he was just plain tired. He excused himself and strolled through the cloisters with their horseshoe arches, looking in the open doors and windows. Eventually he found Tangle.

The corsair was standing before a great and ancient map set in mosaic in the wall. It was an old map and it showed the city of Salé as the center of the world. The British Isles were at the very top of the map. Thorton stepped up to study it. England seemed very far away. Strangely, he was not homesick.

Tangle heard him and turned around. "Peter Rais! I didn't hear you come in."

Thorton stepped forward. *"Isam Rais, salaam."* He pointed up at England. "What is that?"

Tangle smiled. "Your country."

Thorton slipped off his shoes and dragged a hassock over. It was the sort of furniture known as an 'ottoman' at home. He climbed up. "No. This." He touched the map. "Galleys pulled up on an English shore, that's what it is. I cannot read the name. 'Tis Arabic."

Tangle was tall enough to stand on tiptoe to read it. He pronounced the name and explained, "That means 'Moor's Beach.'"

"Moor's beach? Moorshead! I know where that is!" He peered at the map and found more galleys. "That must be Penzance, and this is Bournemouth and that is Landsea!" He marveled. "Galleys on the beaches of England!"

"A hundred years ago we were great mariners, Peter. We raided from the Canary Islands to Iceland. Many towns in England, France and Spain made us welcome." He tapped the map. "My father told me that in the old days there might be twenty galleys pulled up on the sands of an English beach. Some of your dark-haired Englishmen are blood of our blood—you cannot give six thousand sailors shore leave and expect them to remain chaste." He smiled at Thorton.

"Shore leave! Don't they desert?"

Tangle laughed. "Men don't desert gold, Peter. Victorious captains don't have any trouble recruiting and keeping a crew." Then he sobered. "Now we don't get farther than Eel Buff and rarely that. Gabir Rais is accounted a great captain by present standards. Even Kasim imagines that he is a mighty corsair." His mouth twisted.

Thorton moved his hassock to peer at a new part of the map. He found galleys on both coasts of France and Spain, islands in the Middle Sea, the coasts of Italy, and more. A Turkish fleet commanded the eastern Mediterranean. The Atlantic Ocean was studded with lateen sails.

Tangle stared at the map with a long face. He stepped next to Thorton and traced the northern coast of Sallee with his finger. "Look. Tanger and Sebta are Muslim on this map." Tanger guarded the western approach to the Strait of Gibraltar while Sebta was right at the tip of Africa and commanded the Pinch. "They say you can see all the way across the Pinch into the harbor of Gibraltar from the hills of Sebta. I wonder if it is true. Sebta has been in Spanish hands all my life."

A soft footfall entered the room. They turned to look. The new arrival was as tall as Thorton but with a slender build. He had curly black hair and a beard with a few strands of white in it, although he looked to be in his early thirties. He had a hooked nose and intense brown eyes. He wore a Turkish coat of elaborate brocade above dark blue pantaloons. The coat's overall color was oxblood, but it was covered in a pattern of arabesques in jewel-like tones. His feet were thrust into leather slippers decorated with jewels. His turban was dark blue around a dark red fez. A large brooch studded with precious stones was fixed to the front of it.

"*Isam Rais. Peter Rais. Salaam.*" The man spoke Arabic in a tenor voice with a clear and pleasant diction.

Thorton had met a great many of the local dignitaries. He could not remember which one this was. Fortunately, Tangle did. "Zahid Amir. Peace be upon you and yours." Tangle bowed deeply to the man, so Thorton bowed too. Then he climbed down from the hassock and put his shoes on.

Lord Zahid walked forward. He paused to look Thorton up and down, then he said in excellent English, "I have heard you are looking for a surgeon for your vessel, rais. As it happens, I am a doctor. I trained at Cambridge."

Thorton was astonished. He responded in English, "I am very pleased to hear it, sir."

Tangle was curious and feeling a bit left out, so he moved closer. "Do you seek a berth, my lord?" It took him a moment to assemble the English sentence.

"Perhaps. It is more accurate to say that I am seeking a man, rather than a position."

Tangle looked to Thorton to make sure he had understood the English correctly. Thorton translated into Spanish for him. "What sort of man?" the corsair asked.

Lord Zahid walked up to the wall. He stood staring up at the map of past greatness with his hands clasped behind his back. His carriage was very alert and unlike the fatalistic and casual slouch of so many of his countrymen. He turned around and spoke English again. "An energetic man."

Thorton glanced at Tangle who glanced back. They drew nearer. "We're interested," Tangle replied.

"Tanger lies within my father's satrapy. He's an old man, a good man, a man who has grown accustomed to the burdens of fate. But I have been to England, and France, too." He switched to French, "*Parlez-vous français, gentilhommes?*" They allowed that they did. The conversation continued in that language. Thorton spoke it better than Tangle spoke English, and Lord Zahid spoke it better than either of them.

"Spain has suffered her first great defeat. Now is the time to make alliances with the nations of Europe who are enemies of Spain and cast her towers from our shores. If we can do that, why not take Granada too? The French from the northeast, the English from the northwest, and the Portuguese will revolt in the west. Spain will be dismembered. The obscene riches of her American mines will no longer flow into Spanish coffers. Who is perfectly placed to replace her as the arbiter of the Middle Sea and Atlantic trade? Sallee. We occupy exactly the same place, with the same merits of climate and position as she does. We are her mirror image."

It was a grand, impossible plan. But a noble vision. Tangle could see it. He had his doubts, but he could see it.

Thorton was a good deal more skeptical. He said cautiously, "Evicting the Spaniards from Sallee would be an excellent step, but money, sir. Where is the money to raise a navy and an army going to come from?"

"Spain herself. We shall raid her, but instead of dispersing the money as prizes, we will pile it up in a great war chest."

"The corsairs won't stand for it," Tangle pointed out.

"That is why we must have a navy. The corsairs must be promised preferment, of course. Estates and offices, pomp and honors. We must make gentlemen and officers of them. Is that not how your English navy operates, Peter Rais?"

"Aye, sir. However, it is supported by a prodigious amount of money from Parliament. It does not support itself. England is a well-populated and prosperous country. Our American colonies supply us with raw materials, which our manufacturing establishments turn into finished goods and sell back. I admit I have not been here long, but I have not seen much industry in your country. "

Zahid paced away from the map, then turned to look at it. "It is as you say, rais. I have introduced English methods of mining and that has improved our output. We produce a great deal of copper and I have no doubt that we could produce iron, too. Sadly, our timber is in want. We must go far into the interior to get timber suitable for ships and the Zouave tribesmen are not friendly. Some of them are still pagans."

Thorton said, "Our colonies are in great want of iron and copper and other metals, but they supply excellent timber, hemp, pitch, and other naval supplies. I meant to say, the English colonies do." He flushed to remember that he was no longer English so they were no longer 'our' colonies.

Lord Zahid wagged a finger at him. "England will not let anyone trade with her colonies unless they touch first in England and pay duty. When they arrive in the colonies, they must pay duty again. It is a slow and expensive way to do business. We must break it open."

"Smuggling is rampant among them, sir. My father was an American smuggler."

Tangle threw him a sharp look, having never heard anything about his father before.

Thorton's mind was beginning to work. "I do believe it would please the Americans to do business directly with you, since it would make the goods cheaper to them while allowing you a greater profit. The Chesapeake Bay is shallow with many winding roads and islands. It is a smuggler's paradise."

Tangle was listening intently to this. "Smuggling is a dangerous business, but it pays well. It takes a fast, agile ship, one that can defend herself. However, she must carry cargo instead of men, so it is better if she not come to grips with the enemy."

"Your galleys are not that kind of vessel. You will need schooners and ships," Thorton replied.

"We need xebecs," Tangle replied with conviction. "I admit you have no reason to be impressed with them so far, but that is because the *Sea Leopard* is ill-handled and has been poorly treated. Lord Zahid, I wonder if you could do me a favor?"

Lord Zahid inclined his head. "If I can, I will."

"I want my vessel back. Kasim has it." He deliberately omitted 'rais.' "How the Spaniards let a Muslim buy her, I don't know. Shakil Effendi must have arranged it through intermediaries. I want her back. Can you help?"

Lord Zahid began walking around the room in deep thought. "Where did he get the money?"

"He borrowed it from all and sundry. He has investors. My wife and Murad Rais included."

"Then she must call a meeting of the shareholders and put it to a vote. The shareholders own the vessel and choose its captain."

"I don't want to be beholden to the shareholders. I want to own it, free and clear, as I did in the days before."

Zahid studied him. "I will buy it and give it to you, but only if you will accept the position of *Kapitan Pasha* of Tanguel and throw the Spaniards out of Tanger."

A slow smile grew on Tangle's face. "Done."

Lord Zahid turned to Thorton. "What about you, Peter Rais. Will you sail under the Tangueli flag?"

"I go where Isam Rais goes," Thorton replied. "It would give me great pleasure to wage honorable war against the Spanish for the liberation of Tanger."

Lord Zahid smiled. "Excellent. Call on me at eight of the clock in the morning and we will establish the Tangueli navy."

CHAPTER 36 : THE WINDS AS GOOD NEWS

Zahid Amir, son of the Bey of Tanguel, had a powerful vision but almost nothing to build it on. He had Tangle, his reputation, and three galleys. There was little that they could accomplish on their own, so they must run the Spanish blockade of the Strait of Gibraltar to Zokhara and solicit the aid of the much larger and better funded force there. But there was one matter on which Tangle put his foot down.

"You must dredge the mouth of the harbor." Tangle and Thorton were sitting cross-legged on divans. Lord Zahid sat on the divan across from them with the skirts of his long Turkish coat spread around him. The sandalwood windows opened on the cloister and let in the breeze and sun. It was a very agreeable room.

Lord Zahid hesitated. "I have spoken about this with my father. He says that if the harbor is dredged the Spaniards will attack us here. As long as they cannot get big ships into the harbor, we are safe." The conversation was in French as usual with the three of them.

"Nonsense," Thorton replied. "If you float a navy they must attack you because you menace them."

"We are not ready to withstand such an attack."

"Then you must make ready," Thorton replied. "Improve the fort, draft troops, stockpile supplies. Dredge the harbor. Tanger is in the hands of the enemy and Salé City is dead and buried. Exactly where do you plan to establish your Arsenal if not here?"

"Well, I—It costs money. A great deal of money."

Tangle said, "Then you must dredge the harbor. Do you have any idea how difficult it is to bring prizes into Tanguel? Most of the corsairs pass you by to send their prizes into Fezakh instead. How many prizes has your prize court seen this year?"

"I don't know."

"I don't either, but I can tell not many because the snow generated quite a lot of excitement. She's just a tobacco merchant. A good solid prize, but nothing out of the ordinary. Look you, we can probably get the brig in by lightening her, too, but the ship will never make it. The ship is the best prize and she's going to Fezakh. The Sultan of Morocco will get the share your father ought to have. That sandbar isn't very big and the channel isn't very wide. We can clear that in a few days if we work. It will be sufficient to float the brig in. When the brig sails into the harbor, that will prove that it is feasible. Then you can undertake the necessary work to widen and deepen the channel to let ships in."

"It isn't just the channel, the harbor is silted too."

"Then dredge!" Thorton replied in exasperation.

"It will silt up again. In ten years we'll have to dredge again."

"Then find what is causing the silting and put a stop to it," Thorton snapped back.

"It is Allah's handiwork," Zahid replied.

"I hardly think so. In England I have noticed that when fields run up to the streams, they erode quite badly, but in forests it is not so. Tanguel has no forests. Plant trees along the edges of streams and forbid the fields to come right down to them."

Tangle was keenly interested. "There were trees, my father told me when I was a boy, but they were all cut to build ships. The river used to run deep and clear. It was navigable above the old Roman bridge."

"If you want a navy," Thorton expostulated, "then you must order your affairs on land to support it. How you can retake Granada if you are unwilling to defend your own home!"

The last argument told on Lord Zahid. "Yes, you are right. I have been entranced by the successes of the English navy without understanding how they were accomplished. I must study the matter further. Very well. I will order the dredging to begin immediately."

"I shall donate my share of the snow's prize money to the improvement of the harbor," Tangle said. Thorton gave him an alarmed look. Tangle said, "Don't worry. My share, as owner. The crew shall have their prize money to spend as they please. By the way, grant shore leave before we pay off. That way they won't run. They'll come back to the ship because they want their money."

"Aye aye, sir."

"All right," said Zahid. "Now that that is settled, let us move on to the matter of uniforms and insignia." He pulled out a sketch. "This is the uniform. Purple frock coats in the English style, white turbans, white shirts—waistcoats optional in the heat—buff trousers, and black boots."

Thorton stared in horror. Tangle studied the image. It was skillfully done, and he pondered it thoughtfully. "White facings? I think gold bars in the Turkish fashion would be better."

"This is the English way. 'Tis modern," Lord Zahid replied.

"We are not English and should be distinguished from such," Thorton replied tartly. Privately he thought this business of aping the English would make them look ridiculous. He was distracted by another fault in the design. "Falling collars? Those are for warrant officers! Commissioned officers need standing collars so their insignia shows!"

"Oh, is that why they do it?" Lord Zahid asked.

"Perhaps short coats trimmed in gold piping and no collar," Tangle mused.

"I am attempting to design a dignified uniform that will make us look like officers instead of tribesmen," Lord Zahid replied. "Do you want to look like a Zouave?"

"The petty officers will. We ought to at least look like we come from the same country."

"Long coats," Lord Zahid said doggedly. "Long coats, but you can have your gold bars."

"Do you really think purple is wise? The color is very dear," Thorton put in.

"The pantaloons are buff which is cheap enough."

"A midshipman can hardly afford a long coat of purple!"

"We-ell, perhaps we could put the midshipmen in jackets . . ." Zahid replied unwillingly.

Tangle had another objection. "Must we wear stocks? That's fine for the northern climates where they need to keep their necks warm, but we'll suffocate in the heat down here."

Thorton replied, "Of course we should wear stocks. All gentlemen do, regardless of the weather. You'll look like a common laborer if you don't."

"I have never worn a stock and I don't intend to start!" Tangle replied with considerable spirit.

Thorton was not as fluent in French, so he switched to Spanish to carry the debate. Tangle was equally strong in his opinion. Thus the Tangueli navy was very nearly sunk before it was even off the stocks.

Zahid didn't speak Spanish at all, but he understood the tone well enough. "Gentlemen, please!" he cried in Arabic. They stopped and mumbled apologies. Zahid produced a new sketch with the details changed except for the matter of the stock. They studied it.

"That's better," Tangle agreed. "It looks more Muslim now."

"Clearly, something must be worn at the throat. It looks odd without it," Thorton added.

"Well then. Let it be the officer's choice. A stock, a brooch, a cravat, a gorget, whatever he pleases. Then you can suffocate in your stock and I can be left in peace," Tangle suggested. The matter was settled.

A few days later, the officers gathered around the *Santa Teresa's* table in the captain's cabin—Thorton's cabin. They had their new uniforms. Maynard was quite pleased with his new outfit, but Foster wasn't pleased at all. They had their insignia, too, on standing collars. Tangle wore crossed scimitars and star for his rank as Captain of the Fleet while Thorton had crossed scimitars as a captain. Foster and Maynard each had a lieutenant's star. Midshipman Kaashifa had nothing to distinguish himself, but he was allowed to wear the standing collar with gold braid. Bellini fared worse, he had no uniform at all because there was no Bellini present. The brig had not come in.

"Why did it have to be purple?" Foster wanted to know. He was back in his spot as first lieutenant. His ship had come in a day after Maynard. Or, more correctly, she had hove to off of Tanguel and her boat came in. The harbor was in no way fit to receive her. The prize court of Tanguel, unwilling to let such a prize (and its share for their coffers) be taken to Morocco, had convened on board. The cargo was taken off in lighters and the ship assigned to a sailing master and agent (another one of Tangle's cousins) to take and sell in Fezakh. Foster would follow Tangle anywhere, even the assault on Tanger, but that did not mean he was willing to wear purple while doing it.

Thorton rounded on him. "Leave the purple be."

"That's all very well for you to say, Thorton. You're blond. You look all right in purple, but I look terrible." Foster was a redhead and starting to go grey. It was not a good color for him. "Blue is better. Anyone looks good in blue."

"I don't," Tangle said.

"Then why did you wear it?"

"Blue is my favorite color."

"Shouldn't we be talking about Bellini and the brig? He's awfully late. What if he doesn't show up?" Maynard asked.

That three grown men should be reminded of more important matters by a fifteen-year old boy shamed them. They looked abashed, shuffled feet, and cleared throats.

"Exactly so, Mr. Maynard," said Tangle. "He's five days late. The galleys and the sloop will be ready shortly. We leave in three days, with or without him. We will just have to hope he made it into Fezakh. My agent there will send us word if he did."

"Is the xebec coming with us?" Thorton asked.

"I think so. Jamila has persuaded Kasim that we need his protection for our convoy." Tangle's lip curled in displeasure.

Maynard snorted. Foster huffed. Thorton was stiff. None of them liked the way they had to pander to Kasim's vanity.

Tangle looked around at them. "How in the hell did I wind up with a pack of *ferenghi* for my officers?" With Bellini absent it was a mostly white officer corps.

"I'm not, sir," Kaashifa reminded him. He was a swarthy man in his late twenties. The hair that had been shorn to his skull had grown just long enough to twist every which way and refuse to lie flat without being able to form into the curls that were its natural habit.

"Which reminds me. I have nominations for the midshipmen's berths, sir," Thorton said.

"Let's have them. Any Muslims among them?"

"Mr. Nazim. Age twenty-four, a Moor and a Muslim. The other candidates are Mr. Arellano and Mr. Gamarra."

"Excellent. Make a midshipman of Mr. Nazim. Now tell me about the other two."

Thorton was silent for a long while. "Sir, am I captain of the *Santa Teresa?*"

"Of course you are."

"Is it not generally the captain's duty in Sallee to select the officers and crew?"

A tense silence fell. Tangle drummed his fingers on the table top. As a corsair he had made his own officers as it pleased him. As the Captain of Corsairs he had called other captains to sail with him. Those who wished to join him answered, but they brought their own ships and officers with them. It was their prerogative. He could not dictate to them. Now that he was the owner and not the captain, the prerogatives diverged.

"Peter Rais, as the owner of the *Santa Teresa,* I have certain expectations. Therefore I would appreciate it if you would oblige me in the matter of the officers."

Thorton set his jaw. "Aye aye, sir."

Foster had known Tangle a very long time. He'd even been chained next to him in the galley. He dared to interject, "What about Bellini?"

"He's late. The galley needs another midshipman, not to mention, another a lieutenant," Tangle replied.

"You know nothing of Nazim's qualities," Foster persisted.

Tangle barked, "Peter Rais. Is Nazim qualified? I cannot think you would have brought his name to me if he were unfit for duty."

"He is qualified, sir," Thorton replied.

"That settles it. If you bring me qualified candidates you have no cause to complain when I select one of them."

"Aye aye, sir," Thorton replied woodenly. He was thinking dark thoughts about being a captain in name only. How was he to get out of the notorious corsair's shadow and distinguish himself as a captain in his own right? The men would be constantly looking to Tangle to validate his orders.

"Now then. Whom do you recommend for the remaining midshipman's berth?"

"I'd like Arrellano, if it pleases you, sir," Thorton replied.

"Make it so. If Bellini shows up, I'll examine him for lieutenant. If he passes, you'll have a proper number of lieutenants. If he doesn't pass, I'll examine the others. If none of them pass, you'll be short a lieutenant and have to select one of the midshipmen as the acting third lieutenant. It should motivate them to study."

"Aye aye, sir." Thorton's expression was sour.

Maynard had a question. "Won't the Dey be annoyed that you have raised your own fleet? Isn't he your king?"

Tangle shook his head. "Not exactly. The various satrapies, military units, naval units, merchants, landholders, religious authorities, and tribal leaders have their representatives that sit on the Divan. They elect the Dey. Usually one of their own number. You might say he is first among equals. Getting them to agree to anything is difficult. The naval interests are the strongest, so they usually prevail in the discussions. During the winter, policies and plans are made for the coming year. During the summer, those plans are carried out by the bureaucrats. Each of the satrapies is largely independent, but pays tribute and receives protection from Zokhara, the capital. The Sallee Republic in turn pays tribute to the Sublime Porte in Istanbul and receives protection. In truth, we pay tribute and get drafted into the Turkish navy, which is why the Sallee navy has been allowed to fall into such a decline. 'Tis better to be a corsair than drafted into the Turkish navy."

"Can the Sublime Porte draft us, too?" Maynard asked.

Tangle had to think about that. Finally he said, "No. We are corsairs. The Governor of Tanguel can draft us, but Tanguel is in turn the tributary of Zokhara, not the Sultan in Istanbul. Thus the Sultan cannot call us up directly. He can only call on the Dey of Sallee. The Dey in turns calls up those that are obliged to him and so fulfills the Sultan's demand. So he could call on Tanguel, and Tanguel could call on us. Yet even if I was called to the Sultan's service, I wouldn't go. Besides, the Dey wouldn't send me. I'm more valuable here."

Thorton asked, "Even though Murad Rais is the *Kapitan Pasha* of Zokhara? I think it would please him to send his rival to Istanbul and far away from Zokhara."

Tangle fell into a brown study. "I will have to discover the politics when I get there. I cannot think the Dey has totally forgotten me." He drummed his fingers on the table as he frowned, then rose. They rose with him. "Very well. I leave you to your duties, gentleman."

Thorton escorted him to the door and stepped into the passageway with him. "Sir. If I am a captain, pray let me be a captain." He kept his voice low so that the other officers would not hear.

Tangle kept his voice low as well. "You are inexperienced when it comes to command and lateen vessels. Not to mention, your Arabic is inadequate."

Thorton replied calmly, "Then you should not have made a captain of me. If I am not qualified, I would rather be a lieutenant and have the time necessary to learn my duties and earn my promotion."

"Having made a captain of you, I cannot unmake you. That would look bad."

"It will look worse if you are constantly treating me like a lieutenant when I wear the crossed scimitars of a captain. You have made your decision. You must live with it. Stop undermining my authority." Thorton's eyes were grey as steel as he locked gazes with his superior officer.

Tangle did not answer for a while. Finally he said softly, "I want you to succeed, Peter." His voice was placating.

"I appreciate your advice and instruction in private, but I will issue orders to the ship and make decisions about the ship's operations. Your duty is to coordinate the squadron and to give the orders necessary to achieve the strategic goals. Do we agree?"

Tangle gave Thorton a bemused look. "We do. Very well, do you have any orders, Captain?" He kept his voice light, but there was an edge to it.

"I do. When you come aboard, you and Mistress Tangle may have the sailing master's berth. I will keep the captain's cabin. I realize it will inconvenience you, but you shall have to live with it. The men naturally presume that whoever occupies the captain's cabin is in charge."

Brown eyes flared as Tangle stared back at Thorton. "'Tis customary for the vessel's owner to have the best cabin."

"It is customary for the most commodious vessel to receive the master of the fleet. That would be the *Sea Leopard*."

"You know Kasim will not receive me."

"That is not my problem. My problem is how to instill respect for my authority on my ship."

Tangle's eyes were snapping but he whirled away and paced a few steps. Thorton stood stiffly. He ought to have been afraid of Tangle's temper, but he wasn't. He knew in his gut that he was right. Why was Tangle angry?

Pride. Tangle had given up his right to command when he made Thorton captain, but he still longed to command. Kasim and the other corsairs could not be ordered, they could only be lead, cajoled, wheedled, and suggested. Once upon a time men would have done as he wished simply because he wished it. He had had that much influence. But that was before a Spanish galley had broken his reputation and politics had passed him by. He must prove himself all over again.

Thorton walked over to him and put a hand on his shoulder. "Isam," he said softly. "You know I am right."

"I do. But that does not make it any easier."

"If you let me be a captain, it will be easier for you to be a commodore. You cannot direct your energies properly if you are always worrying about me. I won't let you down."

Tangle drew in a breath and squared his shoulders. He straightened as much as he could beneath the low deckhead. "Aye. Very well. I will take the sailing master's cabin."

Just then the thin nasal voice of a man calling the faithful prayer sounded right over their heads. "*Hayya alassalah. Hayya alassalah.* Come to prayer. Come to prayer. *Hayya alal-Falah. Hayya alal-Falah.* Come to success. Come to success. *Allahu Akbar. Allahu Akbar.* God is great. God is great."

A chill went up Thorton's spine. Come to success. He looked around the coach, out onto the deck, at his ship and crew, and back to Tangle, his commanding officer. Was this not success? Had he not grown as a man and officer these last few weeks? Tangle had made it happen. Bishop might have forced him to train his fortitude but never his abilities. Thorton owed Tangle a great deal. Suddenly he saw things in reverse perspective: it was not he who had rescued Tangle, it was Tangle who had rescued him.

He smiled and softly said, "Come to success, Isam."

Tangle relaxed and nodded. "To success," he replied. He went out on the deck.

Thorton lingered a moment. He could see Tangle join the men around a bucket of water, slowly passing his hands over one another, washing his face and ears in the prescribed manner. He noticed the way the man didn't hurry, the graceful, almost dance-like motions of the ablution. Tangle loved the ritual and he was grateful to his God. The God of the Muslims was the same as the God of the Jews and Christians, and He accepted prayers in all languages. They were all

People of the Book. Of this Thorton was certain. He went out on deck and joined the congregation.

The man leading the prayer recited a few verses from the Qur'an. "And He it is Who made the night a covering for you, and the sleep a rest, and He who made the day to rise up again. He it is Who sends the winds as good news before His mercy; and He sends down pure water from the cloud, That He may give life thereby to a dead land and give it for drink, out of what He has created, to cattle and many people."

"*Ameen,*" Thorton answered.

"*Ameen,*" the men chorused with him.

CHAPTER 37 : THE BATTLE FOR TANGER

The *Santa Teresa de Ávila* and her consorts sailed north then east into the Pinch. Kasim Rais had consented to travel in convoy with them, but he ran far ahead and snapped up a slog-bottomed snow to send into Fezakh—he would not send her into Tanguel even if she could have made the sandbar at high tide. Tangle hoped he'd get himself killed but not lose the xebec. It was a complicated thing to wish for and required some very exact wording in his prayers to make certain Allah understood what was wanted.

They put their heads into Tanger and saw very little force there—Spain had called everything she had home to fight the French. The main fort was on the height and commanded the entrance and had a good view of the sea approach. The lower fort was on the end of the mole that improved the harbor. The fort fired on them and they retreated. They made a show of sailing past Tanger, but once they were out of sight of the headland, they hove to until dark.

Tangle knew something about the area, so he put the landing party ashore at the mouth of a stream. Under cover of darkness Thorton and his marines climbed the stream bed to its spring just below the summit. A path lead from the fort to the spring; the path was very clear. They crept quietly along it until they could see the fort. The land wall was not very high. All the guns pointed out to the sea. The top of the hillside had all its trees cut down for a hundred yards around the fort. Creeping through the woods, Thorton distributed his men according to plan.

Thorton and his petty officers were dressed in Spanish uniforms taken from the galleys. Thorton even had a cocked hat with ostrich feathers and gold lace around the brim. His sword—good Toledo steel —had made its previous owner very proud. The ordinary men were dressed in white shirts, dark blue breeches and short blue jackets. They had their checked kerchiefs over their heads instead of turbans. He had selected men who knew how to stand up straight and march in formation, more or less.

"Columns of two," he whispered. They formed on the road just below the crest, then at his command, marched brazenly along the road, over the crest, and into sight of the fort. Thorton's heart was hammering in his chest. It had sounded simple enough. Storm the fort. Overwhelm the guard. Turn the guns on the other fort.

The rear wall was about twelve feet high and very thick. A dry moat ran around its base. A pair of sentries looked down in astonishment. Thorton summoned up his best Castilian Spanish and bellowed, "Reinforcements for the fort! Open up!"

That caused general consternation among the Spanish. No password had been assigned because none was expected to be needed. This required the commandant to be roused from bed. Meanwhile the rovers waited as patiently as they could manage, but they were not marines. The lines began to unwind as some of the men fidgeted. Thorton heard the rattle of equipment and turned around and yelled in Spanish, "Order in the ranks, you misbegotten sons of French whores!"

Up above a dozen men hung over the edge of the parapet to try and see what the fuss was all about. The white crosses on their red hats made excellent targets and more than one Salletine longed to put a musket ball through them, but restrained themselves. Thorton was heartened; if only a dozen men were on duty tonight the fort's garrison must be very small.

"Who are you?" The officer of the guard called down.

"What? I can't hear you," Thorton replied.

"Who—are—you!" the man bellowed back.

"Teniente Don Diego Arrellano y Menéndez of His Most Catholic Majesty's galley *Santa Teresa de Ávila,*" Thorton replied, hitting the lisp on the 'z' and rolling his 'rr' to perfection, but not loud enough to be clearly heard.

"What? I can't hear you."

"What?" Thorton replied as if he couldn't hear either.

Inside the commandant came to the door in his nightshirt and breeches. "Oh, for God's sake. Open the door and ask them who they are."

The drawbridge dropped. Thorton advanced onto it with his men at his heels. When the gate opened, Thorton shot the first man he saw and rushed the breach. The men inside were taken by surprise so Thorton lived, but the man after him was shot in the face and killed. Thorton ran through the gateway as fast as he could go, screaming in Spanish. Men running up did not know who he was at first and were beguiled by the Spanish words, "Go back, get your weapons!" No effective defense was made at the gate.

His marines poured through the gap behind him. There was more shooting; Thorton felt a ball go whizzing past his ear. With all attention on the gate, the sentries did not see the bulk of the troops rush across the field with their scaling ladders made of saplings, throw them up, and climb the walls. The scimitars and cutlasses cut down the guards as they were firing into the interior of the fort. Thorton kept moving; a moving target was harder to hit. His Spanish sword was in his hand and he swung it wildly, slashing a man in the throat. A gush of his foe's blood splattered his coat. He was glad he wasn't wearing his own uniform. Bloodstains were hard to get out.

The fort proved to have only about fifty men in it. After a sharp but brief action, it was his.

"Get the drawbridge up!" Thorton bellowed. "Man those guns!"

The sound of gunfire woke the town. The guards in the lower fort were shocked when the high fort began to fire on them. Meanwhile, the galleys, having heard the gunfire, raced to assault the mole. They fired their bow guns to little effect against the solidly built fortress, but the fortress did not reply. The defenders were busy cowering under cover.

The galleys ran their prows ran over the mole and held their place thanks to the oars. Tangle ordered his men across. The men from their consorts ran up onto the mole without opposition. Men threw up grappling hooks and scaling ladders to assault the walls of the fort.

"Bring the bomb!" Tangle called.

The bomb was a keg of black powder with a short fuse. It was placed against the gate and the men retreated around the corners of the fortress. A moment later, the keg blew. Tangle and his men charged through the smoke and the shattered door into the gateway itself. The portcullis blocked their way. Guardsmen in the gatehouse pointed their weapons down through the loopholes in the floor and fired them. The men trapped in the small space heaved at the portcullis and raised it an inch.

"You can't raise it from here! Out!" Tangle called. They retreated, carrying their wounded with them. They flattened against the walls outside the gate. More men went up the ladders and the sound of shots came from inside.

Meanwhile, Thorton's party was doing a terrible job of bombarding the mole fort. Balls were flying everywhere to pepper the interior of the for, but none of them was doing much actual damage. Thorton cursed roundly in English, then aimed the guns himself.

"Aim for the gate, ye damn dogs!" Thorton bellowed at them. His men were jumping out of their skins with excitement. Somebody dropped a cannonball and it went rolling away. Thorton put a heavy hand on the man's shoulder.

"Breathe, man. Breathe." The sailor gulped in a deep breath and nodded. Thorton let him go.

The assaulting force gained the walls of the mole fort. A small party ran down the steps and fought their way into the gatehouse. They cranked the wheel and raised the portcullis. Tangle heard it creaking and ducked his head around to look. Seeing it rise, he shouted, "Come on men!" He charged into the gatehouse and threw himself on the ground to roll under the partially raised gate. More men followed him.

More cannonballs were crashing into the fort. Thorton had finally got his range and windage. It would be intolerable to be killed by friendly fire, so Tangle hastily ran up to the parapet and waved a white flag.

On the hill Thorton barked. "Cease fire." The guns stopped. "Reload and run out, but hold your fire."

Inside the fort Tangle bellowed, "Lay down your arms!"

A shutter opened and a Spanish voice shouted, "Who are you?"

Tangle grinned and bellowed back, "Sallee rovers! We claim this city in the name of the Bey of Tanguel!"

"What are your terms?"

"Throw down your weapons, depart, and never return!"

So the Spaniards threw their guns out the windows, then the commandant came out in his breeches and shirt. He was barefoot, having barely had time to put his pants on when the firing started. Tangle descended from the parapet and accepted his sword and parole. The occupants of the fort trooped out in disorder.

Tangle put a force into the mole fort to hold it, then returned to the galleys. They rowed into the harbor with their bow guns bristling. Some of the citizens were hastily packing up carts and donkeys to flee into the countryside. Others were burying their silver in the garden or hiding their daughters in attics. The mayor came down to the waterfront under a flag of truce to parley. He had several other men with him. They were older men, portly and well fed, grey haired and respectable. They had even dressed properly, although very modestly to disguise their wealth.

The *Terry* came along side the dock and bumped gently. Oars backed and spilled, and she held her place. Tangle walked out onto the prow with his scimitar in hand. He'd bought it while in Tanguel.

"What are your terms, Sir Corsair?" the mayor asked.

"Fifty thousand sequins, or we fire the city. Deliver it by dawn. Any gold or silver, whether bullion or jewelry, are acceptable. The Spanish officials and all military personnel must submit to Islam and swear allegiance to the Sallee Republic, or be exiled and their goods forfeited. Civilians will not be molested unless they molest us first."

"Who are you?"

Tangle grinned down at him. "Isam Rais Tangueli, *Kapitan Pasha* of Tanguel."

The name made the man drop his jaw. "I thought you were captive in a Spanish galley!"

"Two months ago I was. Now I am in your front yard. Will you submit?"

"We accept your generous terms. If we convert to Islam and swear allegiance will we be allowed to keep our property?"

"Aye. We will occupy you in good order."

"And our positions in government?"

"Yes, if you swear obedience to the Bey of Tanguel and submit yourself to his authority."

"If we don't convert?"

"You will pack up and leave the city immediately, taking whatever movable property you can carry, but forfeiting the rest. You will not be allowed to take any Muslims with you. If you behave yourselves, you will not be molested and your women and children will be safe. Raise a hand against us, and I will cry 'Havoc' and turn the corsairs loose on Tanger. They are eager for blood and booty."

The man made up his mind very quickly. "I testify that there is no God but Allah and Mohammed is his prophet."

"Excellent," replied Tangle. A conversion made under such terms wasn't valid and Tangle knew it. But that was a religious point. The imams could separate the sincere from the faithless when they arrived. The submission of the city was a political point, and he had gained it with remarkably little loss of life.

Tangle kept his men under control. There was no pillage or rape, to the great disappointment of some of the rovers. Tangle sent his agents to demand the names of the burghers who had fled to the hills, then let the rovers break open and loot their houses. Afterwards the houses were set on fire, hastening the cooperation of the others. The ransom was delivered by dawn. When light revealed how few the corsairs were, the mayor and aldermen regretted not making a defense, but the burning of more than a dozen houses warned them what the price would have been if they had tried it.

Tangle collected his men from the mole fort and set a fuse to the magazine. They piled into the galleys and rowed away but not quickly enough. The *Santa Teresa* was peppered with debris from the explosion.

Thorton did the same to the hill fort, but being further away from the city he could carry it out with more leisure. His men were safely in the trees before the fort's powder magazine blew. An hour later the galleys beached and picked up Thorton and his men. Casualties were only seven men killed and twenty-seven wounded. They laughed heartily, except for Maynard, who hadn't been allowed to take part in either landing party. Still, fifty thousand sequins in mixed objects and specie was a marvelous haul. The men were in a great good humor.

After breakfast Thorton dismissed his officers. When they were alone Tangle moved to sit next to Thorton and kiss him. Thorton closed his eyes and felt the familiar tide of desire and reluctance wash over him. He slipped his arms around the man's neck and kissed him back. Tangle pulled him close and kissed him harder, but Thorton broke the kiss and pulled away. "Your wife is waiting."

Tangle sighed and looked away. "I know," he said quietly.

Thorton rose from the chair and walked to the other side of the table. He leaned on the back of one of the chairs. "I need sleep. I climbed up and down a mountain last night. My legs hurt."

Tangle came and knelt before him and bent to kiss his knee. His strong hand slipped down to lift his foot and draw the boot off, but before he could remove it Thorton pulled away. He shoved his foot down into the warm sweaty confines of the boot again. "No."

Tangle looked up at him from where he knelt. Thorton felt the familiar heat swelling in his veins. It would be so easy to resume their affair, but he shook his head. Tangle rose to his feet, trailing his hand along Thorton's leg as he did so.

Thorton pulled away and smoothed down the skirts of his Spanish coat. "No. You're very handsome and virile, but no."

"Why not?"

"You know why."

Tangle's hands slid over Thorton's body. "I don't understand. You want me. Right now you can have me. Why worry about the future?"

Thorton pushed his hands away. "It doesn't matter. I sleep alone." He crossed to the door and opened it. The marine standing guard outside stepped out of the way.

For a moment it seemed that Tangle might not leave, but he finally collected himself and ambled out the door. Thorton shut it firmly behind him and locked it. The blond captain undressed and crawled naked into bed. He had to alleviate the heat in his blood, but as soon as that was done, he was sound asleep.

CHAPTER 38 : ZOKHARA

If the reception of the French had been warm, that of Zokhara was delirious. Women waved their veils and threw flowers and several local bands turned out to play Turkish music. The clanging of the cymbals was a strange and exotic to Thorton's ears, but he recognized the martial spirit. Lords and laborers came down to the quay to see with their own eyes the return of the great corsair. Some Muslim ladies came down in sedan chairs carried on the shoulders of their slaves. The curtains hid them from view, but jeweled fingers drew back the curtains enough to permit the occupants to peek at the scene.

In spite of the jubilation things were done in naval fashion in Zokhara. The harbormaster came out in his gig, inspected them, assigned them berths and collected his fees; the health inspector came out and permitted them to land at the lazaretto; and each of them bowed and smiled to the great corsair. Tangle received them with a grave majesty that suited his fame while Thorton settled the galiot. Well-wishers came out in rowboats and small lateen-rigged sailboats. Here, as in Correaux, there were reunions and glad cries for men returned as if from the dead. About half the Muslims in the *Santa Teresa* had come from Zokhara and its environs; their families, lovers, and friends crowded the quay. As in Correaux, there was a great wailing when the news of the death of a loved one had to be given.

In the midst of all this, bumboats came along side to sell everything from live chickens to alcohol. In spite of Thorton's best efforts a goodly number of each got aboard. However, he did manage to intercept a pair of Zokharan strumpets with bare bellies and kohl-lined eyes. On the other galleys they were not so shy and the women found employment in spite of him. Likewise he found it difficult to hold the men and some of them leaped over the side to the quay or slithered down the starboard side into a boat rowed by friends or brothers.

Thorton bellowed, "Stand your posts! Stand!" Few did.

Tangle came to the foot of the outboard stairs and looked up. "Peter Rais. Let them go. We are home."

"But the ship! She needs a standing crew!"

"Ask for volunteers. Some of them will stay. Some of them will come back after they've seen their families."

With a sigh Thorton did as he was bade. In the end, he wound up with a skeleton crew of thirty-two men. Kaashifa came to touch his fez and ask for leave.

"Be back tomorrow at noon," Thorton told him.

Foster remained and so did Maynard. "Mr. Foster, I'll have a muster roll and quarter bill made up."

"Aye aye, sir."

Before Thorton could give any other orders, a fine figure of a Turk came along side. He was a well-tanned man of middle height, dressed in a short green coat decorated with curls of red braid on the front and cuffs in the Zouave fashion. A heavy gold chain supported an amulet set with jewels. Beneath the short jacket he wore a white shirt and below that red calf-length Zouave pantaloons with a dropped crotch. They were tied just below the knee with gold garters. White silk stockings went down to black ankle-high boots. His scimitar hung at his side in a jeweled scabbard. Rings weighed down his hands. His beard was long, black, and curly. He was accompanied by men dressed in a variety of fashions from the European to the Turkish to the tribal. Half of them had visible scars. They looked both rich and dangerous.

"*Salaam*. Peace be up on you and yours," the stranger called up to Tangle in Arabic.

Tangle, looking over the side, replied in the same language. "*Salaam, Murad Rais*. I hear Allah has been generous to you. Congratulations." From this Thorton learned that the stranger was the man who had supplanted Tangle as *Kapitan Pasha* of Zokhara.

Murad spread his hands and shrugged his shoulders. "You were taken in the galleys. When the Spaniards refused your ransom, we knew they intended you to die there. In the meantime, duty called. I was pleased to accept the honor of following in your footsteps. Allah is most merciful to return you to us."

The words from both men were as polite and insincere as any words spoken in an English drawing room.

Tangle smiled and nodded. "Allah has provided for me. I am now *Kapitan Pasha* of Tanguel." He touched the insignia on his purple collar. Murad's eyes darted to it. Was that a hint of anger that flashed in his brown eyes?

"Congratulations," he replied flatly. "You must come to the palace and illuminate His Excellency the Dey with the details of your escape. He is eager to hear it. As we all are."

Tangle called, "Peter Rais! Join me."

Thorton gave the deck to Foster and said, "See that the ship is bedded down in good order, Mr. Foster." He descended the stair. With every step he took he felt Murad Rais' eyes burning into him. Every inch of the purple uniform was inspected, the insignia on his collar was stared at until he felt its shape burned into his neck. Thorton stepped up next to Tangle.

Murad spoke first. "You always did have naval aspirations, rais."

Tangle's smile thinned a little. "I like it when things are done shipshape. Allow me to present Peter Rais Thorton, formerly of the English frigate *Ajax*. Peter Rais is our rescuer. It was by his courage that we were released from our chains."

Thorton gave a little bow. "Peace be upon you," he answered in Arabic. He understood only the part of the conversation that directly concerned him.

"And also upon you," Murad replied automatically.

"I have made Peter Rais captain of my galiot *Santa Teresa*. I believe you already know my brother-in-law, Kasim. Allow me to also present Namin Rais of the *Silver Star*, Siraaj Rais of the *Fortune*, and Carlos Rais of the *Pearl*. They are all Tangueli men."

The other captains were on their own ships, but Murad Rais looked at their vessels and nodded. Abruptly he turned back to Tangle. "I wouldn't keep him waiting. You know his temper."

Zahid went with them, but Kasim, who had been careful to assert his independence as a corsair, was left behind. Thus did Tangle repay his brother-in-law for the slights committed against him. Murad Rais and his men escorted them, along with a suitable number of marines. They marched in formation and the people in the street waved and cheered as they recognized Isam Rais al-Tangueli.

The palace was magnificent. It was even larger and grander than the palace at Tanguel. It was in excellent condition and well-staffed. They passed through a glassed over courtyard filled with orange trees tended by Spanish slaves. They walked through a hall hung with the trophies of many wars: captured flags and weapons adorned every surface and hung over head. They passed a line of supplicants waiting to enter an office. All the people they met were well-dressed, even the slaves. Thorton realized that with surroundings like this, the ruler of the Sallee Republic had no reason to doubt his nation's puissance. In no way would he see himself as inferior to the hated Spaniards.

At last they arrived in the audience chamber. Thorton didn't know what to do, so he did what Tangle and Zahid did. He got down on his knees and bowed his head to the floor and stayed there. It was a posture humiliating to an Englishman, but not Thorton. He had made the same posture during prayers. He was submitting himself to the Dey, who was Allah's representative on earth. Even Murad Rais had to prostrate himself. The marines were spared the exercise; they had been left in the first antechamber.

The vizier told them, "Rise." He was a thin caramel-colored man in a long blue gown that showed only the tips of his shoes beneath. His turban was large and white, his beard was thin, pointed, and grey. His nose was long, his eyes small and blue.

They stayed on their knees but straightened up. The Arabic was impossible for Thorton to follow, but he gathered that the Dey was displeased with their uniforms and especially with Tangle's title. Zahid did most of the speaking. His tone was earnest and eloquent. Thorton spent his time studying the Dey.

The ruler of the Sallee Republic was a short man who sat cross-legged on a divan. He had short cropped iron grey hair under a pure white turban. A broach of pearls was attached to the front. His coat was in the Turkish style with a full skirt that flared around him in a graceful way. It was black and severely plain, but made of a lustrous and expensive fabric with a refined texture. Pearl buttons fastened it. The chest had white braid in a ladder pattern. Thorton picked out the crossed scimitars and three stars of his rank. The insignia were apparently a topic of debate because Tangle pointed to his own and said,

"One star, Uncle," he replied, using the avuncular title that was the peculiar honor of the ruler of Zokhara. "I do not usurp your authority. I am employed on behalf of the Governor of Tanguel. I have no intention of interfering with the operations of Zokhara."

"Bah. Why does a sleepy little backwater like Tanguel even need a *Kapitan Pasha?*"

"To unite the corsairs of Tanguel and make war upon the Spanish. We intend to drive them from our shore."

Now that they were talking plainly instead of dissembling with convoluted Muslim flattery, Thorton could follow them.

"Feh. Nonsense. If it could be done, don't you'd think we'd have done it by now? They're stubborn dogs, the infidels."

"We took Tanger on Thursday. Would you like us to give it back?"

The Dey paused. "No." He pressed his lips together and stared at Tangle. Then his glance moved thoughtfully over Thorton and the other captains and Zahid. He stared at them for a very long time. Finally he asked, "Do you think you could take Sebta?"

"Not by myself, but yes, I think the Sallee Republic can take it," Tangle replied.

A light started far back in the Dey's eyes. He turned and looked towards the elegant set of triple arched windows with a wistful look. "I would like that very much." He turned back to the guests. "Very well. I acknowledge your rank, provided that your funding comes from Tanguel and you confine yourself to the service of your native province. How they're going to pay for your adventures, I don't know, but that's your problem. Now tell me about Sebta."

Tangle talked. He laid out what they'd learned about the force and layout, then talked about the need for a joint assault. They'd need a large land force and a large naval force. "I think we may have to ask the French to lend us some ships of the line, or else join us for the bombardment. We don't have anything heavy enough to make the assault. Maybe the Sublime Porte will send help when he sees us try it."

The Dey was listening carefully. "The French are our friends, and now the English, too. I signed the accord when Achmed brought it to me. However, the French and Spanish are engaged in heavy fighting off the coast of Cataluña. I do not think the French will be able to assist us. We will have to ask the English to prove their friendship."

Zahid was not able to keep still. "Once we have reclaimed all of Sallee for Islam, we can invade Granada!"

The Dey listened to Lord Zahid, then fixed his gaze on Tangle. "Do you think it possible?"

Tangle gave a blunt and unadorned answer, "No."

The Dey snorted. "Dreamer," he said to Zahid. "Haven't we been longing for that ever since Andalusia, the richest and most beautiful province in all the world, fell into the hands of the infidels?"

Thorton cleared his throat. All eyes were on him. His Arabic was not equal to the task, so he spoke Spanish. "I don't believe it possible any time soon, Your Eminence," (he was not sure how to address a Dey) "but I do believe that in time, if you develop the resources of your nation to a sufficient level, it might be possible, my lord."

The Dey looked at the vizier, who translated for him. "You must be Peter Thorton, the renegade. I've heard of you. Go on."

Thorton remained on his knees. None of them had been given permission to rise or be seated. He pressed his palms down very firmly against his thighs. "England is not a large country, but it is a prosperous one because of the industry of her people. You do not have industry here. Not much, anyhow. You don't have colonies. You don't have markets abroad. England, France, and Spain do. In the end it all comes down to money. Who can afford to fight? If you do as they have done, then you will have money, too. That is my view, sir." The vizier hesitated, but translated.

"That's your idea? That we should become an empire with colonies? I point out to you, we are already part of the Ottoman Empire."

Thorton's jaw worked a little. " It isn't necessary to have colonies, sir. Just to trade with them. The Americans love a smuggler. 'Tis a dangerous business that requires fast ships and brave men, but there is a lot of money in it."

The Dey drummed the fingers of his right hand on his thigh.

Zahid spoke up. "The Americans have timber and hemp and other things we need. We have things they want, like iron and copper. It would be a profitable trade."

The Dey turned his head to the west. The rest of them saw only a wall, but he saw the great grey Atlantic Ocean and all the riches that lay beyond it. "We'd need a better port on the Atlantic side."

"We are dredging the harbor at Tanguel already, Uncle," Tangle replied.

"The Divan will debate it," the Dey replied.

Tangle remarked drily, "Don't they always?"

The Dey shrugged. "We are a republic. I am bound to listen to their views. You will have a hard time persuading them."

"Do I need to? You are the Dey. You can command the navy where you will. 'Tis the corsairs that are touchy about their rights."

The Dey snorted at that. "You and Murad Rais are chief among them. You know our navy is very small. I had to commission you and other corsairs to fight the pirates on our shores. Besides, if we raise a large navy, the Sultan will appropriate it for his own purposes at our expense."

Tangle said, It is possible to both serve one's country and make a profit, but there comes a time when a man must stand for something more than money. Nobody goes down in history because he is rich. He goes down in history because he attempted something great. What could be greater than driving the infidel from our shores? If the Sultan calls for our ships, inform him how you have already put them at his disposal by ejecting the Spaniards from Muslim lands."

The Dey steepled his fingers before his chin. He studied Tangle long and hard. Finally he said, "Make it so. Drive the Spaniards into the sea, and by Allah, figure out how to pay for it! You know the Divan won't raise taxes. They squeal enough as it is."

Tangle was satisfied. "We'll do it. You'll see."

"I will depend on it. Now, Peter Rais, I'd like to talk to you. Your friends will wait for you in the antechamber."

Tangle and the others gave him surprised looks, but Thorton had no idea why the Dey was singling him out. Tangle and the other captains bowed and withdrew, not turning their backs until they reached the door and could step out. The vizier, Murad, and Thorton remained.

"Take a seat, Peter Rais." The Dey indicated a small divan the right size for one man only. Thorton settled himself gingerly upon it. He drew his legs up cross-legged. The full skirts of his purple coat fell around the seat. Murad and the Vizier remained standing. "Tell me about England, Peter Rais."

Thorton had no idea what the Dey wanted to know, but he began speaking. The vizier continued translating. "'Tis a small island country, but very industrious. Her colonies support her, and she supports her navy. If you examine the matter logically, you will realize that there must always be more merchants than privateers, for if there were more privateers than merchants, they would starve for want of prizes. Thus, if there are more merchants than privateers, it stands to reason that the nation prospers more from her merchants than her privateers. The merchants in their turn must have a navy to protect them. One or two frigates can protect a convey of forty sail. Thus we can conclude that it is more profitable for a country to engage in commerce than privateering, even with the expense of keeping a navy. The taxes paid by the merchants will more than outweigh the loot the government receives from privateers."

The Dey's brow darkened like thunder as he stared at Thorton.

Murad snorted and said, "You insult us with such remarks."

Thorton stared him down. "I've seen Zokhara and I've seen the harbors of England. The English Admiralty could put your navy in its pocket and count it as loose change. If this state of affairs offends you, you have only yourself to blame. If you want it to be otherwise, then you must enrich your country through industry and commerce."

Murad stepped forward. His hand went to his side, but all visitors to the Dey were relieved of their weapons before entering his presence. He had no sword to draw. "Why you dog of a renegade!"

"Stand down, Murad." The Dey's voice was flat and hard.

Murad ground his teeth so hard his beard bristled. "Are you going to let him—"

"Yes. Now shut up and let me talk to the man."

Murad's eyes flashed. "He insults the honor of our country, our corsairs, and every man!"

"Whereas you waste my time, which is a far graver insult. You may go." The Dey snapped his fingers and his guards came out from behind the screen to escort Murad Rais from the room.

Murad left in a foul humor. He was barking at Tangle before the door to the antechamber even closed. What happened out there Thorton didn't know, but he didn't think it would be pretty.

"Do you make a habit of insulting your hosts, Peter Rais?" the Dey asked with some asperity.

Thorton worked to control his own temper. Yet he was gratified that the Dey seemed to want to hear what he had to say. He had to figure out how to say what he needed to say without causing any further friction. Finally he said, "Englishmen often take offense when I tell the truth, sir. My previous experience with Salletines had lead me to believe they did not need to be dipped in honey to talk."

The Dey steepled his fingers again. He stared at Thorton long and hard. "You're as proud and stubborn as a corsair, Peter Rais. If I know anything, I know corsairs." He lowered his hands. "Achmed has brought me a great deal of information about the English navy, so I know that what you say is true. By his measurements, the English navy is three times the size of the Spanish navy. Navies are expensive. Very expensive. You tell me your country pays for it with trade and colonies. America is a very large land. It produces silver, gold, timber, grain, and every needful thing in abundance. My country does not. Zokhara contains a quarter million souls. London contains nearly three times that number. Half a dozen cities in England are as big as Zokhara, but Zokhara might as well be a city-state. The hinterland gives us little. It is disheartening to contemplate."

Thorton said nothing. He hadn't been asked a question. The Dey looked to the west again. "My people have long memories, but they do not have foresight. They will not believe you if you talk of such things. I suggest, Peter Rais, that you begin by driving the Spaniards from our shore. Then the Divan will be in a mood to listen to you. If that is the case, I am willing to enact decrees for the support and encouragement of our merchants. I am pestered on one side by corsairs and the other by janissaries. A third to balance them would be most helpful. But that is for the future. For now, go in peace. Please avoid fighting with Murad Rais. I must now pacify him."

Thorton rose from his seat, bowed deeply, and backed out. Murad Rais was summoned back into the Dey's presence.

CHAPTER 39 : PARADISE

As soon as Murad Rais went in to the Dey and the door shut, Tangle crowed like a rooster and slung his arm around Thorton's shoulder. "We did it! He's on board! We will drive the Spaniards from our shores and the country will prosper!" He kept his arm companionably around Thorton's shoulder as they exited the chamber and retrieved their swords.

Thorton laughed and blushed. "Don't hang on me, Isam, people will think you're drunk!"

Tangle laughed and let go of him. "You're dining with us tonight at my wife's house! I shall get to see my children! I must get their presents!" He swerved down the steps of the palace to head back to the galiot. It wasn't far and he was soon burdened down with his sacks like Saint Nicholas bringing gifts to the poor people of his country.

Thorton followed him but demurred. "I do not want to intrude on your family life."

"Nonsense, Peter. 'Tis no intrusion. Do not argue with me! 'Tis insubordinate. I will command you as your superior officer if you make me." His voice was cheerfully indomitable.

Thorton hung back for a moment. Tangle continued blithely down the road unaware that the Englishman had fallen behind. From the rear Tangle's broad shoulders and long legs were obvious. The purple uniform looked uncommonly good on him. Thorton felt a surge of lust and fought it down. There would be no more of that for them. Not when Tangle was home with his family. Where he belonged.

Still, the law was lenient here. Maybe he could find someone to warm his bed. That made him a little giddy. He looked with interest at the men they passed, but he could not tell if any of them were looking at him, or if they were just looking at the strange gaudy uniform. Still, Tangle had had male lovers. Maybe he could help.

He caught up to the corsair, screwed his courage to the sticking point, and asked, "Isam, I wonder if you might do me a favor."

Tangle stopped and faced him. "Whatever you ask, if I can do it, I will. I owe you my life and my freedom, and you have never taken advantage of that."

Thorton licked his lips nervously. "Since you know this city, and you're a man of the world, I thought you might know a gentleman who, ah, how shall I put it? That might like to meet me. And I him." He blushed terribly to ask it.

Tangle set down the sacks of toys and gifts as if they had suddenly become heavy. He was silent for a long moment. "I love you, Peter, but you've been cool to me ever since Jamila came aboard. It pains me to think that you want company but won't accept mine."

"I don't love you. I like you, admire you, enjoy you, even lust for you," Thorton colored brightly as he admitted it, "But not love you. You are a friend, Isam. You have been good to me, and I have learned a lot from you. As strange as it sounds, even when you are angry with me, I am not afraid to speak my mind to you."

"I love you as a friend, too, Peter. But I love you as something more as well. I know that my love is engendered at least in part by the situation, but that does not change the fact that I feel it and you deserve it. I admire you highly. Even when you're stubborn and drive me to distraction. But there is something else about you. Something that completes me."

They stood in the busy street with bullock carts, horsemen, and peddlers going around them. Nearby a demi-galley was raising a cargo net full of supplies to her deck. The naval part of Thorton's mind kept track of all that was going on around him even as he stared into Tangle's eyes. "Yes?"

Tangle rubbed his hands on the skirts of his coat. "You're male. It was not easy for me to marry. I had to learn it. My natural inclination is for my own sex. Yours too, so I think you know what I mean when I say that I desire your masculinity."

Thorton's heart beat faster. "Yes, I think I do. But still, you *are* married! And you love her." It was an accusation.

Tangle picked up the sack of presents with a sigh. "Yes, I do. And the children, too. I want to go home to them. On land, I am a father and husband. But Peter, we will go to sea again."

Thorton's pulse was pounding. "Yes, we will."

"Things will be different then."

"Maybe." Thorton knew himself. He did not think he could withstand the corsair's advances if he pressed his suit on board ship far out of sight of land and wife. "But I would rather have someone of my own. Someone I don't have to share. Someone to be mine and only mine."

Tangle rubbed a hand over his face. Finally he said, "I think you will like my brother-in-law, Shakil. He is a man like us. You will meet him."

They walked the rest of the way to the house. It was a Greek style farmhouse, low, with one story, white walls, and a porch across the front. Smooth Tuscan columns supported the architrave. Double doors let into hallway with a parlor to the left and office to the right. In the office was a thin man dressed in white about Thorton's age. He was working at a drop front secretary desk of French origin, made of birch and decorated with scallop shell carving. He had a simple white cotton cap on his head. He looked up and broke into a broad smile when he saw Tangle. The corsair set his bags down and embraced the man, kissed him on each cheek, then clasped him in a bear hug. At last Tangle made the introductions.

"This is my brother-in-law Shakil bin Nakih and a more honest man you will not find. If you left your virgin sister and a thousand ducats with him, ten years later you would find them both still intact. Shakil, this is Peter Rais Thorton, the man who saved me from the galley." He spoke Spanish for Thorton's benefit.

Shakil was about an inch shorter than Thorton and a good deal thinner. He had a sober demeanor, but he smiled at the effusive introduction. "Peace be upon you, Peter Rais. Thank you for bringing Isam home to us." He bowed deeply with his hand to his forehead.

"I will let you two get acquainted. I have presents for the children. Where are they?" Tangle said.

"In the courtyard. Alexander is digging up the flowerbed again."

Tangle hurried into the inner courtyard. A happy, girlish shriek sounded as soon as he was seen. "Baba!"

"Tahirah!" he cried with great delight. His voice came clearly through the open double doors.

They could see him grab a girl dressed pale pink and whirl her around and around while she shrieked at the top of her lungs. A little boy ran up but hung back uncertainly. Tangle put the girl down and grabbed the boy to his bosom. The boy was dressed in thin blue and white stripes. The girl came back and must be hugged, too. He wrapped them in his arms and kissed them as he knelt there on the black and white tiles.

A line of three—they must be the triplets—came on next, urged by their mother. One of the three was bigger than the other two and held back sulkily. Tangle let go of the oldest two, who were no more than nine and seven, and held out his arms. "Zaafir! Nakih! Naomi!" The two little ones, who looked exactly alike except one was a boy and one was girl, ran to him. Zaafir sulked a little longer, but at last got jealous of his siblings and flung himself into his father's arms. Tangle kissed them all and hugged them tight.

The last child was a toddler. He held onto his mother's hand and put his thumb in his mouth. He was still in nappies under his blue tunic. He did not know this stranger. Jamila knelt down and encouraged him with soft words. "He is your Baba. I know you don't remember him, but he loves you very much."

Tangle let the triplets loose and held out his arms and called softly, "Alexander." The boy hugged his mother and would not come. Tahirah wrapped herself around her father's back and announced, "My Baba!"

Jamila shushed her. "He's Hamet and Alexander and Zaafir and Naomi and Nakih's Baba too!"

Little Hamet went over to his smallest brother and patted his head. "Baba's nice!" He lead Alexander over, but the baby was still shy.

Tangle knew how to cure that. He opened his bag and pulled out a toy horse and offered it to the child. Curiosity overcame shyness and the baby came forward to receive it.

Nothing would do but for Tahirah to have a present too. She clamored and tugged at her father. "What did you bring me?"

Thorton and Shakil stood shoulder to shoulder in the doorway watching. Thorton felt that he was intruding on a very private moment, a moment that did not include him. He turned away.

"Would you like some tea or coffee? You must be tired from your journey. Let me make you comfortable." Shakil's voice was a pleasant tenor.

"Yes, please. A cup of tea would be delightful."

Shakil disappeared for a few minutes, then returned with a teapot on a tray and a pair of cups. A bowl of cream and another of sugar accompanied it. They settled on the divan in the parlor with their cups of tea.

Thorton was not sure how to strike up a conversation. He tried to remember Perry's social lessons from long ago and asked a question. "Are you married?"

Shakil shook his head. "No. Are you?"

"No, and I don't intend to marry."

"Marriage is a happy state. Even Isam Rais has learned that."

"For some men, it is. But I'm not that kind of man."

Shakil looked at him more thoughtfully. "I'm not either." He glanced out into the courtyard. "I love my nieces and nephews, but I would not make a good father. I am too bookish."

"He seems very fond of them."

It was a stilted, awkward conversation, but Shakil was warming to the topic. He smiled as he added sugar to the tea. "He is a wonderful father. It was quite a change in him. I remember the wild corsair Jamila set her heart on. I could never be such a man. Or survive being married to such a man. I don't know how she does it."

Thorton smiled and accepted a teacup. "He's an overwhelming personality. I like him, but sometimes I feel invisible next to him."

Shakil nodded vigorously. "I know exactly what you mean! I am a quiet person. Everyone says I'm shy, but I'm not. I just don't have much to say, unless you're a scholar. Do you like books?"

"I do. And I'm learning to read Arabic. *Salaam.*"

"*Salaam.* I am glad to hear it. Arabic is a wonderful language. Are you reading the Qur'an?"

"I am trying to, but I know very little. I find it hard to pronounce."

Shakil smiled warmly. "I would be delighted to help you study."

Thorton's heart did a slow roll. He smiled back giddily. "I'd like that."

Shakil blushed and added sugar to his own cup of tea. "Maybe you could come tomorrow afternoon, then stay for supper."

Thorton's heart soared. This man was much more to his liking. He was gentle and pleasant, not overbearing like the corsair. "I have a lot to learn. Isam Rais teaches me, but he distracts me, too."

"Yes, I understand that. I'm used to it, but still, he has been gone so long I had grown accustomed to the quiet." Another girlish shriek sounded from the courtyard, followed by a bubbling stream of laughter. "Although it is impossible for a house with children to ever be truly quiet," he said humorously.

"I hesitate to bring up business, but there is the matter of the *Sea Leopard.* Lord Zahid said he'd buy it for him, but Kasim Rais won't sell it. Do you know anything about that?"

"Yes. I keep the family's accounts. I know exactly how much Kasim owes each investor. I was already at work on the figures when you arrived. It must be done quietly, or Kasim will be angry and try to block the sale. Murad Rais will be the difficult one."

"I want Isam to have his ship back," Thorton said.

"So do I." Then his mouth curled into a smile. "So you're in love with him?"

Thorton blushed crimson. "I didn't say that."

Shakil didn't laugh, but his mouth quirked. "I was in love with him for two years when Jamila first married him. I survived. You will too."

Thorton was shocked. "You mean, you—"

"Sh. No, I didn't. I was terrified of him. Besides, I would never do anything to hurt my sister."

"I have nothing to get over," Thorton replied with dignity. "I have been very firm with him. I told him that I will not accept a married man as a lover." His eyes strayed to the window where Tangle was galloping by with one of the children on his shoulders. Shakil just smiled. Thorton sighed when he saw he was caught mooning. "I mean it. I will have nothing to do with him." He drank tea. "Besides, there was someone else I liked."

"Who was that?"

So Thorton told him the whole long story, starting with that rainy morning in London. It took a long time to tell. He was surprised to find it late in the afternoon before he was done. Shakil listened to it all. His hazel eyes were kind, and he either laughed or shook his head at the appropriate moments. He put in a sympathetic word from time to time, asked a few questions, and stared intently into Thorton's eyes when he was speaking. What a delight to unburden his soul to such a good listener! No judgment, no fear of the law or court martial, no shame, no disapproval. By the time he had finished his story, he was in love with Shakil. When he took Shakil's hand in his, Shakil let him.

Thorton whispered, "I want to call on you. Not just to learn Arabic." He was blushing brightly. "Will you let me?"

Shakil blushed just as brightly. "I will."

Thorton slipped off the divan and knelt before him on the carpet. "I want to court you. I promise you are the only one that I will ever look at. I will be true to you."

Shakil leaned forward and brushed a soft kiss across his brow. "You must prove it to me!"

Thorton lifted Shakil's hands and kissed them one by one. "I will have to go to sea again, but I will write. Will you give me a memento to remember you by?"

Shakil replied, "I know a silhouette cutter. We can have our pictures made."

Thorton beamed. "Perfect! Would you like to see my ship?"

"I would."

Thorton was deliriously happy. It had been a long strange journey, but he had found his place in the world. He had found a religion he could believe in and become a captain with a worthy fight before him. On top of that, he had met a man on whom he could fix all his affectations without any of the complications of his previous infatuations. If that wasn't Paradise, nothing was.

THE END

AFTERWORD TO THE SECOND EDITION

I have been crew aboard 'wooden sail' for six years now, which is not very long, but long enough to have my share of adventures. Last year I was aboard a tall ship during Hurricane Earl, which isn't as exciting as it sounds because we were safe in a snug harbor. The day before it hit I hiked up the cobblestones to the Seaman's Bethel and sat in the pew communing with Herman Melville and the ghosts of dead mariners.

I am not a famous author and I don't pretend to be their equals in literature, but for all that, I think my real life experience brings a special perspective to nautical fiction. I was within arm's reach when a half inch steel cable snapped and went whizzing past with a sound like a rifle shot, and I have spent eight hours in an open boat in the middle of winter. I have been bow watch while picking our way through flood debris that included telephone poles, which made me keenly aware that only two inches of pine separated me from a watery doom. Likewise I have been to the top of the mast, keenly aware that nothing but my captain's steady hand was hauling me up in the boatswain's chair. You learn what 'trust' is at such moments.

Most of all I love the ocean, which I call 'the Big Empty.' I like it best when there is nothing human to be seen but the ship herself, but standing watch in fog with stars swirling around the masthead is a close second. I even like a bow watch when the swells are steep enough we strap ourselves to the sheet bitt timber. On the tall ship with which I currently serve, the foredeck has no lifelines or bulwarks; it's entirely up to you to make certain you stay with the ship, no matter how she rollicks.

I came to the ships before I started reading nautical fiction. Once I did start reading, I grew swiftly frustrated by the lack of gay characters. When I read a book, I like to feel a sense of fellowship with the characters, but I found nobody like me—unless he was a minor villain whose sole purpose was to get knocked down by the heterosexual hero to prove how manly he was. After finishing one of these novels, I flung it down in disgust and said, "I'm a writer, I'll write my own damn story."

Lt. Peter Thorton leaped fully formed from my head like Athena leaping from the brow of Zeus. The rough draft of the novel you hold in your hands was written in a white heat in six weeks—usually in the wee hours of the morning before getting up and going to work. I shared it with friends who liked it very much, then posted it to an online forum, where it had the good fortune to win a Sweet Revolution Award for 'best full cast' in a same sex romance. Since then it has won a 4th Place/Honorable Mention Rainbow Award for gay fiction.

At first I had no idea what I would write; I simply followed the formulas of the genre. However, I made several decisions that proved fortuitous. First, I found that the struggles of a gay man to find himself in the Royal navy added an interesting twist to the usual naval heroes. Second, I was sick to death of the Napoleonic Wars. If the reader knows anything about the period, he can guess what is going to happen. Writing in 1838, Marryat passed over Trafalgar by saying, "But everybody already knows what happened there." If it was old hat then, what could I say to make it new?

I decided to write an old-fashioned swashbuckler of the sort that I loved when I was a kid. That freed me to invent whatever events, people, and places I needed for my story. As did *Pirates of the Caribbean,* but I didn't want to go *that* far. No undead monkeys or magic compasses for me! Having devised an imaginary history, I then set out to make it as realistic and believable as possible.

The novel is replete with details about how ship operations are carried out, but written so that the reader doesn't need to be a sailor to understand them. Some readers skim over those sections, but other readers tell me they find the action scenes exciting and easy to follow. 'Ship wonks' are fascinated by the scenes set aboard lateen-rigged vessels—a class of vessel that as far as I know has never been intelligently presented in nautical novels.

I was also interested in developing characters who were heroic but human. All too often fictional characters have alleged virtues that the author does not fully demonstrate. Worse, supporting characters and villains often receive short shrift. I wanted my characters to face challenges large and small and to rise to the occasion (or not) depending on who they were as people. I also felt the villains and supporting characters deserved to be as well-researched and detailed as the hero and his friends.

Pundits have defined as swashbuckler as nothing more than a story featuring adventure, romance, and gorgeous period dress, and *Pirates of the Narrow Seas* delivers on all three. More formally, swashbucklers are a subset of the adventure novel with close affinities to historical fiction and romance. They are descendants of the picaresque novel— Tobias Smollet, author of *The Adventures of Roderick Random* (1748), specifically claimed to be attempting to write a picaresque novel more plausible than *Gil Blas*. (This explains why early heroes were rascals.)

The real impetus to the nautical novel was given by Captain Frederick Marryat, a career officer who had the good fortune to serve as a midshipman under the famous Lord Cochrane during some of his most daring naval actions. Marryat's many novels, such as Frank *Mildmay, Peter Simple,* and *Mr. Midshipman Easy,* are rife with authentic detail that only a man who has lived the life can give his stories, while still being romantic tales of derring do that sometimes reach preposterous heights. I cannot claim to be Marryat's equal—it never occurred to me to have my protagonist escape captivity by stilt walking across France disguised as a girl—but his mixture of utter fiction and authentic detail is one I admire.

Nonetheless, for all my good intentions, sometimes research failed. I found it exceptionally difficult to discover details of daily life in maritime Morocco in the 18th century. I decided it was better to do a good job of writing about an imaginary country than a bad job of writing about a real country. Thus, although the Sallee Republic of the novel is loosely based on the real Republic of Salé, it will only be found on maps containing Ruritania, Florin, Guilder, and Grand Fenwick. However, the feats attributed to the Sallee rovers in the novel were actually accomplished by real Sallee rovers and other Barbary corsairs. Sadly, the atrocities attributed to the Spanish were also real— and worse. For example, the Spanish adopted the policy of executing all Barbary officers and gunners after Turgut Rais (the inspiration for Captain Tangle) was ransomed from the galleys and wrought havoc. Had I been strictly faithful to history, Tangle and Foster would have been dead before the story ever started, and then where would we be?

My real world experiences have given me courage to dare to publish in a field dominated by giants—I have caught even the esteemed C. S. Forester in an error. While I can in no way compete with Forester, Tobias Smollett, Frederick Marryat, Herman Melville, Rudyard Kipling, Joseph Conrad, Patrick O'Brien or Alexander Kent, I can hope the reader will be entertained by what he finds within these pages.

~K~

M. Kei
Perryville, Maryland
18 August 2011

Printed in Great Britain
by Amazon.co.uk, Ltd.,
Marston Gate.